DISPATCHES FROM
LESBIAN
AMERICA

DISPATCHES FROM
LESBIAN
AMERICA

42 SHORT STORIES AND MEMOIR BY LESBIAN WRITERS

EDITED BY XEQUINA MARIA BERBER,
GIOVANNA CAPONE, CHEELA ROMAINE SMITH

BInk *Bink Books*
Bedazzled Ink Publishing Company • Fairfield, California

978-1-943837-64-9 paperback

Cover Design

DESIGNS

Bink Books
a division of
Bedazzled Ink Publishing, LLC
Fairfield, California
http://www.bedazzledink.com

This book is dedicated to Lesbians in every country of the world, especially those who are suffering the most. May we know our true worth. May we achieve our full freedoms in this lifetime.

PREVIOUSLY PUBLISHED WORK

Terry Baum's current play "Awaiting the Podiatrist" is the longer version of "Dutiful Daughter," which is her short play that we published in this anthology.

Joanne Fleisher's story, "Married to a Man and in Love with a Woman," was adapted from a blog she wrote for the *Huffington Post* in December of 2012. As a result of this submitted blog, Joanne was invited to become a blogger for the *Huffington Post*.

A segment of Judy Grahn's book *A Simple Revolution: The Making of an Activist Poet* has been included in our anthology, specifically pages 122-134. Judy's book was originally published by Aunt Lute Books, in San Francisco, CA, c. 2012.

Bev Jafek's story "Malena the Maddened One," is an excerpt from her novel, *The Sacred Beasts*, published by Bedazzled Ink Publishing Company, in 2016.

Heal McKnight's story "Other: Driving the Land In Between," appeared originally in the magazine *Brain, Child*. It ran in the print edition of Vol. 5, issue 3, Summer 2004.

Regarding the short story by Dr. Bonnie Morris, the author says: "A few pages of my material on Mothertongue also appeared in a different version, in an essay called 'Writing in Women's Bars' in *NIMROD, the journal of the University of Tulsa, Oklahoma*, v. 59, n. 2. It was in their issue called *Mirrors and Prisms*, spring 2016."

Ashley Obinwanne's short story "Let it be Known: My Coming Out Story," originally appeared online at her website: lesbiansovereverything.com

A segment of Francesca Roccaforte's memoir "Beyond the Wooden Spoon" was previously published in *She is Everywhere, volume II*, c. 2007.

IN MEMORIAM: POLLY TAYLOR
MAY 31, 1929 – JULY 26, 2016

We are saddened to learn of the passing of one of our elder authors, Polly Taylor, in the three years time this book was in production. Polly has a short memoir in this collection, entitled "My Urban Forest," which we are proud to have included in our book. Polly was born in Haverford PA into an old Quaker family whose beliefs helped to shape her life-long commitment to peace and social justice for all. She graduated from Wellesley in 1951 and later earned an MSW in social work. In 1961 she started a psychotherapy practice in Buffalo, NY, developing concepts of feminist therapy. In 1977 she and her partner, Marge Nelson, set off in an RV to find other older feminists and lesbians. They eventually settled in San Francisco in 1978 where Polly lived until her death. Polly was a life-long political activist, working for civil rights and social justice, doing draft-resistance work and counseling during the war in Vietnam, including driving hundreds of young men across the border into Canada. She helped create options for older women at the San Francisco Women's Centers, co-publishing Broomstick Magazine for 15 years, and working for lesbian visibility and equality. Inspired by her life-long struggle with asthma and Chronic Obstructive Pulmonary Disease, she was also active in the disability rights movement. Polly is survived by Marge Nelson and a caring community of lesbians and other friends and family. Polly's papers will be archived at the San Francisco Public Library James C. Hormel LGBTQIA Center atchives.

ACKNOWLEDGEMENTS

This project was made possible by the support of many women. First on our gratitude list is our publisher, Bedazzled Ink Publishing, or more specifically, C.A. Casey and Claudia Wilde, who gave us the means to take an idea that the three of us found exciting and turn it into the book you now hold in your hands.

The editors wish to extend our profound appreciation, as well, to each contributor for entrusting us with the safe passage of her story from manuscript form to finished product. For patiently bearing with us as we requested various revisions—and sometimes even revisions of revisions!—and for always so graciously allowing us to perform our nips and tucks without complaint: to each and every one of you we offer many, many heartfelt thanks.

Gratitude goes, as well, to each woman who submitted work that we were unable to find space for in this book. Were this an e-book with endless capacity for an unlimited number of stories, we would have been glad to include many more pieces. But, for better or worse, all three of us are old school lovers of the "analog" book for which no battery charger or internet connection is required. (Although, of course, you do have the option of reading *Dispatches from Lesbian America* as an e-book.)

Finally, our thanks go to you, our readers, for choosing to read our anthology.

Cheela "Rome" Smith

There are many people to thank for assisting us with this literary effort and for sustaining enthusiasm about this project. I echo Cheela "Rome" Smith in beginning with a big thanks to C.A. Casey and Claudia Wilde, our publishers, for making this book actually see the light of day. They believed in it from day one. I may not remember everyone, and I apologize for that in advance. But I would like to extend my gratitude to a few specific women whose ongoing consultation, input, and excellent life-saving ideas over these three years have really helped us in the process of shaping of this collection. They include Dr. Frankie Bashan, Max Dashu, Pippa Fleming, Bev Jo, Lenn Keller, Jeanne Lupton, Denise Mauldin, Doreen Perrine, Luan Stauss of Laurel Bookstore in Oakland, and all the members of my Riff Raff Radical Writers writing group in Oakland, California (you know who you are!). You have all made a big difference in helping us to think about this book and expand our vision of what it was, to what it is now. *Mille grazie!* Finally, a big thank you to Xequina Berber and Cheela "Rome" Smith, my co-editors, for three years of hard work, and our continuing to hold onto the vision of this book together, until we were finished.

Giovanna Capone

All the above goes for me too, but the biggest thanks and recognition goes to Giovanna Capone who was the true inspiration behind this book. Her energy, publishing experience, and vision saw us through to the end.

Xequina Berber
Oakland, California, October, 2016

CONTENTS

PREFACE

This anthology was Giovanna Capone's brainchild. It was 2013, and we were at Thanksgiving dinner, sharing our written stories with each other. We talked about how few venues exist for good lesbian writing. Giovanna suggested we publish an anthology, and enlisted Rome and me as co-editors. Giovanna's vision was for a collection of lesbian stories; our stories, both fiction and memoir.

We began spreading the word to the local community, asking for work. Giovanna then said this collection should not just reflect the voices local to the San Francisco Bay Area. Why not have it include the entire United States? So we put out a call for manuscripts through *Poets and Writers*, a national magazine. Once we did this, work began flooding in.

Then began the long and painstaking process of reading and choosing between the pieces we received. Many were interesting stories, but required too much editing in order to make them publishable. A very few were not appropriate, or didn't fit the focus of our book. We were surprised at the breadth of work we received: we got a story from a woman in prison in the South; an account from a lesbian whose partner transitioned; several memoirs submitted by lesbians living in other countries.

Despite the enthusiastic response, we noticed women of color were not well represented, and we wanted to increase the racial diversity of our collection. We personally contacted women we knew, or who were recommended to us by others. We republished our call for material three more times, focusing on encouraging lesbians of color. Working tirelessly, Giovanna also found valuable and pertinent work online, and contacted those authors for permission to include their work.

With a lot of solid, compelling work in hand, and a tentative book title, we worked hard to find someone who would publish our anthology. We approached several publishing houses, but found no interest. Finally, Giovanna found a local lesbian-focused publisher who was excited about the anthology. They told us this was the direction they had been wanting to move in, and they accepted the manuscript.

Then began the final editing and preparation of the manuscript for submission. We continued to work up until and into the eleventh hour. After three years, we are now finished. It is our hope that you will love this collection of lesbian writing, as we have loved it.

Xequina Berber, Co-Editor
Oakland, California
October, 2016

OPENING REMARKS
PIPPA FLEMING AND GIOVANNA CAPONE

To dispatch literally means to send someone to a specific destination for a particular purpose. A dispatch is also a report on the state of affairs. Dispatches can be written messages sent with speed. In this new book, *Dispatches from Lesbian America*, we have more than forty lesbian correspondents sending you the most current information representing our collective lesbian consciousness that we've seen in print format in many years.

We invite you to immerse yourself in these stories by lesbians from a variety of backgrounds, cultures, and ages. They represent the experiences of lesbian women mostly from the United States, but also including one Canadian, one woman from the Netherlands, one from Aotearoa/ New Zealand, and one from Australia. There was also one story which, for privacy reasons, was contributed anonymously. We welcome every single voice. It has been years since the voices of this many lesbian writers, this many female born women, have been gathered into one book. We hope you will cherish its arrival.

Why the need for a lesbian-focused book at this time? Now more than ever, there's a need for lesbians to identify ourselves, in our own voices. Now more than ever, we need to speak on our own behalf, define who we are, and what our lives are about. We have a right to speak for ourselves on what we know best: our own lives, and our richly lived experiences.

As you embark on this journey of sisterhood and self-discovery, please find a comfortable place to sit down. Take a deep breath and settle in. Release your breath, and please consider a few questions. There are no right or wrong answers; we just ask that you be as authentic as possible.

- When did you first discover you were emotionally and sexually attracted to women?
- In how many situations in your life today are you "in" or "out" of the lesbian closet?
- Do you have a strong support system of lesbian friends/romantic partners? If not, why not?
- How do you currently feel about your lesbian mind, body, and spirit?
- What changes would you like to make in your life to feel more grounded and powerful in your identity, your sexuality, and your presentation?
- When was the last time you attended, hosted, listened to, or visited a female-born lesbian: party, dance, potluck, concert,

- sports event, ritual circle, land or farm gathering, art show, theater production, film series, business, bar, medical clinic, bookstore, spa, sex shop, or poetry reading?
- What are you willing to do today, to help re-create a visible, viable lesbian community and culture that is a place of honor for ourselves and each other?

A few months ago, Pippa and Giovanna shared a dinner together. Pippa served Giovanna a bowl of delicious homemade chicken soup in her home, as a cold El Nino rain was falling outside, and northern California was attempting to pull itself out of a long drought. It was not unlike the drought we were about to discuss that evening.

We began by reminiscing about when we first met, back in July of 1987. We were both in our twenties. We had been working tirelessly for United Communities for Human Rights, a feminist-led women's fundraising organization, which to our delight had the guts to consider women's rights to be human rights. We worked with teams of other women every night, canvassing neighborhoods throughout the San Francisco Bay Area, raising capital for local women's organizations like Bay Area Women Against Rape, Las Casa de las Madres, Child Assault Prevention, and Chrysalis, a women's alcohol recovery home. We chuckled about the boldness it took for a mostly lesbian crew to knock on doors night after night and solicit money from the public for women surviving rape and domestic abuse. Remembering that time many years ago, we held a meaningful pause. Now, thirty years later, we both understood why it was time to get real about publishing a lesbian-focused anthology.

"The climate for lesbians today is dire," Giovanna said. "The L of LGBT is becoming smaller, weaker, and less visible. Some lesbians are even going back into the closet to survive."

"Hell, I know it, girl," Pippa said with emphasis. "To make matters worse, lesbians are policing and attacking other lesbians! Don't they understand how they're internalizing systemic homophobia?"

"And internalizing misogyny too!"

"What about the Michigan Womyn's Music Festival? We just saw the last one take place after forty years," Pippa said.

"I was there!" Giovanna added. "Women were grieving. They were outraged. They didn't want to leave the land."

"Of course not. You saw how our own—*other lesbians*—actually helped shut down the Michigan Womyn's Music Festival?" Pippa said, in disbelief. "Why do we keep falling for that same old divide and conquer tactic?"

We were both feeling our anger that night, but at the same time, we were wracked with a deep sadness. It's clear to us that we live in a fear-based, sexist, racist, and patriarchal society that demands our unfaltering allegiance.

Our existence as lesbians is a threat. Our strong, woman-centered culture is dangerous. Therefore, we're a target. The footholds that we as lesbians have diligently created from our social and political organizing over the last forty years are now under threat of dissolving—collapsing and disappearing. Our bookstores, businesses, clinics, bars, cafes, restaurants, and female-only spaces are being targeted or eliminated altogether. Even worse, they are going out of business due to lack of enough lesbian patronage. This could be rooted in a growing apathy, the result of being disconnected from our physical community spaces, the ones many of us remember and knew so well, and on which we depended for our survival. Butch lesbians in particular are being attacked and disappeared. They are perhaps being hit the hardest. We all need to put ourselves back on the map.

This is why we need a lesbian-focused book today. It's also why we need to work to preserve and re-establish our lesbian-focused spaces, conferences, gatherings, and circles. That is where our culture comes alive. Now, more than ever we have to gather our forces and hone our collective wisdom into a powerful storm, the perfect storm to combat the misogynistic, lesbian-hating atmosphere we are currently faced with.

In today's era, social media has become the new bridge that many people use to build community, to organize, and to create social change. To some extent, this is helping lesbians all over the globe to find one other, to connect, and talk for the first time in history. This is great, and it can be very empowering. Many of us have solid radical friends here and in other cities and countries through our online communities.

But it's also true that lesbian voices and radical feminist contributions both in and outside of the LGBT community are too often getting blocked from pertinent conversations. Some of us are being kicked off Facebook or banned for thirty days because of our viewpoints. Our most courageous and truth-telling warriors are being de-platformed and removed from conference panels online and in real life too. There's infighting in our community spaces. Male-controlled social media platforms like Facebook and Twitter are in some ways being used as leveling campaigns against lesbians and radical feminist women, and against our longstanding woman-centered culture. This has created fear, confusion, and doubt in our personal lives, in our relationships, and in our precious organizations and community spaces. Fewer and fewer all-female spaces even exist. That's a real problem, because we have a right to those spaces. We fought for decades to create them. Considering all this, as of today it's time for us to say a loud and collective "Basta! Enough!"

As we recoup our energies, we have to ask ourselves, how does an ancient tribe of lesbian women heal itself from invisibility and silence? This world is in desperate need of strong women who aren't afraid to speak up. It's in desperate need of strong women whose anger is aimed and focused in the right places. How can we restore what's been stolen from us, co-opted, or lost?

The answer lies in our innate power as women and in that long-held lesbian ability to reinvent ourselves from the beginning, even while our cultural "through lines" are being attacked and destroyed. Women like us may be frightening to those who don't understand the power of the divine female. So be it. Their role right now is to listen to us and learn. This is a challenging time for us. But we are rising again, re-inventing ourselves, like we always do.

Every lesbian has a story of her own awakening: that exquisite moment in time when we each became aware of our love for other women, when we first glimpsed our own reflections in each other. Our lesbian culture is as diverse as the cosmos and no matter what our age, class, race, ethnicity, nationality, ability, or life circumstances, each lesbian life is worthy of celebration and respect. Each of our lives is a victory, a story worth telling and preserving for future generations.

It's time once again for a cultural renaissance—a lesbian revolution. We are challenged with re-birthing ourselves and our lesbian tribe. In the powerful words of Audre Lorde, our silence will not protect us. In fact, our silence = our death. Today, we are being asked to hold an undivided devotion to one another. Only in this way can we preserve our stories and our unique culture for ourselves and for future generations of lesbians. Those lesbians, once they untangle the lies and finally come out, we hope will feel guided/dispatched to a safe haven, assisted by the existence of this book and others like it. Our intention is to save ourselves, and also to create a destination for future lesbians, a collective culture that is ours, a place of reverence and sanctuary. That is our challenge now: to re-create lesbian culture and to go on re-creating it. If not now, then when?

Dispatches from Lesbian America is a testament to our living legacies. In this book, we hope to raise the collective lesbian self-esteem by offering you more than forty heroic stories and life experiences. We pray that this book will be one among many more to come in response to the erasure of lesbians, a giant push back against the social pressures that would rather see us silenced and made invisible. No more!

In this book we say, "This is who we are. This is where we stand. We draw our boundaries here." We invite you to pick it up and share it like a brilliant jewel wherever you go. We hope its light will re-awaken your spirit, cleanse your soul, and re-unite us in a strong lesbian sisterhood. And so it is. Ache`!

Pippa Fleming and Giovanna Capone co-wrote the Opening Remarks for Dispatches from Lesbian America. Pippa has been a vocalist, writer and performer since her teenage years. Her early creative interests led her to study theater, photography and film.  After a brief stint in the Army as a Media Specialist, Pippa attended the University of Massachusetts where she majored in African Studies, was a Pearl Primus dance scholar, and further trained in theater and dance with Andrea Hairston of Chrysalis Theater and Joi Gresham. Blossoming as a young Black lesbian in the San Francisco Bay Area in the late 80's, Pippa had the good fortune of having mentors and teachers like Pat Parker, Audre Lorde, Gwen Avery, and Angela Davis to light pathways of growth and understanding. The opportunity to study and develop with such dynamic women propelled Pippa into a life of artistic activism; which eventually lead to her becoming a co-founder and co-editor of Ache magazine and an event producer and Disc Jockey for DaddiGirl productions. Pippa's mid-life travels and living have taken her from London to Hawaii where she has produced works in film, theater, music, television, and has shared stages with the likes of Margaret Cho, Mario Africa, and Big Island Conspiracy. In her continued efforts to celebrate and preserve Black lesbian "butch" identity, Pippa appeared in Debra Wilson's Showtime award-winning film "Butch Mystique" and recently premiered her theatrical cabaret "Living in the Mainstream," A Griot's Tale of Survival, at the Museum of the African Diaspora in San Francisco. She is currently writing her memoir, *Walking In Between Storms.*

WHERE ARE YOU SISTER?
ARTEMIS PASSIONFLOWER

Artemis Passionfire came out in 1981 in Boulder Colorado, the same year she got her black belt in Tae Kwon Do and the dyke witches brought her onto the path of the Goddess. She moved to the San Francisco Bay Area for her sexual freedom. She taught amazon mysteries for twenty years at a Women's Spirituality Festival near Mendocino, California. For twenty-five years she worked in the union electrical trade in California, where butch lesbians through the Feminist Tradeswoman Movement,  agitated to get women into the building trades. The great recession with up to 25% unemployment in the trades destroyed her career, and she and her butch spouse had to move to rural Nebraska where her partner has supportive family. They are legally married. There are few butch lesbians here and no organized lesbian community. Artemis and her spouse bought their home in Nebraska in 2015, jobs are plentiful, and for the first time in thirty years Artemis can work on a garden again. Artemis is raised Jewish and proud of her NYC Jewish heritage. Her poem is memoir.

I LOOK FOR you everywhere I go. On the job, in the grocery store, at the hardware store, in the factory, at the restaurant.

Here you are rare and elusive. I have one at home; but we are two alone. We have no community; but still I hunt and search for you elusive breed soul sister of mine in your Dykely sensibilities like me. The way you carry yourself, the way you take up your space. Your sensual Butch Being.

We shop in the men's department, we like big watches, our hair short, boots and sensible shoes close to the ground. I think I see you; but find you are with a man carrying a purse, no, an imitation. Disappointed, I recalibrate. These country women look like you but are not you. In my isolation I begin to mourn.

I have my mate, but no companions. We are drowning in a sea of conservative heteros. Others name themselves differently, flattening their breasts, hiding their plumage, imitating males; but not you, that female juxtaposition, that rare breed of Amazon holding her ground, her strong female gaze, who breaks into new territory as a female.

My Butch sisters; everywhere I hunt for you. I spy one in a Target, two at a small Pride event calling themselves by male names, but are they you? Or will they hear the siren song of hormones and surgeries to pass as male, leaving our tribe in the dust?

My love for Butch Dykes is my love for myself as one, and loving another; but one cannot love what one what cannot see, forever an anomaly.

It is your strong gaze, your powerful stance, the full embodiment of dyke unashamedly. Some camouflage themselves for a moment as men for safety in this world from those who cannot see who she truly is. Once in the safety of her Tribe, she reveals herself fully as Butch Amazon female taking up her full space.

Where are you my sister? Are these territories too hostile for you?

You who break through every barrier men erect, daring to pass through them, claiming new territory for yourself. You who dare . . . It is your strength and defiance I love, hearkening back to our Tribe of Strong, Defiant women who love women,
the Amazons of all time.

CARRY ME HOME
CHARLENE ALLEN

Charlene Allen's short fiction has been named a Top Ten Finalist in the Tennessee Williams Literary Festival Fiction Contest, judged by Michael Cunningham. Her nonfiction has been published in the Sage Press. She holds a B.A. in writing and literature from the University of Massachusetts at Amherst, and a J.D. from Northeastern University Law School. She lives in Brooklyn, New York, where she also writes middle-grade and young adult fiction.

"WHAT I'M SAYING to you, Raylene," Reverend McElroy boomed, his steady brown gaze pinning me to the spot, "is that difficult times don't have to remain so. Preaching is a powerful balm, especially for those like you and me." He settled back on Mother's sofa and crossed his arms over the lettering of his double XL t-shirt: *Tithe If You Love Jesus, Anyone Can Honk.*

Reverend Mac could be an easygoing guy if he wanted to, but the fire in his eyes told me he hadn't made this particular house call just to be sweet. Mother seemed to agree. She hovered by the windows, quietly pouring a constant flow of iced tea.

"People like us?" I asked the Reverend, hoping to lighten the mood. "You mean fat people?"

He rewarded me with a chubby-cheeked grin. "Speak for yourself," he said. "I meant talkers, community people. Leaders from the word go."

I stared at him then, struck by how well he thought he knew me. Because maybe he did: maybe I was the one who'd forgotten who I was. Still, I was sure of one thing. Whatever he thought my "difficult time" was all about was light years from the truth. Even Mother, with her powerful radar for my business, hadn't figured out what I was hiding. And for that, I thanked the Lord.

"Preaching's in your blood, Raylene," the Reverend said, going grave again. "Take the pulpit for just one Sunday and I promise you two things. You'll learn something new about yourself. And . . ." he made a toasting gesture toward Mother with his tea glass, "your mama will die a happy woman."

Mother had the good sense to leave at that, wandering down the short hall and busying herself with dish towels just inside the kitchen doorway. The Reverend and I glanced after her. Making my mother happy meant something to each of us. For me, it was relief from the icy disapproval that peeled off her skin like a bad batch of Jergens since I'd deferred grad school and come home. For the Reverend, on the other hand, Mother's support was glue for his crumbling church. She drove forty miles every Sunday, stayed through community hour, and showed the congregation that even if you moved to the white suburbs, the black church was still a part of you.

"You came home for a reason," the Reverend said, reaching to stretch a fatherly arm around my shoulders. "But you haven't made it all the way yet, have you, Ray? I believe taking the pulpit will help you make that final step. I think your father would agree."

He'd picked a good trump card. I let my head fall back on his ample arm, taking in his rich B.O. and missing my dad more than ever. Since I'd been home, I'd taken to pulling out his preacher's robes from the back of my closet, touching and sniffing them late at night. I didn't know if Daddy would have cared, one way or the other, if I did a sermon at the Reverend's church. But it wasn't like I had a better idea.

"Sure, Reverend," I said, letting me eyes slip closed. "I'll give it a shot."

THE BOOKS PILED up on our coffee table.

"It'll be just like one of your school projects," said Aunt Cecile, my favorite aunt and Mother's sister-frenemy. She pulled well-worn library books from her bag, *Sisters on the Pulpit: Sermons by Black Women Preachers* and *Lord Hear our Prayer: Sermons that Satisfy.*

"Not now," said Mother, brushing them aside and handing me a book from her own assembled pile, *Son of a Preacher Man: Black Families and the Pulpit.* "Read this one first. It has a lot on Paul and Silas. You know how the congregation loves our righteous brother Paul!" She laughed, settling me into the La-Z-Boy with her book.

A grin crept onto my face as I read. I'd never thought much about Paul's famous "Advice on Marriage," but it struck me now that he might have had some very personal reasons for his support of men remaining single. Was the righteous brother Paul as queer as a rainbow-covered cross? Glancing back toward the kitchen, I wondered what Mother would say to my theory. Not that I'd ever ask. But Mother was nowhere in sight. It was a new skill she'd picked up lately, and one I definitely appreciated. I relaxed even more, preferring to think about Paul's predicament rather than my own.

I wouldn't have thought it possible, but the tension in our house was melting away with the fifteen pounds I was always trying to lose. Privately, I put myself on a different kind of diet: no sexy movies, no biscotti, or jasmine tea. No memories, if I could help it. I still woke up wet and anxious, miserable when I realized where I was. But at least it was morning when I woke, not two a.m. with a long, cold night ahead.

Maybe it really is in my blood, I thought, when the big day came. My mind felt light and my body strong as we walked up the sidewalk to the Walker Street AME Zion, my copper silk blouse brightening the fitted black suit, Mother's gold cross glinting on my chest. For the first time in forever, my head was where I wanted it, *here* and now on a sunny day, enjoying the tingle of stage fright as I held tight to my notes and practiced voice inflections in my head.

"Raylene, look how beautiful the programs came out!" Mother hurried past the chatting parishioners to grab the folded pages from an usher. "Look!" She folded back the cover with its black-and-white sketch of the church, and my own face stared back at me in living color. I snatched it from her hands.

It was my graduation photo: blue cap and dangling yellow tassel. Guilty brown eyes and bitter, plastic grin.

"Mother . . ."

"It came out nice, didn't it?" Mother said, beaming.

"This picture? What were you thinking!"

"I know you look a little chubby," Mother whispered, yanking me to her with vice grip fingers. "But keep that kind of noise to yourself. This congregation is proud of you for graduating college!"

I wrenched my arm free just as Reverend Mac bounded through the side door of the church, robes flowing, ample arms outstretched. "Come on, preacher girl! Let me show you the way."

Mother grabbed me again as I turned away. "Just a minute." She leaned in, her breath hot in my ear. "I was going to surprise you with this, but you're acting so peculiar I'd better tell you now. I sent an announcement out to your college people—the ones we met at graduation."

"You . . . ?"

"I don't know for sure if they'll come, but—Ray, what is the matter with you?"

People were moving towards us from the parking lot, the sidewalk, the restaurant across the street. I was suddenly searching their faces so hard they became a blur. Was one of them tall and caramel-skinned? Elegant and lovely?

"Come on now, getting late." The Reverend guided me out of the glaring August sunshine, down a darkened corridor and to his office. He had a hand on my shoulder, helping my feet to follow as my mind drifted three hundred miles south.

The last time I'd seen her was another sunny day. Graduation.

The Dean's reception in the cozy tenth floor conference room. Anata stood in the doorway, stunning in a sleek royal blue dress. We had a deal. She would meet my family like any other friend; we would all go out to dinner. But she had only crossed half the carpet when I knew I couldn't do it. She was too familiar, too beautiful. Too much.

"Ray!"

I felt the stiff smile slide into place, my head tilting to the side as if greeting a stranger.

"I just wanted to say congratulations," Anata said.

"Thank you." I took Mother by the hand and turned my back.

"Ray? Did you still want us to take your mother to dinner?"

"I'm sorry, I promised Henry . . ."

"We wait here until the organ stops," the Reverend said. "That way all the eyes come to us when we enter." He'd brought me to the door that led to the chapel and opened it a crack, then pointed out the hymn book and the fresh glass of water he'd placed by the lectern for me. I searched the pews, but it was no use. I could only see a small corner of the room, twenty people settling in with their Bibles on their laps.

The music faded to the last, ringing chord. Up the burgundy-carpeted stairs the Reverend led me, to our place at the polished lectern. I thought there'd be time then to collect myself as he gave the Call to Prayer, sang with the choir, announced the offering. But there was only a timeless void where my heart banged crazily and my mind went white with overload. And then the Reverend was pressing me forward, melting away to his seat at the back of the stage.

A sea of faces swam before me. There was no whispering or hip shifting. Every head was turned to me.

"Let the church say amen!"

"Amen, sister!"

"Let the church say AMEN!"

"AMEN, now!"

I blinked until the faces came clear: Mother and Aunt Cecile, front and center, the deacons' wives flanking them. It was hard to take them all in, but I didn't see her anywhere.

Maybe it would be all right.

"Brothers and sisters, it is my honor to be before you, to share what I have learned through your nurturing care and the Lord's abiding love. This morning, I invite you to remember that when God reveals His mysteries . . ." I paused. I'd chosen the next words because they honored my Daddy's style. But that didn't mean I could pull them off. "When God reveals His mysteries . . ." I repeated, *the devil will soon be history!"*

"All right, now!" came the church's happy response.

I started to relax. It was like the Reverend said; the congregation fed me. But there was something better than that: I felt Daddy up here—his calm, steady energy—almost like he was standing beside me. Maybe that's what the Reverend had been trying to tell me—and Mother, too.

"Brothers and sisters, let me tell you about Paul and Silas. The Word tells us that Paul and Silas got locked up for the sin of believing in the Lord."

A wave of head shaking crossed the church. They knew the story as well as I did, but still they hung on my words. Acceptance warmed the stained glass windows. Love came back to me.

I began to revel in the power of my own voice. "Well, now. There's nothing new in righteous people being used and abused for doing the right thing!"

"No, sister!" The flock settled in, ready for the long haul. Even mean old Mrs. Tippin there, so sour-faced we called her the sock puppet, looked happier than I'd ever seen her. And next to her was . . . Anata.

"The story, brothers and sisters, the story goes . . ."

Anata sat smack in the middle of the church, wearing a shimmering, sea green blouse. How had I missed her? How could she be here? It was as if both things couldn't be happening at once—Anata in front of me, and me on the pulpit.

"The story . . . Paul's story is about . . . about . . ."

I trained my eyes on my notes and read each word carefully, my mind fighting to fly off on its own. *Did she think I had sent the invitation, instead of Mother? What did she think it meant?*

" . . . about faith. Because what did Paul and Silas do?"

The green shirt was the one she'd had on the first night I came to her and wound up in her bed. Had she worn it on purpose? If she was trying to make me remember, God help me, it was working. I saw myself standing in the doorway of her apartment, pulse beating a racket in my ears, wondering how anybody could be so perfect. Golden brown skin, deep dimples, a long, lean body. All that and med school, too.

"They stayed strong, sister!" Aunt Cecile called out, lifting a hand in the air. "Paul and Silas stayed strong!"

My eyes slid from the green silk blouse to Aunt Cecile's flowered jacket, to Mother's pale beige suit. Sweat trickled down my sides.

"No sin in being curious," Anata had said to me that night.

"Preach, sister!" called the congregation.

I turned to Reverend McElroy behind me, opening my mute mouth, blinking, spluttering. Reverend Mac stood up, inclined his head towards the guest lectern. "Brother Thompson," he whispered, pointing to the old deacon sitting in back of the stage, "the reading."

I shook my head; I hadn't chosen a guest reading. But Reverend Mac nodded again, picking up his own Bible and flipping through the pages. He held it out, showing me a passage.

"Let us turn to the Word," I said into the mike. The congregation opened their Bibles, and I turned again to the back of the stage. Reverend Mac had worked quickly; Brother Thompson was bringing his long, creaky body to a stand. He took the Bible from the Reverend and made his way to the lectern, one hand raised to God.

I closed my eyes in relief as he began to read. When I opened them, Reverend Mac was at my side.

"Ray," he whispered, pulling me back to the deacons' seating. "What's happening? Are you ill? I can't believe it's stage fright . . ."

I sat down in Brother Thompson's empty chair, sipped the water the Reverend handed me, closed my eyes. The memory came back whole, starting with the moment she asked me . . .

"Listen, Ray. Was there something else you wanted?" She fingered a biscotti from the plate on the table, a single dimple showing.

I had come to her apartment to talk about an article for the black student newsletter; Anata was our graduate advisor. She made tea and answered my questions. It got late, and I didn't leave. "I just didn't want to print the wrong thing," I said. "You know. And get us in trouble."

"Hmmm." She looked straight at me, taking a nibble of her cookie. "Because maybe you heard some rumors about me. I mean, word has it that Anata Emerson is a big old bull dyke. Did you hear something like that, Raylene? No sin in being curious."

"I'm sorry," I said, butterflies zumba dancing in my stomach. "It's none of my business."

The kettle boiled again. Anata went back to the kitchen part of her studio apartment, turned off the burner, and leaned against the counter, facing me. "No worries," she said, "you're not the first."

I looked away, inexplicably hurt.

"Ray?"

"Hmmm?"

"I just mean, I don't mind your being curious. You can ask me anything."

I nodded. I didn't have a question, or even a clear thought. Time seemed to pass as my eyes wandered her room: bookshelves, iPod speaker, a nest of pillows surrounded by texts. I knew I was on dangerous territory, though I couldn't say why.

"Or . . ." Anata poured the tea, looking down as she filled the cups. "I could help you in another way . . ."

I swallowed saliva, looked up, forced my attention back to the church. Words floated back to me in Deacon Thompson's commanding, old man's rasp. " . . . the wicked will *not* inherit the kingdom of God!" The congregation was rapt.

"Help me with what?" I asked Anata.

"Your curiosity." She was grinning now, mocking me. "I'm a medical student, aren't I? I know how to treat it."

"I told you I was sorry, Anata. I should go."

"It's simple," she said, ignoring me. "Like the test for diabetes, this treatment. A touch test. Only no blood." She was babbling, and that made me more nervous than ever. And then she was crossing the room, closing the distance between us, and my heart was pounding like a desperate prisoner as the jailhouse door banged shut.

"I," Anata said, halfway across the floor, "a self-avowed lessss-bian . . . will touch you. If you feel nothing, you're forever relieved of further curiosities. If, however, you feel a little tingle, a tiny little spark . . . then further testing is indicated."

"I hope you don't think I'm . . ." I said, digging through panic to find my voice. "I didn't say I was curious that way." I trailed off. She was in front of me now, rolling up her sleeves like a TV surgeon. She was taller than me, thinner, stronger. I smelled the jasmine on her breath when she brought her hands to either side of my neck, her fingers kneading my stiff muscles, moving down my sweater-clad arms.

I was trembling. There was no way to hide it. Her hands intertwined with mine, caramel skin on cocoa. She bent her head and brought soft lips to the edges of my eyes.

"I don't think you're doing too well," she whispered, resting her forehead against mine. "But since I've never administered this test before . . ." The tip of her tongue brushed the corners of my lips. She pulled back to look at me.

I stayed perfectly still. Until I kissed her back.

Brother Thompson's voice grew soft. He closed the Bible and raised his head. Reverend Mac peered at me as the church said "Amen." I nodded, gripping the edge of my seat. My insides vibrated with wanting, guilt, sadness. But there was one more emotion, and that was the one I grabbed onto. How dare she do this to me! I had told her what I wanted. I wasn't proud of the way I'd ended it—a note under her door, a request to send my things to a P.O. box. But I had settled it. She had no right to stir it up again.

Reverend Mac smiled encouragingly as I stepped back to the lectern. I pulled in a deep breath, smelled worn wood and velvet upholstery, kept my gaze on the back of the chapel.

"The Bible tells us," I began, though I had no clear idea what the Deacon had read to them, "that Paul was so dedicated to the Lord's service that he counseled, at times, against marriage. He applauded the single life for men. This was due to his enduring faith . . ."

I read from my notes, ignoring the pulse in my belly. The congregation was content, I told myself. The Apostle Paul was a crowd pleaser, and they were focused on him, not me. There were only two pages left now, and I read them without a glance in her direction. Finally, I reached the last refrain.

"Blessed be the offering of these humble words." It was Daddy's traditional closing. Tears welled up in the back of my eyes.

"Amen!" The church responded in a single, satisfied release as the first slow organ chords began to rise. Reverend McElroy took my hand, raising our arms overhead for the benediction.

It was over.

After a long, shaky hug, Reverend Mac and I walked together down the center aisle to the door, where our parishioners would greet us. I made a plan. I would welcome Anata like any college acquaintance, show that she hadn't gotten to me. With each greeting, I searched the queue.

"Sister Inez, Sister Lugenia, Brother Bob . . . I'm so glad you enjoyed it . . ."

"Of course I was nervous, until I saw your smiling faces . . ."

But the green shirt was nowhere in sight.

Old Mrs. Tippin was the last to leave, asking the Reverend to walk her to her car. Mother and Aunt Cecile were huddled with their friends at the bottom of the outside steps. I could have left right then, pretended I hadn't even seen her.

"I left some things in the Reverend's office," I shouted to Mother. "It'll take a few minutes." Turning my back before she could answer, I unhooked the heavy church door so it would shut behind me.

Anata stood in the doorway that led to the Sunday school rooms. Creamy silk pants flowed beneath the green shirt. As chic as ever. Heat rose in my nipples, spread down my body.

"What the hell," was what came out of my mouth.

"Yeah," she said. "Just what I was thinking." Her natural hair was shorter than before, making her prettiness even more stark.

"Look," she said, her eyes sliding over me. "I didn't mean to mess you up, up there. I just had to know if . . . well. I heard the sermon, so now I know."

"I don't know what you're talking about," I said, wondering if she'd noticed my missing fifteen pounds, hoping I hadn't gone too far and lost the roundness she'd loved in me.

"Your feelings for me," she said. "I know now: the pain that has to be history."

"What?" I shook my head, glad she was pissing me off again. "Anata, not everything's about you."

"Mmm. Just a coincidence then, your preaching the Bible's biggest homophobe. Whose idea was it, Ray?"

"Homophobe!" I was outraged. "That's ridiculous, if anything I think the man was g—" A cone of sunshine cut through the dark chapel. Behind us, the church door was opening.

"Well, there you are!" Aunt Cecile thrust her head through the crack in the door and my gut flooded with bile. "Just came to see what's keeping you. Oh, yes!" She glanced at Anata. "I thought you looked familiar. You must be a friend of Ray's from school."

"Pleasure to meet you, ma'am." Anata's dimples popped with her easy smile. I rushed to tell Aunt Cecile I'd be right out.

"No hurry now," Aunt Cecile said. "I'm gonna take your mom on home and you can make it back when you're ready. You're welcome to join us, honey," she added to Anata.

"She has to get back to Chapel Hill, Aunt Cecile. Tonight." I didn't look at Anata as I said it, or as Aunt Cecile disappeared through the door. I closed my eyes, took a breath, and finally turned to her.

Her gaze, brightened now with tears, was still on the door. "I never understood," she said, "what the hell happened that weekend. I know it freaked you out having your mom at graduation with us. But still. You threw everything away and you never even told me why."

"I did tell you!" I said. "I had Mother asking a million questions—wasn't there some man I wanted her to meet, and where was I going to live next year. I couldn't take it. Something had to give!"

"And I was the weakest link."

"Mother's not strong since Daddy died!" I seethed. "I couldn't do that to her."

Anata hugged herself. She reached into her bag and pulled out a folded copy of the church program. Taking a seat on the front pew, she smoothed the pages on her lap.

"What?" I asked, irritated.

"Your mother's not the point, Ray," she said softly, "but here." She took a sheet of paper from inside the program, an insert. "This was inside the program your mother sent me. I noticed it wasn't in the one they handed me at the door."

"Mother sent you this?" I asked, sitting, too, as I took it.

I read with disbelieving eyes.

Famous words of the Apostle Paul

Do you not know that the wicked will not inherit the kingdom of God? Neither the sexually immoral, nor idolaters, nor adulterers, nor male prostitutes, nor homosexual offenders.

I Corinthians 6:9-10

"The mom's usually the first to know, baby," Anata said. "She threw down the gauntlet when she sent that to me. So I took the challenge—and now I know. You might not have known she sent that verse, but you gave the sermon, Ray. You had to know about Paul."

My mind was suddenly sharp as it moved from one awful thought to the next: Mother being gentle and funny, handing me the book about Paul; her being so pleased when I told her I'd use it in my sermon. I heard Deacon Thompson's voice uttering the very scripture Mother had sent to Anata " . . . the wicked will *not* inherit the Kingdom of God."

Wrapping my arms around my silk clad belly, I tried to absorb the sucker punch. What a fool I was! I'd played right into Mother's manipulative, prudish, cowardly hands. For a fleeting moment, I thought about Paul, and how I'd thought he might be gay. Poor fool probably was. We'd be two peas in a pod, him and me, buying into our own destruction.

Anata's hand was in her bag again, taking something else out: a silver chain with a delicate charm on the end. "I made this for you a few months ago," she said. "It's a boomerang. It was supposed to help you come back to me." She gave me a sad grin. "You know, the lesbian boomerang test. Anyhow, just keep it now."

She lifted the two ends of the chain to my neck, leaning over my shoulder to fasten them. My pulse went wild.

She stood up.

But I reached around and unfastened the chain. "You keep it. I don't need it," I said. I was playing for time, praying the mess in my brain would resolve itself. Because I could see now that she was right. Gay people could be plenty self-hating. My question was, how did she keep from being that way?

"Fine," Anata said, holding out her hand for the necklace.

I stood up. Still trying to make sense of my thoughts, I turned to the lectern where I had gone through so many emotions. Instead of seeing myself up there, or Reverend Mac, I saw Daddy. His smile was mild, like it always was when Mother flipped her lid a little too high.

I held tight to the necklace.

"'Nat," I said, false confidence in my voice again, as it had been on the pulpit. "Come home with me. Like Aunt Cecile said."

"*As . . . ?*" Anata looked scared.

"My friend from school! Please, give me some time . . ."

The tiniest corner of her lip turned up. She took the necklace from my closed fist and slipped it into my jacket pocket. I felt its weight, close and comforting.

I pictured the scene in my mind as Anata took me in her arms. I saw myself walking through Mother's door, pleased and proud, introducing my school friend with perfect calm. I was furious with mother for what she'd done. But the Reverend was right, I'd learned something about myself from taking the pulpit. It was Daddy who I'd felt up there today, because it was his spirit that still lived inside me. Breathe, Raylene, he'd tell me now, a big, steadying hand on my back. The Lord never said it was a race.

Slow and steady, I thought. Just like him. Until I'm strong enough to claim my own life. And fill it with everything I want.

PATSY CLINE ROLLS AROUND IN HER GRAVE
MARI ALSCHULER

Mari Alschuler is a poet and writer who received an MFA in Poetry from Columbia University in 1982. Her poetry has been published in *American Poetry Review, Shenandoah, Berkeley Poets Cooperative*, and *Pudding Magazine*, among other journals and anthologies. A poetry chapbook, *The Nightmare of Falling Teeth*, was published in 1998 by Pudding House Press. Her story, "Revealed," is featured in the new anthology, *Lock n Load*, (to be) published in 2016 by University of New Mexico Press. Mari teaches creative writing and prosody privately and is certified as a poetry therapist. She has contributed textbook chapters and scholarly articles on applications of poetry therapy. Currently based in northeast Ohio, Mari is an Assistant Professor of Social Work and MSW Program Coordinator at Youngstown State University. She is also in private practice for psychotherapy, poetry therapy, and clinical supervision. She is a quilt maker too. Her story is fiction, but it's based on an actual experience.

THE DRIVE TOOK her along Alligator Alley at seventy miles a clip. Amber knew that it would be a good four hours before she reached her destination, a sleepy retiree town near the Gulf Coast. Two of her closest friends—a lesbian couple in their sixties—had recently relocated to Gulfport, and were regaling her with promises of "so many gay women" and "really gay friendly," as if they were wooing her there as well.

As she traveled along the four lane road, Amber remembered a trip she'd taken with her father along this same route, then a dusty two lane path between the east and west coasts of Florida. The car had broken down and they'd had to wait for a tow. She and her father, both reformed smokers, had lit up Camels at the gas station, making secret promises not to tell her mother of either the breakdown of their cigarettes.

Amber was in her mid-forties. She had been single for over five years, since leaving her lover of fourteen years in New York City and moving to south Florida. Now she was lonely and bored, depressed, bordering on suicidal. She'd been celibate—not by choice—for over three years.

Her ex, Sandy, had changed careers drastically after being fired from the art gallery she had managed for over two decades. She floundered for months until she landed a job at a high-end bakery. There, she'd met a younger woman who belonged to a group that believed in space aliens living on earth. Soon, Sandy too became immersed in their cultic lore. She could barely talk to Amber about anything else, and Amber gradually lost all respect for Sandy. She made the hard decision to not only leave her, but to also leave New York and the city she loved.

Amber passed street signs that warned of approaching fog masses, something wonderfully named "Corkscrew Sanctuary," and ads for tours of the Edison and Ford winter mansions, long abandoned. Amber could understand how the huge empty mansions might feel, visited only occasionally by some vacationing midwesterner with four tow-headed tykes, oohing and aahing over mahogany *etagères* and *trompe l'oieul* frescoes in the overdone dining rooms. She recalled the last time she'd visited her father's estate in Palm Beach, wandering from room to room, feeling displaced and replaceable simultaneously. His new wife, Soraya, was a designer, and had outdone herself in their new residence. Her famous dictum was "Always bring the outdoors in."

Now Amber was outdoors, her legs cramping after two hours. She visited a rest stop somewhere near Fort Myers. She'd had the car's accelerator floored via cruise control, God's greatest gift to the automobile, she thought. But still her legs and lower back felt stiff. She used the rest facilities and returned to the road. Traffic between Sarasota and Tampa was sporadic. For stretches she would keep her cruise control in place; at other times she had to return to driving, as the other cars and SUVs were weaving in and out of the two lanes heading north on 75.

Within two hours, Amber arrived in Gulfport. First she passed strip malls and a super Kmart. She had been using Mapquest directions, which were miraculously accurate. She noticed a rainbow flag and a Gay Pride carwash a few blocks from a suggested left turn and wondered how a gay car wash would differ from a heterosexual one. She laughed to herself as she made her left.

Pulling into the complex in which her friends lived, she noticed each building was named alphabetically. She meandered around the one-way alleys between identical buildings, scanning for Jamestown, Groton, Harvard, Ithaca—it was like a cluster of dorms at a northeastern prep school. She pulled into a guest parking spot and dialed her friends' number.

Annette called down to her, cell phone in hand, "Yoo-hoo! Amber! We're up here! You should park closer to the awning."

So Amber backed the car out and drove around the parking lot, reaching a better guest spot. She unpacked her small overnight bag and a grocery sack of ripe strawberries from the farmer's market in Davie, near where Annette and Claudia used to live when they were just a mile down the road from Amber's own apartment.

She found the elevator and realized she didn't remember their apartment number, but she was able to find A. Resnick and C. Linus in the resident listing, apartment #319. She took the elevator to the third floor.

Their front door was wide open. The breeze was warm and strong, whipping the tops of the palm trees below them like a teenager's long hair. She stepped in and met the embrace of Annette, the elder of the two women. Her body felt warm and moist beneath her tie-dyed tee shirt worn over khakis. Her partner, Claudia, sat at the dining room table. Amber then approached Claudia, saying, "I've missed your wonderful full-body hugs, babe." She waited for Claudia to rise slowly and the two hugged warmly. Amber noticed her friend's weight loss and the paleness of Claudia's body and face. She had been suffering with lupus for a long time and the ravages of chronic illness were taking their toll.

Claudia and Annette gave Amber the five-minute tour of their new condo, lined with soothing waterscapes Claudia had painted over the years. Three of these were hanging over Amber's own bed back in Davie, a housewarming present when Amber had abandoned New York and her ex-lover to return to the Florida she had originally left for college nearly thirty years earlier.

This evening's plan was to have dinner at a local café in downtown Gulfport, then go to a Patsy Cline performance by a look- and sound-a-like entertainer. Amber was not partial to country music of any kind, with two exceptions: k. d. lang and Mary Chapin Carpenter. She was not particularly looking forward to the show but her friends had told her it would be mostly a lesbian crowd and there might be dancing. Annette and Claudia were on the lookout for a new gal pal for Amber. They had encouraged her to visit them as soon as they finished unpacking from their move three months earlier. "There are tons of women here, Amber. You'd have your pick."

Around five p.m. they left for the Grouper Gallery, a small homey café on a side street. The walls were decorated with work by local artists and craftspeople. The emphasis on the menu was local seafood—grouper, yellowtail, mahi-mahi. They squeezed into a side booth beneath a black-and-white painting of a man holding a child's hand. The paint had been slathered on with a palette knife. Amber looked at it, remembering similar strokes executed by her grandmother, also a painter. She herself had learned to use a palette knife long before learning to wield a paintbrush. Amber gave up painting in grad school when she became a busy substance abuse counselor. These days, she limited her artistic musings to visiting galleries and museums and having artistic friends. She enjoyed work-ing with clients who were musicians, writers, artists—her kind of people.

After dinner the trio of friends walked around the village. "Actually, Gulf-port achieved city status. It's no longer a village," said Claudia. Amber thought the stores were quaint, the houses small and cottage-like. She fantasized about renting a house for the summer to work on her writing. It would be nice if there were a special someone in that house with her, she pondered. Maybe she'd meet someone tonight.

Around seven-forty p.m. they walked into the casino where the performance would be held. It looked a lot like an Elks Lodge somewhere in the Midwest, or a church's recreation hall. Amber recalled being in similar rooms for various twelve-step meetings when she had been training to become a substance abuse counselor a while ago. She looked around the white-walled, uncarpeted space and the long tables covered in red plastic tablecloths and suddenly remembered it was Valentine's Day. She'd forgotten that.

The tables held two paper plates festooned with hearts. Heart-shaped individually-wrapped strawberry-and-cream hard candies were piled onto the plates. A drink doily was laid at each place, encouraging the audience to visit the bar on the other side of the casino.

Amber excused herself and bought a Smirnoff Ice. It tasted like lemonade with a little kick. The label said 5% alcohol, less than wine. She settled down in her white folding metal chair and looked around the room as people came in and found their reserved seats.

Annette and Claudia were relatively new to Gulfport but had been visiting long before finally moving there. So their table was full of faces familiar to them, and they walked around greeting friends and being introduced to new ones. The women at their table were all lesbians, mostly over fifty-five.

Amber sat at the other end, closer to the stage. A guitar rested on a stand on one side. Two large Valentine's Day balloons festooned either side of the stage. A big bouquet of white flowers graced the back. An off-white cowboy hat was plunked forlornly on the front left side of the stage.

And then Amber noticed. Far from this being a "mostly lesbian" crowd, the people who were milling around the bar, finding seats, and greeting one another were actually mostly straight couples on their Valentine's Day dates—with their spouses and other married, heterosexual couples.

The news these days was full of debates for and against gay marriage. Just that morning on her drive, Amber had listened to a radio talk show on NPR in which two gay people—a man and a woman—shared their opinions and personal experiences about gay marriage. Amber had listened until the station faded out somewhere near her entry into Collier County. Amber wondered if she might one day legally marry a woman she really loved. It seemed so unbelievable at that moment in time.

Many of the straight couples in the room were wearing western-type clothes, to go with the Patsy Cline theme, Amber guessed. She observed the people surrounding her. They looked happy, dressed casually in rhinestone-sequined blue jeans, fringed jackets, with mother-of-pearl buttons on their faux-western shirts. The men held chairs out for their wives and ordered drinks for them at the bar. As Claudia and Annette were taking their seats nearby, Amber turned to the woman sitting next to her, who'd introduced herself as Lila, and said, "I feel like I'm visiting from an alien planet here. Look at all these straight people!"

Lila smiled. She had arrived with her female friend named Rick, which was short for Patricia, they had all learned. "Why not Pat?" asked Claudia.

Rick rolled her eyes and smiled. "Because every butch named Patricia is nicknamed Pat," she answered. "I guess I wanted something different." They all laughed.

Suddenly the lights dimmed. From somewhere behind the stage, a disembodied female voice rang out in a sultry, deep alto.

A door opened and out stepped "Patsy Cline." She wore a white polyester scarf tied around her neck, a dark brown wig, a red skirt with sequins, white boots, and a white shirt with fringe and red hearts. "Hi, y'all! Happy Valentine's Day!" she shouted.

This Patsy Cline double launched into several songs that Amber recognized and several that she didn't: "Jambalaya," "I'm Walkin'," "Your Cheatin' Heart." Then she asked the audience if anyone knew what Willie Nelson's real first name was. Some guy yelled out "Belvedere!" Amber believed him. Belvedere Nelson. Hell, it was no worse than Marion, John Wayne's real first name. "No, no," said Patsy. "It was Hugh! Hugh Nelson." Big deal, Amber thought. Who the hell cares?

"Patsy" had begun the evening in a good voice. In between songs she continued to offer the audience some tidbit in the persona of Patsy Cline, about her life, her husbands, her recording career. She talked about divorcing Gerald Cline and marrying a man named Dick. She said she couldn't go on stage as Patsy Dick. "So the best thing I got from Gerald was his name—Cline, Patsy Cline."

Every lesbian at their table cracked up. Most of the straight audience laughed, too, though in a slightly more subdued, self-conscious manner. Amber turned to Lila and said, "Would *you* have come to a concert by Patsy Dick?" Lila chuckled and shook her head no.

"Shhh!" warned Annette.

"You're not really going to shush us for *that*, are you?" Claudia glared, jerking her thumb in the direction of the stage. "Let's leave after intermission, okay? I'm tired and she sucks," Claudia whispered.

Amber and Annette agreed to an early departure. Aside from Patsy's lackluster performance, they were concerned about Claudia's failing strength and lack of stamina.

"Patsy" soon completed her first act and the audience broke for intermission. On her way to the bar, Annette said, "Anyone want something to drink?"

"I'll go with you," said Amber. She rose and followed Annette to the other side of the casino.

As Amber and Annette walked away, Amber could distinctly feel Lila's eyes following her. She thought Lila might be appraising her as she walked away. Amber felt something toward Lila, too. That is, she thought Lila was attractive, but there was something else too, which she couldn't quite figure out. Was part of her left arm missing? Amber wasn't sure. The room was dark, but she was fairly certain she'd only seen that one hand Lila had produced to shake hers when they'd first met. Amber bought herself another Smirnoff Ice.

Annette bought two diet Cokes and returned to the table to visit a few new friends for the remainder of the intermission. Amber walked around, finishing her drink. She returned to her seat and began eavesdropping on Claudia and Lila's conversation. They were talking about stocks, the housing market, and the Gulf Coast weather in Florida.

"Give me your business card and I'll call you when I'm ready to buy another property," Claudia was telling Lila. "A good handyman or woman is a great thing to know about."

"Byron is really terrific. He shows up and does what he says he will," said Lila, handing Claudia her card. Claudia pocketed it.

"By the way," Claudia said to Lila, "we're leaving after intermission."

When Annette returned to her seat, Claudia stood up. She sidled over to Amber, put her arm around her waist, and drew her close enough to whisper in her ear, but far enough away from the others for privacy. "Hey, someone's had her eyes on you tonight."

"What? Who?"

"Your tablemate, Lila," she continued. "She was checking you out. The minute you stood up and walked away with Annette."

"I thought I felt her eyes on me," Amber said. Then she batted her eyelashes at Claudia teasingly. "But at first I thought it was you, you old perv."

"Anytime, baby, you just tell me," Claudia joked back. "But seriously, are you interested?"

"Sure. She seems nice enough, and she was easy to talk to. I just don't know."

"You mean about her arm?"

"Well, we're four hours apart by car. Would it even be worth exploring?"

Amber also had to admit to herself that Lila's missing arm did make her stop and wonder. She had first noticed it when Lila had asked Rick—the butchest one at the table—to open her bottle of water for her. Amber glanced down and realized that the blazer sleeve on Lila's left arm was pinned together midway past where an elbow should be. There was no hand.

"I don't know what to think about Lila's arm," Amber said. She had peeked at it a couple of times again, to see if she could determine where the appendage actually ended. It wasn't the kind of thing you asked a stranger about on first meeting. Amber had gone to elementary school with a couple of boys whose moms had taken thalidomide. Stevie had a few fingers that sprouted from under his shoulder; Mike's arm ended at his elbow and he'd been fitted with an early prosthetic, an awful, claw-like contraption that at least allowed him to hold a pencil in class. Maybe Lila's missing arm was due to that, or to bone cancer, or to an accident. Hell, it could be anything.

Intermission came to an end with a flicker of overhead lights. Annette motioned to everyone to stop talking as "Patsy" had regained the stage and was doing her sound check. Amber took her seat next to Lila. Amber was looking at the stage, but watching Lila from the corner of her eye, because Lila sat between her and the performer.

Amber wondered if Lila was interested in her too. She began to wonder what it would be like to go to bed with a one-armed woman. She figured that Lila must compensate with the other hand and arm. Maybe her other hand's fingers were strong and supple. She imagined a stump ending just below the elbow, a smooth rounded end solidly healed over. She started to fantasize what a stump might feel like between her legs and caught herself blushing in the darkened casino. Would it feel sexy? Amber wasn't sure.

"Let's get going," whispered Claudia to her partner.

"Ok, but I want to hear her sing 'Crazy,'" said Annette, pointing to the program. "It's the next song. Then we'll go. Alright?"

The trio agreed to leave after that most famous of Patsy Cline songs. "Patsy" completed her mike check and began singing "Crazy." But after just two minutes of the song, her singing was flat, overly controlled, and emotionless. Not nearly crazy enough.

"Okay, let's go," whispered Annette once the song ended.

"Well, it was nice meeting all of you," Lila whispered to Claudia, Annette, and Amber. Lila extended her hand to shake theirs.

Amber smiled, shook Lila's hand, and said softly, "Good night. It was really nice to meet you." Lila smiled back and remained seated next to her friend Rick. The three friends rose quietly and walked to the area near the exit.

"Can I see Lila's card?" Amber said to Claudia as they exited the casino.

Claudia reached into her pocket to give Amber the card. It had a picture of a house and said Palm Tree Properties, with Lila's name, address, phone, and fax number.

On their way out, Amber looked back once more at Lila, who was looking back toward the exit and not at the stage. Their eyes met momentarily. They smiled at each other and Amber's heart jumped for a second. Maybe she would give her a call the next day to inquire about possible rental properties in Gulfport.

ROUGH DRAFTING
JOAN ANNSFIRE

Joan Annsfire is a poet, writer and retired librarian who lives in Berkeley California. This piece is non-fiction, based on her experience working at the San Francisco Water Department in the early eighties. Her memoir pieces have appeared on websites most recently in *Anak Sastra, Stories of Southeast Asia. Aunt Lute Press*, as well as *Harrington Lesbian Literary Review* have her published stories. She has a story in *Identity Envy* and an excerpt from a longer piece in *Uprooted: an Anthology of Gender and Illness*. Her poetry has appeared in *13th Moon, Sinister Wisdom, Harrington Lesbian Literary Review, Lavender Review, Milk and Honey: a Celebration of Jewish, Lesbian Poetry*, and Counterpunch's *Poet's Basement* to name a few venues. In 2015 Headmistress Press published a chapbook of her poems, *Distant Music*. She has a blog, Lavenderjoan, somewhere under the rainbow, at the following address: http://lavenderjoan.blogspot.com/

I HAVE ALWAYS been good at job interviews. This survival skill paid off when I landed a job in 1982 through CETA, the Comprehensive Employment Training Act. In the field of drafting, women were considered part of an under-represented minority. Actually, the entire field was a veritable wasteland regarding any female presence.

On day one upon entering my new workplace, I felt a chill in the room that was like walking into a meat locker. Worse yet, apparently I was the meat. Six men, each of whom looked incredibly old, were already hunched over their drafting tables and there was a glass-walled office up front for the top banana. Heads lifted and eyes locked on me as I walked through the door. Being female and in my early thirties, it soon became clear that I was entering a foreign land where I was totally unfamiliar with the language and the customs.

It didn't take me long to realize that these men were not happy about this strange new addition to their work environment. Their closed faces said it all. As the boss was taking me around, one guy named Odie, which I later assumed was short for Odious, glared and refused to extend his hand to meet mine. I had to remind myself that I would be making good money here, not expanding my social life. This concept became a mantra in the coming two years. I had to try hard to maintain a semblance of sanity on the frontlines of this war zone known as the San Francisco Water Department.

Word of the "new broad" in the drafting room spread like wildfire. In the parking lot that first day, an older guy in well-worn workpants whose name I later learned was Joe, approached me and said accusingly, "Why are you taking a job away from a man?"

"Maybe you haven't heard, but women need to eat too."

"You don't have to take a drafting job. You could work as a secretary."

"I would have to be able to type then, wouldn't I? You can work as a secretary if you like," was my response.

In addition to the perpetual undercurrent of testosterone-infused hostility, the drafting room was awash in numerous alien rituals. Lunch was one that seemed insurmountable. Every day some of the plumbers, carpenters, and machinists would venture in from "the field" to play cards and smoke cigarettes, turning the drafting room into an aging men's fraternity.

Their conversation often centered on team sports and not-so-subtle sexual innuendo. It was banter loaded with bluster and bravado and it left me with one pressing need: to get away for the hour. The smoke, the chatter, the male-saturated environment—I had to flee. So I would walk through the industrial neighborhood to one of the few sandwich shops, pick up something, and eat in my car until the smoke cleared, the cards were put away, and the gang dispersed.

One of my co-workers was "fast Eddy" who, at forty-eight, was the youngest and horniest of the group. He looked me up and down in a way that made me nervous. Even though I only wore pants, had short hair, no makeup, and walked like an axe murderer, in 1983, it would never occur to these dudes to think of me as anything other than heterosexual.

I would often be sent out "in the field" with Eddy to measure pipelines. We'd hold some measuring tape, jot down some numbers, and ten minutes or so later we'd be in Red's Java Hut along the old Embarcadero waterfront, one of Eddy's many hangouts. Eddy would usually begin chatting in a time-trusted way. "My girlfriend doesn't understand me," he'd say, making me feel as though I had a part in a really trite soap opera.

"Such is life," I would reply, trying to steer the conversation in another direction. The subject of our co-workers seemed better. Maybe I could recruit an ally in the drafting room battles.

"Does Odie have a stick up his butt or what?" I asked him. The situation between me and Odie had recently deteriorated into a war between his cigarettes and my electric fan.

"Oh, you know, he's all wrapped up in the black church thing."

"Is it charitable to treat me like garbage?"

"He's just old and set in his ways. Don't take it so personal," Eddy advised.

Perhaps he had a point. I've always had trouble distancing myself from everything, whether it's offhand comments or direct insults.

"I can talk to you better than I can talk to my own brother," he said out of nowhere.

"That doesn't say much for your relationship with your brother," I commented dispassionately, wondering if conversational bullshit like this actually impressed straight women.

The problem with these weird interchanges was that once we got back to the office, Eddy would gather some old boys around him and allude to sexual improprieties between us that had transpired only in his imagination.

Once I overheard him telling his buds that he'd gone to my flat. Another time I caught him trying to convince uptight, straight-laced old Odie that he'd kissed me.

"If you buy that one, I have a bridge to sell you!" I interjected as I walked by. What would they do if they knew I was actually a dyke? I certainly wasn't ready to find out.

At times, I tried to join with the guys in their drafting room chatter. That proved to be a big mistake. One time they were going on about politics and Roy referred to a prominent female politician from California as that "hebe broad." It was too bad because my banter with Roy, an old white dude, was okay most of the time. After that comment of his, I stayed away from group conversations.

The closest thing I had to a friend in that room was Justin, a Chinese-American guy who was in his early fifties but could pass for forty, easily. An intellectual, loner type he was unmarried and didn't seem interested in folks of either sex.

"I'm a Chinese-school dropout," he confided one day. He lived in the Richmond District, a part of San Francisco that was heavily Chinese and Chinese-American by the eighties. He claimed his family was one of the first settlers. "They didn't want us here," he said. We compared notes on ethnicity and neighborhoods, since my family had confronted similar issues as Jews living in Ohio in the forties and fifties.

Ken, on the other hand, was my immediate boss. He was a tiny Korean immigrant. His English was good but he had a thick accent. He might have been in his late fifties or early sixties, a diminutive male, he was barely five feet tall. Our interaction was awkward from the get-go because of where his eyes would fall on my five-foot, six-inch frame. And old Ken was full of surprises. One day when we were both working in the vault, which was a tomb-like locked room where the old hand-written records of the Water Department were kept, he confided that the first thing he saw when he looked at a woman was her vagina. He told me how he would visualize its color, texture, and elasticity. I was at a loss for words.

Encounters like this were frequent and expected in that male, blue-collar work environment. I was so naïve, it had never occurred to me that little old Asian guys could be perverts. I pretended not to hear his comments and we continued working side by side in the vault, reading and amending old records.

Suddenly one day, I felt something wet on my ear. It was Ken's tongue. He'd moved in closer to me and was licking my ear.

"Ken, get the fuck away from me!" I yelled. Then I left the vault to speak with the head honcho of our department, who was his boss.

Tim Rooney, the top banana, was an engineer. He described himself as old San Francisco Irish, a working-class kid who went to college and made good. A bit more sophisticated than the others, he was the reason I had gotten hired in the first place. "Ken did what?" he said in disbelief.

"You heard me. He began philosophizing about women's vaginas and then commenced to lick my ear."

"I'll talk to him," Tim promised. "It won't happen again."

Meanwhile, Eddy was beginning to open up emotionally on our field measurement days. He told me that he hated to be called Eduardo, and that he felt that being of Mexican ancestry was demeaning. He had joined a local yacht club, even though he didn't own a boat and nor had any real intention of buying one. He would brag about how he was successfully passing for Italian-American in all his ventures.

Water Department interaction between the guys was laden with ethnic slurs. I tried to think of it as a *when in Rome* type of thing. Maybe it was like the way puppies play or dudes punch each other and insult someone's mother. Joe, the stationary engineer from across the hall, would regularly pop in and yell at Eddy, "How's it hangin', Spic?"

And Eddy would chime back, "Thick and hairy, Wop."

Tim and the management boys sometimes went out for lunch at a restaurant called Dago Mary's. I kid you not. That was the actual name of the place.

Being an active member of the obsessively politically correct lesbian community, it was a stretch for me to maintain a detached attitude. I rationalized it all as their culture, a bit abrasive and shocking but essentially light-hearted. But my perspective began to shift when I first heard the tradesmen referring to the black guys who hung out together as "The Cotton Club."

Their sexism was the same: thorough, insidious, and unrelenting. Still, I was persistent and determined, and I believed that time was on my side. They would get used to me, and finally come to terms with having a female co-worker.

Months passed and nothing was really changing. After I'd been there half a year, I was still battling with Odie on a daily basis because his cigarettes made me sick and my electric desk fan made him cold. I was still hearing rumors about my budding romance with Eddy, and I now felt closer than ever to coming out as queer. I figured at least it would throw a wrench in their gossip machine.

Even though Odie was perpetually angry about my fan, he refused to smoke less. A diehard military man, he was not going to let some female work in his job classification and try to treat him like an equal without a fight. He was also suspicious about my lunchtime ventures. Bayview was a mostly black, working-class area—a mix of small homes and industrial developments. One day he just came out with, "Where do you go in a neighborhood like this?" delivered in an accusatory tone.

"To get a sandwich, Odie, where do you think I go at lunch?"

"You're a tramp. You're nothing but a tramp," he concluded in his most odious, self-righteous manner.

"You're right, Odie, I'm a tramp. I didn't want to say it, but I guess you've figured out that I spend my lunch hour moonlighting at a brothel down the street!"

Overweight and balding, Odie sometimes spoke of his years in World War II as though they'd been the best ones of his life. A few times he'd described his service as "I was over there liberating your people," by which he meant the Jews, as if this country ever cared about any group other than the rich and powerful!

"Well, you did a bang-up job. If only you'd begun a bit sooner," I'd reply. If he wanted to take credit for winning WWII, he should certainly take the blame for all the missteps as well. He told me he was an original member of the Tuskegee Airmen, one of the first all-black Air Force regiments.

I have never been closeted about my own ethnicity. My unusual-featured face and kinky auburn hair might be a dead giveaway but mostly, the main clue of my ethnicity comes from my big mouth. I have trouble keeping the details of my life and my opinions to myself. But here at the Water Department once you were identified as Jewish, it became a filter for everything else.

One other Jew who worked there was Jay, the machinist. In his late twenties, Jay was queer as hell and obviously Jewish because his last name was Birnbaum. He would sometimes set up a little table in front of the Water Department at lunch to do his second job, selling scarves and costume jewelry. It irritated the hell out of me that he played into stereotypes by doing this, but Jay himself was cool about it. He had neatly cropped, dark hair, just a touch of eyeliner, and an amazing black leather motorcycle jacket.

"Jay, don't you think you need a few more zippers on that jacket?" I teased him. It was festooned with studs, zippers, and all sorts of potential openings.

"Oh honey, you should see the matching pants!" he cooed in his campiest voice.

"I think I'll pass on that one."

In the bathroom I ran into Flossie, also a secretary, in the ladies' room. She was their queen bee. She began airing one of her major gripes against Diane, another secretary, who I'd thought was her close friend. "She is hoarding things in her desk again," Flossie began. "The big bottle of whiteout, the good stapler, she keeps them all so no one else can use them. You know those Jews, they think they own everything."

"Diane is Jewish?" I inquired, surprised. I knew about Jay but hadn't realized there were others.

"Oh yeah, of course she is, that's why she wants to take over the whole show."

In this situation, my replies to Flossie were based on a technique I'd learned in self-defense class. It involved using the force that's being directed at you against the enemy who's attacking you. Just let them lunge at you and, as they do, gently guide their body down to the floor. Their own hatred and anger will do the rest.

"And you're not Jewish, Flossie? Somehow, I always thought you were." This was a blatant lie on my part. At this point I just wanted to get her goat, as they say.

"You did? Was it my eyes, my hair?" I could hear the panic rising in her voice.

"I don't know for sure. It's just a vibe or something." Flossie was looking distraught by now.

"I'm Jewish too, you know," I announced.

"Un hunh." Clearly this information had already circulated in the clerical quarters.

"So you really can't expect me to support you when you make anti-Semitic comments against Diane."

"You people really stick together, don't you?" Flossie said, perturbed.

During all the tumult of my work experience, the Tradeswomen group that met once a month was a lifeline for me. It consisted of other women in trade jobs around the city who, like me, were just trying to keep on keepin' on. Often we were isolated from one another, as management seemed to prefer having only one female employee in any given "male" job classification at a time.

The Tradeswomen supported my struggles as a woman and a queer, but they had more trouble understanding the ethnicity issue. Integrating myself into this blue collar world was much more complicated than it seemed to be for most of the others. Except of course for Elaine, who was black. But Elaine kept to herself and held good boundaries, which I tried hard to emulate.

Sally, a stationary engineer, had a straight forward way with the guys and was totally able to keep them in line. Her background was rural, full of horses, church bazaars, and 4H club meetings.

But the one person who really kept me sane at that job was Mickey, the laborer. I'd run into her in the room with a couch that led into both the women's bathroom and the locker room. She was relaxed, a lesbian who was out with her co-workers. Our early encounters ran on too long because once we got started talking, we just couldn't stop. One fateful afternoon in the women's locker room, she took out some cocaine, an old favorite drug of mine, and we did a few lines together. It was wonderful. All the petty problems of the work-place just melted away and I felt sure I could rule the world.

Thus, our ritual began. At about three p.m. each day, we'd meet in the women's locker room and we'd do a few lines of coke together. Then we'd yak and shoot the breeze for about twenty minutes more, and then I'd return to work re-energized and refreshed.

I looked forward to getting high and speculating on every facet of human nature with Mickey. After a time, I lived for both things. The drugs and Mickey became the highlight of my days. Cocaine made me feel certain I could succeed at anything, and Mickey was an odd and interesting soul. Unbelievably, she had exchanged a life of prestige and status for this one. Although she had a master's degree in history and had been a lecturer at a community college, she'd gotten tired of it and decided to chuck it all, and work with her hands.

"I got tired of all the butt-kissing in academia," was usually how she'd sum things up. She was on the other end of the spectrum. She felt as comfortable and accepted here as I felt shunned and disliked.

As time passed, my mirror and my skills with half a razor blade and a sprinkling of white powder smoothed over any rough terrain on the job. It was like a ritual of worship during which we had to work quickly. The fact that it was an act of subterfuge made it even more enticing.

I became a pro at laying out the floury substance into neat delicate lines and rolling dollar bills into straws that we would snort from, licking it all clean afterwards. The light would shift and I'd feel at peace with Mickey and every corner of that imperfect universe.

Due to this new dimension in my life, my work at the Water Department was becoming almost tolerable. My day was divided by my treat schedule: coffee at eight-thirty in the morning, lunch at twelve-thirty or so, then at mid-afternoon, my break-time of snorting and chatting with Mickey. An hour more of work and it was time to go home.

The beehive bullies had always harbored resentment, but now, at each little birthday celebration, Flossie would divide the cake into pieces for each person she liked and label them with their names. If I went looking for some, she'd say they didn't have enough because all the slices had already been assigned. I would just find a big piece labeled for one of the guys.

"I'll take this one. Ronald won't mind," I'd say, and go off with it. Even if I didn't eat it, I made sure I made a dent in her birthday cake control wagon.

My work environment became commonplace, even boring, until the day that word got out that there had been shooting at the Sewage Treatment Plant a few blocks away. The story I heard was that a black low-level worker who was rumored to be a drunk had shot a white boss. Sewage treatment jobs were literally full of shit, especially at the bottom rungs of the ladder. He didn't kill the guy. He only got him in the shoulder. The boss returned to work but the laborer did not. They said he'd gotten thirty years to life for attempted murder.

After this, things began heating up around the yard. The racial tension was palpable. Now the division between black and white began to feel more like a chasm. People hurried by in groups of their own kind.

The strain took other forms as well. I noticed that Jay no longer was selling his wares in front of the building. I asked Mickey about it because she had the inside scoop on everything. She said Joe, the same stationary engineer that harassed me that first day, had called him a "kike faggot" and was spreading false stories around the yard about him and his "sexual proclivities."

The anti-female attacks spun out of control too. Joe came in the next day looking for a file of some kind. After pulling out the metal drawer of the cabinet he exclaimed, "This file is tighter than a pussy!"

"Then Joe, why don't you try to slam your dick into it!" I said, almost reflexively.

"I never heard a female talk the way you do!" Joe was floundering a bit.

"That's because, one, you don't know any females and two, you don't listen."

Joe stomped out of the room muttering the words "fucking bitch" under his breath.

I was still going on field runs with Eddy, who was now creating elaborate fantasies of sexual encounters he'd supposedly had with me at my flat. I know it wasn't the wisest move, but I couldn't take it anymore. One day I broke up the huddle and said, "Eddy can't even get to first base with me, boys, and you know why? It's because I have zero interest in any man. In fact, show me a woman who won't stay in her place, and she can stay in my place."

They just looked and me, guffawed, and looked at me again. After that, when other tradeswomen came in to pick me up for lunch, the room fell silent and all eyes turned to watch me and whoever was going off with me. I realized they thought I was screwing every gal in the place. One day Odie made some comment about my bevy of girlfriends.

"You're just jealous because I'm getting so much more than you are," I said loudly.

Coffee was the elixir of life at the Water Department. Everyone drank tons of it. As a non-smoker, I probably drank a bit more than most since I had no cigarettes to waylay or divert my attention. I rewarded myself with a cup almost five times a day. Between that and the coke, I had almost stopped sleeping entirely.

Because the coffee room was just behind the wall of my desk, I heard more than I ever desired from Flossie and the beehive bullies. When the room grew quiet, I could listen to their conversations. One rainy day I heard someone say, "Should we tell what's-her-name that she left her lights on?" I thought it very well could be me although I didn't realize that they didn't use my name in their gossip. When I went out to the parking lot, I found that, yes, it was in fact my car to which they'd been referring.

It was then that I heard that Jay, the machinist, had gone out on medical leave. Someone had put a cracked bench vise at his station and it broke while he was machining a piece of metal. His wounds were from metal, piercing him like shrapnel. Once it was removed, they said he would recover, at least physically. But last I heard, he was out on stress leave indefinitely.

Now each day before leaving, I would check beneath my car. I tried to do it surreptitiously, so as not to give anyone ideas. I'm not sure that I would have recognized a bomb or something evil if I saw it, but it couldn't hurt to look.

This proved to be a good policy, because one evening while leaving work, I found a piece of wood with nails sticking up behind one of my front tires. I then started parking my car on the street, in different places in order to feel safer.

At this time, my partner, my sister, and her boyfriend and I were in the midst of buying a multi-unit property in San Francisco. When the sale finally went through, several co-workers asked me about it. I told them yes, that I had just completed my FIRST purchase of real estate. It was like the time Roy asked me if I had a trust fund and I told him, "Yes, all of us are issued them at birth."

A few months later, things got tight financially for the city of San Francisco and I got a pink slip in the mail. Now, it was official. My time here was drawing to a close. As I worked those final weeks, women from Tradeswomen were nowhere to be seen. Only Mickey, my stalwart drug buddy, gave me a parting gift on my last day: some lines of coke and a free lunch. No one else said a word. Maybe the others were worried that I might lose my house. Most likely, they just didn't know what to say.

Back then, losing jobs was no big deal for me, but their generalized fear was starting to become contagious. The day I finally left the Water Department, the silence that followed me out the door was deafening.

In the space between jobs, my feelings of depression and uncertainty were mixed with an overwhelming sense of relief. I was glad to be gone from there. As usual, before my unemployment benefits ran out, I managed to find another gig. This one involved a new drafting program called CADD (Computer-Aided Design Drafting) which, in a few years, would render all those old drafting jobs obsolete. I simply led my prospective employer to believe that I already had experience with this new technology. I planned that, if anything stumped me, I'd just explain how the system I'd trained on was slightly different than the one they were using.

I wasn't too worried. With jobs, my guiding motto has always been: *Forget about love and war, all's fair when it comes to economic survival.* And, like I said, I have always been good at job interviews.

state for lesbian/gay marriage and so we opted to plan for a wedding. A few months before we had set our wedding date, Chris started dropping hints and saying that she was contemplating getting chest surgery. The surgery, it was hoped, would make it possible for Chris to be perceived as "male" in our public life. At first this idea made me wonder and worry. But when I stopped to think how much more comfortable Chris might be with this alteration, and when I also admitted that her breasts always remained completely covered whenever we were sexual, I decided that this was basically something I could support. Mainly, I wanted Chris to be fully comfortable and I was willing to go the extra mile to ensure that.

Also at this point, I was reading about and being told that people exist who are the opposite "brain" sex of their biological sex, and that they had this nebulous feeling of their "identity." I decided that I could handle top surgery if it made Chris happy. I certainly didn't want Chris to feel tormented. Our wedding took place as planned. We had a small ceremony and invited only a few friends to the reception.

A few weeks after our wedding, Chris arranged to have top surgery. She had been seeing a therapist for several months now, who approved a referral for a surgeon. The results were consistent and luckily there were no major complications. But Chris never shared with me these "results," still preferring to keep semi-covered whenever we made love. However, Chris seemed happier, and for this I was relieved.

But, that happiness only lasted for a short while because as it turned out, Chris began to feel even more freaky in public and dissatisfied with external appearances. One day, not long afterward, Chris explained to me a growing desire to start taking testosterone, well "just a little bit," in order to be seen publically as fully "male." Two times when we were out together in public, we were still referred to as "ladies," and that was very upsetting for Chris. More than once, I would watch Chris fall into a moody stupor, which ruined the rest of the day for the two of us. Maybe a somewhat lower voice would help stop this from happening, and then, as Chris promised me, the testosterone injections would stop altogether.

I hated seeing Chris suffer so much. But to be honest, by this point, I was starting to feel nervous. I was having thoughts about our future, what it would be, and whether I could stay in this relationship. But, by now I was emotionally and financially invested. I was married and I felt bound to support Chris, whose happiness had become paramount to me, even more paramount than my own feelings and doubts. So I tried to push down my nagging misgivings. I started paying more attention to other things in my life, like the organic vegetable garden in our backyard, and my career. I worked in retail for a European furniture company and I was learning a lot about current trends in interior design and all the latest styles coming here from Europe. I got a discount on the merchandise and so I bought us a few things for our living room and made it beautiful.

Fairly quickly, the testosterone injections began. I knew without having to talk about it that my own reservations and queasiness at Chris's decision to take testosterone were expected to take a backseat to this seemingly torturous life Chris had had as a woman. So I accepted these changes and tried to read more about transgenderism.

Unfortunately, I did not really come across any radical feminist analysis or any other trans questioning type of writing at that time. I had no other means to understand or sort out what I was going through. I wish I had, because I was becoming increasingly troubled and scared, and I was yearning for a variety of viewpoints or discourse that might bring me more clarity. I loved Chris, but I was feeling so divided. Even while I thought Chris's rights and feelings must be fully protected, at the same time, I felt that I had some rights too. I was aware that I had been squashing my own growing feelings.

I loved Chris more than I'd ever loved anyone in my life, but I worried. I'm the partner. What if these changes were not going to work for me? I knew they would irrevocably change our relationship. I worried every day about our projected future. Could I live with it? Not wanting to answer this question, I disregarded my own queasiness and gave all my empathy to Chris.

Fairly easily, Chris was getting testosterone from a local doctor. All that was required were these continuing visits with the therapist a few times. Chris talked about a longstanding feeling of gender dysphoria since being a young child. Based on this therapist's support and recommendation, a doctor prescribed hormone therapy—testosterone in particular—and Chris starting injecting every day.

Again, I felt it was my duty to support Chris's right to transition regardless of my own misgivings, which I decided not to share with Chris at this time. Because I had no exposure to any other viewpoints to understand what we were going through, I felt that I *had* to follow through. If I didn't, what kind of an ally or wife would I be? I felt I had no choice.

One morning I watched Chris take this daily injection. A feeling of concern and sadness came over me. After that one time, Chris did these injections privately and never told me how much or how often they were happening. All I knew was that, despite being told this would be a temporary measure only to achieve a slight voice change, the testosterone injections actually continued.

I could see some physical changes occurring within the first year we lived together. The injections went on well after the first and second years of our marriage. Today, in hindsight, I wonder if Chris had always planned to continue with hormone therapy in order to completely pass as a male in society but just didn't want to tell me this up front for fear of my withdrawing my support and ending our marriage.

At about this time, I was also competing for a managerial position in my job. I was now a buyer for this European furniture store and they were opening a new outlet in another city. The business was expanding and they were promising me a promotion to store manager, but only if I accepted a temporary job re-location first. They wanted to see how well I did in managing a new outlet they had planned to open in ten months. So they asked me to re-locate to their new store in another city to help set it up for business. This re-location meant that Chris and I would have to live apart for at least eight to ten months while I focused on getting this new store set up and helped to train my newly hired staff. Although I didn't want to live apart for so long, part of me felt it might be good to have a period of time in which we both got some breathing room, especially me. I needed to focus on my career and learn to work with my staff in this new location. I would still be in close relationship with Chris through phone calls and Skype and occasional visits.

This is how I explained this period of relocation to myself and to Chris, who wasn't too happy about it. I also knew an old college friend named Nina who lived in the city that I was being re-located to. She had a large house with a guest bedroom. She was paying off some longstanding debts from graduate school. So it was convenient for both of us to room together at this time. I decided to take the opportunity. I admit that I wasn't fully aware of my own mixed emotions. I was in some denial about how this time apart might affect Chris and me.

Within two months of living in another city, in an apartment that I was now sharing with an old college friend, I started googling "wedding annulment." At first, this was out of curiosity. But later, I began researching it more seriously as a legal procedure, including any statute of limitations that might be involved. I felt enormous guilt about this and so I mentioned it to no one.

Chris and I spoke on the phone regularly, and sometimes we Skyped. Months ago, I had agreed to share in the cost of the initial testosterone injections with Chris, feeling it was my role to be as helpful as I could be. But as the weeks passed and I adjusted to my current life in a re-located city, a life which included a substantially higher rent, I realized I was now beginning to resent what felt like an inequitable financial agreement between Chris and me. Although I was okay about helping out initially, I had never agreed to ongoing testosterone injections. This ongoing cost was not cheap either. It was certainly becoming more than I had bargained for, both financially and emotionally. In retrospect, I should have started talking about these feelings right away with Chris. But yet again, I suppressed them and tried to continue as usual. Several more weeks passed.

To be fully honest, on one occasion, I did attempt to air my concerns about this with Nina, my trusted longtime friend. I wanted to see what she thought, so I spoke as honestly as I could about my situation. She listened and tried to be supportive but really didn't know what to say to help me sort out my feelings. She suggested I find some online support. Maybe there was a group of some kind that would help.

I thought this was worth a try. I found a new butch/femme forum online, and tried to chat with a few women there. But I was not finding much support for the particular situation I was in. It seemed like I was the only lesbian femme who ever experienced something like this, where my butch partner was now transitioning, and all that that entailed. Perhaps I wasn't finding the best resources. I kept trying, but I was starting to feel very isolated and alone. I didn't have much support in real life either. I was only sharing these concerns a little bit with my family. They tried to be helpful, but they really had even less familiarity with these issues than Nina did, and besides that, my mother had a tendency to be homophobic, although she meant well. She had dropped a couple of annoying comments and I didn't feel safe confiding in her.

At this time, the one way I had to soothe myself and de-stress was to become better and better as a buyer at my job. I signed up for training classes on product marketing and on the latest small space design ideas from Europe. I studied various kinds of fabric for comforters, and got better at creating attractive store displays with our new merchandise. My staff and I were getting better at working together too. I actually love this line of work, and I'm good at it, so this was a productive place for me to be putting my energies. After five months, I got the promotion they had promised me, with a modest raise as well. This gave me a boost emotionally, and served to divert my other worries too, at least for a while.

In our long distance phone conversations, I think that Chris could sense that I was not fully on board with the changing circumstances of our relationship. From my side, I could sense some growing anger on Chris' part as well, especially after one attempt I made to talk about our financial arrangement and my discomfort with it. One day, I hinted that I wanted to stop contributing toward medical expenses for the injections that were only supposed to be temporary anyway. Somehow, I managed to find a way to say this. I knew it was time to get honest.

The conversation did not go over well. Chris got really angry with me and reacted in a volatile and excessive manner. It wasn't the first time Chris had gotten incredibly angry with me over the phone, and displayed a temper that scared me. This time, I had less patience than the other times. I threatened to hang up the phone. Actually I did hang up twice, but then I called back a few minutes later. I told Chris to monitor this tendency to throw a temper tantrum because I didn't deserve to be treated this way. After hearing the firmness in my voice, Chris calmed down, but basically, accused me of reneging on my previous agreement to help out with medical costs. At the time, I felt guilty. Was this true?

In retrospect, I don't think I was reneging at all. Instead, my feelings were starting to change and I was getting stronger about finally speaking up. Also, I had never agreed to indefinitely help out with medical costs. Besides that, when we talked on the phone, the now much deeper voice I was hearing on the other end of the line was becoming increasingly uncomfortable for me. I tried to convince myself that Chris was the same person I had met nearly three years ago and that I simply needed time to adjust. Not only that, but my adjustment was crucial in order for Chris to live a happy life.

The physical changes in Chris were occurring more rapidly and becoming more noticeable, including voice, hair, and face. They were difficult for me to grasp over Skype, but I knew I was not finding myself comfortable with them. One night, after we Skyped, I felt sad. I went to the closet and took out our old wedding photo. I was shocked to see a photo of the handsome butch I had married, compared to the person I had just spoken to online. The smooth, handsome butch face I well remembered and loved had now changed from a good-looking butch to a middle-aged man's face which was familiar, but I did not fully recognize it. I saw vestiges of the handsome woman I had fallen in love with but that was all. I also saw a different person. Someone else. Chris's skin texture and manner seemed to change as well, all of which left me with a profound sadness. The person who I fell in love with was disappearing right before my eyes.

We were due to spend time together in two weeks. I was getting scared. A month prior, I had agreed to fly back home as soon as possible for a much needed vacation. I thought this would give us some time to catch up with one another again. We hadn't seen each other in about six months now. I took my luggage out of the hall closet, knowing I would need to start packing some clothes soon. In one suitcase, I came across a few more photos of us, including more wedding photos. I held them up to the light and stared at them in disbelief. I had the oddest feeling.

The woman in the photo, my partner, barely resembled the person I had just been Skyping with a day ago. A deep sadness crept over me. At that moment, it occurred to me maybe I shouldn't fly back home at all. I felt a sense of dread just envisioning it. I put the photos away and decided to go to bed and not think about this dilemma until tomorrow. But all night long, various scenarios were seeping into my half-conscious mind and I couldn't get restful sleep. I woke up crying, at one point. I remembered Nina had given me a few Ambien to use on sleepless nights, which I seemed to be having more of lately. I took 10mg of Ambien and tried to go back to sleep.

The next morning, I realized I was in a precarious emotional state and I needed to just keep what little wits I had about me to get through my work week and the demands of my job. I was glad to at least have my job to distract me. But as a new manager, I had to be responsible. I had to be on the ball.

Soon after this, I started numbing myself with alcohol a few times after work, seeking to alleviate some of the anxiety and guilt I had about possibly not flying back home to Chris. Ironically, after a couple of drinks, my mind would wander even farther. I let myself consider even more serious plans. Maybe this was all too much for me, more than I had bargained for. Maybe I needed to leave our marriage altogether. I was concerned about indulging this new line of thinking, which I would only let myself consider after two or three drinks. I felt miserable and lost, like I had no one to really sort out my thoughts with.

One night, after managing to finish most of a bottle of red wine by myself, Nina came home to find me on the couch staring at the TV. I was wrapped in a puffy indigo comforter, which I loved. It was one of my employee discount purchases from the store. She looked at me still in a stupor from the wine I had consumed, and sat down.

"Laura, what is this?" she said, picking up my empty bottle. "What are you doing?" She got up, walked into the kitchen, and returned a few minutes later. She sat down again near me and all I can remember is her familiar brown eyes staring at me, and me feeling really out of it. Nina said she was concerned about what I had been going through. She was worried for my safety and my well-being. She suggested I postpone my trip back home until I was more clear-headed and definitely ready to see Chris. "Think about it," she said. "You can't keep doing this. It's not a solution." Then she went to bed.

As I sat there, I knew she was right. I realized that I was resentful that the early promise Chris had made to me not to transition was not kept. I had asked that question very clearly well before we got married, and the answer was a firm "no." I was angry and I felt manipulated. I was also afraid that my original attraction to Chris was never going to return. On top of that, this was my first "gay" relationship. I was ashamed that we weren't doing so well, especially remembering my mother and her occasional homophobic comments and her negative prognostications about my "gay" life. I had enough doubt and worry, I didn't need her crap along with everything else.

Then my thoughts wandered back to Chris and our relationship. Actually, I did have doubts, serious ones. But they weren't about my attraction to women. I wondered: What have I gotten myself into with Chris?

Also, I was concerned about Chris's current mental health situation. It was scaring me, the angry outbursts and the ongoing expectation of financial help coming from me to pay for the injections. Why? I had not signed up for that and it wasn't fair to expect me to keep that up, especially with the burden of my higher rent right now. Also, I was sensing that Chris had stopped going to therapy. This was the same therapist that had okayed the initial injections. We had not discussed it recently. But I was fairly certain that Chris had stopped going altogether due to being unable to afford the payments, and possibly choosing to prioritize the injections instead. I knew Chris had a couple of friends, but aside from them, Chris probably lacked enough emotional support, not to mention anyone else to share day to day concerns with.

I felt deeply sad about this. Then I realized, there I was, worried about Chris again. Dammit! I realized that my own mental health was seriously suffering now. I was drinking heavily and I was depressed and scared. My friend and my family were concerned with how distraught I was becoming over this relationship.

In recent days, I had also started experiencing acute colitis. I would get abdominal pain, cramping, and bouts of diarrhea that would send me running to the bathroom, even when I was at work. I knew it was because my anxiety was at an all time high now. I was not coping well. I still loved Chris and I didn't want to hurt this person whom I had spent three years with. But staying in this marriage was hurting me too much. I didn't feel emotionally safe anymore.

To make a long story shorter, I decided not to go back home for that visit. Instead, Chris and I had several emotional phone conversations and one Skype. I finally announced in our third talk that I did not feel safe anymore and I was unsure of why I was in this relationship, given all the changes. It was not unfolding as I had expected. Our geographical separation had helped me to finally understand this. And lastly, I finally said it: I decided I wanted to file for a divorce. This was huge, and I was afraid, but once I managed to say the words, it was as if a lead weight had been lifted from my shoulders. That lead weight was the stress of guilt and sadness that I'd been carrying for so long.

At first, I let a few weeks pass and did nothing. Two months later, I sent divorce papers to Chris at our old home. First I called and left a phone message saying that I was doing this. I hated doing it but I knew that my own health and well-being had to come first. I could no longer remain in this marriage. At first the papers were completely ignored by Chris. I called again and then sent them once more. Finally, Chris signed them and sent them back. Our divorce judgement was legal. It was finalized in four months.

Chris and I have not spoken since then, which was more than a year ago.

Even with that much time passing, I still think about Chris every day. I'm still sorting out my feelings over what we went through in those three plus years together. I've been in therapy and I got into AA on my therapist's urging. That is, I found a local twelve step group to make sure that I stopped drinking and got sober again.

In retrospect, I want to tell other women, and other lesbians especially, to trust yourself. Have compassion for yourself. As a woman you are conditioned to be accepting and kind, supportive of everyone, but most especially the one you love. But you have to remember to love and support yourself too. You have a right to speak your mind, express your reservations, voice your doubts or even your outright disagreement with your partner. You have to include your needs and yourself in the relationship.

If you are ever in a situation where your female partner decides to transition, remember that your desires are just as important and valid as their desire to transition. You have the right to not feel comfortable with any of it and to not be ashamed that you are not emotionally equipped nor willing to stand beside your partner if your partner wishes to pursue such a drastic and permanent alteration. Your desires matter. You have the right to leave the relationship and you don't have to feel guilty about it. I'm saying this to you now, but it took me years to finally get clear on this myself. So I'm passing this on from my own extremely difficult experience.

Additionally, let's also remember this. If you are a woman attracted to butch lesbians, butch lesbians are not synonymous with men or with "trans guys." Butches are a completely different type of person. Number one, they are women. Gender non-conforming women, yes. But butch lesbians possess a strength that is unique and compelling, as they move through a cruel world that harshly sanctions and punishes females who refuse to conform to a stereotype of how women and lesbians are supposed to be. Butches do not perform culturally mandated, gendered notions of what it is to be female and a woman, and that's perfectly okay. Actually, I find it admirable and amazing.

As for me, I still struggle with my life today. I wish I had trusted myself more and sooner. I wish I had found the strength to have voiced my opinions earlier and more often about my lover's transition. I wish I wouldn't have cared so much, seeking to spare Chris's feelings so that, in the end, I was hurting myself and I was so confused. I was left with a lot of unresolved questions which I still sort through in retrospect. I still feel sad. That was a loss that has permanently changed me, because that was the lesbian relationship in which I came out all the way and in which I discovered with great excitement and enthusiasm, my love for other women. That was my "coming out relationship," in which I had wanted to feel pride and happiness for finally embracing my love for other women, and look how it ended, so sadly, and with so much pain.

In the months that we were separating, I began and haven't stopped reading radical feminist analysis of sex and gender. I started questioning decisions people make to surgically and chemically alter their physical selves in an attempt to gain peace with their physical bodies. I'm not sure where I first began, or which feminist authors and websites I first started reading, but I learned that gender is really just a conglomeration of culturally enforced sex role stereotypes. It's socially constructed from day one. Women and lesbians are especially being oppressed as a class by these rigid stereotypes. It affects our relationships and our coupling too. It affects the ways we think about our own lives.

As I have learned firsthand, the social construct of gender can have really damaging effects on us, and serious repercussions for children, women, lesbians, and society as a whole. My feeling about it today is, change society not yourself. You are okay the way you are, whatever that is. Regarding my own identity, although I hesitated many years ago to call myself a lesbian, today I realize that it doesn't matter what "type" of woman I am attracted to—they are all women, as I am myself.

Today, I identify now as a strong femme lesbian, who is attracted to other women, butch lesbians in particular. I desperately wish that gender non-conforming women, butches, especially those of the younger generation, will come to realize their unique and powerful beauty as females, just as they are, and also to realize the rich history of lesbian women who came before us. I pray that we can come to love and respect lesbian women and our precious lesbian culture. As a lesbian femme who adores butch lesbians, I especially want to say: Please understand this: You are perfect just as you are, and we love you exactly the way you are.

SOLILOQUY
ROXANNE ANSOLABEHERE

Roxanne Ansolabehere's "Soliloquy," is part of a larger anthology of connected short stories set in the Central Valley of California. She is originally from the Central Valley and well understands the particular pains and joys of growing up lesbian in a disapproving and repressive environment. However, like most places with a small town character, there are glimmers of endless acceptance and even love. It is this very human and universal quality that her fiction tends to explore and celebrate.

A WHIFF OF varnish and industrial cleaner. Scrubbed. Ordered, but dim in the corners from low wattage lights. Cinder blocks with coats of cheery paint over what had been a squat collection of buildings owned by the government for draft induction and testing. The complex had sat vacant for three years when a group of determined and well-meaning citizens descended like a pestilence on the local government and forced Sheffield to ask for the return of the buildings. No one wanted much to do with the armed services. This was 1976, the draft was three years dead, and try as the country might to cleanse its palate, the Vietnam War was still a bitter taste. So the government handed it over without much of a fuss and the town decided they'd do some good and make money in the bargain, so they opened the only school for the deaf in the central valley. The closest other one was six hours north. It was a good bet they'd get students, but they weren't prepared for the flood of applications. After initial confusion and much debate, as only a small town can offer, they decided the only way to keep everyone happy was to give preference to local kids, and Sallie Ann was enrolled.

It wasn't the picture she'd imagined when two weeks ago her mother sat her down, barely containing her excitement and told her the news.

School.

Not the summer school where she'd gone every year so she could learn to sign and read lips. And not the public one where she went during the year and tried to make sense of it, which was like trying to live in the world with her head wrapped in gauze—always behind, always fending off instead of taking part. She'd stuck with it because her father said she had to or else they would come to the house and arrest her. Had to sit where she could see the teacher's face, always in the front and not in the back where the secret games and fun were. Had to stand on the edge of everything and watch others laugh, a small but tightly fisted group of girlfriends whispering to each other and she alone, apart with her restless hands shoved in her pockets.

"Everyone there is deaf. Like you. A school for you. And it's all year long," her mother had said barely hiding her own excitement. "You'll make friends, honey. It'll be different. They're going to teach you how to use your hands better—to sign better, you won't have to read lips so much."

Sallie Ann clenched her fists. She had, from the time she could remember relied mostly on lip reading, not from a school, or a tutor, but she had taught herself. She had become so good that little escaped her. But the chance to be around others like her, to learn to use her hands to talk to others like her, others her own age, made her heart pound.

A new school. Everyone like me.

Excitement was too flimsy. It was something bigger, deeper, and wider, like the bass thrum of music when the volume was turned up high and she leaned against the speakers. It filled her.

Her mother placed her hands on Sallie Ann's shoulders. "They're going to teach you how to get a job, how to take care of yourself. You're a big girl now, sixteen—almost seventeen—you're old enough. You could start thinking of a job. When I was your age I was waitressing. But you have to do some growing up. No more of this nonsense of doing what you want when you want. You have to answer to people. You can't just get up and leave school when you get upset. They have rules. You have to follow them. And you have to start sticking up for yourself. You just let things burn in you and burn in you and then when you can't stand it anymore you just take off. You can't do that, honey. You just can't."

Sallie Ann blinked. Her mother sighed and turned away.

She wore her best dress on the first day and bit her nails from nervousness as she and her mother walked down a long, dim hallway and turned left to enter the front office. It was a large spacious room that had been divided into a few small sections with two nearly identical women sitting at desks, gray and small.

The woman closest to the door looked at Sallie Ann's mother and then at Sallie Ann. Although her face was worn, her eyes were kind. Sallie Ann watched the woman's mouth, she was saying something about the director running a little late and did they want to have one of the school's volunteers come and give them a quick tour before the appointment.

When Sallie Ann's mother spoke she must've agreed because the lady smiled. Suddenly the door opened and all the air seemed to gather itself in a whirlwind and a woman entered. Her age seemed indeterminate since Sallie Ann had never seen anyone like her before. Not in Sheffield. She was tall and thin, mannish, but it was her calmness that stood out. She walked slowly into the room, bringing with her an air of authority and strength and a whiff of what Sallie Ann thought might be lemon cologne, but she had never smelled anything like it before. There was nothing frilly about it. It was clean and strong and each breath pierced Sallie Ann at her deepest, nestled there until it made her restless.

The room's drabness faded. Sallie Ann understood from the exchange of pleasantries that this was the school's director. She was beckoned closer and there was a thrumming energy about the Director that, coupled with her assurance, made her compelling. Sallie Ann barely breathed.

The Director wore a pair of blue pleated gabardine pants, belted carelessly and a starched, cotton blouse, so white it was blinding. Her brown curly hair was cut short and from what Sallie Ann could tell she didn't use hairspray to keep it in place. Her appearance, her confidence, her gentleness made Sallie Ann want to nestle in the crook of her arm, breathe in her lemon cologne, take her in slowly, slowly, and then all at once. Sallie Ann, so used to looking at the floor, raised her eyes to take in more of this woman and met the steady gaze of her cornflower blue eyes.

Sallie Ann was in love. A thrilling sharp stab followed just as closely with fear. What was this?

The woman came over to where Sallie Ann and her mother stood and before she said anything to her mother she took both of Sallie Ann's hands in hers. Nothing was said, nothing signed—the two simply looked at each other and Sallie Ann felt for the first time that someone who understood was looking at her. At her. Sallie Ann ventured a slow, shy smile and the woman tightened her grip on Sallie Ann's fingers. For a second her eyes flicked toward the others in the room and then she said directly to Sallie Ann and as she spoke she signed slowly and carefully, "The girl who is going to take you around and show you the school is here. Her name is Rose Clare."

But Sallie Ann wanted to stay there. Stay being held by this woman. Stay. It was a new feeling. New, thrilling and dangerous.

Reluctantly, Sallie Ann turned and saw a girl around her age with wispy, thin blond hair and flat, depthless brown eyes. Sallie Ann tried another small smile and the girl smiled back, automatically, but her dark brown eyes remained lifeless and impenetrable.

Rose looked over at the Director who turned toward Sallie Ann and like a true teacher never missing an opportunity, signed, her fingers, graceful and expressive, formed the words she spoke out of thin air. "Have a good tour. I will meet with you again after."

Her mother faded, gone, the Director placed an arm around her and they approached the young girl. It was in a sweeping blur and then suddenly Sallie Ann was in the hallway, alone with the girl, Rose Clare, who looked at her and motioned for her to follow.

They took off at a brisk pace. As they walked down the hall Rose pointed dramatically, stabbing the air for emphasis and with clumsy, halting movements she signed and said, "This is the girl's bathroom. This is the boy's." Suddenly the girl stopped and whatever she had been saying was lost. It occurred to Sallie Ann then that no one had told her guide that she could read lips. No wonder Rose was using exaggerated gestures and clumsy signing. She thought Sallie Ann could only communicate with crude hand gestures.

As they moved on, Sallie Ann thought about letting her know in some way that she could read lips, but something told her to hold back. She tried to keep level with the girl so she could see her mouth as the girl spoke, but Rose was too fast for her. She skip-walked so Sallie Ann was able to catch snippets.

"Art . . . painting . . . lunch . . . over here . . . there . . ."

The girl turned to Sallie Ann and motioned her toward an exit sign and said more to herself, "I'm tired."

They walked outside the double doors that led to a small courtyard where a bench sat underneath a large scrub oak tree. It was a beautiful day, early September, the trace of summer heat not yet over, but the light had changed and there was the exciting rush of fall in the air. The two girls sat side by side on the wooden bench and stared back at the squat, drab building that held so much hope for Sallie Ann. Sallie Ann closed her eyes. She could smell the musk of the crushed leaves of a tree that had given up early and there was the faint wisp of a thick, perfumed sachet from Rose. She opened her eyes and turned to see if Rose was ready to continue, and was startled to see Rose staring back at her, unblinking and without expression.

"This place is a dump," Rose said and then frowned. "They've tried to make it nice, but it's still a dump." She narrowed her eyes at Sallie Ann and said, "You can't understand a word I'm saying, can you?"

Sallie Ann blinked. There was about this strange girl something that was astringent, wiry, and angry, which reminded her of her father, the same coiled anger, the hard eyes and thin lips. Sallie Ann knew her type–knew her every day of her life.

She sighed and crawled down into herself and waited. It wise to stay still, watch, and hide as best she could.

The girl stared at Sallie Ann, measuring her, and finally turned away. But she didn't stay quiet for long. Whatever it was that was bothering her was going to spill out. It was just a matter of time. Sallie Ann had seen this with her father.

"I bet you think you're lucky. This fancy school for kids like you. Everybody acting like they care." She paused. "I don't think you're so lucky. You can't hear. You can't talk. You have to go to a special school. That's not lucky at all. It's sickening how they cart people like you off to crumby little places like this so you don't get in the way."

Rose looked at Sallie Ann with pity. Sallie Ann didn't blink, she hardly breathed. She didn't know why, but she was prey. These situations happened to her all the time. Suddenly people around her were mad. Suddenly they cried. Suddenly they left, they came. The hardest thing about being deaf was not hearing the nuances of others' moods so she could get out of the way. Instead, she became a runner. Which is what they called her at school. When it became too much, too baffling, too scary, Sallie Ann just left. Started walking and didn't stop.

"You don't even know what I'm talking about right now, do you? You can't understand a word I'm saying." Rose shook her head in disgust then looked away, the storm having passed for the time being. The girl drew circles in the dirt with the tip of her shoe. After a few minutes she stood up and fetched a stick and came back and sat on the bench next to Sallie Ann, but she didn't look at her. Using the stick she drew a spiral over and over again and once she reached the center she stabbed the ground, then dragged her foot across the dirt to wipe it clean and began drawing again. As she drew, her lips began forming words that even sideways Sallie could easily read.

"God I hate this town. And everybody in it. I just want to go away and never come back. Just get in a car going somewhere—anywhere—and never have to come back here again." Rose sighed. "I need a getaway plan."

The girl pressed her lips together and looked out at the distance, lost in thought. "If I could, I'd get on the highway and head straight north. North. There's a place up there—a school where I want to go." She shook her head slowly back and forth. "I want that more than anything."

She whipped the stick back and forth. "I knew as soon as I saw it that I wanted to go there, but Mama wants me to go to the university. She says it has more prestige. Prestige."

Rose dug the stick into the powdered earth deeper. "Mama never saw Cyrus. Just the pictures and Daddy only said, 'Too rich for our blood.' But I talked to a woman up there and I could get financial aid—"

Rose stopped. "I don't know why I'm talking about this."

She drew an elaborate spiral and let the stick fall. She wiped the dust on her pants and sighed. "Cyrus is nothing like anything here. It's green and pretty and the people there are smart. It could be a place for me. Just for me."

Sallie Ann almost nodded, but then remembered she was playing as if she didn't know what the girl was saying. She watched Rose closely and just before the girl looked over at her, Sallie Ann cut her eyes away and looked blankly around her.

After a few seconds scrutinizing Sallie Ann, reassured her words were going nowhere, Rose looked away and Sallie Ann turned back and watched the girl's mouth. Her mother always said, "If you look people straight in the eyes, Sallie, they'll think you know something." So Sallie Ann kept her eyes averted and stayed hidden.

"It's not so much Cyrus itself, although it is beautiful. It's the feeling I have there, that I could be anything I wanted to be, I could do anything I wanted to." She paused and dropped her head and if Sallie Ann could have heard the next sentence she would have known it was whispered, as if Rose herself could barely have had the courage to utter it: "I think my world starts there."

Sallie Ann looked away from Rose and took in her new school. Rose's words fit her in a strange and synchronistic geometry. The "School for the Deaf," as it was known, was a collection of small, squat cinder buildings with old floors, a tired, sagging, used quality. And yes, it was a dump as the girl had said. It was the best Sheffield could muster for its "handicapped." But to Sallie Ann it was as magnificent as Cyrus was to Rose. It wasn't the walls, it was the promise they held and its eventual fulfillment that struck her. Sallie Ann felt that here, in this school, she would finally have the world for which she abandoned her exile in the tree almost six years earlier.

Rose picked the stick back up and began pounding it in front of her. When Sallie Ann looked over, the girl's face was pinched and white, furious, " . . . trapped by her all the time wanting me to do what she wants. I've got that whole family on my back and they won't leave me alone. They won't LET ME GO."

Suddenly the girl looked up, startled and seemed to focus at a point behind her. Sallie Ann turned around and saw a group of girls around her age coming out of one of the doors, signing furiously and laughing. She smiled, despite herself and longed to go over and be with them. She turned toward Rose and saw her smirking. She looked at Sallie Ann full in the face and said, "I don't know what I'm worried about. None of you can hear a word I say. Oh God."

She sighed, rolled her eyes, and sat back. "The truth is I think everybody here is just trying to make something nice that's not. The kids, that director who thinks she's a man, you, everybody. You're stuck and don't even know it or care. Don't even want to shake the dust of this place off you. Dumb. Dumb. Dumb. In more ways than one."

Rose leaned in. "I'm only doing this volunteer stuff for my college resume. I found out the president of Cyrus has a deaf brother and I thought it'd look good if I worked with the deaf. Smart, huh? My mom didn't want me coming out here–she thinks this place is as bad as Porterville."

Rose studied Sallie Ann and when there was still no response she looked satisfied and went on. "Porterville. Now that's a dump."

Rose remained still and pensive for the longest time. When she started talking again, Sallie Ann wasn't sure her guide even knew she was there, sitting next to her.

"We used to drive out there every summer on our way home from our vacation at the beach. The first time we went Mama told Daddy to drive by and so we got off the highway and went down this long dusty road. At the end there was this place, kind of like this, but a lot bigger and there was this . . . playground . . . I guess and it had a big cyclone fence around it. You know out it the middle of nowhere with tumbleweeds all pushed up against the fence and so many dust whirlwinds, but there was a whole playground full of these . . . retarded people . . . some were like forty years old and they were riding bikes and wearing diapers, you know, some of them, and they were grown, you know. And they were living their whole life out there."

Rose took a deep breath, like the short, strangled attempt of someone drowning.

"And Mama said to Daddy, 'Will you look at that.' And then she said to me, 'There but for fortune, Rose. There but for fortune.'"

The girl was still. Sallie Ann saw panic and guilt struggle for dominance and suddenly, despite the girl's meanness and anger, Sallie Ann felt a stab of pity for her.

"We sat in the car and watched these . . . people . . . riding tricycles and laughing over not much at all. Mama and Daddy didn't say anything, they just stared and I watched this one woman. She went around and around in a circle and she was laughing and hitting the handlebars with her hands. She looked older and I just knew she'd been out there forever and I wondered, 'Who cared about her? Who loved her?'"

Although she had turned away quickly, Sallie Ann saw that Rose had begun to quietly cry. She bowed her head and waited for the moment to pass.

After a few minutes Rose dragged the back of her hand across her eyes and said, "They didn't tell me why, but we stopped there every summer on the way home from the beach. I never thought too much about it. Then one summer, we were sitting watching all of them ride around on their bikes and play kick-ball, when my mother all of a sudden sat up and leaned forward. She didn't say anything, but she put her hand on my father's arm and he looked where she did. And they both sat there staring at the playground and my mom made this sound—like a kitten, this little mewing sound and my father threw his cigarette out the window and he leaned forward."

Sallie Ann frowned, not sure where this was going.

Rose looked up at the treetops. "I was twelve, the girl they were watching was a big girl with this powder blue ribbon in her hair. She was about seventeen or eighteen, I think. It was hard to tell. I have long blond hair, so did she. I have a pug nose and brown eyes, she had a pug nose, and I bet if we'd gotten closer she'd had brown eyes too. She looked exactly like me except she had that look that retarded people have, you know, like nobody's home, but sweet. Mama always talked about her first child—the one who supposedly died three days after she was born. It happened a few years before she had me. She was always talking about how lucky they were to have me, that she wasn't built for childbearing and stuff and how lucky I was to be alive and all that. But that baby didn't die. She'd lied."

Rose shook her head. "I had a sister. I just knew it. So much fell into place. The visits to Porterville, why there was no grave. The special gifts Mama bought at Christmas and sent to Porterville saying it was charity. All a big lie. I had a sister, but she was born retarded and they didn't keep her around. That's what people do with kids like that. They get rid of them." Rose scanned the sky as if there were answers there.

"It could have just as easily been me. I could be the one riding a tricycle out on some slab of cement in Porterville, wearing a blue ribbon in my hair that somebody else put there." She stuck the stick in the ground in front of her. "That's what people do with the different ones, I guess." Rose punched the dirt in front of them with the stick, but there was no anger in it.

"I never asked them about her. I didn't have to. And we never went there again."

Sallie Ann looked away. Suddenly this girl with her strange ways made sense to her, her fury, her sadness, her traps, but Sallie Ann was tired and wanted to go away. She didn't want to know this girl's secrets and haunts. She wanted this day to be hers and not another day where she had to hide from others around her. She wanted to see the Director again. Be close to her. She wanted to go join the group of girls like her who were just this minute disappearing back into a classroom, signing to each other—a group—her first friends like her, she hoped, and Sallie Ann wanted to be with them, not stuck on this bench pretending she didn't understand anything.

Suddenly Sallie Ann stood and began walking toward the classroom where the girls had disappeared. She was aware that Rose was following her, trying to keep up with her, and trying to grab her elbow to get her attention. But Sallie Ann would not stop. Suddenly the Director was before her and Sallie Ann stopped when the woman put a cool hand on her shoulder. She turned around long enough to see Rose explaining, her face red, ". . . I showed her those and then we sat a little and she just took off. It's hard to get her attention. She doesn't sign or read lips . . ."

Rose stopped. The Director was shaking her head and Sallie Ann saw her form the sentence, "But she does. Sallie Ann is a champion lip reader. She doesn't miss a word."

The girls locked eyes and there flitted across Rose's face a parade of fear, anger, shame, and finally the knowledge that she had once again been betrayed.

Rose said, "You understood me?"

Sallie Ann nodded.

"Everything?" Rose's eyes pleaded for a "no" and for a quick second Sallie Ann pictured the lost sister. She closed her eyes and saw it all so clearly, could almost feel the wind whipping her face, the fine dust finding the creases of her ears, her mouth, ceaseless in its intimate ways. She could feel the cold hard metal of the cyclone fence as she pressed her face against it and watched the strange car visiting year after year, sitting out past the playground, a stream of gray from the tailpipe as it idled outside the fence, its windows blank in the sun's glare, the eerie quiet, the strange waiting and then it turns and goes. She could see the whirlwinds follow its leaving, pass across the desolate and barren country and the tumbleweeds roll and catch against the fence, scratching her shins. She could see only the empty landscape and the sky the color of spent ash. Without knowing the why of anything or the who of anyone, she could reach up and almost feel the satin of a bow at the top of her head. As Sallie Ann looked at Rose she wondered who showed her love. Who?

Sallie Ann shook her head "no" and Rose's face relaxed back to its natural blankness, the faint hint of a now unsure smirk. Then, Sallie Ann was curved into the arm of the Director, pressed against her side, she was heady with the scent of lemon cologne, her strong arm, the crisp white shirt as the older woman pulled her toward the school, toward her future and away from Rose.

When Sallie Ann looked back, the girl was gone. She never saw Rose again.

DUTIFUL DAUGHTER
TERRY BAUM

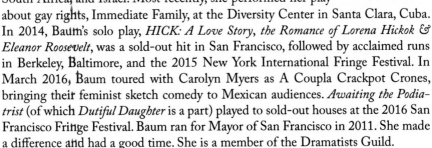

Terry Baum has had her plays translated into French, Dutch, Italian, Spanish and Swedish and produced all over the world. *Dos Lesbos* (1981, with Carolyn Myers) was the first time many lesbians saw their lives accurately portrayed in the media. It inspired the first anthology of lesbian plays (*Places, Please*, 1985) and offended the Pope during World Pride 2000 in Rome. As a solo performer, Baum has toured the U.S., Canada, Europe, South Africa, and Israel. Most recently, she performed her play about gay rights, Immediate Family, at the Diversity Center in Santa Clara, Cuba. In 2014, Baum's solo play, *HICK: A Love Story, the Romance of Lorena Hickok & Eleanor Roosevelt*, was a sold-out hit in San Francisco, followed by acclaimed runs in Berkeley, Baltimore, and the 2015 New York International Fringe Festival. In March 2016, Baum toured with Carolyn Myers as A Coupla Crackpot Crones, bringing their feminist sketch comedy to Mexican audiences. *Awaiting the Podiatrist* (of which *Dutiful Daughter* is a part) played to sold-out houses at the 2016 San Francisco Fringe Festival. Baum ran for Mayor of San Francisco in 2011. She made a difference and had a good time. She is a member of the Dramatists Guild.

(ALEX AND MOTHER ENTER MOTHER'S LIVING ROOM, REPRESENTED BY A COUCH AND END TABLE. ALEX IS A MIDDLE-AGED DYKE DRESSED IN COMFORTABLE CLOTHES, CARRYING A SUITCASE. MOTHER CAN BE EITHER AN ACTRESS OR A PUPPET. IN THE ORIGINAL PRODUCTION, SHE WAS A PUPPET ON ALEX'S HAND, SHAPED LIKE AN OVEN MITT, WITH BRIGHT RED HAIR, WEARING LOTS OF MAKEUP AND VERY NICE COSTUME JEWELRY.

MOTHER
(TO AUDIENCE) It's so nice that my daughter flew down from San Francisco to spend some time with her poor old mother in Los Angeles.

ALEX
Mom, Daddy's been in a coma for three weeks. We're all the family we've got now.

MOTHER
Too bad you weren't here on Chanukah. No party, no nothing.

ALEX

I TOLD you why I couldn't come down! I had a very important . . .

MOTHER

(MOCKING) YOU had something IMPORTANT?!?

ALEX

Damn right, I . . . Oh, never mind. I'm here now!

MOTHER

What's the point? Chanukah's over. And I spent it in the hospital by Daddy's bedside. Terrible. You should move to Los Angeles so the same terrible thing doesn't happen next year.

ALEX

You want me to give up my work, my friends, my apartment—my whole life in San Francisco—and move to L.A. to be with you on Chanukah?

MOTHER

You're not going to be a dutiful daughter?

ALEX

(TO AUDIENCE) Those two words, when linked together, send a chill down my spine. "Dutiful daughter." (SHE SHIVERS. TO MOM) Absolutely not.

MOTHER

(TO AUDIENCE) It figures. I was a dutiful daughter to my mother. My mother was a dutiful daughter to HER mother. But is my daughter dutiful to ME? Little did I know that I was to be the end of a long line of dutiful daughters. Where's the justice? (TO ALEX) If you move down here to L.A., to take care of me, you'll finally have some purpose in your life. I won't charge you any rent.

ALEX

Mother, I'm not going to even respond to that.

MOTHER

(REMINISCING) Yes, I was always the perfect dutiful daughter. Your grandma was lucky to have a daughter like me. Daddy was lucky too, until now. He enjoyed his work, made a nice living, had a lovely family. Yes, he was a lucky man until this stroke. (PAUSE. SHE TURNS TO ALEX AND ACCUSES HER.) Of course, he *did* expect at least *one* grandchild to comfort him in his old age.

ALEX

Yeah, Mom, I guess the worst thing that ever happened to Daddy before the stroke was *me* coming out as a lesbian.

MOTHER

Well, when he was a soldier in the Pacific in World War II, that was no picnic, believe you me. (REALLY GETTING INTO THE STORY) Once he was out on patrol, and everyone was killed except him. He had to crawl down a river for three days to get back to base camp! (PAUSE, TURNS TO ALEX) But you're right. You coming out as a lesbian was worse.

ALEX

Know what I love about you, Ma? You have no subtext. I never waste time searching for hidden meanings because everything is right there on the surface, smacking me in the face.

MOTHER

You're too sensitive.

ALEX

I admit I'm sensitive. Perhaps I'm *very* sensitive. But I'm not *too* sensitive. I'm just sensitive enough.

MOTHER

No, you're *too* sensitive. I don't understand you. You do what you please. Then you complain I don't approve of you. Other people live for their parents' approval. Why not you?

ALEX

(TO AUDIENCE, BOILING WITH ANGER) It took me fourteen years of therapy to get to the point where she just can't bug me anymore!

MOTHER

(IGNORING ALEX'S ANGER) You know what? All that sensitivity of yours makes me tired. I'm going to take a nap. (SHE LIES DOWN)

ALEX

(TO AUDIENCE) You think this a sweet little old woman? This is a force of nature! She drives me . . . (MUMBLING TO HERSELF) Fourteen years of therapy . . . (TRYING TO CALM HERSELF DOWN, SHE BRINGS OUT A BOOK FROM HER BAG.) I've decided to try something new: Buddhism. (SHE SHOWS THE BOOK TO THE AUDIENCE.) *Everything You Always*

Wanted to Know About Enlightenment but Were Afraid to Ask. (READS A LITTLE.) "Buddha's First Noble Truth: Pain is inevitable. Life is difficult." (ENLIGHTENMENT DAWNS:) Buddha is right! This whole big mess is just a part of life! There's nothing unfair about my mother having no respect for me. I'm not entitled to an easy life. No one is! (ECSTATIC) Life is difficult! I accept it! I embrace all of life, even this! I feel so much better! Maybe Buddhism can help Mom too! (RUNS OVER TO MOTHER) Mother! (SHAKES HER AWAKE.)

MOTHER

What? (SHE WAKES UP, IS VERY IRRITATED.)What is it?

ALEX

I'm reading this book about Buddhism. And it says here that Buddha's First Noble Truth is that life is difficult.

MOTHER

Difficult for everyone?

ALEX

Yes.

MOTHER

That's a depressing thought. I've never heard anything so depressing. Not everybody's life is difficult. I personally know several people who live without any difficulty at all.

ALEX

But Buddha's first noble truth certainly applies to you and me, and it helps me . . .

MOTHER

Well, if that crap helps you, that's fine. But it doesn't do a damn thing for me. Why are you reading about Buddhism anyhow? Buddhist schmoodist. You're a Jew. You should read what the Jews say. Do the Jews say life is difficult?

ALEX

I don't know.

MOTHER

(YELLING) You should find out what the Jews say.

ALEX

(SHE WRITHES IN AGONY) Your voice is like fingernails on the blackboard of my soul.

MOTHER

(HOVERING OVER ALEX, EVEN LOUDER.) You're too sensitive! I bet the Jews don't say life is difficult! (NORMAL VOICE) I'm going back to my nap, and don't wake me up again, just because you found a new religion! (SHE LIES DOWN AGAIN.)

ALEX

(TO AUDIENCE) My dad's in a coma. My family has been reduced to a remnant. My mother spends Chanukah alone. Most of her friends and relatives are dead. And she *still* refuses to acknowledge that (SHOUTING) LIFE IS DIFFICULT! (PAUSE) Why am I trying to change her? I want to do something for my mother, to make up for not being a dutiful daughter, but introducing her to Buddhism is obviously not the answer. (GETS OUT BOOK ON BUDDHISM, LEAFS THROUGH IT) What does Buddha have to say about my mother refusing to accept that life is difficult?

(READING & SKIMMING THROUGH PAGES) The lessons we learn from pain . . . how it helps us to grow spiritually . . . OK, I must embrace my mother's refusal to embrace the fact that life is difficult. (TURNS A PAGE) No, no. First I must embrace my OWN refusal to embrace my mother's refusal to embrace that life is difficult. (TURNS ANOTHER PAGE) Wait a minute. Before I do that, I have to embrace my mother's refusal to embrace my refusal to embrace her refusal to embrace . . . (SHE LOOKS UP IN CONFUSION TO THE AUDIENCE.) I think I'll just embrace myself. (SHE WRAPS HER ARMS AROUND HERSELF. SHE SMILES. THEN SHE LAUNCHES INTO A SNIPPET OF THE GERSHWIN SONG "EMBRACEABLE YOU.")

(SINGING HAPPILY) I love all the charms about you. Above all, I want my arms around you. Embrace me, you irreplaceable you! Embrace me, my sweet embraceable you! (LIGHTS FADE TO BLACK.)

UNNATURAL LOVE
XEQUINA MARIA BERBER

 **Xequina Maria Berber** has been writing since third grade. She holds a Master's degree in English Literature and another in Women's Spirituality. She is of Mexican-American descent and the author of *Santora: The Good Daughter*, a novel loosely based on her strange life, and a children's book, *The Mermaid Girl*. She came out during early middlessence and now makes up for lost gay time through her creative endeavors—short stories, comic strips, and paintings celebrating lesbian themes and personalities. She also re-writes songs to honor dyke culture, which are then performed for the community with her partner Rome. She is currently at work on a portrait of Rome as Saint Sebastian, the Patron Saint of Queers. Xequina lives in Oakland and works as a school librarian. *Unnatural Love* is a mostly true story based on her partner's extensive experience with dyke drama.

CALL ME CYRANO. It's not my real name, but you can probably guess by the title I had to change the names to protect the guilty. The dyke demi-monde is so small and incestuous, everyone knows your business. We inbreed out of the need to survive as a community. No, this is not foreshadowing for making it with my sister. What I mean by incestuous is how ex-lovers tend to become family: my ex's best friend is my current lover, and my best friend will be my current's next girlfriend, and that ex will be my best friend after a year or two, and her's will be—you get the idea.

I don't know why I agreed to this. Yes I do, why lie? I was trying to keep my girlfriend and my best friend, and look cool even while my world was falling down around me. This is how it started: Layla (not her real name), my girlfriend of four years, came home one day and told me she'd had a major epiphany about herself.

"My authentic nature is to be polyamorous. What that means is in order to achieve true erotic fulfillment, I need to have more than one lover at a time."

Layla had been reading all this literature on ethical polygamy. I'm sure part of what lead her to that conclusion was empirical research—she'd cheated before and thought I didn't know. This new self-realization would justify her cheating, only now she could do it in full view. But her news flash wasn't over.

" . . . so I'd like us to open up our relationship and invite other people in. And the first person we should invite in is M."

M. My best butch buddy. The only butch I'd ever gotten to know and get close with.

"She's the perfect choice," she went on. "We're all close, she really loves both of us, and we always have a good time together. M. admires us, and she thinks you're so cool." Note that Layla didn't ask if I was okay with it, nor did she invite any discussion about it. "Come on, Cyrano. It'll be really fun," she said through clenched teeth.

Fun for you, I thought. But I went along with it because I'm a sucker and a wuss, and because I knew Layla. She's willful and stubborn, and when she wants to do something, she does it. Also, I was outnumbered. Layla and M. had been fooling around already. I'd seen the lust-laden looks that passed between them, and heard them flirt when I was nearby.

I have to take some of the blame for this whole fiasco. I'm the one who started her even thinking about my friend. One day a few months back, Layla was looking at her butt in the mirror, complaining how fat and unattractive she was. She is neither, far from it. So I opened my big mouth and said, "No you're not, lots of people think you're a fox."

"Like who, besides you?" she said disgustedly, like my opinion didn't count for anything.

Now Layla may be hot, but she's also bitchy, and lots of people hate her. Unwary, I mentioned the first person who popped into my head. "Well, like M. She calls you a traffic-stopper in Butchtown."

"Really? M. said that?" She checked her high, firm ass one more time and stood a little taller than she already was. "Hmm. That's interesting." Then she tossed her long, strawberry red hair and walked out of the bedroom.

After that they started hanging around each other more. The three of us worked at a book distributorship. Layla and M.'s offices were right next to each other, while I was way out in the warehouse, stuck in a small, windowless room, hunched over a computer, hacking into their e-mail accounts. M. was hanging out at our apartment a lot, and it wasn't long before they were doing things without me, like leaving me at work if I wasn't at the car by the time they got there. They seemed to have forgotten I still existed.

Why did I put up with it, you're wondering? Well, I was depressed. I had no stamina, no fight, and no backbone to resist the situation. So I just smiled like everything was all hunky-fucking-dory with me and tried to act worldly and jaded.

One Friday evening I got home from work (I'd had to take the bus) and the apartment smelled great.

"Hey, what's cooking?" I called. I heard laughter coming from the kitchen. Layla and M. had cooked dinner and were finished eating when I came in. The kitchen was completely trashed. The laughter died when they noticed me and they stopped talking.

"Oh, hi. Have some spaghetti," Layla said. *Was that a curl on her lip?*

Just as I sat down and was pouring myself a glass of wine, they got up and started getting their jackets. "Hey, where you going?"

"We have to get to a movie at the Piedmont. You'll be a sweetie and clean up, right?" Layla said, kissing the air in my general direction, then taking off into the dark with M. They were like a pair of scheming witches.

So I sat down to a lonely dinner, the kitchen a complete mess. There was even a spray of spaghetti sauce on the ceiling. After I ate and cleaned up (it took an hour and a half), I sat there feeling miserable and sorry for myself. I was trying to read while finishing a second glass of wine when the phone rang. It was Layla.

"There's a meet-n-greet at the Polynesian Lounge. Why don't you come over?"

My spirits lifted. Maybe she did still care! So I spiffed up, adding a tie to my shirt and exchanging my sneakers for wing tips. The Polynesian Lounge is a dive with a jungle painted on the outside and a big wooden tiki love god grimacing in the doorway, next to a fake palm tree and an equally fake waterfall fountain. A greeter handed me a name tag.

"Hello, I'm Joan. This is a singles mingle put on by Yikes We're Dykes! Are you single?" I glanced over her shoulder and saw Layla talking to two butches I didn't know.

"Uh—my girlfriend is," I said. The greeter laughed like I was joking and waved me in. I stood at Layla's elbow for several minutes, but she didn't introduce me, didn't even say hello. Finally I asked if I could get her a drink.

"Yes, a Delilah Punch."

"What's that?"

"They'll know," Layla said, giving me a look that said, *"Get lost."*

So I went and stood at the bar, waiting for the bartender to notice me. It was really busy so I had to waitin a long line, and as I stood there watching Layla attracting more and more attention from big, hunky butches, I could swear I was getting shorter and smaller, which must have been why the bartender kept overlooking me.

I finally got our drinks. Layla took her Delilah Punch without a pause (or a thank you) in her conversation, and the butches closed ranks around her—literally, they sealed up all the spaces between them and shut me out. I felt like a mole in a forest of stately redwoods. I went back to stand at the bar. In the mirror behind the bar, I watched myself getting uglier and tinier by the moment. Worst of all, my nose was staying the same size—in fact, it was growing. I turned my head; sure enough, the bump was four times its normal size and the tip stuck out about four inches over my mouth, growing more grotesque by the moment, like what happens to male salmon when it's time to mate. Maybe this was nature's way of telling me to call out one of those butches. Then I heard a familiar voice:

"Hey, Cyrano, having a good time?"

M. slid onto the empty seat next to me. Layla must have brushed her aside too, and I tried very hard to feel sorry for her. Soon we were taking about stuff like sports and movies, just like old times and I started to wonder if maybe I really could be okay with M. cuckolding me. Then she cleared her throat.

"So, bro' . . ." she paused, and I was sure she was going to say something about my nose because she couldn't take her eyes off it. She even looked at it from the sides. "Can I ask you something?"

"Sure, go ahead. You want to know why it's so big, right?"

"Huh? Why what's so big?"

"Never mind. What were you going to ask?"

"Layla says the three of us should get together."

"Oh yeah? And do what?" I asked, thinking about kayaking or peewee golf.

"You know, have sex."

I inhaled beer and choked. M. had to throw me over her knee and smack me on the back.

"Bartender!" she barked. "Water!" Of course, the bartender turned to her immediately. M.'s a butch to be reckoned with, unlike me, Mr. Mouse.

"No—*cough*—Delilah Punch," I said in choking agony. Might as well take advantage of the bartender's attention. Except when it arrived, M. grabbed it and forced me to drink it. She set me back on my feet.

"You okay now, bro'?" she asked. Except for the alcoholic cross sightedness, I was fine.

"So . . . how about it?" asked M.

The punch taken with beer and no doubt the wine earlier, went straight to my forebrain, effectively lobotomizing me. I nodded in a debonair way. "Sure, why not?"

"Hey, great, bro'! You are so cool!" She slapped me on the back and knocked me over. M. went and whispered in Layla's ear. She jumped up and down like a cheerleader, kissed each butch good night, and came over to me.

"I'm so glad you're going to join us!" she said. "Let's go!"

"You mean—you want to do it now?" I squeaked. "Shouldn't we have another round of drinks first?" Like wine, beer, and Whore Punch wasn't balls enough. But Layla and M. were horny and impatient. They dragged me out of the bar and back to our place. Layla and M. got naked right away. They looked like Aphrodite and Athena. And then there was little peon me, paralyzed and modestly clothed.

"Come on, don't be shy," said Layla. "For crying out loud, we go to the hot tub together all the time."

"All the time" was once, but being naked wasn't the issue. I was afraid if I took my clothes off, nothing would be there. They grabbed me and ripped them off. I looked down. Sure enough, my body was insubstantial, almost transparent in fact. Luckily Layla and M. didn't notice because they weren't looking at me. Layla did give me a really nice kiss, but then M. moved in.

As it turned out, the sex wasn't bad; it wasn't all that different from what it always was, except Layla had M. to kiss while I was working on her. At least I got to go first, and then I conveniently passed out so the trauma of watching M. do my girlfriend was minimized.

> *A little old man was running down the street grabbing his head, crying "Oh no—I'm a victim of my own philosophy! I'm a victim of my own philosophy!" until he stepped into an open manhole where I was hiding and landed on my head.*

I woke up, my head throbbing like they do in the cartoons, *doo-wah, doo-wah,* swelling to twice its size with each broken heart beat. I was alone; Layla and M. probably went out for breakfast. I staggered to the bathroom. I had a hangover so bad my face was swollen. Even my hair hurt. But I'd done it. I was *the man.* I flexed my biceps in the mirror:

I'm the man! I told my reflection.

But I wasn't convinced, and besides, the effort hurt. The bright light and loud Saturday morning noises like a cat mewing down the street was killing my head. I went into the kitchen and fixed a Bloody Mary before going back to bed. The pillow over my head felt like a cinder block.

AFTER THAT LAYLA and M. invited me to join them for sex a few times, but I always had excellent reasons to say no, like needing to paint my toenails. Layla was spending several nights a week at M.'s place now. Those nights I couldn't sleep, obsessing about them together; on the nights she stayed home she giggled and cooed on the phone with M., then fell asleep with her back to me, as far away from me as possible. I was more depressed than ever, and I was avoiding mirrors like a vampire hiding from what he is.

A couple of weeks later M. invited me to go on a hike. To be a good sport, I went and we actually had a great time. I was reminded why M. was my best friend. She's sharp, witty, well-read, fun; just because she was fucking my girlfriend didn't mean we couldn't still be buddies, did it? After the hike, M. suggested we go to the Crab Shack. We had beer while we looked over the menu.

"So . . . bro' . . ." she began.

Remembering another ominous conversation beginning that way, I carefully swallowed and set down my beer.

"Yes?" I said.

"You and me should get together sometime."

"Yeah," I said. "Today was great."

"I mean, you know, differently."

"Uh, no. What exactly *do* you mean, *bro*?"

She leaned into me. "Have sex," she whispered.

"Have sex," I repeated. She shushed me, even though the nearest person was on the other side of the restaurant. I studied M., drumming my fingers pointedly.

"M., are you really into all this poly horseshit, or are you just taking advantage of the situation? I know you never get anything off those straight, married women you're always chasing."

"No, I just don't think sex is a big deal, Cyrano. We were practically together that time with you, me, and Layla. And it's not as if we're straight."

"Oh, so you mean because we're lesbians, it's okay?"

"Well, yes," M. said. "Why not?"

I ordered another beer and thought about it. It couldn't be any worse than the other night, could it?

"Okay, sure." What I wouldn't do to make Layla happy. Because this had nothing to do with M.

She smiled. "Great, bro', I knew you'd come through. This calls for a *real* celebration." She signaled for the waiter. "A dozen raw oysters, please!"

"Oysters?" I asked. "*Raw?*" The only way I'd ever had oysters was in a cracker.

She winked. "It's an aphrodisiac."

I was definitely going to need that.

They arrived, disgusting, slimy things like egg whites, only gray. M. showed me how to put lemon and salt on them and a spot of hot sauce. "They're still alive, that's how you know they're fresh," she said. "Bottoms up!" She tipped her head back and swallowed it whole.

"So first I torture the poor thing with acid and chili before eating it alive?" I asked. I thought I saw one move.

"Best way." M. fixed another and held it to my mouth. "Open up!"

It went down so fast I could hardly taste it. So I had another, quickly followed by a big swallow of beer. Not bad, if you could ignore the slime.

We ate the rest of the oysters, drank beer, and ate buttered French bread until we were stuffed. Then M. invited me to her house, and I said yes, which meant I was drunk enough. Usually I avoided going over there because M.'s place is a complete and total sty. It smells like a roadside bar bathroom and moldy socks. Once we got there we had another beer. The next thing I knew, we were crying and saying how much we loved each other.

So, holding each other up, we lurched into the next room. I tried not to look at the bed, which was a complete mess, the sheets old and greyish. I wondered about Layla putting up with it. She made me change our bed every week!

We started taking off our clothes. We looked at each other in our boxers and started laughing. Then we got in bed and started trying to make out. It was sort of like two leads trying to dance. After a couple of kisses, I pushed M. down on her back and started to get on top, but she outclassed me by at least a hundred pounds. She knocked me off, pinned me down, and climbed on top. We started fooling around some, but it was more like wrestling—she'd start to move her hand toward my breast and I'd grab it and hold it fast, then she'd grab me in a headlock over her enormous breasts.

Then I put my hand on her groin. It was like someone dumping cold water on my head. I felt stone cold sober and wasn't into this one bit. Maybe I wasn't really a lesbian. But when I thought of kissing men with their big, hairy bodies and oozing dicks I felt sick. M. had let go of me and was digging around in a drawer. I sat up and looked around the filthy room. The walls started wobbling and I smelled garbage.

M. loomed over me. "What's wrong?" she asked.

From somewhere she had gotten a giant purple jelly dildo with veins and huge balls. I shoved her away and ran for the bathroom, making it to the toilet just in time. I hawked and threw up beer and whole oysters and half-digested bread. Then I let go of the toilet bowl and collapsed around the filthy commode until it was time to make another sacrifice to the chthonic gods of plumbing.

I woke up sometime around two a.m. M. was passed out, spread-eagle on the bed and snoring. That purple dildo was on the floor like a mound of decanted grape gelatin. I had another throbbing hangover. I put my clothes on and staggered home.

M. must have told Layla what happened, because Layla told me that I always ruined everything, that I obviously didn't want to work on a relationship between the three of us, so although it was really sad, she and M. were going to have to proceed without me. But I couldn't worry too much about Layla and M. anymore; I had problems of my own to work out. Not the least of which, I was drinking too much.

Not knowing what else to do, I made an appointment with a friend of Layla's who was a homeopath and a psychic. Delpha lived down the street from us. Her apartment was small but serene, painted shades of turquoise, sparely decorated except for lots of plants around the windows. She was a small woman with short blond hair who used crystals and drumming in her work. She gave me a pot of ginger tea, then took my health history. After that she did some psychic work on me, assessing my aura and moving energy.

"The first issue that has to be addressed is your depression. I can prescribe a remedy for that, but alcohol is a depressant, so limit your drinking. Have four liters of water and juice or herbal tea every day, because you're dehydrated. Also, your work environment is bad for you in several ways: you're being stifled in darkness, obsession, and positive ions. Those are the bad ones."

Her energy work left me feeling better than I had in weeks, and I now had some directions to move in. Ice water became my drink of choice, and my general well-being improved. I could think clearly for the first time in years. I bought a car and found a job at a vegetable distributorship in South City. I started on the night shift, so I never had to know what Layla was doing. On the weekend I had appointments with Delpha and started going hiking with a couple of new friends. Layla must have missed me, because she started leaving me little love notes. Sometimes there were notes from M. too. I put them all in the compost.

One day I was climbing the stairs to Delpha's apartment when the door opened and Layla came out.

"Cyrano! How did you know I was here?"

"I'm not here to see you."

"But you brought flowers." She put her hands out to take them and I held them out of her reach. Delpha came out of her apartment and I gave them to her.

Layla put her hands on her hips. "What's going on here?"

A little devil got to me. "Layla," I said, "you're on the right track. Being poly is great fun."

"Excuse me," she said. "You're not poly, *I* am." She glared at us. "Delpha is my friend."

"So was M.," I reminded her.

"But polyamory is about being honest with your partner. We never discussed this."

"Layla, *we* never discussed anything. You did all the talking, and I went along to make you happy. Except you're *never* happy."

"That's because you never *say* anything. You always just sit there, going along with everything." She turned to Delpha. "You can have her. You'll see what it's like taking care of her." Layla whirled and headed down the stairs. "I never want to see either of you again!" she shouted.

I had an impulse to run after her, tell her I'd been joking—Delpha was only my homeopath, and the lavender was for a spiritual cleansing for me—but all I could do was stare after her, going along, as usual.

"What just happened?" Delpha asked.

"The inevitable," I said, but the relief made me feel so much taller.

Layla moved in with M. the following weekend. I cleaned the apartment from top to bottom, rearranged the furniture, and burned a sage and herb mixture for cleansing and starting over. I was surprised to find that I didn't miss Layla.

THROUGH THE DYKE grapevine I learned that Layla and M.'s relationship didn't last very long. Turns out sex *was* a big deal for M. when Layla was *her* girlfriend and she was having sex with other people.

Much later, I met with Layla, who told me she wished I'd been honest with her because I was the one she loved, and ours had been the important, stable relationship, while the others were just flings. Crying, she said, "I wish you had fought for me, told me that my being poly wouldn't work for you. I would have chosen you."

It was hard to believe, but maybe she was telling the truth. Maybe her cheating had been an act of desperation to get me to commit myself, or do *something*. Instead I'd been a wimp and a yes-man, going along with everything she wanted, to try and keep her. I didn't tell her the whole situation had been feeding my depression and self-loathing for years and I needed to get out; she would have thought I was blaming only her.

ONE DAY AT the neighborhood café I saw M. She invited me to sit with her. We shot the bull for a while, and it was almost like old times. Then, avoiding looking me in the eye, she said, "I'm sorry about what happened, about my part in breaking you two up. This might be hard to believe, but losing your friendship was a bigger blow than things not working out with Layla."

I shrugged, and there was an awkward silence. Finally I said, "So, M. . . . what do you think—wanna try again?

She looked surprised. "Friendship?"

"No, fool," I said. "Sex."

Layla wasn't the only one with ideas about radical sex.

LOVE IN A MOTOR HOME
ELIZABETH BERNAYS

Elizabeth Bernays is a biologist and writer. She grew up in Australia, became a British Government scientist in England, then a professor of entomology at the University of California Berkeley. From there she became Regents' Professor at the University of Arizona, where she also obtained a MFA in creative nonfiction. She has published 39 essays in a variety of journals. The story here is a memoir piece.

I LOOKED DOWN from our motor home through pines and junipers with their long, early morning shadows, to a blue lake and rocky bank beyond. I was at Fool's Hollow campground, Show Low, back in Arizona after three weeks camping in Utah. Retired, future uncharted, I was learning to feel free, to give up ties to the academic life and write my story. Samantha, grudgingly awake, appeared at the door and I looked up, waiting for that first grouchy greeting from my unschooled lover.

"Babe, your patience has been evidentiary. I wondered if we should have went to Colorada."

"Bub, this is our holiday, or as *you* would say, vacation, and Utah has been splendid."

I cooked the eggs then spread English Marmite on a slice of bread, making Sam smile finally.

"Still eating marmoset, eh, babe?" Then, "Is that cool or *what*," as a black-headed grosbeak landed nearby, and Sam's newfound birding spirit soared. I felt a strange melting within, that came whenever Sam's delight took wing.

"Bublet, I love you," I said.

"I love you too, babe."

We lazed through the morning. Sam, tanned, young-looking, and boyish in shorts, waited for birds to photograph. She moved my chair into the shade at intervals and tried not to talk. I'm sure I looked like the pale academic I had been for forty years, as I mused on the past weeks of travel through canyon lands, and how love had prospered in spite of our being total opposites, how laughter had proved such a brilliant counterbalance to what seemed a mismatch to many—how the laughing had enriched our embraces!

On our first day out of Tucson, we decided to camp near Cottonwood. I studied guidebooks and settled for Dead Horse Ranch. Sam had a good geographical sense, but I usually went for maps.

"It looks as though you need to take the next one to the northwest and go about three miles," I said, "and maybe the turn will be on Tenth Street." I continued suggesting other possible routes.

Sam looked across at me. "You need to circumvent the parallaxes and intercept at the peripheral, and then figure out the cerebellum and dissect for the angle of proximity to the vortex." We laughed and found ourselves at the park without any of my study of maps.

I had been used to planned camping trips and sleeping on the ground in the bush, but this time there was no itinerary, and no definitive return time. I had qualms about the vagueness and about RVs sardined into treeless campsites by freeways, but Sam knew I was addicted to peace, and happily, Dead Horse Ranch with its mesquite and cottonwood trees along the fast-flowing Verde River was quiet. We settled in, and on the first walk, our Labrador Bailey played in a muddy flume.

"Bailey, get outta that dirty water or y'all get kama sutra."

"Giardia." I laughed, throwing a stick over her shoulder without thinking.

"Son of a *bitch*," Sam said, "I thought that was a snake. Scared the *fuck* outta me."

I smiled. Almost anything would *scare the fuck outta her*. After cooking dinner on the barbecue grill we sat watching the sunset.

"I'm freezin," complained Sam, though it was warm. Then, "I'm burnin up."

I was used to this, with Sam in the throes of menopause. Coats or bedclothes came on and off. And she often had *tummy take, booboo, spasm*, or *painful finger*. Sam was, by her own admission, a *wuss*.

Next morning, watching goldfinches at a feeder, I remembered how I had once tried to tell Sam about their habits, but Sam was not yet ready. "It's just a little yella *bird*," she had shouted.

Now, watching in silence, Sam said suddenly, "Sorry for that." I looked at her questioningly. "Sorry about the fortuitous when you could hear but a breeze so you couldn't smell it."

It took me a minute to realize she referred to a fart. Earlier she had coined the term "elevator" as a result of a fart in an elevator. After a bathroom trip she would sometimes shrug, *just elevator*.

From Cottonwood we drove to Glen Canyon where, crossing the dam, an array of cliffs greeted us. The waters of Lake Powell extended into every nook and cranny of what was once, according to David Brower in *Let the River Run Through It*, a hundred paradises. The apparatus of electric power in the form of dozens of giant steel pylons with high-tension wires stood as industrial ornaments on the red, rocky heights. I had read Edward Abbey and listened to Richard Shelton read his poems. Clearly Glen Canyon was one of those places that should have been preserved, though I had no concept of its glory before Glen Canyon Dam, before the making of Lake Powell. It was late afternoon

With some impatience at her need for new places I said, "Maybe I need some time alone."

"You have no symphony for me. Usually you so gratuitous and grateful with your time and I always in your despair."

I looked at her and smiled, and mollified, Sam set up the tripod and sat with a little more patience than usual for the great picture. "Look, babe, quick, come 'ere."

"What?"

"Can't you see that sucker?"

"Where?" So quick to see the birds, she had seen a little mountain chickadee I had missed.

By midday we were ready to see the great cities of towering rocks in Bryce Canyon.

"Come look at this tiny flower—in the family Asteraceae," I beckoned from a canyon rim.

"Sons of *bitches, you* come over *here*," Sam yelled. "You's too near the edge."

I obeyed, and we embraced, enchanted with the rock and mountains, sun highlighting patches with gold, and shadows enhancing the three dimensions.

Walking back to the campsite, we passed the camp host. Sam saw the Texas license plate and called, "Hi, where y'all from in Texas?" Immediately the camaraderie was on while I stood by, silent.

"Used to fish at Galveston."

"Yeah, all along the coast."

"Any good fishing round here?"

"Oh, sure, there's a good lake up the road. Just go north over the crossroads and up the road and y'all find Pine Lake. Rainbows and browns there, easy. Great place, nobody up there, and y'all see plenty a deer and elk. Get the paste bait at Ruby's."

"What's the limit?"

"Four of each."

So we planned on Pine Lake next day as we ate barbecued steak. The meat was too tough for Sam, but I like a good chew. Suddenly Sam coughed violently and I rushed to pat her on the back.

"Is okay, got caught on my hangy down guy."

"You're just woofing it down aren't you?"

She always needed dessert to follow—sticky coffee cake, chocolate-coated graham crackers, Hershey's chocolate kisses filled with peanut butter, or shocking-pink and lime-green cupcakes. Suddenly Yoyo, our kitten, began climbing on the screen door and clung to the wire.

"Bub, she is having trouble disengaging her claws," I called.

"*Disengaging*," Sam shrieked. "*Disengaging*! You little encyclonic. What's wrong with 'getting her claws out'?"

"Disengage," I said again, laughing, and kissed her forehead.

"Oh, babe, you want to make a grapht out of it? A spreadsheet? You always with pearls of wisdom on your oyster tongue."

We held each other as we laughed and I gave up on my magazine, no longer caring about Handel's biography. The laughter was a carefree comfort that quickly turned to a passionate embrace.

The next day we explored the rocky scenes in earnest. My avocation was, as always, for the sights and sounds of nature and ready for a few miles at least, but Sam cared little for long walks.

"Such pain in my laigs. My knees are killin' me."

Later, in bed early, I started my book.

"What's that book then?" Sam asked.

"It's a book of essays, mostly about the Grand Canyon—nature stuff and travel sort of thing," I replied.

"Well, read some to me, I'm tired and that'll put me to sleep."

I looked for some passage that could be read out of context and still have some meaning, and began in the middle of *Gone Back to Earth* by Barry Lopez:

> We're aboard three large rubber rafts, and enter the Colorado's quick, high flow. The river has not been this high or fast since Glen Canyon dam. Jumping out ahead of us, with its single oarsman and three passengers, is our fourth craft . . .

Interrupted by loud laughter, I looked at Sam rolling in the bed with her legs kicking. "Craaaft, raaaft, you so fancy smancy, so eengleeshy, so very queenie."

And the laughter was unstoppable, irrepressible, contagious, as silly things will often be when two people are close, so ready to enjoy humor based on nonsense.

"Always you tease me," I gasped.

"Yes, I a-teasa you, I teasa you, you little contigenera. I teasa you, you doctor doctor." And she grabbed me into her arms. Whether it was the reading, the exhaustion of so much laughing, or just simple weariness, she fell quickly asleep, allowing me to finish the essay and ponder Lopez's final thoughts in relation to the splendid scenes we had witnessed in recent days.

> The living of any life, my life, involves great and private pain, much of which we share with no one. In such places as the Inner Gorge, the pain trails away from us. It is not so quiet there, nor so removed, that you can hear yourself think, that you would even want to; that comes later. You can hear your heart beat. That comes first.

Pine Lake was surrounded by alpine meadows with high mountains beyond, and Sam was quiet, concentrating on lures and movement. In an hour she had four rainbow trout, and we headed home.

"I'm freezing, time to put on long pants."

Then, "Ah, I'm burnin' up. And look, oh my thumb so sore where that fishhook went in. Toxins vacillated into my cubicles."

As we were leaving Bryce, Sam went into excited mode: "Look at them Dutch-look midgets . . . look at that girl's shorts tucked into her fat butt crack—need tweezers to pull them out . . . look old fuckers . . . look at that Mexican . . . there's a raven . . . look bunny . . . there's a Texas license plate . . . look they got a Jesus thing by their motor home." I couldn't keep up with her long litany of rapid observations, but I laughed as I looked at Sam's face full of fun, vision rushing ahead of her thoughts.

The road meandered northeast along byways of red cliff and boulders, white rock canyons dotted with the dark green of pines, to Capitol Reef National Park. Our motor home struggled up hills, and at the high pass over Boulder Mountain we stopped to walk among aspens, dressed in new greens quivering among the white, black-lined trunks.

"Get me some chocolate," Sam commanded.

"You are incorrigible."

"Yes I always incognito. I need chocolate."

We laughed and I left the passenger seat and selected four Hershey's Nuggets. I unwrapped them and handed each to Sam, who smiled. "We might could go fishing somewhere tomorrow."

Next day, on our return to the camp from the cliffs and red rocks of the park, there was a *cluster fuck*—headaches, booboos, and a grim, seventy-mile dash to a vet for antibiotics for a sick Bailey. Storm clouds and lightning, dead elk on the road, speeding on narrow country roads through sagebrush country and over mountains, past lakes and through small towns. But the following day was calm, in a green valley under the great red cliffs of Capitol Reef National Park. Golden eagles glided high and Sam, for the first time in earnest, became excited by birding. It was to be her first day of making lists.

"Oh, my God, those goldens, babe!"

We sat among the cottonwoods, leaves flashing silver in the breeze and fluffy, falling cotton wafting through the air like summer snow. Bullock's orioles, Western tanagers, and hairy woodpeckers flew among the trees; brown-headed cowbirds and American robins foraged in the grass, and an occasional chukka partridge marched across our sights. We idly watched summer and ate *apple pah*. There we were, a sixty-five-year-old academic and a fifty-one-year-old Texas dropout; Australian egghead versus fast-brained, street-smart photographer with a short attention span. The one work-weary and disciplined, the other unschooled, a free spirit. But we had love, and it was gentle that soft summer day.

"I'm an adult toddler," Sam said.

"And I am a toddling adult," I replied.

We went northeast to the town of Green River, through yet more canyons red and white, and mountains yellow and grey, to camp on the Colorado River in Moab. It was a shady site with wireless Internet, good for using computers outside.

"Fuck, I got a bug on my computer screen. What is it?"

"Oh, just a chironomid fly," I replied.

"Yeah, yeah, I hate chrysanthemums on my screen."

We laughed and I settled down to write, but it was not easy to concentrate with Sam there.

"Whatchew got there, bucko?"

"Just revising stuff and adding some anecdotes; nothing much, Bub."

"Okay, you put in some antidotes? You just writing for your bemusement, eh?"

"Hmm."

"Hmm yes or hmm no?"

"Hmm," I repeated, to annoy her. We had been through this one before.

"You talkative little chipmunk," she chided, and I knew she would have liked more chit chat, but was happy to take her *professor doctor* for the quiet person I am.

"Well, adios amoebas," Sam called as she went off to shower. "Seeya, wouldn't want ta beeya."

Later we lay in bed in each other's arms as a dust storm raged outside.

"Holy fuck, *sons* of bitches," Sam said.

As dust storms went, it wasn't much. I just held Sam as memories of research in the Sahara Desert ran before my eyes, and my so-different life swept back from the corners of my consciousness. It felt good to stop holding on to the professor's hat and simply feel the bittersweet of nostalgia as I savored this new life and love.

"Talk to me, babe," Sam pleaded.

How could I explain my complex emotions? I said simply, "I love you."

"I love you, babe, you doctor-doctor."

The road south from Moab became flatter with occasional buttes that resembled statues carved from red stone, the last remnants of strata not yet weathered away. Sagebrush took the place of juniper and pinyon pine until finally, the red earth was barren. We kept our eyes ready for dark silhouettes in the sky.

"There's a bird," Sam would say; she was always the first to see one, a dark spot in the blue. We would wait until it was closer, and usually it was a common raven.

"Raven," Sam shouted.

"Raven," I shouted back.

Back in Arizona we climbed into the White Mountains and ended up at Fool's Hollow Lake Recreation Area, with piney smells and west wind. Above the lake ospreys soared and Sam got her prize photo, and here we relaxed with the memories of our three week trip.

In bed, Sam, "freezin'," had a heating pad below her and an electric blanket above. At "burnin' up" times she emerged and lay on top of the bedclothes. She had her iPad for a last game of poker and I lay with a new book, Aldo Leopold's *A Sand County Almanac.*

The bedclothes were suddenly thrown off.

"I'm burnin' up."

I came out of my reverie and took the blanket for myself.

"Freezin'." And we were both under the blanket again.

Lights out, skin on skin. The comfort of being held with love before sleep carries one to another world that recedes again with a morning embrace.

SAM FISHED WHILE I wrote on my laptop under the trees with newfound peace. There had been aimless travel in lovely places, living in a small space, mixing love and laughter, moving closer with all our differences and contrasts.

"Sad," Sam said, who, childlike, wanted the journey to last forever.

"Why sad?"

"Because coming to an end."

But I wasn't sad. It had been good, and would become embedded in memory, joining the stores of sweet nostalgia that enrich the years. I thought of the close partnerships I had seen through my life. One factor stood out in the best ones: humor. An ability to laugh at each other and at one's self, and not to take oneself too seriously were perhaps the crucial features, freezin', burnin' up, and laughter.

THAT DELICATE BLUE STREAK
LYNN BROWN

 **Lynn Brown** is a lover of friendship, gardens, birds and writing poetry especially loves to read and engage creatively loves to cook and be at peace writes poems, memoir and this piece of fiction.

AS WE SAILED down the open road, my eyes were riveted by a delicate blue streak of horizon pulling us gently forward. It soothed my inner twitching and gave the outer landscape a tranquil smoothness, a patina that erased all the commotion of a modern roadside.

Cara and I pulled our trailer over to a small rustic café where an old neon beer sign kept flashing its last breath in surprisingly spotless windows. The interior of this cafe was intimate, with soda fountain seating directly across from the entrance. There were only three other customers, one of whom was using her laptop, a wiry haired woman with a lovely soft plaid flannel shirt. She was typing with the concentration of a bulldog. I think she might have been a dyke.

We sat down in a booth with a red speckled Formica table top and squished ourselves into the worn soft cushions. A ceiling fan twirled lazily. The windows were framed by pale green floral curtains tied in the middle. We ordered hearty breakfasts with a side of small, thin buckwheat pancakes. The waitress was a bit flirty in her blue jeans and dark blue tee shirt with slashes of color on the sleeves. Her hair was glossy black, short, and spiky. She took our order and skipped to the back kitchen. It appeared that she would also be preparing our order behind those closed doors.

We sat there staring at the landscape, salivating in expectation of food. Cara asked me, "Lin, do you think these women are dykes?" then she blurted out, "Look!"

I turned my head to catch a small tawny deer outside, little nubs on its forehead, munching away at a clump of weeds, oblivious to the man-made tarmac just beyond. I sat spellbound, taking in the vulnerability of this small wild creature, grateful to see her. In our excitement, we were kicking each other under the table.

"Oh, the parents just strolled across the lane," said Cara.

Then out sexy waitress returned to the table with our dishes in her outstretched arms. "Every time I see deer it makes my heart quicken," she said.

Speechless and frozen, the three of us watched these sweet creatures breathe and live while we took in every second of their presence like a last supper. I was thinking, given the way we treat the world, who's to say when the wildlife will disappear or go completely feral?

The moment dissipated and we slipped into gorging ourselves on the delicious breakfast. Even the eggs wowed me. After a while we slowed down, drank our decaf lattes and talked about what might happen next. Our bellies satisfied, we imagined the road ahead as we continued to fantasize about our next adventure.

We were having the time of our lives, dragging our tiny trailer from one breathtaking vantage point to another and we found lesbians everywhere out here. Cara, once my lover and now a dear friend and sometimes lover, was a blessing to travel with. Thirteen years had helped us to know each other better. Her complaints were easy to accommodate and she was totally present when we needed to get something done. I couldn't have dreamed up a more endearing companion and I think she felt the same.

We started out looking for birds and canyons, and to explore any community that interested either of us. In our first encounters near the Four Corners, Cara tolerated my foray into a Hopi healing ritual that wound up lasting three days and even danced in the circle and let out her whoops along with the rest.

I wrote in my journal every day about our road trip.

Months after being lovers, then moving towards friendship, we decided to travel westward, brave the possible discomforts and explore what was still wildish. We were open to the intimacy this might bring. Cara had her habits, which had ended up serving both of us in tandem. She kept fairly regular hours and had good health, considering she had arrived at almost eighty years of her life. She was still bright and full of optimism, though the shadows sometimes closed in around her.

We both wanted to see the wolves in Yellowstone National Park and we were determined to create this possibility. We stocked our little trailer with the bare minimum of supplies and also brought some of the things we couldn't bear to be without. She had her vibrator. I had my soft downy pillow. She brought her daughter Rebecca's quilt for the bed and had been able to forgive my voracious snoring.

Just yesterday we awoke to the smells of rain and a dust storm. We battened our hatches and watched through the window as balls of thick round twine twirled desperately in the air, grasping for a stronghold. There was a mangy dog not too far away foraging for rodents.

"Thank the goddess we didn't leave our chairs out!" I had said. As it was, our underwear might not have hung onto the line we had strung from tree to trailer. We had named our coach Rosie and referred to her occasionally as another person.

After the dust storm, we brewed coffee and toast, got out the huckleberry jam and fake butter in Cara's faux camping containers. None of these little daily rituals seemed to bother us. We didn't talk much until there was something tasty to entice our communion. Cara didn't have her newspaper but there were plenty of magazines mailed to us and there was the beauty of it all, the never failing glory of breathing in the real world out where it hadn't been spoiled too much.

Two weeks ago we slowed down into a group of RVs big enough to house a feudal castle inside its fortress of vehicles. They were parked in a circle like an old-fashioned western wagon train, ready for an attack. We were the outsiders but we were pleased to discover it was Birchlog Retreat, the old womyn's camp ground we had heard so much about in San Francisco. They had camping down to an art. They had a communal indoor and outdoor everything, from bathing to cooking. No children, except the occasional brave visitors from home. Most of these womyn were lesbians who didn't want to toe the line on someone else's land and had the know how to do it differently on this land. I was surprised that Jess, our old friend, had not already been here and told us about it. She had been everywhere in her ninety-some years.

They even had a small printing press outfit running from a shed someone had hooked up to the generator in their enormous camper. They had already published a short memoir and three books of writing, one with hand-drawn illustrations that tickled me silly.

Birchlog Retreat had shady caverns and open trees spread over five acres, with running water on the edge. They'd already harnessed the wind for their water power use and planted an orchard with figs, olives, and lemon trees. They had chickens, goats, and two lamas for long walks off their land. They were refined, gnarly, and welcoming in a way I hadn't dreamed of since leaving my community in San Francisco.

On our first evening there was a bonfire, tables and chairs and blankets all around, with a hearty stew and crispy-edged polenta. Someone had made brownies for dessert. They also served elderberry wine mashed from the sweet berries on their land. What a little heaven they had made for themselves. Cara immediately channeled us into telling our stories. We were even doing little enactments that had the whole bunch splitting their guts with laughter! We went to sleep that evening in silence, so happy. That night of howling wolves in the distance only softened our dreams.

Before we purchased our caravan wagon, Cara and I had fantasized decorations of red paint with cream embellishments, wanting Rosie's name to be somewhere prominent on her body. We had different thoughts on the subject at the beginning of our trip, and my stubbornness just couldn't let go. But Cara is no pushover. She knew from the beginning that she wanted to identify our chariot plainly on the door. It made me feel a little vulnerable but who needed to know that? I always wondered if we could make our decisions together without alienating each other when they didn't match up. It turned out that we trusted one another enough to move forward without attachment to our own positions. This approach usually made for a good blend. I have felt deeply respected and appreciated by Cara, and hope that she feels the same when it comes to how we relate to each other. I want it to be so.

There have been so many opportunities for the flaws in a human being to be recognized and touted over the beauty and the possibility of us working together. It has been a relief to hang out with someone who wants to support our side-by-side arrangement and doesn't feel the need to be on top. That's how it is right now and I love it. I don't take it for granted.

After we pulled away from the café where we'd stopped for breakfast, taking along some berry pie for our evening repast, we headed northwest toward the mountains. The sun was on our left side and a soft wind was wafting through our car in the open air. We were heading away from the four corners, away from hot days and cool mountain nights toward the big peaks on the California horizon that we barely got to see. I was energized by the proximity of their vision and faint expectations of gorgeousness.

Whenever we pulled off the road, it was often to stop and watch a raptor circle and swoop toward its prey. By now the hawks were becoming our old friends and we had an idea of which ones we were seeing when we looked through our binoculars. The land was open and wide, reddish with a bright sun-washed fade that made our eyes ache. I felt saved by the sunglasses I had finally purchased! So it was with delight that we set our sights on the highway and possible volcanic eruptions.

One evening, Cara was explaining something to me about the effect of light on what we saw and how each of us interpreted the variety of sightings along the road. Then she began quoting Adrienne Rich's *Diving into the Wreck* and I was swept along in the tempo and color of her strong recitation. Hints of her southern Virginia roots were in her voice and they only deepened my admiration and enjoyment of her. It was like this all the time; the way her aliveness tickled my pleasure.

In a former life, when I lived on land in Oregon, I hitchhiked up and down the California coast and only went to Mount Shasta once. There was something inviting and mysterious about this mountain that loomed over Route 5, so intensely present and majestic. There are California myths dating back over time that Shasta contains a hidden valley that housed the inhabitants of Lemuria, a continent of highly adapted and advanced humans, which sank into the ocean centuries ago.

Cara and I had alter egos, named Bobo and Lyone, a brown bear and a young lioness. We were both game one day, so we began driving our trailer northwest into the beginning of another day. The towns we passed through were often interesting and we stopped to explore one that looked like a picaresque western movie set. Nobody was wearing a gun or chaps. Cara decided to relax inside the trailer while I wandered around the town exploring. They had a bookstore and the young woman clerk looked approachable.

I leaned on the wooden counter and asked if she carried any lesbian literature. Without blinking and beaming a smile, she indicated the corner bookcase where I found shelves of women's writing. I returned to the counter and enquired about the bounty of these books. Where did they get them? I was excited because there was a copy of *Moon Moon*, which I grabbed on the spot and bought.

The young woman then explained, "My mom bought this place about thirteen years ago and slowly got women to come and visit. She's a lesbian and was hungry for community when we moved to Romona. We were strangers to the small town life. She's happy here now and she found someone who cares about her. Me, oh I'm ok. I miss Sacramento, the Delta, and some friends. When school starts I'll have more fun. I really love to read too, so this isn't a bad place to be."

"My name is Lyone," I said. "What's yours?"

"May, and my mom is June Miller. Nice to meet you." She smiled.

A few minutes later, I left the bookstore and kept walking. There was a small five-and-dime store that reminded me of the ones that were always around about fifteen to twenty years ago. Oh, and there was a soda fountain! I walked back to get Cara and shared some ice cream with her.

The inside of the five-and dime-store was so much like what I remembered that it felt like a rewound film. When Cara saw the place we poked each other again, a little giddy at our find. We straddled the bar stools and looked at the menu, put some money in the juke box and laughed when a Chubby Checkers song spun out over the speakers. We both ordered pie a la mode; Cara wanted the apple and I got blueberry. It wasn't too sweet either.

Now it was almost twilight and we were at the base of a large mountain, gearing up for some campgrounds ahead, so maybe another two hours of driving. It was going to require our patience as we were both exhausted from the long drive switching back and forth, always stopping for bird sightings and jackrabbits.

"Why can't we just sprawl here, off the highway, and lounge?" Cara said.

"Onward and upward!" I answered. The road was a twister, requiring a twenty-five mile speed limit, up and down, with nothing else on the road side.

"Oh!" Cara said as we hit the trail and watched the trees. There was mountain dogwood in bloom and incense cedar, even hemlock. The smells were swoonable, deep musty scented fragrant air and earth arias of life which curled into our nostrils. We loved it and we sang our love out loud. It was solitary and inviting as we sailed our little craft into the forest silence, gently caressing the mountain sides. We let the dust fall from our minds as we rose into the embrace of this looming mountain.

Ninety minutes later we found the marker to our camp area and pulled into the evening quiet. There were a few other vehicles and tents settling down for the rising darkness. We found a lone spot without neighbors nearby and decided to open the trailer's top and camp in the starlight. Smells from still smoking fires and dinners made us salivate, so Cara and I brought our chairs and wood out to the fire pit and we made a roaring fire.

We heated up some leftover grains and veggies inside and ate outside, just happy to have our tushies in the chairs and slowly coming to rest our bodies in the rhythm of the forest. We sprawled now, our muscles and skins releasing the tensions of driving. Our attention was drawn inward. We squeezed hands and our bodies smiled. There was the sound of water somewhere nearby. I put that aside to pursue the next morning. We would want to swim and, if we could find an accessible entrance, our bodies would follow. Meanwhile, we drifted quietly in our chairs until the fire died down, the embers smoldering. Finally, we packed our tired limbs off to dreamland.

Waking from a deep sleep to lots of light as the sun began to spread across the sky, Cara suggested she make us breakfast while I find the water source we heard the night before. Then we could decide on an afternoon swim.

"Okay, I'm down for that, but it might take a while," I said. She offered an hour. I dressed, washed, and ambled off to see what was around. I could feel the warmth already, so finding a swimming hole would be delicious. There were several trails around. I decided to ask some women on my left with a banged up, green station wagon what they had discovered. They pointed me to the western edge and I loped around the corner, filled with the scents of tree smells and the brackish sound of jays.

Maybe fifteen minutes later I was staring at a full running river or creek bed, wide enough to need care in crossing. There were boulders in the water's path. I walked around, looking for a still pond or pool somewhere and, sure enough, it was there. My dream wish came alive! Happiness flooded my heart and I turned around, excited to tell Cara that we had a place to play.

Cara was sitting outside with her binoculars, looking into the trees. There was a little picnic set up with our dishes waiting. She had made biscuits and sausage and coffee for us. I sat down ravenous but restrained.

She said, "There are woodpeckers up there but I can't find them."

"Let's eat," I begged. Very agreeable, Cara filled our plates, beautifully decking them with sausage, broccoli and biscuits. I adored her, knowing that she put the green there just for me.

After we were done, I cleaned up and then Cara asked, "Did you hear anything last night? I woke up to scratching noises but felt too tired to explore." For safety, we decided that no one of us went exploring at night alone.

There were flowers here and berries. I wasn't sure if we could eat them. Earlier, I had gathered several handfuls in my hat and took them back to our camp. Cara was sitting down drawing. I stood off to the side and watched her concentration until she felt me. Unbelievably, she said, "Those are olla berries!" I was so excited. I promised to go back to pick more and Cara promised some kind of berry cobbler sooner or later. We passed the morning easily. I wrote about the water and the berries. Hours passed. We lay down and snuggled inside our trailer.

Soon we were down by the water with our chairs, books, and Scrabble. It was pleasurably warm on the boulders as we watched the water flow by, caught the rays, and then cooled ourselves off with a dunk. We were drunk on the luxury of our pool, sharing it with two kids from the campsite above. I tried to keep my hands to myself but I was tempted to touch Cara. Being in water with my friend made me go all silky.

When we were drenched with dunking and sunning, Cara and I returned to our chairs and set up the picnic basket at a table with the Scrabble board on top. I was always hesitant to engage in this game, as Cara was such a good Scrabble player. I knew she loved to win, especially when I was trying to beat her, and that gave me pleasure and an excuse to draw my guns. But Professor Cara won by ten points, which was a close and competitive game!

Now we sat and indulged, watching the sunlight on the water and the kids in their big inner tubes floating past us from upstream. We read to each other until it felt like time to return to camp, and think about building a fire and what we should have for dinner. Cara liked her twilight cocktail and she fixed a very mild one for moi as well. Thank the goddess for the electric light inside Rosie, as darkness was falling fast. I built a nice fire and we decided to make hot dogs and smores right over the fire. It was a no fuss operation and we could continue to relax without much preparation. That was the glory of being on the road.

Soon we could hear music, live music, soft guitars, and some wind song. Never too tired for something new, we walked a short bit from our site to find a small group of women playing and singing for one another.

"Just our luck," Cara whispered.

We were invited to join them and introduced to Cody, Jill, Rain, and Rola. There was a mandolin and someone who could play it. The women were quite talented and unpretentious while we lingered for several hours, telling our her-stories and listening to their saga of adventures and mishaps. Jill was a writer for an alternative paper on the east coast and she shared her experience of living through the 9/11 attack in New York. Each of us remembered that and honored our feelings as they came up. Then we sang some rounds together. We told them about the swimming hole we played in earlier and suggested they try it out with us tomorrow. It was clear they were lesbians and we feel elated walking home in the velvet dark after such unexpected good music and companionship. Cara had invited them to have dinner with us tomorrow night, with my help of course.

A new day and Cara barely had time to run to our swimming hole, get back, and begin the meal. There was sweet corn and boiled artichokes with hollandaise and trout, fresh from the fish mart in town.

Our guests arrived. Everyone was feeling good and hanging around the fire. After dinner, we awaited dessert. I didn't even know what Cara has created. Wow! It was a lemon sponge, gooey delight and we were all in heaven. Jody, the flautist, who daylighted as a graphic designer (she could even work on the road, but didn't), began to nip at the stem of her mouthpiece and Rola picked up the guitar. Soon we were all crooning away. There was beer, wine, and someone passed a pipe. We were streaming a delicate blue, a clear open feeling of freedom, just letting go in our quiet corner of the woods. How blessed we were to have had what we had, to have found birds of a feather and got together.

Oh, now they were singing "Girl from the North Country." I was swooning. I was alive and the light was pouring out of us on this dark new moon evening as we radiated our love to the cool universe. If this was the path to the Old Lesbian Abode, then I was skipping and rolling right down it.

Too soon, we hugged, said our good nights to the quartet of new friends, and tippy-toed to our soft bed without a word. Praise be.

The next day was another gorgeous morning, only slightly overcast. Cara said, "Okay, let's drive into town and see if they have any films we'd like to see or maybe just find some ice cream."

I asked her, "Do you remember anything from the paper we picked up in Mayhen, that pea-sized town from a week ago?"

"Nothing much except the title of one film called *Sarah's Key* that sounded interesting. I doubt there's much out here in the way of art films, but it is California!"

Two hours later we were strolling through the Shasta streets checking out the local vintage and looking for mischief of some kind. I spotted a theater. "Hey, it's a theater and they have some good stuff! Let's go see this one. I've heard about it but never read the book. Would you be up for it darlin'?"

"It starts in ninety minutes."

"So we have time to fish around for other stuff."

There were a lot of touristy shops, selling crystals and stylish western apparel. I found some gorgeous bandanas and bought four to use as napkins, bright red beauties. Lo and behold another soda fountain! I felt just like some desert rat finding water after a month in the sun, but I think it was only a week or so ago that we had some ice cream. We slithered in and found all kinds of edible delectables including our favorite flavors. Cara was squealing because of the butter pecan and I was so excited by the sight of real peppermint pieces sticking out of the flavor I wanted.

The young woman behind the glass display case told us that it was all in house, homemade, when she saw our pleasure rippling everywhere. I asked what her favorites were and she liked the dipped cones with sprinkles. That wouldn't be my choice however.

There was also a bunch of Mexican art work, candleholders, decorative candles with colored designs and melted metallic dots. There were some table-cloths that caught our eyes and a beautifully designed mirror made of copper. We decided to get out before more indulgence overcame us with shopping for extras we didn't really need today. The film loomed ahead, so we skipped to the theater like children from the fifties on a Saturday afternoon.

WE HAD A heated argument last night. It was a major barrier to our fall-ing asleep. Our backs were facing each other across the silence, as Cara slid into sleep and I stayed awake pouting over the tiny thorns sucking at my marrow.

It was so stupid, so silly for us to have confusion about where we wanted to go next. I didn't really care. Maybe Cara was just tired of the driving. She wouldn't really say. She just got upset as we talked about our plans and asked for quiet time. I got nervous when she wouldn't talk to me, but it was always the way she handled her feelings. You'd think I would have been comfortable with it by then.

It had been three months of slow traveling to places we both wanted to explore. We'd exhausted our almost five-week stay on Shasta. What a great experience of community, swimming, writing, music, and general good will. I believed Cara felt the same way, but something had changed. Oh, well, maybe tomorrow she'd talk more about it.

By the next day, it seemed that Cara wanted to either drive across the country for a fall experience on the east coast, or go home. She was so clear when she spoke.

"I know you don't like the driving so much but I haven't been near Virginia for sixteen years and my heart wants to be there," she said. "I'm nervous that you won't be interested and that will leave me without support."

I, on the other hand, was happy to work with this, and I told her so. She gave me so much of what I wanted and this seemed like an easy accommoda-tion. I was relieved that this was the issue, which was simple to remedy. My only concern was, I just hoped our little trailer would hold up.

We decided to spend two more days on the mountain, loving the water and getting our fill of stillness before the journey to Virginia. There was a full moon out this evening and we made love slowly and then fiercely for the first time in several weeks, hungry to tell each other how much we wanted and desired one another, to make our marks on wrinkled skin and re-affirm our affection for each other. It seemed to last forever. The glow was still around us when we said our goodbyes to this generous community and began our descent down the mountain.

The maps were out again, and we were plotting what to drive through and where to linger. I told her that I wanted to see Wyoming and Chicago at the least. Thank the goddess the weather was still holding sweetly. Neither of us was ready for any wintry signs while we drive.

It was amazing to look at America and realize how little of it I had seen. It was hard to think of ever returning to Detroit, where I grew up. I went to Miami too many times last year for the death of my mother and to help my sisters with support and with our Mom's house. I was happy not to relate to where I have been. Maybe there would be visions across the Midwest that would enchant me, although I couldn't imagine it now.

"How about changing with me darlin'?" Cara said. She probably didn't realize that she could get anything she wanted when she talked with those southern charms that always undid me. Of course, I said yes.

We were back on the freeway and it was endless, flat, and monotonous. I forced myself to stay alert and we drove for four hours. We were way out of California now and on our way back east. I kept my eyes focused on that delicate blue streak of horizon, what little there was, pulling us forward. It was late August, just past my birthday, and the weather and horizons were soft and gently cloudy, with maybe a hint of storm in the distance. I could feel Cara slipping away like a baby from the motion and gravity of long distance driving. It meant that I had to remain extra alert. Eventually the changing sky would encourage me to pull over and find us a cozy retreat for the evening, under a green canopy or an open field where we could park our cabin on wheels.

"HEY SLEEPY BUTT, time to rise and shine!" Cara said. "You were restless last night. I woke up twice to you mumbling and tossing and wondered if I should tickle you out of your discomfort or what. I see that you made it on your own."

My eyes opened slowly. The door was ajar and I smelled coffee, maybe stewed fruit. I was dreaming deeply last night about a woman named Janice, who was my friendship nemesis. We had a rough interaction that never got resolved. Our connection had withered over the years. I couldn't remember what was going on in the dream, nor why I dreamt of her, but she was sticking all over me this morning. I got out of bed and went to see what this new day was like.

Cara was still in her jammies and our Rosie was parked off a road in the middle of a field. There was my honey in her red flannels in a pocket of tall something, maybe corn gone to seed, drinking her café and strutting. I made tea and grabbed a biscuit with some fruit soup. I sat on a step and drifted lazily between the yummy tastes and Cara's lovely-to-look-at form. She pranced for me and sang a song from the thirties which made me break out in a wide smile. That was how it was with us, a dazzle and a razzle, enough to make our glue. We both wrote and often we took time in the mornings to let our thoughts spill out on paper. Once in a while we'd read to each other from our own work.

In the middle of our morning reverie we heard strange rustlings nearby, like animals pushing through grass. Soon we saw the sweet faces of baby goats pushing their way into our little camp. There were five tiny bleating creatures with very soft mouths. We were petting them like cats and they were sucking our fingers. They must have smelled the food. Then three girls came trailing behind them.

"Hello," I said. "These are so cute. Are they your goats? Is it okay that we pulled off here?" Nervous and surprised, we stumbled over our greetings.

The three girls were just taking their babies for a roundabout and couldn't be less startled by our presence. We offered them some tea but they seemed to want to continue their walk. They told us about a farm ahead that sold home-made bakery goods and canned foods. We thanked them and decided to stop by there later in the day.

Back on the road, Cara had been telling me stories of her life in Virginia before she left to come out west. I was amazed by how much she remembered and the many details of her grandmother's history she was able to recount. We came from different channels across the U.S. to find community and self-expression for our souls and feelings, to be supported by other women of similar minds and hearts. Oh, and bodies, of course!

Cara insisted that the existence of feminism and the women's movement changed her outlook on life so thoroughly that she leapt from motherhood and a loving relationship with her husband into the arms of a female colleague and traveled across the country to escape having her life be constrained by all that she'd been taught she was supposed to be. From where I stood, it had turned out to be a blessing, because it freed her spirit to flourish in such openness that even indecision was a character enhancement. She was still deeply connected to her daughters and they to her. What I saw was the beauty of their commitments with each other, and their consistent caring.

Equality and fairness were qualities we both wanted in a relationship. It was too easy to hurt one another. As for me, I had a long-term male lover in my twenties and quite a few other women lovers. Live-in relationships had eluded me on a long term basis, but I was compensated by my need for periods of solitude. Feminism had made both Cara and myself aware of the position of womyn in the world and the absolute need to support other womyn like ourselves. The struggle for womyn to have equal access to all kinds of resources based on our strengths and abilities, including race and disability, always needs to be asserted and honored. There are constant backlashes coming from everywhere, seeking to erase years of womyn's accomplishments with a quick blink, and a nod to patriarchy. I've had my separatist leanings going back many years, but there are deserving men and I've had my share of support from them as I've grown older. However, lesbian feminism is my leaning. It's where I bond most deeply in the larger picture of our world with all the brave and courageous efforts of womyn on a global scale. That's where my heart resides.

Laced throughout our wandering together was the philosophical thread of creating what we wanted right in this moment. Our driving and stopping had allowed us to be responsible for where we were and what we wanted to do at every moment. It was not all pleasure, because we still had the scabs and scars of our old baggage that we were healing. Gratefully, we were conscious enough to engage that emotional work within ourselves. I was impressed we had come this far and we were still laughing with and at each other and also still able to find something funny or odd about all that we held sacred.

Back on the road, that delicate blue horizon kept pulling us forward. Clouds billowed and formed cartoon abstracts.

"Look at the emu smoking a pipe! There's Santa in her rocker!" Cara said.

The night skies twinkled with mystery and reminders of what had come before. We were part of the larger puzzle and we fitted snugly into the big picture, both next to each other and apart. Cara loved to pull the thread out, exploring parts of our conversation that had nothing to do with the original chatter. I loved going down this road with her, having my mind titillated by an untested truth or a mental challenge to get at what she was thinking. But most of the time we were simply quiet with each other, letting our eyes and mouths feast after we'd stopped driving and were amply ready to stretch and caress one another.

At this point, we'd traveled overland to the east coast. We were now driving across the terrains of Kentucky and Tennessee looking for southern land dykes as we skirted the busier cities. Cooling or global warming was interfering with the steamy air currents. That didn't stop us from pulling into some obscure little campsite as we settled down in the Appalachian Mountains.

Now we were about seven or eight thousand feet above sea level. The lake near us was a deep blue and we didn't care if it was cool. We changed into bathing suits and locked the camper and almost ran across the grassy knoll to the beautiful deserted sandy beach with a brilliant expanse of quilted water lapping at our toes. We dipped in. It wasn't cold!

Cara grabbed my hand and tugged as I was always the slowpoke in new places. The lake bottom was clear and silty soft as we slipped into the water. The grit moving between my toes felt exciting. We were fearless and bold and we dove under water and rose like merwomen from the deep. We flopped around and splashed each other. We blew kisses in playful happiness at the refreshing bath of water on our skins.

We rushed back to our camp and flopped on our beach towels. It was so lovely as we spread out in the waning sunlight. I borrowed some of Cara's lotion just in case. You'd think I was brown enough! We burrowed down into the clean sand and napped peacefully together.

A while later, I woke up to a chill and to the smell of food. I had such a deserted feeling that I got goosebumps and felt abandoned until I heard my name being called.

"Over here, Bobo!" I yelled back.

Cara called for me. She had started fixing a little snack before dinner, some grapes and cheese with a shared toasted biscuit, a wonderful fruity cocktail for me and some clean bourbon for her. We sat in our chairs outside and listened to music, enjoying the great nothingness as it sat with us. We heard some birds but we didn't know what they were. By tomorrow we'd be in Virginia, entering the place of my dear one's birth.

At daylight's end we gathered wood to make a small bonfire and relaxed in our chairs. We'd been on the road almost six months now, and home back in San Francisco was tickling my mind. Cara was pensive, deep inside herself. Then she began to tell me of her deep appreciation that I had been willing to accompany her on this journey home, how happy and grateful her heart felt that her companion, me, chose to support her dreams sometimes. I was blushing in the dusk.

Cara was loving me out loud and across the fire and I was taking her love into my heart. We'd come shining across so many miles, still whole and intact, still feeling satisfied and satiated with our fullness and the beauty of our hearts' desires being met.

NEW SHOES
GIOVANNA CAPONE

Giovanna Capone is a poet, fiction writer, and playwright. She was raised in an Italian American neighborhood in New York, whose strong immigrant influence still resonates in her life. She lives in California, but will always be a New York Italian. Giovanna's first book was *In My Neighborhood: Poetry & Prose from an Italian-American* (Bedazzled Ink, 2015). Her work has also appeared in various publications including *Curaggia: Writing by Women of Italian Descent; Bless Me Father: Stories of Catholic Childhood; Unsettling America: An Anthology of Contemporary Multicultural Poetry; Avanti Popolo: Italian-American Writers Sail Beyond Columbus; Queer View Mirror 2, Lesbian & Gay Short Short Fiction;* and *Fuori: Essays by Italian/American Lesbians and Gays.* Her recent short fiction has appeared in *The Paterson Literary Review.* An interview with Giovanna appears in *Daughters, Dads, and the Path Through Grief: Tales from Italian America,* ed. by DiCello and Mangione. Giovanna's play, *Her Kiss,* was produced and performed to sold out audiences in San Francisco by Luna Sea Women's Performance Project, in their Dyke Drama Festival in 1999. She also co-edited *Hey Paesan! Writing by Lesbians & Gay Men of Italian Descent* with Tommi Avicolli Mecca and Denise Nico Leto. This was a Lambda Literary Award finalist in the year 2000. Giovanna works as a public librarian in the San Francisco Bay Area. Her website is: www.giovannacapone.com. Her short story "New Shoes" is memoir.

THE WALK TO my junior high school takes about fifteen minutes at a fast clip and I'm moving pretty fast on this cold winter morning. Cold air rushes to fill my lungs. It feels like tiny icicles are cutting the inside of my nose as I breathe. I push my hands deeper into my pockets, my textbooks wedged under one arm.

Early this morning, a clean layer of December snow had fallen and its fine white powder blankets the ground. The tree branches above my head seem lifeless and scraggly against the sky. Their bark is coated with an icy girdle freezing them in place. Even the wind can't make them bend. My breath forms a cloud as I walk step step step step on my way to school.

On the main street trucks and buses whizz by and cars are honking. I can hear the distant rattle of the subway rails and the slosh of dirty gray snow flattening under car tires. I turn off the main street and walk through the neighborhood, past the brick-attached, two story houses, their porch roofs laden with white powder. Already the neighborhood is decorated with Christmas lights and Santas and Madonnas. Every once in a while I see a lit Menorah in the window for Chanukah. On our block there are a bunch of Italians, some of us right off the boat, like the Nardones, my neighbors. There are a few Jews, and a few Irish too. The place really gets lit up at the end of December. Some people go all out, with their lawn displays and hanging flashing lights and even putting herds of reindeer and Santa sleighs on their rooftops. There are two of our neighbors who try to outdo each other, their front lawns covered with holiday artifacts usually a week after Thanksgiving.

Every day I walk this route back home for lunch. Sometimes Ma has a bowl of macaroni and meatballs steaming on the kitchen table, leftovers waiting for me from our Sunday dinner. They taste even better warmed up the next day. I'll eat lunch with my brothers and sisters, Vinny, Dominic, Theresa, and Rosemarie. As I walk, I think about that warm bowl of macaroni, holding my books and shivering.

Most mornings I give myself fifteen minutes to walk. Junior High is much farther away than elementary school was, so that's barely enough time. I'm often late. This morning I only gave myself twelve minutes, which means I have to walk fast, which means it won't be an enjoyable twelve minutes. I don't care. Most days I really don't wanna get there anyway. I'd rather be anywhere else but school.

Anyway, I walk to school on this cold December morning, past the decorated houses and lawn displays, past the parked cars covered in snow. I'm wearing a black zippered jacket that looks warmer than it actually is. Really, I'm freezing.

But this jacket is special. Not because it's new. It's actually a hand-me-down. It belonged to one of my cousins, Dominic or Anthony or somebody, and it's a boy's jacket. It's a little worn, but I like it that way because it doesn't look at all frilly or pretty. It looks cool. I hate all the coats they have in the stores for girls my age. All those dumb frills on their collars and weird looking buttons and belts. I picture those coats as I walk, racks and racks of them in various seasonal colors. I feel like I could suffocate under them. I could lay down in the store, under the racks, and suffocate and no one would ever notice or care. I hate those coats and the way I look in them. I won't wear them, refuse to even try them on when I'm with Ma at Korvettes Department Store.

"Try this on."

"No."

"Just try it on for size, goddammit!"

"I don't want to!"

I move down the racks and end up in the boys' section. I don't look for it. I just move toward the coats I like, and that's where I always end up. That's what I like. Why do *they* get all the good clothes? I turn around to find my mother. When she sees me in the boys' section, a look of horror spreads across her face.

Therefore, this black, worn, hand-me-down jacket will work just fine for me, although it's not really warm enough. It's better than a girl's coat, and you can't have everything. You can't have a new coat that looks good on you and is also warm. That would be having everything, and I don't deserve that. Why should good money be spent on a boy's coat for me, a new boy's coat, when I ought to be wearing girls' coats and besides, girls' coats cost less? So I wear the old coat, the black coat. Black is good anyway. Black feels right when I see myself in the mirror with it. My Aunt Tessie wears black all the time. Why can't I?

So I walk to school in the snow, freezing. I hunch up my shoulders and grind my teeth till I get there and it's almost like not feeling the cold at all. I plunge my hands deep into my pockets and watch my feet as I walk step step step step past the houses with their porch roofs buried in snow, past the holiday decorations, on my way to school.

I watch my feet and before I know it, I'm at the short cut. I have only to climb over the stone wall, cross the field of crab grass and dog shit, swing from the silver pole and drop down to the sidewalk on the other side and I'm there. I love this short cut. The playground is right around the corner. I made it and I wasn't wearing a sweater under my coat or a hat, or anything. I never wear a hat. They're too dorky. I hate the way my hair looks when I take it off: all flyaway and frizzy. I never wear a hat, no matter how cold it gets, especially since I discovered this way of getting to school. Hunching up my shoulders and grinding my teeth and watching my advancing feet until all of a sudden I'm there at the stone wall. I never wear gloves for the simple fact that it's not good to have too many belongings. Same goes for a sweater under my coat. Too many things are not good because if you have to make a quick getaway in an emergency you won't be able to. If there's an air raid, or the school's on fire, you can't have too many things to gather up if you need to make a quick getaway, and you never know when you'll have to do that: for example, escape a burning building or run from exploding bombs because the Russians just attacked us. You never know when you'll have to run for your freakin' life.

I walk onto the playground and see some boys lined up near the girls' doorway. They're firing snowballs as the girls dash inside. The snowballs are ice-packed and whizz by the heads of the girls. I hear the hard slap as they hit the side of the building. The girls are screaming, ducking, and running inside. I decide to slip inside the boys' door, passing the monitor in the hall. I climb the stairs to my homeroom. No one stops me. Once again I made it inside. Hey, all you dumbshits! I made it inside this building, past the monitor, and up the stairs AS A BOY. No one hit me in the face with a snowball. The patrol didn't stop me and ask questions. I made it inside! Screw all of you! I'm a GIRL, and I'm proud. Don't tell me what door to go through.

I rush up the stairs and go to my locker, thinking of the times I almost didn't make it inside, like the day a tall eighth grader grabbed my arm when I was walking home from school. He was a tall black kid and he said, "Punk, omma kick yer butt!" His fingers tightened in a death grip. "Gimme your money, punk!" It was cutting off the circulation in my arm. Finally I blurted out, "I'm a girl! I'm a girl!" I confessed what I was and he let me go, asking if I had a brother 'cause he was gonna kick *his* butt.

But today, once more, I made it through the boys' door. I didn't have to use the girls' door where iceballs are whirling through the air or sliding down the red brick walls of the building, having missed their targets. The girls' door is farther away from my homeroom anyway, so I didn't use it. No one came up to me and said, "HEY! WHAT THE FUCK ARE YOU, A GIRL OR A GUY?" and nobody wanted to beat the shit out of me or kick my ass just because I walked by and actually looked them in the eye, instead of staring at my toes like I usually do when I walk onto the playground. Today nobody wanted to beat me up. I made it into homeroom with my books and my pen before the bell rang for sixth period.

Now I'm sitting at my desk while the teacher is putting notes on the board. Today is the day we'll do auxiliary verbs and I'm thinking about my shoes.

Miss Barrett is putting vocabulary words on the board: parsimonious, pernicious, precarious. I copy them down, remembering what that girl Robin said on the bus about my new shoes. We were both coming back from downtown last Saturday. I was trying to be Robin's friend. She's in my English class. She has so many friends and always throws parties at her house. I wanna get in those parties and I thought maybe someday she'll invite me. It's the holidays and there's bound to be tons of parties. So I invited her to go shopping with me. Oh what a dumb idea! Whatever made me think it would be that easy? Dumb dumb dumb! Nothing's that simple, you idiot!

I copy down more words: perspicacious, pertinacious, pestilent. I'll add these words to my collection. Tonight, I'll look them up, break them into syllables, place accent marks, define them, and use them in a sentence.

At home, I have a green index box filled with Miss Barrett's words. I'll add these to my "p" words. Knowledge is power. The poster over Miss Barrett's classroom door says so, and she's constantly pointing it out. She marches in front of the class in black low-heeled casuals, toes pointing, hands on her hips, gray hair parted and combed perfectly. Little gray wisps of hair curl on either side of her forehead. She stares at us through black-rimmed plastic glasses. "Knowledge is power!" she yells, pointing at the poster above her door. She repeats herself several times a day, so that when we're all sixty years old her opinions will still ring in our ears: "Knowledge is power!"

Well, if that's true, I have a lot more vocabulary words to collect, because "I have not yet begun to fight!" and "Give me liberty or give me death!"—two more slogans written in giant letters across Miss Barrett's walls. I'm arming myself with words. Don't mess with me, motherfuckers!

They say Miss Barrett used to be a nun. She was a nun for fifteen years, and then all of a sudden she had to leave the church. No one knows why. Now she teaches seventh grade English. The joke about her is "She kicked the habit!" Another one is Miss Barrett, the flying nun, because her hair sticks out like wings on either side of her forehead.

I'm copying down her vocabulary words, still thinking about what Robin said on the bus, coming back from downtown last Saturday, the day I was trying to strike up a friendship with her. I'm still worrying about my shoes. I'm also worried about the auxiliary verbs. Today we'll stand in front of the class and recite them one by one. I'm wearing those new shoes I bought. Damn, maybe I shoulda worn my sneakers.

A line is forming in front of the class. Miss Barrett has called on seven kids to start reciting the verbs. They stand like wooden soldiers in front of the blackboard. Miss Barrett's slogans are above their heads, her famous quotes from history and literature: "A man's reach should exceed his grasp, or what's a heaven for?" "This above all, to thine ownself be true." "Thinking is the intrepid effort of the soul to keep the open independence of her sea." What does all that crap mean? You have to strain your brain to figure it out, but she keeps hollering it day in, day out. Another thing she hollers a lot is "Burst, burst, burst!" because "burst" is the only verb that stays the same through all three conjugations: past, present, and future. There's no such thing as bursted, bust, or busted. In fact, it's practically illegal to say those words in her classroom. She'll kill you if she hears 'em. It's burst, burst, burst. Another thing you should never say: "Miss Barrett, my pen ran out." She'll just point down the hallway and say, "Well go out there and run after it!"

She's standing at her desk now, studying her troops. "Come on," she says, "I want you to rattle off those verbs! One by one. Get up there and rattle 'em off!"

It's performance time. The curtain is rising, and if you can't pull it off, Buddy, it's curtains for you! What bothers me is, I know the auxiliary verbs. I memorized every one of them weeks ago. Who cares about the stupid auxiliary verbs? If it wasn't for what Robin said on the bus, I wouldn't be sitting here worrying.

We went to Cross County Shopping Center. We took the #51 bus. She was looking for shirts. I was buying some shoes. So she goes into Popular Cottons and tries on these two paisley print "blouses." That's what she calls them. Not shirts, blouses. One's dark red, the other's pale pink.

"What do you think?" she asks me.

I look at them and shrug.

"Well, do you like the red one or the pink one best?"

"The red one," I say, because I hate anything pink.

"You don't think it's too dark?"

"No." I don't tell her my favorite color is black. So she buys the red one.

Then we walk into Sear's Junior Miss section. She tries on this and that blouse. She goes into the fitting room with five different ones, tries them all on, and hands them back to the clerk. I'm amazed. She actually goes into fitting rooms and tries things on. All I ever do is glance at stuff on the racks. I figure if it doesn't look good on the rack, it's not gonna look good on me.

Finally, Robin comes out in a bright yellow blouse. I watch her standing in front of the mirror straightening the collar. Her honey blond hair is pulled back with a blue head band. Her blue eyes match the headband. Whatever she wears, she always matches. Maybe that's why she's popular. She knows what to wear. Even now, her yellow hair matches the yellow blouse, which is long-sleeved and has little bits of white lace on the collar and cuffs. Lace? I dunno. It looks like something a doll would wear.

Five minutes later, she's at the cash register paying for it. Boy do we have different taste!

On the way out, she stops at the jewelry counter to look at earrings. She almost buys a pair that look like yellow butterflies.

"Do you have pierced ears?" she asks, reaching to touch my ear lobes.

"No," I say, flinching slightly under her scrutiny.

"You should get them pierced," she says as we leave the store. "Then you can wear earrings."

I wonder about piercing my ears as we walk down the avenue. Would I want to wear earrings? Not really. We pass a few shoe stores: Stride Rite, Payless, Tom McCann. I look in the windows at the shoes.

"Don't you wanna go in?" Robin says in front of Tom McCann.

"Don't need to."

"Why not?" she says.

"I can tell from the windows which shoes I like, and I don't like any of these." I sweep my hand past the glass windows of shoes.

"How do you know that fast whether you like something or not?" she asks.

"I don't know." She smiles and we continue walking.

It's like that for two more hours. We walk up and down the sidewalk, stopping at the windows of every shoe store. At this point, I'm starting to get a little worried. Robin has already bought all the blouses she's going to buy (five in all), and I really have to buy some new shoes. TODAY. Besides the fact that I need them, it was hell convincing Ma and Daddy to let me do this by myself. I can't come home empty-handed, after all that. They'll never let me go shopping for myself again, and I hate the clothes *they* buy me.

We pass Payless for the second time, and this time I really look carefully.

"What about that pair?" Robin says, jumping up to the window. She points at some brown suede platform shoes. I shake my head.

"I hate platform shoes. How can anyone walk in those clodhoppers?" I say, and we continue down the street. Guess I can't blame her for trying to help me. It's already four-thirty and we have to catch the five-fifteen bus home. I'm starting to get really depressed. Why can't I ever find anything I like? Maybe I'm too picky. Maybe I expect too much. Why is my taste so different from her's? Let's face it, most of the girls in our class dress like her, not me. So what's *my* problem?

"Here's a pair!" Robin practically sings she's so excited. She's standing near another window. "Come see!" I move closer. They're these sandal type black shoes with open toes.

"I don't like sandals, Anyway, it's winter," I say, moving on, but I'm really thinking, Shit! I'll never find something I like. And I'll never be one of Robin's *good* friends. We're too different. I'm not like the other girls. I'm not like anyone on the entire planet. I'm too weird. Why do I have the same problem with shoes as I do with coats? I just can't figure out who in their right mind buys all these ugly girls' shoes. But they just keep making 'em and making 'em and sellin' 'em and sellin' 'em. They gotta be crazy! I hate shopping! I hate clothes! I'll just wear my sneakers all the time, my black converse high tops. They're the best. Who needs a stupid pair of shoes anyway? It's just a waste of money. I'll wear my sneakers till the soles wear off.

I continue down the street, feeling lousy and alone. We pass a few more store windows in silence. Finally, in the window of Tom McCann a second time around, I actually see a pair that catch my eye. I can't believe it. What a relief! They look kinda cool. They're brown leather oxfords with flat rubber soles and dotted designs across the top of the leather. I can't believe I missed them the first time around. They're the only decent pair I've seen all day, and they're not too expensive. I move closer to the glass. They look kind of Italian, like a pair of brown leather shoes I've seen in my father's closet. They were made in Italy. I decide to go in and ask for some in my size. I look around for Robin. She's a few feet away on a bench.

"Hey! I'm going in," I yell, pointing at the door.

"Okay, great!" she answers. "I'll wait here."

A FEW MINUTES later we're running to the bus stop just as the bus is pulling away from the curb. We rush after it.

"Stop!" Robin yells at the driver and bangs on the folding door. He snaps it open, grumbling. We pass him quietly, shopping bags in our hands. Then we just bust out laughing and make a dash for the first empty seats we can find. We end up in the back, holding our hands over our mouths and laughing, which makes him even madder. He glares at us in his rearview mirror as the bus swings out of the shopping mall, heading for home.

On the ride back, we bounce in our seats. The bus turns onto the main road. I open my bag and take one shoe from the box to look at it again. Sharp! I hold it in my hand and rub the leather with my fingers. I can't believe I actually found a good pair of shoes in my size. At the last minute too! I'm so relieved!

And they're well-made, which is great because they're gonna have to last me the whole year. Wait until I show them to Ma and Dad!

"Pretty cool, huh?" I hold one up for Robin to see. She looks at it and suddenly looks out the window.

"Look at the designs on the top," I say, pointing out the dots curling in circles. Robin looks at the shoe again, shrugs, and turns her face back to the window.

"What do you think?" I say, moving the shoe closer. "Cool huh?" She keeps looking out the window and won't say anything. I gaze out the window at the stores and gas stations whizzing by. What's so fascinating out there?

"Do you like them, or not?" I say. She doesn't answer. She just kind of smiles and shrugs. "You hate them, don't you?" I say. She turns back to the window.

"I don't hate them," she says. We bounce in our seats again as the bus descends under a highway overpass.

"What's wrong with them?" I say, holding up one shoe. "What's the big deal? "For Chrissakes TELL ME!"

Her face is still turned toward the glass. "Well they're kind of—"

"What?" I push her.

"Well, I don't know . . . *masculine*," she whispers, as the bus dips down under the bridge and everything becomes dark.

I fall against the back of my seat. My throat feels tight, like I can hardly breathe. Did I buy a pair of men's shoes? No! They were in the women's section.

"They're *not* masculine," I say in the shadows. "They're just a stupid pair of shoes!" But the bus is shaking and the brakes are screeching so loudly as we descend that no one hears me.

SEVEN MORE KIDS are called to the front of the classroom. I hear my name called among them. I walk down the aisle and stand at the very end of the line. Robin is somewhere in the middle, wearing her bright yellow blouse with the lace collar. I hunch up my shoulders and grind my teeth. I know these verbs inside out and I'm gonna do it. I stare straight ahead at the posters on the back wall of the classroom. Miss Barrett is at her desk, supervising. She paces back and forth, hands on her hips.

She's inspecting us from top to bottom. "Okay, when I give the signal, I want you to rattle 'em off. Okay? Ready, set, go!" The kids start one by one, all down the line. I barely hear a word. I lock my knees and keep concentrating on the posters on the back wall, waiting for my turn.

Robin goes, but I don't hear a thing she says. When it's finally my turn I take a step forward. "Am is are was were be being been have has had do did shall should will would may might must," I say, in a blur.

"Again!" Miss Barrett yells.

"Am is are was were be being been have has had do did shall should will would may might must," I repeat. I feel my knees sink a little. I look down at my shoes.

"Excellent!" she yells with a big smile and calls up the next row of kids as the first bunch of us march back to our seats. Going down the aisle, I have the urge to yell out, "Burst, burst, burst!" just for the hell of it.

AT HOME THAT night, in my bedroom, I sit before our ten gallon aquarium. Ma is cooking supper in the kitchen, and the smell of eggplant parmesan fills the house. I sit in front of the aquarium and watch the fish gliding through the water. Bubbles from the filter's plastic hose rush to the surface and disappear. I listen to the quiet hum of the motor.

In a smaller tank, I watch Bacciagalupi, the pet turtle we've had for years. She's grown larger and larger. Her green shell has hardened over many feedings of chop meat, tuna, and lettuce. Every month I give her calcium baths for added strength. I watch her paddle through the milky depths of the bathroom sink. She's the one who outlived all the other turtles we bought from the pet store at Cross County Shopping Center. The one turtle whose green shell miraculously did not grow soft, whose eyelids did not close over with a horrible sickness prone to turtles raised in captivity. I watch as she paddles through ten inches of water, then plunges to the depths. The red gravel at the bottom of the tank swirls as her webbed feet pass over it.

I keep thinking about her shell and those milk baths. Her shell, and all those coats on the racks in Korvettes Department Store. I picture those slogans in giant letters on Miss Barrett's walls. "Give me liberty or give me death." "I have not yet begun to fight." "This above all, to thine ownself be true." And I decide right then and there that if the boys hurl ice balls at our heads, or if the Russians drop bombs on our house, or if some punk at school wants to beat my ass—motherfuckers, let's do it. I'm ready for you.

SUMMER SOUNDTRACK, 1977
SUSAN J. CLEMENTS

 **Susan J. Clements** lives in Buffalo, New York, with her wife, Kay Patterson, and Stella, a rescued pit bull. Her work has appeared in *Uncertain Promise: An Anthology of Short Fiction and Non-Fiction, The Buffalo News, Pyramid Lake Women Writer's Anthology*, and *In the Air: Your Stories*, a Talisman anthology. She has received honorable mentions for her personal essay in the Writer's Digest 2004 writing contest, Hudson Valley Writer's Guild 2010 Short Fiction Contest, and Hudson Valley Writers Guild 2014 Nonfiction Contest. "Summer Soundtrack, 1977" is memoir.

IT WAS TWO o'clock in the morning and we sang to keep ourselves awake throughout the night. We had embarked on the drive across Death Valley in eastern California at midnight, when temperatures dipped to the low nineties. There was no air conditioning in my Chevy Vega, and the hot wind made it hard to listen to the radio or hold a conversation. A sign in Barstow warned "Last gas for 200 miles." I would not have been surprised to see a sign for "Hotel California" blinking out of the darkness.

In 1977, gas was thirty-four cents a gallon and even though my car burned two quarts of oil for every fill up, it was still pretty cheap to drive across the country. I started out in Buffalo with my college roommate Teri, a guitar, and three hundred bucks in my wallet. A Rand McNally Road Atlas was our only guide in the pre-GPS era. We had no specific route, just a list of friends and relatives to stay with, and a deadline date of five weeks to get from New York to California and back. Once across Death Valley, we'd dip our toes in the Pacific Ocean before turning eastward again.

Teri was not only my college roommate. For a while she had been the love of my life. That relationship ended when Teri, a devout Catholic, put an end to the cuddling, hand holding, and kissing that were rapidly leading somewhere she refused to go.

I met her my freshman year and we were immediately attracted to each other, though neither of us would call it that. Raised in the sheltered suburbs of Buffalo, I was only dimly aware of Stonewall and gay liberation. Teri was a small town girl from upstate New York, with a sister in the convent and a brother destined for the priesthood. We quickly became close friends who gazed into each other's eyes, pressed our bodies together on the narrow dorm room bed, and kissed each other on the lips.

One afternoon, we lay entwined on my bed, the door locked and curtains drawn. We were feeding each other saltines between kisses. I placed a saltine between her lips and started nibbling on the other end until we met in the middle, kissing with urgency. Her lips parted, and I was about to experience my first French kiss, when she sat bolt upright.

"We can't do this. It's wrong. We can't do this ever again."

The new rules: no lying down together; no kissing on the mouth; no locking the door. I complied because I was besotted with her, but my frustration grew.

In those days, music was a huge part of my life. I played the guitar and wrote songs, often romantic ballads to woo girls I had crushes on. "Sunrise, sunrise, you warm me. I was cold, I was alone . . ." That was Teri's song. "And if you stay for just another day, I'll be happy. And if you say you'll remember me when I'm gone, you'll be the dawn in my memory . . ." I seemed to know it was not going to last.

That summer at the camp where I was working as a lifeguard, I met Anna, a kitchen worker who exuded vulnerability. We played guitar together, staying up singing and talking long after campfires had been put out. Furtive embraces quickly progressed to a level of intimacy I had not yet experienced. I felt like I was cheating on Teri, but couldn't seem to stop myself. I wanted to take that final step, and Anna was more than willing.

I came to know that Anna was unstable with a volatile temper. When fall came, I returned to college and my chaste relationship with Teri. Anna did not take it well. Twenty page letters arrived every few days and she called incessantly. Long distance charges went down after eleven p.m., so I was plagued with late night phone calls. Her father was abusive and she often threatened suicide. I worried about the state of her mental health and her father's abuse. I truly felt sorry for her, but her rages at me were terrifying. I felt trapped in the relationship—unable to help her, unable to escape.

The planned road trip offered an out. Anna lobbied hard to go with me. Teri didn't push. I still loved Teri deeply, and the situation with Anna was scaring me half to death. Ultimately I chose Teri as my traveling companion, and in July of 1977 we pulled out of my parents' driveway and headed west.

By that time, I knew the relationship with Teri was also going nowhere. I was coming to terms with being a lesbian, but I was confused. I desperately wanted a relationship with a woman, but had no interest in the celibate one available to me with Teri. My hometown, Buffalo, was no haven for gays at the time, and beyond college and camp, I had no idea where to start looking for better prospects.

I had a lot of time to think during the long days on the road. God knows, Teri and I were not talking about what had happened between us. I didn't even want to bring it up. I was relieved to be out of Anna's reach, and I'd given up on anything beyond friendship with Teri. Music loomed large in my ruminations. Like Paul Simon looking for America, I felt empty and lost. I ached with inchoate longing for a clear path forward.

West of the Mississippi, AM radio was filled with Grand Ole Opry tunes and fire and brimstone preaching. We sang through the regions of dead air. Driving along that winding highway celebrated in Woody Guthrie's song, lyrics popped into my head unbidden. Ascending the Rocky Mountains, we hollered out a John Denver tune as we crossed the continental divide. Singing as we cruised Ventura Highway made the L.A traffic seem less intimidating.

In a dusty western town, I stopped the car and we both climbed out. Like many before us, we stood on the corner in Winslow, Arizona. Everything unsaid between us was in that Eagles song. I knew by that time her sweet love would never save me. I had to move on, but was afraid I'd never love someone else as much as I loved her. And to make it worse, I couldn't tell a soul about it. I suffered alone.

Every phase of my life has had its accompanying soundtrack. That summer, I favored songs of the open road, unrequited love, and yearning. It was the era of folk rock and the singer-songwriter, of earnestness devoid of irony.

Back in Buffalo, we parted ways. Teri had graduated, and I would start my senior year that fall. The seasonal structure I had grown up with was coming to an end: school years punctuated by summers spent outdoors. That cross-country odyssey with Teri had probably been my last chance for an extended road trip.

I saw her just a couple of times after that. We lost touch entirely, but many years later, I found her through our alumni directory. She was teaching in a private school, and still lived in the same small town where she grew up. Perhaps it was significant that she'd never gotten married.

Anna also disappeared from my life. I learned through friends that she was living in her late parents' house. I later realized her problems were rooted in a troubled family life, and there was nothing I could do to change the situation that entrapped her. My attempts to fix it had just made matters worse. I hope she's found some healing, and some peace.

Many years later, most of my youthful questions have been answered: love, requited; yearnings fulfilled; mortgage paid off, and now mortality is in sight. It's a different world than it was in those covert days.

In my twenties I continued searching for someone like Cat Stevens' hard headed woman—strong, smart and accepting. I found Kay in 1984, and twenty-eight years later we got married—legally—in New York State. She challenged me to do my best, and as the song says, the rest of my life has been blessed.

Now thirty years later, Woody Guthrie's words of the open road still ring true. The frontier has opened and the road is beckoning, as my longtime wife Kay and I head out for some new adventures.

Songs referenced in this essay:
"Hotel California" by Don Henley, Glenn Frey and Don Felder
"America" by Paul Simon
"This Land is Your Land" by Woody Guthrie
"Rocky Mountain High" by John Denver
"Ventura Highway" by Dewey Bunnell
"Take it Easy" by Jackson Browne and Glenn Frey
"Sunrise" by Susan Clements
"Hard Headed Woman" by Cat Stevens

PADDLING SLOWLY FOR ANOTHER COAST
a youth in movements
ELANA DYKEWOMON

Elana Dykewomon is the award-winning author of eight books foregrounding lesbian heroism, including the novels *Riverfinger Women, Beyond the Pale,* and *Risk.* Her most recent, *What Can I Ask–New & Selected Poems 1975-2014,* was published as a Sapphic Classic by Sinister Wisdom/Midsummer Night's Press. Elana is a longtime social justice activist, editor and teacher. She lives happily in Oakland, stirring up trouble whenever she can. See: www.dykewomon.org for info on her writing classes, editing & publications. *Paddling Slowly for Another Coast* is memoir.

This is a condensed excerpt of chapters 1-3 of a memoir in progress. It switches between the third person, where I am a character in my past, and the first person, when I am a reflector in the present. Some large chunks have been edited out.

1.

MY NAME IS Elana Dykewomon. I made it up. The name change is what most people ask about first. Why would a serious writer, a thoughtful radical, pick a name that almost repels book sales, even among movement lesbians with senses of humor, uncomfortable reading a book by "Dykewomon" on the bus?

My New York Jewish father who had Latvian parents used to sing a Scandinavian round when we were children in Puerto Rico, where he moved us when I was eight. Dropping us off at the small school house by the sea, my father thought to amuse us, singing, "My name is Yon Yonson, I come from Wisconsin, I work in the lumberyards there. When I walk down the street, all the people I meet, they say, 'Hello!' I say, 'Hello!' They say, 'What's your name?' I say, 'My name is Yon Yonson . . .'"

After his funeral, one of my sisters-in-law asked, "What did he think he was doing, moving you here?" All of us, my two brothers, my mother who loved New York (the theater, the newspapers, the politics, the food, her friends, her family) were marked by the boundaries of beach, a new sense of distance, heat, language, culture. But my father was content, lawyering in "paradise," happily taking cases against corporations, often late to dinner in his quest to be a benefactor to the little guy.

"Of course he thinks it's paradise," my mother would draw in her breath with a hit of nicotine, "he doesn't have to deal with vegetable shortages or worry about mildew or wait eight hours for the plumber who comes without the right part—" She gestured and let the rest hang in the air. They were used to mainland middle-class conveniences, the humming post-war infrastructure. Puerto Rico is a different country, scarred by U.S. economic exploitation for generations.

Soon after the women's movement—the Second Wave—started, started for me, I changed my patronymic. I was standing in a cemetery in New England, looking at the headstones, and realized that every woman buried there was defined by a man: loving wife, beloved mother, daughter of Tom. It was 1975, and "dyke" was an edgy word. It still is in some places, but not in San Francisco, so it's easy enough to forget how powerful that word can be. A weapon, cutting in at least two directions at once. A labrys. Other women were changing their names to flowers, seasons, animals, daughters-of, or going by only their first names. I chose "dyke" for the power, and "womon" for the alliance, for the understanding that gender is used as a categorization of power, and I was choosing to make common cause with women as a class.

And I changed my last name because I was afraid. My first novel, *Riverfinger Women*, had just been published. It was the first novel ever advertised as being about lesbians in the *New York Times* (while *Rubyfruit Jungle* was on the same full page ad, the word lesbian wasn't in its description). I was afraid of success–the ordinary, documented women's syndrome. Now that I have distance, I believe I was also afraid of being marked as a Jew, linking me to a long line of rabbis by blood and male writers by association. Perhaps, among these many reasons, I also took the name to spite my father. But it was primarily fear that success would make me "different" in ways that would keep me from the community life I wanted. Still, the shortest honest answer to why I changed my name is that I wanted to be not a "star" but a cultural worker, a member of the community from/in which I write.

In many ways, that desire stems from having been locked up as a child after two suicide attempts at thirteen, the last one very close to successful. Institutionalized for the better part of two years, when I got out, I walked a thin line between being a queer, fat, crazy, egghead trouble-maker and wanting to be one of the gang, wanting depth and friendship. Somewhere along the way, I glued together the broken pieces of childhood suffering and revolutionary ardor, and this memoir is that story.

2.

AT THE MAIN entrance to Johns Hopkins Hospital in Baltimore stands a marble statue of Christ, his hands spread open at his sides in the come-unto-me gesture, two stories tall. In 1963, a week after Elana's thirteenth birthday, at one a.m., she and her mother stood in the shadow of that statue while getting directions for the psychiatric ward where Elana would spend the year.

TWO YEARS EARLIER, her mother, Rachel, started taking her, some-times with her brother, to the Tapia theater in old San Juan. They had lived in Puerto Rico for three years, her father Harvey's law office requiring him to head up the San Juan branch. Rachel was delighted when culture came to town, by which she meant New York's theatrical road productions, replicas of Broadway's temples. The children both saw Marcel Marceau (the French mime who made miming famous), and stood in line to get the playbill autographed.

And then Rachel and Harvey took Elana to see *Death of a Salesman*. She was ten or eleven. Because it was Mildred Dunnock, her mother said, who'd played the mom on Broadway, and someone else famous, or famous among those who followed New York theater. She was a little young, maybe, her father thought, but old enough to be quiet and appreciate the treat of great theater. "Oh, I see," she said, unsure about what "taking the pipe" meant. But Elana did get that Willy Loman killed himself in the end. Killed himself! What an idea, what a wonder, what a possibility! And if a grown man could, why not a child? Why not anyone?

A twelve year old is barely born. If you look closely, womb fuzz and umbilical grease would still be clinging to her smooth, spongy skin. Children experiment with their bodies, not just in joy, as baby whales crash out of the sea for the splash, but to understand human pain and violence, which they see everywhere. No wonder they hurl themselves at TVs and broken glass, hit their siblings, roller skate until they can't breathe. What is the body? Where are its edges? How much is it worth?

But conceive plans to kill themselves? Elana did. She found a miniature version of the *Rubyaiyat of Omar Khayyam* that belonged to her parents, and was keen for the verse about the potter's hand shaking. Unlovely, misshapen vessel! Fling yourself back in the fire since you came out wrong. And she must be wrong. She was angry, angry to sleep downstairs alone, angry about the man behind the counter at the San Juan Hotel who pushed her hand on his penis in exchange for comic books, angry about her changing body, being expected to wear girdles and make up, angry about going to the big Presbyterian school after graduating from the tiny one-room-to-a-class elementary one, angry because she'd found a cache of Holocaust novels and exploitative war literature which she read by flashlight instead of doing her homework, angry because she knew she was not a girl like the other girls, she didn't want what they wanted, and she had an image, a sense from who-knows-where, that girls like her ended up in leather jackets in back alleys in New York, estranged from their families, angry that she was on an island and couldn't get to New York to find out about the thing she didn't understand.

Elana told some of her new classmates that she was going to kill herself. She had been a straight A student in her old school, and now she was failing algebra, despite the fact that she had a crush on the algebra teacher, a woman who looked like Lena Horne—at least as far as she could make out from the album cover, one of five they'd brought from Long Island.

She was a year younger than everyone in her class; her Spanish teacher made jokes about the Jewish kids who stayed out on the High Holidays. More likely, she said something like, "their people killed Christ, and now they want special days off to be lazy." She had taken to writing sketches of her new classmates, and someone looked over her shoulder, taking it in. The other kids said she could predict their futures; she had a moment of popularity writing about them that seemed to backfire, and cause them to think of her as weird.

Then she conceived of a science fair project in which she would find that thing in the human brain that made humans different than other animals. She spent hours in the school library with tracing paper, trying to overlay cat and monkey brains on human ones, to see, exactly, the seat of the soul. She had to get that science project in. Her father would kill her if she flunked science.

"Elana," her mother said one afternoon, motioning her to come sit and have some iced tea, "one of the other mothers called me because her daughter said you wanted to kill yourself. Is that true?"

"Oh, Mom, it's just something kids say. Don't worry about it." Elana was genuinely surprised that her school life was colliding with her mother, that her mother had any interest in her anymore, beyond buying her clothes, exasperated because she was so hard to fit, or taking her to diet doctors. Her mother was distracted. Her back hurt, her spine had been operated on twice, she was about to be president of the Puerto Rican Hadassah chapter, she was working on being a life master at duplicate bridge at night with Harvey, she and Harvey were fighting more, she ran a book club. The children seemed fine, most of the time, left to their own devices.

"All right. But your father and I think you should talk with someone. Next week we're taking you to see Dr. Providencia Castro Caro de Gonzalez—she's the sister of your pediatrician, Marissa. Remarkable—five sisters, four of them doctors, and they all married doctors. Anyway, I think you'll like talking to her. You'll be all right until then?"

"I am all right, Mom. Don't worry."

"DON'T WORRY," DR. Providencia Castro Caro de Gonzalez said, "lots of girls your age think they're homosexuals, but almost none are. I can assure you that you're not."

"What's a homosexual?" Elana asked.

Oh. So there was a name for it. And apparently it showed, and apparently it was a thing-not-to-be. And as soon as she got the word, she knew that's what she was. No way to wiggle out of it. But Elana reported instead fantasies about boys in her class, maybe Martin, the polite, buttoned-up son of her Algebra teacher, trying to give the psychiatrist what she wanted.

The science project was going nowhere. She could not find the seat of the soul, and she could not tell either Dr. Provi or her father. She was still getting felt up behind the San Juan Hotel counter for comics and candy bars. And she was angrier than ever.

THE DAY OF Elana's first suicide attempt she stood on the roof of the San Juan Hotel, her and her brother Dan's favorite hangout. She knew the back staircases and unlocked doors, took the elevator to the next to the last floor—the twelfth—and walked up the last two flights to the roof. She'd been there before. She and Dan had gone to look at the view, at the tiny people playing in the pool and beach below.

Elana watched the sunrise over the Atlantic and looked over the ledge at the gravel parking lot, the bushes ringing the hotel. What if she didn't die, or didn't die right away? What if she got pierced by the bushes, and ended up looking like Saint Sebastian? Puerto Rico was a Catholic island, and she was going to a Presbyterian school. She didn't think she was afraid of dying, but she was afraid of living through the fall. Of being in pieces, but still conscious, in pain, capable of being humiliated.

Elana was up there a long time, long enough to take a shit in a corner of the flat graveled roof. Then she was afraid that she'd die with dirty underwear, something her grandmother had counseled her against. "You never know, when you go out of the house, what can happen. You could end up in the hospital." Definitely. The sun was bright and then her father was on the roof with a couple of big policemen, who were edging around the ledge toward her. Did they think they were invisible? That she couldn't see them doing their delicate, beefy side step, afraid that they'd fall, but hoping still to tackle her?

"How'd you know I was here?"

"Your brother told us where to look for you," Harvey said. He must have said other things, like "please come down" and maybe he promised presents or trips. Eventually he said, "Your mother's downstairs crying."

"Crying? Really?"

"Of course. Of course she's crying."

"If I come down to see, can I come back up?"

Her father looked her in the eye and said, "Yes. Just come down."

She knew he was lying. But she knew she couldn't jump. Not anymore. Not with dirty underwear. Not in front of these policemen and her father. The roof must have seemed like a pretty sure bet, like Willie Loman driving his car into a tree. At the time, she didn't have any other means. She had considered and rejected driving a knife through her own heart, and probably suicide by slashing your wrists hadn't come up yet.

One step off the ledge and the *policia* grabbed her—two big men dragging her down the stairs like a sack of corn. Her mother was not crying. But Elana was docile now; maybe they injected her with something like they do the big cats that come down out of the hills in drought. She only remembers concrete lions on a stairway across from her father's office at the edge of Old San Juan, the fortress city, where they must have gone to make phone calls and do paperwork. Then they took her out in the country, to a Catholic hospital for the insane.

This was 1962. Puerto Rico, most of the U.S., had no facilities for adolescents, let alone pre-teens. She was in a private room close to the door of the locked ward, guarded by twenty-four-hour private nurses, to protect her from the other patients, they said. It was a woman's ward. Most of the women were heavily sedated. Inside of the locked ward there was another locked ward, with a small security window that she sometimes stood on her toes to peer through, though there wasn't much to see—sometimes a woman who'd wrapped sheets around herself, head to toe, a tall woman clutching the sheets to her chest like a ghost.

Her parents brought books. Mostly *The Wizard of Oz*—the whole series, deemed much safer than Holocaust literature, safer than the *Hardy Boys* or even *Nancy Drew*. Her parents had never read them and didn't know they were full of communist/socialist imagery—from each according to their ability, to each according to their means was how Oz was run. *That's all very nice*, Dorothy said, *but it would never work in Kansas*. Why not? Thinking about the bigger world was better relief than thorazine—which she got—it made her nod agreeably when her mother said her school friends sent their best wishes, although she knew they did not, except possibly for the son of the Algebra teacher.

She wasn't in the Catholic hospital for long, a month, maybe. Rachel and Harvey had arranged to bring her to the psychiatric ward at Columbia Presbyterian Hospital in New York, where a cousin, or a friend of a cousin, was an eminent child psychiatrist. From there, they would look at one of the few longer-term facilities for children, somewhere on Long Island. Elana was very drugged by this time, and having half of the long list of thorazine side effects. Although she had no pleasure in eating, in doing almost anything, she gained fifty pounds very quickly; her joints seized up—in occupational therapy they gave her a kit to make a leather belt from interlocking pieces that had to be manipulated together in a series—child's play. But her fingers were so stiff it was hard to do. She walked lopsided and shudders started somewhere in her nerves, spreading through her in quick, short convulsions which no one seemed to notice. No one asked.

On the ward, time was slow. She'd spend an hour watching the second hand of the clock move, click, click . . . relieved when someone threw a fit. One woman, a young woman, not older than twenty-five, although eighteen would have seemed old to Elana, was being given insulin shock therapy. They would shoot her up, wrap her in something, put her in an adult crib while seizures coursed through her body.

Somewhere down the hall, a doctor suggested to Mrs. Nachman that they try shock therapy on Elana. "She's just a child," her mother said.

"We've had good results with children," the doctor persisted.

"Her brain is still developing. I won't give my consent." An act of courage in the face of doctors in whom her parents had abiding faith under most circumstances. Rachel was not the blame-the-mother stick figure here, only a young woman herself, navigating without a map, a heartbreak no theater, no art, had prepared her for. In that moment of resistance, she saved Elana's future mind.

Rachel rented or borrowed a car and drove Elana to the facility for adolescent girls on Long Island. A woman in an office, alone with Elana, asked her if she was a sadist.

"What's a sadist?" One thing about getting locked up, it's good for your vocabulary.

"Well, for instance, do you like to pull the wings off flies?"

"You have girls here who like to pull the wings off flies?" She was appalled. She would not come here. Time to get self-directed, drugged or not. She swam up from the deep thorazine passivity and told her mother she wanted to come home. Really, really, she wanted to come home.

The doctor at Columbia Presbyterian gave her a new round of tests. Although she had answered honestly, or defiantly, the first time she'd been give the Rorschach, this time she said she saw women singing, praying, diving into a pool. She saw children playing with rabbits. It's really not hard to fool grownups. "A temporary psychotic break," the famous doctor pronounced. "Keep her on medication and therapy, move her bedroom upstairs, and she should be fine."

RACHEL TOOK ELANA home. It was the beginning of the summer. At the end of the summer, just before ninth grade was going to start and she would have to begin studying for her Bat Mitzvah (how could she stand up in shul, everyone looking, looking at her, knowing what she'd done?), her mother was going to take her on a trip to Saint Thomas, just the two of them, a special treat.

Elana was good, she was quiet, she was stocking up pills in a small purse she hid in her bureau or under the mattress. They were giving her, and maybe her mother too, Seconal to sleep with. She knew where her mother kept them, under her slips. She snuck out one or two at a time, two or three times a week. Thorazine the same. By the night before the flight to St. Thomas, she had forty pills of one, sixty of another, twenty of some other barbiturate in the house. She went back to the tiny copy of the *Rubyaiyat*:

... And this was all the Harvest that I reap'd—
"I came like Water, and like Wind I go."

Somewhere in the suicide note she wrote "The Moving Finger writes; and, having writ,/ Moves on: nor all thy Piety nor Wit/ Shall lure it back to cancel half a Line,/ Nor all they Tears wash out a Word of it." Anyone raised with religious liturgy can fashion a blade out of poetry.

She didn't care about the trip to Saint Thomas, she no longer looked forward to her grandmother's visits, which used to make her glad; she saw that she had no hope to set her heart upon, that there could be no future in the family for a fat girl who loved girls. She took a hundred and twenty pills with one glass of water somewhere around midnight, and was not found until the following morning, in a coma.

3.

I DIDN'T IMAGINE this, nor did I dream it. I moved from my corporeal case and body surfed on wispy clouds over the hills of Puerto Rico, the countryside my father liked to drive us through on Sundays, proclaiming that the painter Rousseau had scoured Paris for every shade of green, when all he had to do was come here.

In that green cacophony below my floating, disembodied self, children were playing on a mountain slope. A game with a ball, or hide and seek. They were engaged with each other, but I could not contact them. Loneliness flooded me, and something more than loneliness–yearning. What a twelve-year-old yearns for is a mystery now. But then it was enough to pull me back from being dead. I knew I didn't want to leave the other children.

Someone was cutting my throat, in the body I had almost left behind. Later I found out I had developed pneumonia from lying still for days. They couldn't give me anesthesia because they were unsure about how many drugs I had taken, what kinds. Since I was in a coma, they might as well put the tracheotomy tube in without any sedation. I stuck my tongue out at them, while being wheeled from the operating room.

MY OLIVE GREEN COAT
HALEY M. FEDOR

 **Haley Fedor** is a lesbian author from Pittsburgh, Pennsylvania. Raised in a Catholic household, she learned how to be a lesbian from the Internet. Her work has appeared or is forthcoming in *Section 8 Magazine, The Fem, Guide to Kulchur Magazine, Literary Orphans, Crab Fat Literary Magazine,* among others. She was nominated for the 2014 Pushcart Prize, and is currently a Ph.D. student at the University of Louisiana at Lafayette. Her story is non-fiction memoir.

We were drunk and stumbling home on liquor snuck into the movies, a hip flask each. Liz fell asleep halfway through the film; her snores were loud and drawn out, and earned a few hushes from other patrons. Her loose change and keys and phone kept falling out of her coat. They made a racket that rivaled the action sequence in the film.

I poked Liz awake at some point, helping her to see at least part of what she paid for. She had drool on her chin and was rigidly heterosexual, but I loved her a little anyway. We were the last ones to leave the theater, struggling to pull on our coats against the winter chill. I liked how Liz tried to rearrange her now-mussed hair as it cascaded long and dark across her shoulders. I liked that it was late enough that we were the only two walking on that part of the street, our shoes crunching through a thin layer of ice and snow.

The more functional of the two, I was going to walk Liz back to her apartment and then head home. Both of us had apartments downtown, so the walk would only be a few blocks total. Crime was a big problem in Huntington, West Virginia. Walking around after dark, especially as a woman, was always tempered with a caution that penetrated even the foggiest moment. Liz's roommate John warned me to avoid driving down side alleys at night, because gangs liked to jump out and stop the car, then rob and beat the shit out of luckless folks.

I remember the freezing winter air, and pulling my puffy coat around me more tightly. It was a real Air Force aviator's jacket, meant for high altitudes, olive green on the outside with a hunter orange inner lining. I'd found it in a Paris thrift store for 35 euros, and it was the warmest thing I'd ever owned. Wearing that coat, with my shaved head and baggy jeans, I felt like the butch I was always meant to be.

The air was bitter, the kind that stung at exposed flesh. I felt my ears and the skin of my shaved head burn, but I was preoccupied with making sure

Liz stayed upright. She stumbled down onto the crosswalk and her long hair flipped out into a sable half-halo.

"Red light," I said, indicating that we could cross. When she didn't move, I gave her a little push to the small of her back. I looked at the backs of her legs in her tight pants, her boots. Reluctantly, she began to walk forward.

"They need to slow down," Liz replied, pointing down the street.

A car was speeding toward us and toward the light. They weren't slowing down.

Liz stopped in the middle of the street, looking at the Mustang with a scowl and yelling at them. My palms pressed to her back, pushing her towards the sidewalk.

As we neared the curb, the front of the Mustang passed just behind our knees. I felt the motion of it brushing hot against my jeans. The Mustang glided to a stop in the middle of the intersection, but reversed quickly over the lines.

"Hey! You almost hit us!" Liz yelled at the driver. She backed into the curb and wobbled—maybe with anger—but still managed to be fierce.

"Motherfuckers!" I yelled, indignant, watching the passenger window go down.

A man in his early twenties leaned out, looking drunk or high or *something* enough to make his eyes red. I was closest to him and took an involuntary step back even as I cursed at him.

"Nice coat, you fat fucking dyke!" he yelled.

"What the fuck did he say?" Liz demanded. Her eyes were wide. "Fuck you!"

"Fuck off!" I added. My voice wasn't as loud as Liz's. I took another step back when I heard him swear. Then the driver's voice chimed in, the two of them creating a muddled stew of profanity.

When they started to get out of the car, I panicked.

"You fucking dyke!" one yelled.

"Fat fucking cunt!" said the other one.

I kept backing away.

"What did that asshole call you?" Liz demanded. "Why don't you both suck on a dick!" she screamed.

Her words were brave, but we were both backing away and turning the corner. Liz's apartment building was halfway down that street.

I knew that if we had to run, we wouldn't make it.

They started to follow us, but flashing blue and red lights made everyone stop. The police were standing outside Sharky's, the local dive bar famous for its karaoke nights and fistfights. There were six officers milling about or in the process of getting back into their squad cars. I'd never felt more relieved to see the cops.

Both men stopped at the sight of the cops and backtracked to the open doors of their Mustang. The light was still red and they revved the engine loudly. A string of curses sloughed from the open window. Even on the curb with policemen around the corner, I didn't feel safe.

Liz yelled at them again, something creatively vulgar.

The light turned green and the Mustang peeled off down 4th Avenue.

"What the fuck..." Liz said, trailing off as we watched their red tail lights. When they were out of sight, she started a fresh rant, going on about entitled assholes who thought they could do whatever they wanted. I was close to tears. And cold.

I was just starting to embrace my identity as a butch lesbian, but I still wore skirts to teach in. I always had big earrings and makeup on in the classroom. As a graduate student, it was my first year teaching at Marshall University and I wasn't *out* at work yet. I had just come out to my deeply religious parents two years ago. It was all so *new*. As much as I tried to embrace this delightful new part of myself, there was always a tendril of fear, ready to latch on.

I walked Liz the rest of the way to her apartment, past the idling cops at Sharky's and over smashed bottles ground into the sidewalk. There was always so much glass, green and brown and white pebbles that made strained noises as we walked, like a note held too long in a song. It was one of a long list of downsides to living next to a bar, but Liz and her five other roommates overlooked it all for the cheap rent. The entire time, Liz was frothing in anger over the men and what they tried to do, but I wasn't really listening. I felt hyper-aware of everything going on around us. My heart was pounding and I was breathing hard.

"Are you okay?"

I didn't say anything. I couldn't.

We looked at each other for a long moment, and she hugged me tight, offering to let me come inside her place and sleep on the couch instead of walking home. I stuck out my jaw and shook my head, insisting that I would be fine. What I really wanted was another drink and my own bed.

"Promise you'll text me when you get home, okay? Please?" Liz asked.

"I will. I'll be fine."

Liz was leaning against the doorframe of her apartment, and I was sure she wouldn't be awake long enough to read the text I'd send, let alone respond. But she hugged me once more and wished me a good night, before disappearing into her darkened apartment.

It felt colder without her there.

I walked past the cops again, aware by now that some of them were watching me. Sharky's was still lively despite an apparent bar fight and lingering police that had been called to stop it. The path to turn the corner and away from all of this stretched out impossibly long.

That tendril of fear that had never left now coiled tighter at the base of my spine. I never really noticed how many bars lay between our two apartments downtown. How many strange, older men would be outside smoking, watching me with suspicion. I wished for a hat to cover my head, to cover my short hair. To be fair, my ears were also freezing. I wanted a cigarette so I'd have something to do with my hands, my mouth. Even if it meant freezing fingertips and flashing my rainbow-colored fingerless gloves. But my hands stayed firmly in my jacket pockets, and I avoided looking anyone in the eye as I walked.

Even though the Mustang was long gone in the direction I was now headed, I kept looking behind me to see if I was being followed. There were only smoking bar patrons and a few homeless folks but I flinched all the same. I picked up my pace, my fat thighs rubbing together almost painfully. The sting of the cold through my too-thin pants and the burn of friction on my inner thighs meant I was miserable even if my coat kept the rest of me warm.

I felt stupid for not taking Liz up on her offer to crash on the couch. John and her other roommates were probably working their way up to the hard liquor, and I could've mooched at least a drink or two.

But I just wanted to be alone.

When I got into my apartment complex—a ratty old hotel transformed into studio apartments—my thighs and ears were numb. There was a glass wall with over-sized blinds at the front of each apartment, making it easy to tell if someone was home or not, awake or not. I contemplated knocking on my neighbor's door, but Angie was already asleep.

Earlier that year, I had broken up with Angie. She was only the second serious girlfriend in my short gay dating life. I was twenty-three and the lesbian dating scene in West Virginia was dismal. Even the online dating apps were mostly filled with attached women looking for a threesome. I met Angie due to a housing arrangement fluke, when we were both stuck in the college dorms. She was a junior and I was a first-year grad student, and I caught her staring shyly at me a few times around the elevators.

Angie was short with floppy, dark hair that always curled in impossible, adorable ways. With her love of good food, tea, and books, she always joked that she was like a queer hobbit. I asked her out and we dated for six months. They weren't very spectacular months, but I think loneliness drew and kept us together more than anything. Despite being a young white woman living in the twenty-first century, Angie thought that she had the core animal spirit of a wolf.

Months prior, weepy and drunk after our breakup, I heard she had gotten down on all fours on her apartment floor, and growled like the wolf she proclaimed to be. Our mutual friend Mark texted me that night after two a.m., asking if I was still awake. He added that it had to do with Angie, but I didn't respond. I heard sobbing through the (thin) shared walls of our apartments, and then what I thought were yells.

After drinking too much and weeping about her dissolving relationship and family issues, Angie got down on all fours and growled, howled, and bared her teeth at Mark. Usually, when she got too drunk she would play a few rounds of Mario Kart or another videogame and fall asleep. This time was different. The rest of the alcohol was dumped and, after a tense half hour of negotiating with her she-wolf self, Angie resumed her weeping.

Mark texted me again, but I didn't know how to go over there and negotiate with her in that state. While Mark sent me long, laboriously typed text messages about what had happened, I listened as my ex-girlfriend wept through the wall for minutes before quieting. We had broken up due to intimacy issues and an inability to communicate what we wanted to each other.

Even knowing that Angie really believed she was a wolf, I contemplated waking her up that night after leaving Liz. Despite the wolf incident, I still spent time with her and occasionally contemplated texting her for a booty call. Instead, I went into my own apartment and left the overhead light off, drinking in darkness in front of my computer and hating the fear that refused to go away.

I felt that fear whenever Angie and I held hands in public, or whenever I went to and from the only gay bar in town, appropriately named Stonewall. Huntington was an inhospitable place for young queers. I had heard stories of harassment or all out beatings. The Gay-Straight alliance on campus had meetings throughout the semester, but it had dwindled down to a handful of people and only one or two of them were friends of mine.

That night after the incident with Liz, I worried that Huntington would actually be the death of me. I was a visible butch lesbian and completely unable to "pass" as straight. What if I had to let my hair grow out? Or go back to wearing the femme clothing my mother kept buying for me? Every year she bought me a new winter coat in the hopes that I would abandon the aviator jacket. My mother would present me with blouses, skirts, and dresses every time I went home to Pennsylvania to visit. These presents always included talk of me joining everyone to visit the oppressive Roman Catholic church of my childhood. The church that had numerous sermons on the "evilness" of homosexuality and the threat of damnation.

I knew I could never go back to living like that: closeted, full of self-hatred and denial, feeling uncomfortable every moment in clothes that may as well have been as binding as corsets. I could never go back to long, impossibly thick hair that my mother refused to let me cut above my ears.

The first time I shaved my head, I laughed with the joy of it. Before grad school, I was home for the summer and fed up with my long blonde locks, now in a multitude of braids, that would take forever to brush out. I remember standing over the sink, holding my father's electric clippers and relishing their vibrating hum in my hand. My blonde-brown hair pooled under the leaky faucet, and I couldn't stop smiling. I used the smallest clip and shaved my hair almost down to the scalp.

That night, my mother stopped in the doorway of the dining room while the rest of us were eating. She looked at me for what felt like a long time.

"I'm just wondering what happened to my beautiful little girl," she said, voice wavering and tears forming.

She had to excuse herself to the bedroom, but we could all hear her crying. My siblings were mad that I had upset her and my father. They thought I was irrationally pleased with myself.

Actually, I just felt free.

As my hair began to grow back, I couldn't stop rubbing my hands over it, as though I had become my own lucky charm. I was proud of my short hair and it felt *right*. My mother's unwillingness to accept me hurt, but I knew then that I couldn't go back to the way things were just to please her—I would be miserable.

I tried to put the incident with the Mustang out of my mind. The next Monday, I taught my students in pants and a button-up, feeling comfortable for the first time in ages. I felt better, more confident. All of the terrible things I thought would happen…didn't.

When I called Liz the next week, she remembered very little about our walk home. What little she did remember, she chalked up to men being assholes. Liz didn't remember the fear, our walking backwards until bathed in the red and blue lights from squad cars. I felt irrationally mad at her, even though she had been so drunk it was a wonder she could remember anything at all. I realized that she didn't have to live with the same kind of fear that I live with every day, and when confronted with hatred, she forgot about it fairly easily.

"Are you okay?" Liz asked me, concerned.

"I'm fine," I lied.

I told her what she wanted to hear, buried the fear deep in my gut, and convinced myself that I was being irrational about the whole affair. I tried to put it all behind me, but that fear never left me.

Two years later I moved to Lafayette, Louisiana, even further south of the Mason-Dixon line. I had gone down there for school. Shortly after I moved, I was walking home from the library one night. A man in a Ford SUV drove by, slowing down for a moment.

Suddenly he yelled out the window, "Dyke!" and tossed his soda in my face as I walked by. Then he sped off. The sticky brown liquid of the soda clung to my face and my hair. I could feel it pulling at the hair on my arms as it dried into shiny rivulets, flowing downward.

I stopped on the sidewalk and stared down at myself for a long time, my face wet, my chest feeling tight. There was a coldness in my belly as my old fear came back, stronger than ever. It was the same fear from the night Liz and I were accosted by the two men in the Mustang. I hurried home and tried not to think about the fact that I didn't have a washing machine yet. About the fact that I would have to carry these clothes, covered in sticky shame, to a laundro-mat. Sometimes, fear is necessary. It's a survival instinct. But after these kinds of incidents, I wonder how much of my life will be spent in survival mode instead of living.

While I have met some truly remarkable people in this new city, I feel the same trepidation about going out in men's clothing, in *my* clothing. I still worry about the short length of my hair, my visible butchness, and whether or not it will draw the ire of some random hateful person. It has taken me years to become comfortable with my butch lesbian identity and my queerness. Years to shed the conservative homophobia of my childhood. I wonder how long it will take me to shed this intense feeling of fear. Will I ever shed it?

MARRIED TO A MAN AND IN LOVE WITH A WOMAN
JOANNE FLEISHER

Joanne Fleisher, LCSW, has her license in clinical social work from Bryn Mawr Graduate School. For over twenty years her private practice has specialized in women's issues and lesbian concerns. In 2005, she published a self-help book, *Living Two Lives: Married to a Man & In Love with a Woman.* Following her appearance on the Oprah Winfrey show, she became the leading expert for helping women who question their sexuality after marrying a man. Today, she uses the experience of her practice, her personal journey, and her long-term relationship with a woman to help others. Ms. Fleisher conducts a private practice in Philadelphia as well as consultation sessions both nationally and internationally regarding this specialty. Her web site lavendervisions.com provides resources and an active online support community for these women. Her certification in family therapy and Imago couples therapy gives her specific skills for working with couples and families who need support and help in their relationships. Trained to teach Mindfulness Meditation, she incorporates it into in her therapy approach. Ms. Fleisher and her partner raised her two daughters together, co-parented with her ex-husband, and is a grandparent of four children. With the exception of names, this piece is non-fiction.

MANY YEARS AGO I decided to leave my husband of twelve years—not for another man, but for another woman. In the process, my definition of integrity changed as well. It was 1979, the year that Donna Summer topped the charts with "Hot Stuff." I had fallen in love with a woman, had an extra-marital affair, lied about it, and broke my marriage vows. My life's trajectory changed in the moment that I made love with Gabrielle. In the afterglow of our lovemaking, I was overtaken with complete joy, then terror swept through me. For the entire next year I questioned everything: my fluctuating feelings, my beliefs, even my character.

I felt like a stranger to myself. I discovered that I was capable of behaviors that were "not me." While I was captivated by a confusing illicit affair, I began neglecting my children. I would spend time with Gabrielle, then fabricate stories of my whereabouts—I was attending Gestalt workshops, visiting out-of-town friends, going to conferences. I had been so sure of my future; I had been so confident as a parent. Suddenly I couldn't make a single decision. What I had taken for granted about who I was; all those assumptions were now open to question.

Throughout my twelve year marriage I had feared there was something broken in me, that I was unable to fall in love. Even before Dave, when I dated men, I never felt the vulnerability or aching desire that my friends seemed to have.

Now I was in love, but I no longer recognized myself. *I can't be a lesbian—I've always been straight and I'm married to a man!*

My husband Dave and I were thirteen years old, in seventh grade when we first started dating. We married at twenty-two and raised our two daughters together with pride. We were a great comedy team. At social gatherings he was the six-foot-one bearded jokester, and I was his petite "straight man." Dave cherished me in his own way. He would often tell me he loved me, but the words felt empty: he didn't reveal his emotions nor empathize with mine. I recall later telling my therapist, "Dave is a brilliant attorney, a good provider and a kind, loyal husband. The only things missing from our otherwise-perfect marriage are emotional intimacy and good sex." The therapist just smiled.

I was restless and lonely in my marriage. In an effort to improve our sex life, we tried sex therapy and even tried outside sexual experiences. It was 1977, a time of women's rights and sexual revolution. Experimentation of all sorts was in vogue. Dave was basically satisfied with the status quo, but perhaps to avoid conflict, he accommodated my request to open our marriage. We attempted to redefine our traditional marriage, but neither of us anticipated the consequences.

Then I met Gabrielle. An out lesbian, she was smart, funny, a powerhouse of will and personality, and *cute*: close cut auburn hair, a short curvy body, and dark brown eyes. She walked with a swagger and laughed constantly at her own jokes. She ended up occupying my daydreams far more often than I chose to admit. I found myself awestruck by the red gold of the leaves on the elm tree in Gabrielle's yard that October as we fed our curiosity about each other's lives. Sex became a natural outgrowth of our new romance. Although I didn't understand this kind of love, it was impossible not to act on it. By now it was 1979. I had never heard of a "straight" woman falling in love with another woman. Surely I was the only married woman facing this kind of problem. I was in love with Gabrielle, but I didn't "feel" like a lesbian.

I eventually recognized that open marriage didn't match my values. Infidelity felt wrong, but my heart and body were way ahead of my mind. Three months into my affair, I decided I couldn't lie any longer. One night after the kids were in bed, I told Dave we needed to talk. I expected a joke or sarcasm, but he looked concerned. Still, he remained characteristically impassive.

"Dave," I said, "I haven't told you the full truth. You said you didn't want to know who else I'm seeing, but I left out a big piece of information. The person I'm seeing is a woman. Gabrielle. And I don't know what to do."

Dave's face remained blank, but his voice was grave. "I asked you not to get involved with any of our friends or with a woman."

It was true. I remembered his request, but had no clue where his idea of my being with a woman had come from. Nevertheless, I had been unable to honor even that simple request. Dave shifted quickly to his usual problem-solving approach.

"We should start marriage therapy."

I felt a strange sense of relief. The question about what to do with the rest of our married life hinged on my decision about whether to continue exploring my awakened love for a woman. Would I, could I, love other women? I was terrified that if I decided to leave my marriage it would destroy my kids, who were just seven and nine years old at the time. How could the children survive a divorce along with the stigma of having a lesbian mother? Today's broad acceptance of gays and lesbians was unthinkable back then.

I vacillated constantly, deciding at one moment to stay, and the next, to leave. I was wracked with remorse and guilt. Finally, I just followed my gut. I hadn't known how to identify my sexual orientation, but this powerful new experience of love was beckoning to me to find out more.

My relationship with Gabrielle eventually ended when she decided to leave town for a more promising, unencumbered partner. I was on my own when I separated from Dave, and these many years later I am grateful for that: it helped me realize that I wasn't leaving for anyone but myself.

Just three months later I met Judy, with whom I shared thirty-one wonderful years until her death in 2011. She and I were from different worlds. She was a wispy red-headed androgynous lesbian with a gentle voice and a powerful body. Judy loved poetry, math, and physics, and had a deep spiritual life. I was grounded in my psychotherapy work, feminine in appearance, and practical in my approach to life. We didn't understand each other, but we discovered that our mystery was a powerful magnet. I was happier than I ever imagined I could be, sharing a deeply devoted life together until her death from metastatic breast cancer many years later.

At her memorial service my daughter Lisa read aloud the following passage:

> "My mom has loved an amazing woman, and she loved her back. We grew up surrounded by a love based on a profound appreciation of the other person exactly as they are. My sister Beth and I soaked up this lesson about how love can be. And isn't this what a parent does? Without out you even realizing it, they influence you, influence the choices you make. Without thinking about it, I have said 'I want to be loved like that. I want to create a home like that.'"

When I heard Lisa's message, I was flooded with relief. Any lingering fears that my search for happiness had been at my children's expense were dispelled.

DURING THE COURSE of my transition to a lesbian life, I made promises to myself that I am still keeping after all these years, promises that have helped me face life's upheavals with resiliency and resolve. Each year I am reminded of these resolutions, which have proven to be timeless.

- I now choose to pay attention to all of my senses because I don't want to be numb to life. It's hard to recognize when my feelings are dulled, but I know the signs: when I feel bored, restless, or just generally dissatisfied. I was born with a whole range of emotions and sensations and I am determined to feel them and use them all for guidance.
- I will face my guilt and use it as motivation to improve myself. When my marriage was breaking up, it did not seem possible to forgive myself for my affair, the deceit, or the upheaval of my loved ones' lives. Finding compassion for other people was always easier. Yet I now know that when I am consumed by guilt, my authentic needs and desires are lost. So in order to love myself, going forward I must learn with compassion what is behind my behavior in order to accept it.
- Before making decisions, I will face my fears. I have learned that fear has a tricky way of clouding the truth and creating deceptive behaviors. During those early days, I avoided confrontation and change by lying to my husband and to myself. I know now that avoidance usually creates more problems than the ones I've been imagining.
- True integrity includes honoring the importance of my own happiness. Sacrificing my own happiness is not the answer to making my loved ones happier. Finding my path to a joyful and peaceful life will reverberate in, and enhance the lives of others.

The uncomfortable reality of being married to a man and in love with a woman was a catalyst for me to understand the meaning of love and integrity. Once I acknowledged my feelings and honored them, I was able to make choices that moved me forward to a satisfying life. One of my choices has been to develop a career specialty that focuses on helping women married to men, who are attracted to other women determine a course of action consistent with their personal values. Since 2003, I've conducted workshops in Philadelphia that bring women together from all parts of the country to share in that process. Using my personal and professional experience, I wrote a self-help book on this subject and continue to serve this specific group's needs. Today I do an online support group for women married to men, and the women who love them. The stream of e-mails I receive from clients and readers informs my sense of having contributed something important to this particular path of coming out. I know this path because I myself have walked it.

EXCERPT FROM
A SIMPLE REVOLUTION:
THE MAKING OF AN ACTIVIST POET
JUDY GRAHN

Judy Grahn is internationally known as a poet, writer, and cultural theorist. Her writings helped fuel second wave feminist, gay and lesbian activism, and women's spirituality movements beginning in 1965 when she picketed the White House for Gay rights, and wrote her first article, "A Lesbian Speaks Her Mind," published the next year in *Sexology Magazine*. She co-founded Gay Women's Liberation and the Women's Press Collective in 1969. She taught writing, literature, and spirituality in Oakland for fifteen years, sometimes in collaboration with Paula Gunn Allen, and Betty De Shong Meador. She graduated from California Institute of Integral Studies with a Ph.D. concentration in Women's Spirituality, after doing research in South India. She has published three poetry collections, eight chapbooks, and two book-length epic poems tracing Helen of Troy as a version of Sumerian goddess Inanna. Much of her work has been dramatized, danced, and put to music. For instance, an acapella chorus, "She Who," does some of her She Who Poems. Judy is a performer, collaborating with singer-songwriter Anne Carol Mitchell; their CD is called *Lunarchy*. Judy has also published an ecotopia novel, short stories and articles, and four nonfiction books, including *Another Mother Tongue: Gay Words, Gay Worlds*, and *Blood, Bread, and Roses: How Menstruation Created the World*. Her latest collection of poetry and prose is *The Judy Grahn Reader*, and her newly published memoir is *A Simple Revolution: the Making of an Activist Poet*. Judy is a professor in the Women's Spirituality Master's Program at Sofia University in Palo Alto, Ca. She co-edits an online journal based in her theory of menstrual ritual origins of human culture: *Metaformia Journal*, www.metaformia.com. The following is an excerpt from *A Simple Revolution*, her memoir published in 2012 by Aunt Lute Books.

We Saw Each Other

EARLY IN 1970, Wendy (Cadden) and I moved out of Capp Street into a flat on Lexington Street, just around the corner from Valencia Street in the Mission district (of San Francisco). The Lexington apartment was meant to have one bedroom, but it also had a large pantry, a front room, a dining room, and a narrow kitchen with a table—an unimaginable wealth of space.

We used every bit of that space, including a wide part of the hall as a bedroom, and soon five people lived there. M., Anne, J., Wendy, and me. I had met Anne Leonard when we both worked at Presbyterian Hospital in the summer, and had taken her to a CR group; she and her husband J. soon took up residence with us. Wendy and I slept in the dining room, and our various art projects began to take up the remainder of our allotted space. Now that Wendy and I had more room, our projects, like goldfish in a larger tank, grew much larger. She built a real dark room in the basement, so she could more easily develop her photographs, and we could use the bathtub for bathing. I had the valuable front living room, and its spaciousness allowed me to begin imagining a larger project than simply writing my own poems. Maybe Wendy and I could collaborate on a book of drawings and poems by women, for women. We had been talking about some kind of artistic collaboration for a while.

All kinds of intensely focused lesbians were now swirling around us as we held weekly meetings of Gay Women's Liberation (GWL), one week at Alice and Carol's place on Benvenue Street in Berkeley, the next week at our flat on Lexington Street.

The first all-women's dances of our movement were in Berkeley in 1970. Poetry readings were connected to them. As Cathy Cade, an organizer and photographer recently said, "the poets would read, and the poetry somehow united us as a community, and then we would all dance together." Women-only dances were happening at that time in New York and Boston as well, and perhaps other places, indicating that lesbians were on the move, outside the bar scenes. A communal erotic beat took hold of us, we began to dance with whoever was there; not as a flirtatious arrangement, but as a soaking up and spreading of a new exhilarating vibrational rate. The guarded quality of bar life fell away for a while: we saw each other anew. In that first rush of sexual solidarity, we saw each other as a group of warriors, GWL handsome warriors. We saw each other, and we liked what we saw.

Having been told so often, in so many ways, how ugly we lesbians were, how plain, how old-maidish, how "no man would want you," how criminal, unwomanly, undesirable, dishonorable, disorderly, filthy, manhating, whorish, inhuman, insanely jealous, and just yucky we were in our very existence, we were astonished to discover our collective beauty. I was not the only one to experience ecstatic exuberance and all-encompassing, heart-opening desire at the women's dances; to feel again, as I had at earlier times, but never this strongly, swept up in a river of sheer beauty—sexy powerful gorgeous clit-distending, nipple-raising, lip-swelling, hair-shaking, spit-flowing, cunt-glowing, eye-flashing, hip-rotating, knee-twisting, thigh pumping, pheromone coursing, fingers expressing, sultry spicy sweat smelling complexly exhilarating female potentiality. We raised up storms of change with our dancing, not because we were dancing, but because our dancing celebrated our commitment to each other. Aesthetics begins with erotic love, and now because we had a viable movement we had an aesthetic; we had beauty and courage and loyalty, toward each other, and toward ourselves. We had hot hot desire, tongue-dangling nipple aching cunt surging desire, that seemed to start as hunger in

As women out in the world, we also had no personal identities. To the men in Newsreel we were "the girls." To the men at the Express Times, I was "the type-setter." To my boss at work I was "the medical transcriptionist" (and somewhat suspect, as I had become surly).

To the Gay Women's Liberation women, Wendy and I were now respected as individuals, as persons, and also as a couple together, as lovers, the lovers, the stable model, the activists, the artists, the leaders—even in a movement that disclaims leadership. "Lover" became a new title of distinction and connection. We were Lovers. This was a step into Outness from the old Washingtonian secrecy of the word "Friend," said with a slight emphasis. "This is my lover, Wendy." Across an ocean from "this is my Friend."

Wendy still did not claim the term "lesbian." "I am a woman who just happens to love Judy," she explained herself. Bisexuality was not a term of the day, not understood, not believed, and not tolerated. Our movement, like others, needed and demanded all or nothing, "the real thing." So in the Native movement some people dyed their skin to be dark enough to fit in, and in the Black movement afros, formerly despised, now became the only way to wear one's hair. What had been only bad now became only good. In our move-ment dyke clothing and posturing were indications of the full commitment to dykeness that had become the acceptable, even glorified way to be, with little tolerance for variation.

So I would guess that at this time Wendy and others with her same open-ness, like Susan Griffin and alta, had to either surrender lesbian community or hide the part of themselves that loved, was lovers with, men. "I am a woman who happens to love women" was one definition of who we were. I did not think of myself as "a woman who happened to love women." I was a lesbian, a dyke, and a lifetime homosexual. It seems to me I was always gay, even in the womb, where my mother said, "you kicked like a boy." For the first time I now had license to be myself, and to be desirable as that self.

In 1970 I wrote a few stanzas in my poem, "A History of Lesbianism" to encompass both positions, Wendy and me in the same poem, making up the term "women-loving-women" who "walked and wore their clothes/ the way they liked/ whenever they could." Some of us embraced the term "dyke" (dike, alternative spelling) while others thought it was a terrible, pejorative term. The poem continued, "In America we were called dykes/ and some liked it/ and some did not." Dyke is a good term because it refers to an individual and to her mannerisms and ways of being. A dyke is a dyke whether or not she is involved with lovers or a lover. Those of us from the old days, the bar culture days, tended to embrace this term; we had been called dyke by rough fellows, some of whom meant us harm, but we had also embraced the term as descrip-tive of our way of life. "I was a dyke by the time I was five" referred to, say, our fighting to wear pants and play sports. The poem ends with a feminist political statement: "the subject of lesbianism is very ordinary/ it's the subject/ of male domination/ that makes/ everybody/ angry."

The line: "in America we were called dykes" would be picked up and quoted, re-quoted, i.e., "In Amerikkka they call us dykes," for various purposes for decades afterwards. But in our 1970 GWL movement, those of us who had come out in earlier times or who felt we were "born that way" were called "bar dykes" or "old world dykes" by younger women who had another perspective, who thought that becoming a lesbian was a personal, and political, choice. The choice, they said, was to be free from male domination. Overnight, "dyke" had gone from the status of a Category 5 hurricane to the only possible site of rescue from harm. Our independent way of life was to be emulated, to be "chosen." The view from here was dizzying.

Standing Up for Ourselves as Dykes

MORE AND MORE varied women were coming to our meetings, like Red Jordan Arobateau, a mixed race, working-class writer and artist with street smarts who immediately began teaching self-defense for women. Middle-class white women came, like Marnie Hall, who would become a writer and lesbian therapist, and activists from the old left labor movement, Brenda Crider and Louise Merrill.

The weekly meetings swelled, and we began to plan actions to draw the attention of straight, leftist, feminist women. For instance a group of us stood in a long line at the front of a NOW meeting holding hands and announcing ourselves into what seemed shocked silence. Some of us made T-shirts that read "East Bay Dykes" in big letters, and wore them, as Pat Jackson said, "to the ice cream stores"–meaning the places mainstream Americans gather.

Straight feminist organizers Beth Oglesby and Laura X began attending our meetings, listening to our heated discussions as we criticized every institution and every theory of social progress, trying to define who we were. Ann Leonard remembers going to the Benvenue meetings:

> [It was] a big room full of lesbian women, even though I didn't iden-
> tify (yet) as a lesbian woman, I was there; I remember the feeling the
> group had of wanting to be heard and recognized as a lesbian woman–
> by straight women and also by the Left. There was a lot of different
> opinions, and a lot of feelings, why were we doing this and how were
> we going to do this . . . militant, very enthusiastic, very devoted, very
> personal, each person . . . it was very personal that they were doing this.
> Everyone was there for personal reasons but something bigger was
> being created. I had no idea about left politics, I came from a small
> town outside Philadelphia, and even though I lived in L.A. for a time
> it was only when I got to San Francisco that I was learning, I was

listening very closely while pretending that I knew what was going on. Though of course I knew what it was all about because I could feel it inside.

If theories of social change excluded, defamed, or criminalized us as lesbians, why should we accept their basic premises? We argued about our relationships to men, to straight women, to gay men, to the use of violent tactics, to feminism and socialism, to the radical left, to the psychiatric establishment. We discussed racism, including our own. We had no end of subjects. We continued our actions; a group of us attended a lecture by a well-known, thoroughly published psychiatrist, an "expert" in female homosexuality. From the audience, we questioned him, what was his authority based in? What real reasons did he have for pathologizing our lives? For emphasis, we stood up, scattered throughout the audience. There were at least a dozen of us, perhaps more. We didn't yell or threaten, just stood. At our standing up, declaring our sanity to him, he gathered his papers, and fled the room. We felt like Dorothy discovering the Wizard as a tiny behind a curtain of false authority.

In that year of 1970 our group of determined activist lesbians took seriously the idea that we were a vanguard on behalf of all women, that we were a warrior brigade. We wanted women's bodies and sexualities liberated for each woman to inhabit for herself. We wanted battery and sexual assault against women to stop, we wanted the streets to be safe and pleasant for women to walk, we wanted mothers to be supported with childcare and in other ways, we wanted women's ideas and creative thoughts to be taken seriously. We wanted equality for all. We wanted women brought out of the Middle Ages. In short, we wanted a simple, but complete, revolution.

Woman to Woman—A Revolutionary Anthology

BUT THIS IS a love story of course. It asks the question "What does it mean to love women?" And specifically, what would it mean if men loved women— really loved women? What would that be like? If women loved women, and themselves? How do I love women, and then one single woman? If you make a social movement that loves women, what does that accomplish? What does it mean? What if we had religions that loved women? A culture that cherished women and sought their leadership?

I handed out materials at the meetings, my own articles, including the satire "The Psychoanalysis of Edward the Dyke," my new article "Lesbians as Bogey-women," and reprints from *RAT Magazine,* a left voice, which had been seized by Radical Lesbian Feminists in New York. Martha Shelly and Rita Mae Brown had both published articles I thought were important, so I copied those and handed them out too. Out on the West Coast, with so much activity and so many people avidly reading things we handed out at meetings, Wendy and I decided the time had come to start gathering material to do an anthology of women's poetry and graphics that would change the images and therefore the way women thought about themselves. We began gathering the materials from every source we could think of, including our neighbors, and of course women we were meeting through Gay Women's Liberation. We were perfectly coordinated in this endeavor, one of our best collaborations, and one in which we were inordinately creative as we had no idea what we were doing. What on earth was "women's poetry"? Who would decide? I collected some poems, some by well-known authors (Amy Lowell, Gertrude Stein), some by published feminist authors (Marge Piercy, Marilyn Hacker, alta), and some by women we were meeting lately, our neighbors, people who heard we were doing such an outrageous project. I included my "Common Woman" poems. I gathered sixty pages of manuscript and handed them out to women, along with a form asking such questions as: Which poems affected you? Which do you consider poetry? What would you like included in a collection? The answers were surprising, some of the biggest "names" didn't make the cut; some of the least "poetic" had the biggest effect. In the end, I chose for impact, positive *and* negative. Most liked my poems, though one responded "Common as a telephone directory . . . this is not poetry." I included them anyhow, as they were spreading around town; I would find pages posted on people's refrigerators in the new households consisting mostly of women.

Wendy's friend Vicky Jacobs showed up one day and pulled out some cash for us to buy paper so we could print our book. Then Naomi and Pat Jackson came over with money that Gay Women's Liberation had gathered for us to buy a mimeograph machine, an office copy machine that used ink; you typed the text on a limp, blue, waxy sort of template and then draped it over a fat rotating barrel. The ink squeezed through the letters and printed on the fresh blank pages. They had bought the machine from Diane DiPrima, who had been in the Bay Area poetry scenes for years. I was including one of Diane's poems in the anthology, though not necessarily with her permission. I was grabbing poetry from everywhere, taking the author's name off, going for pure content, and breaking down the elitism that I felt—despite the heroic efforts of the Beat poets—still dominated poetry.

The physical design of the book was inside out: we used heavy paper for the text, thin paper for the cover, and onionskin paper for the graphics. A dyslexic design sense on my part. I was certain that the ink on one side would leak through to the other, so insisted on backing each graphic with a blank sheet of the heavy, lavender-tinted paper. The cover, delicate as an aged leaf, was red, and carried a powerful graphic by Wendy and big letters for the title: *Woman to Woman.*

The boldness of the book described us as well. Our erotic connection was fueled by how competitive we were toward each other. When we struggled it became physical, not in any violent sense, just in the juggling we did for territory, our constant negotiations; who would run the mimeograph machine? We crowded shoulders and hips together to jockey for positions. Laughing, while knowing the seriousness of our personal quests for self-authorization, as well as for women's voices in the world. We wrestled heedlessly, testing and finding our strengths, exhilarated at the pitch and heave of our equality. Members of GWL came over to help us collate, so this became "our book," a collective enterprise. And the book, filled with women's art and poetic opinions, got printed, and was both strong and beautiful, if flawed in its design.

Meeting Parker

ONE DAY SHORTLY after we had started this project, probably March or April of 1970, Linda Wilson stepped gracefully through the bright paisley cloth that draped the fine arch into my room. "I've brought someone to meet you," she said in her resonant voice, and in walked a tall black woman, neatly dressed in pressed slacks and blouse, high cheekbones, thick glasses, and handsome in her own striking way. Here was Pat Parker. Pat was gregarious, athletic like Linda and Wendy, while at the same time her thick glasses and high forehead gave her the intellectual look of an introvert, a book-reader, or librarian. She emanated a wave of warmth, charming, like a lot of Southerners.

"I hear your drink is Southern Comfort," she said, handing me a brown bag with a pint bottle of amber liquid in it. Linda excused herself, Parker sat down (by now I had a couple of chairs) and, sipping the bitingly sweet liquor, we began talking about cowboy clothes, poetry, activism, Civil Rights, where we grew up, how we were with regard to feminism, the need for revolution, the bad deeds of the power structure, and by the time the bottle was empty we were connected. I showed her the rows of pages Wendy had meticulously lined along the floorboards of my room, spilling into the room next to it. Pat promised to bring me some of her work.

I included four of Pat's feminist poems in *Woman to Woman*, which was ready for distribution in late summer of 1970. "Child of Myself" is a signature Pat Parker poem ending "I, Woman must be–the child of myself." Pat was writing black woman identity, black activist political, and feminist poems. She was not yet writing anything pro-lesbian, though she had begun a love relationship with a woman.

THE ROAD TO FREEDOM
FELICIA HAYES

 Felicia Hayes is a recent graduate from California College of the Arts where she earned her MFA degree in writing. She is currently working on the first of a series of memoirs that chronicle her coming of age and coming out experiences. This memoir focuses on her grappling with her same-gender attractions while being raised in a strong Christian household, followed by becoming a member of Reverend Moon's Unification Church, then leaving it twelve years later once she realized that being a lesbian is not something she could "pray away." This paradigm shift and dawning self-awareness lead her on the path to her own inner freedom. "The Road to Freedom" is a survey of the first memoir.

I OFTEN WONDER what my life would be like if I weren't a woman-identified, Black, Buddhist lesbian. Each of these identities, including other uniquely-me aspects of my character, are connected to the pain of my various oppressions. I wasn't aware of these intertwining walls of oppression until I bumped up against them with the agency my adult independence granted me. I couldn't quite make out the full shape of this layered oppression, its size, nor how deep it went. I do know that my coming out process as a lesbian was halted often as I grew up. I wasn't even aware that I was "coming out;" I was just being who I was, and an adult or peer would say or do something that brought me shame and my natural self would go back into the closet again.

My indoctrination began as a baby—I was the pride and joy of the elder pastor of the American Methodist Episcopal church in Chattanooga, Tennessee. Our family was like royalty in the Black Community, as the preachers there had credibility and clout. My grandfather being a pastor in a Bible Belt state maximized my grandparents' clout. This in turn made my grandparents very image-conscious.

While my dad was in college, he discovered jazz. He met my mom in Nashville and she would sing while he accompanied her. This was the "devil's music," according to my granddad. But my dad would not stop playing the "devil's music," and so he was banned from my grandparents' house.

This was a few years before I was born in 1961, a time when my mom and her siblings participated in civil right sit-ins and had to use "Blacks only" entrances and designated spaces in public places, such as having to come in through the back entrance to get to the balcony section of movie theaters.

Mom and her twin sister had a double wedding and my parents were soon on the road to Florida where they both had teaching jobs. Mom was pregnant with me and about to give birth. They looked frantically for a hospital that would allow her to come in the front door instead of the back entrance for Blacks. Mom couldn't climb steep stairs in her condition. They got denied access and they had to go back to the car and continue to find another hospital. My mom's twin sister was also in the car to help. They had a flat tire and for a moment thought Mom would give birth in the car. Finally, a Catholic hospital that didn't participate in segregation accepted my mom through the front door and she didn't have to climb any stairs. I was born.

Both sides of my parent's family were middle class. Along with this came middle class values and ethics, and the desire to assimilate into white society by becoming good consumers and having all the items that signified a healthy financial status. It was all about status and being a "good Black Christian." My paternal grandfather worked for the U.S. Post Office as a mail carrier when he wasn't doing his church duties. His wife, my grandmother, was a housewife who was subservient to him. She watched soap operas and gossiped, mostly with her sisters, of which there were many.

We always had to be cleaned up when we went outside, and walk with dignity due to the heavy racism that greeted us. She dressed me in frilly dresses and patent leather shoes just to go to Newberry's down the street. I didn't understand it, and was not aware that we were navigating sections where we weren't welcome, sections that were meant for us to "know our place."

My great-grandmother, whom I called "'Nother Momma," lived in a big house on a hill. She had an apple orchard in the back of the house, and there was a vacant lot with exposed red dirt next door. When her husband died, she lived there alone and tended to things herself. I was very impressed by her. She had twin sons, one of whom died. The other was my granddad.

I enjoyed my time with her. In the mornings, my brother and I would wake up to the smell and sound of coffee percolating. Two large white porcelain coffee cups on matching saucers were waiting at the center of the kitchen table when we walked in to sit down. We watched the steam swirl and rise as she poured the coffee about halfway into our cups. She added cream and a few teaspoons of sugar. I have never tasted coffee as delicious as hers since those days. She loved *The Lawrence Welk Show*, and we would gather around to see the one Black performer who tap danced on every show. All of us were excited to see someone Black on TV. She chopped her own wood and fixed things in addition to tending the garden and cooking. She taught me to read and play "Blessed Be the Tie That Binds" on the piano. She had a signature pound cake that no one could replicate and took the recipe with her to her grave years later.

'Nother Momma had a chamber pot in her room, and when my brother and I visited, she put one in our room because it was pitch black in the house. My brother and I would lie in bed at night and hold our hands up and ask each other, "Can you see my hand? Here it is. Can you see it?" We hadn't yet learned to be afraid of anything, not even the dark. We were so protected from the harsh realities that were just outside our front door.

On my mother's side, her mother became the breadwinner after my grand-dad became ill and had to quit his job as a chef on a train. He took care of her and the children while Grandma taught elementary school and sold insurance. She was very active in her church and was the president of various organizations including the local branch of the NAACP. She was very busy and had little time to be with her children. Granddad was sick a lot but he sang in the choir and kept an eye on the children. He sang bass line to all the programs on TV including the commercials, a habit I picked up later in my life after teaching myself bass guitar.

When I was still a baby, my mom and dad moved us to California. They took us on a very dangerous road trip through the southern states from Florida. This trip was due to a "vision of an angel" that my dad had one night who said that we should move there. All was fine, as far as I was concerned until Mom and Dad began arguing. This was soon after my dad had started going to the mosque, a change which I'll describe more fully a bit later.

The process of my development as a young woman included having my first crush. Wendy, a girl in my third grade class, was so beautiful to me. I remember being shy around her, but mesmerized. I'd be in my mom's car and would hear that song on the radio: "Who's peeking out from under a stairway/calling a name that's lighter than air/who's bending down to give me a rainbow/everyone knows it's windy." I would chime in on the hook, "Everyone knows it's windy," replacing the word "windy" with "Wendy" while staring out the window at the sky. The clouds would dissolve into Wendy's face. The happier I got, the more animated her face became. Petals of rainbow colors would form around her head. She would be in the center of a psychedelic flower, "ba-ba, ba-ba, ba-ba, everyone knows it's Wendy."

I had no need to tell anyone about it, because it wasn't an "it." I had a simple childhood crush, just as I did for our babysitter, Roberta. She was a Black teen who had beautiful long, black, thick (pressed) natural hair that went down to her mid-back and milk chocolate skin. She was a teenager and I always wanted to be around her and engage her in games when she came by to watch us.

My younger brother and I watched a lot of television in those days. In the afternoons, after school, I would take out my Etch-a-Sketch, or crayons and paper and work on some art while watching *Mr. Rogers*, *Sesame Street*, and *The Electric Company*. I had a huge crush on Rita Moreno. I also watched *The Jackson Five Show*, and would enjoy being serenaded and winked to bed by Carol Burnett, "I'm so glad we had this time together . . ." after watching *Love Boat*, *Laugh-In*, *Cher*, and the *Lucille Ball Show* while eating a TV dinner on a TV tray. It was the late sixties.

We lived in a big two-story house in Los Angeles on Second Street near Jefferson, just down the street from my first Catholic school. My dad lived with us. He was a jazz musician and taught music at the university. He had a music room where he would go to compose and arrange his music. It was off limits to me. That was fine; I would find other things to play with and I would sing around the house all the time.

When I was in the den watching TV, I sat with my nose touching the screen so I could see. That's when I got checked for glasses. It turned out I was very nearsighted. When I walked to my babysitter's after school, the older girls began to snicker, point, and make fun of a rash I had gotten behind my knees. It was atopic dermatitis, which I had gotten over eighty percent of my body. This was the first time shame was associated with my body, and it became embedded in my emotions.

When Dad started going to a mosque, and got involved with the Nation of Islam, our lives suddenly changed. In addition to going to our Christian church in Pasadena, where our cousins and my aunt also attended every Sunday, we would also go to the Nation of Islam mosque for meetings. It was strange. As we approached the mosque my dad and baby brother would go through one door, and my mom and I would go through another door. We were searched. The women would struggle, trying to help Mom pull her mini skirt down below her knees. Then we would proceed through the main part of the big hall. Women sat on the left side, and there was a divide in the middle. Men sat on the right side. All the women wore headscarves. It reminded me of the headgear of the Catholic sisters at my school. We had to wear something on our head there too, a sort of white material with lace.

As it turned out, Mom didn't want to stop eating pork, clean out every pan in the kitchen, nor become subservient to my dad. So their arguments increased. I started scratching, and a "person" in a full-body leotard with cat ears began visiting me in my room at night. It was quiet, it never said a word, it just looked at me. I told mom about it and she knew something had to change. She told me later in life that these visits were hallucinations. The next day they asked me who I wanted to live with, Mom or Dad, and I chose Mom. I didn't understand, at seven years old why I had to choose, and in my choosing I thought for years afterward that I had caused the separation between them.

Another question Mom asked me: "Do you want to continue to keep going to Catholic school or do you want to go to public school?" I had no idea. So when we moved to Altadena, I went to my cousin's school, a public, mostly Black school. That is where I met Wendy.

Mom couldn't afford to be home much now. She was teaching far away in Watts. She had just gotten a divorce from my dad and we had moved closer to her older sister in Altadena, California. I was seven years old at this time. It was 1968.

It was in this mostly Black school that I became very independent. I would roller skate around abandoned businesses, jumping off steps and going up and down slopes, much like kids riding skateboards do today. I didn't have any friends who did this with me, but I never needed any. I would jump with my pogo sticks and play baseball with my brother and his friends with my shirt off. I swung on the swings at a nearby school alone. I was very athletic and boys would be surprised, but I didn't know why it was such a big deal then. Besides, at that time, their opinions about what I as a girl could do didn't matter to me at all. I was labeled a "tomboy" and I embraced that label.

One time, while playing on my favorite monkey bars and swinging on the rings next to it, a boy saw my new baby blue cat glasses on the ground and he stomped on them. I jumped off those bars and ran after him. There must have been twenty students who saw what he did who started chasing him for me. When they caught him, they held him against the wall while I unleashed all of my anger through my flailing arms on his face, head, and stomach with some strong kicks thrown in. He was crying by then, and when the adults came, the students told them what had happened and he got in even more trouble. I felt empowered by these students who I didn't know well, supporting me.

Another time, I was standing in the lunch line and a song came on over the loud speakers. All the kids, mostly Black, joined in. As they played, ate, and braided each other's hair they sang, "To be yooooooung, gifted and BLACK! Oh, what a lovely precious dreeeeam . . ." I'd never heard the song before, but my heart swelled. I didn't know why it was a precious dream, but I did know I felt pride hearing this song.

By the time I reached nine years old, my chest "buttons" began appearing. I didn't really notice them much except when I bumped into something there was pain. At this time, my mom introduced her new boyfriend to us. He was going to live with us. He was quiet.

Things began to change around me. We started going to a lady's house a few blocks from our house after school so she could watch us. There were many boys and dogs there, running around, cursing, being rude to each other. The dogs humped on people and each other. I sat on the couch and just stared at the TV because it made me feel safe. Sometimes I would be enticed by these boys to climb the ten-foot-tall chain link fence to play on the school yard behind their house. It felt wrong, but I did go a few times. Then one of the boys came over to our house to babysit us. I woke up with him between my legs in my mom's bed. I didn't know what happened, but I felt ashamed and strange. I went into the bathroom not sure what to do, but stayed there until my mom and her new boyfriend got home.

On another day, I was on the swings alone at the school near my house when I heard someone whistle. I couldn't see who, or why, but they kept doing it. There were trees and hills surrounding the perimeter of the school playground.

Finally I became afraid, as that whistle seemed devious and sinister. I never played alone there or anywhere around there again. It felt as though I had escaped something potentially dangerous on that day.

It wasn't long before things at home got uncomfortable. Mom's boyfriend would get me and my brother alone and say things like, "Let's play a game. I will heat this spoon over the fire, and ask you a question. After you answer the question, you stick out your tongue, and I'll put the hot spoon on it, if it burns, that means you lied to me. If it doesn't burn, it means you told me the truth."

He also took me to a scary movie, alone, and during the scary parts he would shake my chair, intensifying my fear. I began to sleep with my neck covered after a vampire movie that we went to. I slept that way, far into my teen years.

Once while outside playing kickball with my brother and his friends, the girly-girls next door who played with dolls all the time and always wore pink and frilly lace, pointed at me and said, "Oooooh!" I looked at them puzzled, and they sang with a shaming tone, "You don't have a shirt on!!" I looked over at my brother, and his friends. They didn't have a shirt on either. I still looked puzzled. Then one of the girls said, "You are a girl. Girls are supposed to always wear a shirt!" Later I asked my mom about this and she agreed with the girls, and told me, "From now on keep your shirt on. Soon you will need a bra because you'll be getting bigger there." I felt shame once again about my body. That negative message embedded itself.

One day, I was shaken awake by one of the biggest earthquakes in California's history. It was 7.1 on the Richter scale. I jumped out of the top bunk of a bunk bed that my brother and I shared. Everyone was gathered at the front door, but somehow I ended up behind the door in the den and I prayed, "Heavenly Father, Allah, God, whoever you are, please protect us! Save us!" When it was over, I was still shaking. I would continue shaking anytime a big truck would pass, or a train would go by until I was in my mid-thirties years later.

That one year of my body and property being invaded by boys and men, and the earthquake happening, it taught me that men can be very dangerous. Mom's new boyfriend took us on trips in the mountains where he would drive too fast around the curves and it would terrorize me. The last straw for my mom was when he beat her with a belt in the next room. Her cries and her begging and pleading and the continuous whips and bangs were the scariest sounds I had ever heard in my life. Before then I had never heard my mom cry, let alone scream. She was trying to be quiet so we wouldn't hear her, but we were tuned in. I had to put my hand over my brother's mouth as he was about to cry, because I just knew that if he did, that man in the next room would kill us. We were completely terrified.

We had been terrorized the whole time that man was in our house. My aunt bravely confronted him one day, and the police came and took him away for a day. We were quickly out of that house and Mom whisked us away to stay at her friends' place as soon as she got out of the hospital. When we visited her in the hospital she was wearing sunglasses, but I peeked underneath and what I saw made my heart sink and my protected world shatter. Her eyes, all of the white parts were deep red, and puffy. One eye was completely puffed closed. Her teeth, her face—it was so scary, and so sad. She tried to make it seem like it was okay when we asked her what happened. She said she fell down the stairs. I was extremely naïve and tried to connect the sounds we heard happening in the next room to the destruction on my mother's face. I also didn't have any critical thought. I accepted everything people said to me and was gullible. Because of the religions we practiced, I was taught to obey authority. It was never questioned.

A few weeks later, we were flown back to Nashville to live with our maternal grandparents. My grandmother rented out the top floor of her house, an apartment, to students. The apartment was available, so Mom, my brother, and I moved in as my mother healed and got on her feet.

In Nashville, I explored alleys, played congas on car hoods, built shacks with found materials from the alleys, played Ouija boards, played board games, wrestled, and played sports with my cousins. One day, the girl down the street invited me to her house. It was full of other girls. I was polite, but it was a bit boring as they only talked about boys. I wasn't interested, so I never returned.

After a year of being in Nashville, Mom went to L.A. to get a place for us, and then she sent for us. That would present a new host of challenges, and I would fall in love with a female friend two years later.

When Wanda and I first met, she cursed me out. It had to do with a seat she wanted that I was occupying on my first day at Monroe Junior High School. I responded with something that made her laugh and after that, we became best friends. We were both good at basketball. We played often, and other girl athletes joined us. We hung out together on the courts all the time. Boys never won a game against us, but they kept challenging us. We were proud, and a bit arrogant about our abilities.

Wanda had green eyes and I enjoyed gazing into them. She had the same complexion as me, her nose was prominent, and her hair frizzy and brown. She spoke through her nose and had a soft, barely audible wheeze. She spoke like a sailor, and that would always make me laugh because I hadn't been raised this way. Her brashness as well as her agency was impressive. I made her laugh a lot as I was sort of a class clown, and I would get a rise out of making people laugh.

I was filling out my bra by now and my hips were small, so I was drawing unwanted attention from men in cars and on the streets. I would just smile and look down. I knew men could be dangerous, so I didn't want to provoke them. However, Wanda would give them her middle finger and yell curse words at them. My heart melted at her bravery. I adored her and put her on a pedestal. When we talked on the phone she would say odd things like:

"Right now I'm taking a shit! Hahaha!"

I would think, *how rude*, but then the infatuation I had for her would skew my logic and I would think, *Oh, but she has me in the bathroom with her, an intimate moment.* She obviously didn't feel the same way about me, but I was glad just to see her every day.

During this time, while I was in an alley, one boy who I didn't really know too well, called me into a garage to "show me something." He led me to a mattress, and then pushed me. I was still too naïve to know what he was attempting, but what I did know is that no one makes me do anything I don't want to do, so I fought him off. He ran away. The wrestling matches I had for years with my cousins had paid off. It was after I told my mom what happened to me that I absorbed her fear and then I got a sense of how serious it was.

Mom dated during these years. She narrowed her suitors down to three men and asked us which one we liked. She married that one, and much to my surprise we were told that we were now moving to Austin, Texas. All I heard was "BOONDOCKS!!" I was so angry, and sad, and heartbroken. My cousin was visiting us and he had gotten to know Wanda too. He had a strong attraction to her as well. We were both broken-hearted that we weren't going to see her anymore. I didn't let him know how I felt about her. It was much like Celie and Mister saying good bye to Shug when she gets married and moves away in the book, *The Color Purple*, by Alice Walker. Both my cousin and I were in love with the same girl.

It was in Austin, Texas where I would have a new series of female crushes, all unrequited love. I didn't have anyone to talk to about my feelings. I learned that it wasn't okay to be "funny." That was the only term I had heard for homosexuality. I decided to visit the library to find out what was wrong with me. I came home with stacks of books from the psychology section that dealt with same-sex attraction. I finally found out there was a word for my condition: lesbian.

I wondered, was there a cure for the "lesbian" condition? How did I get it? Why do I have it? Will I have to go to a mental hospital? I didn't want shock treatments. The information gave me clarification but it also terrified me. I realized I was in danger. If my mom or anyone else knew, I could be dealt with in an unpleasant way.

After this, I poured all of my attention and energy into playing pickup basketball and my bass guitar in my room. I isolated myself from people except for the person I was in love with, who I had met at my church. She was very flirty with me, which kept me hooked, but no one mentioned the "L" word. She dated boys a lot, smoked weed and cigarettes, and she lived a bit on the wild side. I just wanted to be around her because I was smitten.

That was in 1976 when the song "At Seventeen" by Janis Ian came out. I thought she was singing about me. If I wasn't with my new crush, I was alone.

It was safer. Racism was blatant in Texas and I steered clear whenever I could. I was in the orchestra, drama club, and was getting more involved with our church musically. We had to go to church at least three times a week for Bible study, choir rehearsal, and of course Sunday service. Our new stepfather was strict, and he didn't talk much. We had to do whatever he decided that we do, and when he was ready to go somewhere, we all had to be in the car immediately or the "wheels are rolling," he would say. Church members would witness me or my brother or even my mother barely getting into the car as he began driving us away with the door open and someone's leg hanging out.

At this time, I felt I needed to change myself somehow to get over the lesbian disease in me. So I joined a large, city wide choir and we travelled from church to church in Texas performing, and sleeping in the pews. I went to gospel workshops, concerts, religious rights demonstrations, and candlelight vigils. I kept crushing on women and fell deeply in love with my best friend. I enjoyed church because everyone wore their best clothes and the women looked mighty fine. It was like a fashion show and it kept my hormones leaping.

Once my mom went out of town and left us alone with our stepdad. I was late getting up, and he was angry. He threw me across the room. After that, Mom decided, for my own protection, that I needed to go to live with my aunt in California.

There I joined an all girl funky, R & B band called "Hot Ice." I fell in love with one of the band members. She had light brown eyes and was light skinned, and we both giggled a lot when we were together. I was surprised to have someone blatantly flirt back with me. The "L" word was still not used, and so we were free to grow close together without shame. It was still under the cloak of "close friends," but we moved into an apartment together and did all the things couples do except have sex. However, if she had initiated, I would have let go and given in to my intense desire.

One day, she invited a friend of hers over who was a Unification Church member, more commonly known as the Moonies. It wasn't long before we were in the mountains at the end of a seven day workshop when we both decided to join this church. Over the first couple of years, the church slowly separated us. She left the area when I was traveling with a fundraising/propaganda team that went from city to city, staying three weeks in each city. By then I was in love with a female Japanese church member whom I had connected with in New Orleans.

Her team arrived in the U.S. from Japan and she slept next to me in the big house that we all stayed in during our time in the city. For the next year, we would travel together on the same team and we got to know each other. She was very affectionate toward me and I began to loosen up in my homophobic body, which until then had been paralyzed with shame and guilt. On the other hand, we listened to Reverend Sun Myung Moon's speech on a videotape where he talks about gay people being satanic and how people need to love the gay person, but not the gay part. He also told his members that if they are gay, they must repent and pay indemnity, which means they must suffer to overcome it. He said, "Can you imagine, two men with beards, kissing?!" The audience would roar with laughter. I smiled externally, but shame was building inside me.

Through my relationship with my Japanese girlfriend, I developed an extremely intimate way of connecting because we couldn't have sex or we would have been banished from the church. I believed the church was going to heal me from my lesbian "problem" when I went to their mass wedding/baptism ceremony.

The only physical touch we could give each other that was acceptable was massage. So she would wake me up with a sensuous massage in front of all the women in the room. When we were walking alone together at dusk one day, I was teasing her and I squeezed her butt. Her eyes got wide, her smile big and she started to giggle, looking around to see if any leaders or members were behind us. Still, the "L" word was never used, nor was any other word about what we'd just did or what it meant. Nothing was ever vocalized or articulated.

Our connection had grown so deep, and our desire for each other so intense, it only took a touch to satisfy me, or a smile. She often fed me from her plate with her chopsticks during dinner, raising some eyebrows. She was subtle, yet bold.

One day when we were in Houston, an Italian member who was getting close to me popped up and asked my girlfriend with intense anger, "Why do you have to give her a massage all the time? She's an adult, she can wake up herself!" That began an argument between the two of them. I stayed under the covers, hoping nothing would change.

It was in New Mexico that she would finally tell me through tears that she loved me. No one had ever said that before and meant it like she did. I didn't know what to do. I wanted to believe her, but, it would take a few years before I really understood. Soon after that, the Unification Church sent her on a mission to California, effectively separating us.

It was years later, while I was in a new "mission" cooking at a camp in the San Bernadino mountains, that she visited me and announced that she was given a new mission by the church to go to France to live and be with her matched spouse (whom she would always compare to me). She cried copiously. I didn't realize that I would never see her again after that day.

I went through their mass marriage in Korea and stayed there doing the work of the church for three months, then I returned for six more months. In Korea I had a few crushes. A Korean and a Japanese female member flirted hard with me. I fell in love with the Japanese woman and we snuck off to the Seoul Land Amusement Park one day to celebrate our birthdays, which were a few days apart. We had a nice buffet, and then the evening set in. I was staying in a hotel and I wanted her to join me. She knew where I was staying, but neither of us talked about it until she was about to go back to the church's host family, where we both lived. Time stood still when she asked me, in Korean, if I wanted her to stay with me that night or go on to the church. I struggled with my ethics so hard in that moment. It would be a sin, and a blatant one, if we did this. But desire was pulling at us. Why was she making it MY decision, I wondered? Was she testing me? Would she go to the church anyway, but was checking to see if I was faithful? Or was it something she would honor in me? That was one of the most painful decisions I had had to make, and finally I said, "Ka, Ja! Kyohe ka say yo!" (Go, go to the church). And with that, she released my hand and hopped into the subway train just before the doors closed.

I cried all that night and didn't get a wink of sleep. If I had said nothing, perhaps she would have waited too long and missed the last train. That is one of my lingering regrets. I should have gone for it.

Unification Church rules dictate that after you are matched and "blessed" (that is, mass married), you take three years to get to know your partner and to bond, after which you begin to move in together, get legally married in court, wait another forty days, and consummate your marriage in a three day ceremony full of symbolic gestures. My time had come; the three years were up, and I was expected to go live with my new spouse. He was an acquaintance from a project we had worked on together in the church at Aetna Springs in Northern California. So it was a surprise when we were matched together. He was a gay man from Sri Lanka who had gone through the mass wedding before, but it hadn't worked out.

Neither of us were in the least bit attracted to each other, but we both wanted to save the world by becoming a positive role model in this new society we were building. He didn't know that I was a closet lesbian, and I didn't tell him. We both procrastinated having the consummation ceremony where we had to have sex. Just the thought actually made both of us scrunch up our noses. He criticized me in the first letter he wrote that he sent to Korea. He thought I was too fat, too Black, that I needed to close the gap in my teeth, etc. When I arrived, he wanted to make sure I lost weight, so he signed me up with a gym membership and bought me a car, because Ossining, NY, where we were at the time, was a small town and he didn't want people to see me riding the bus.

It was Spring of 1993. As our day of coming together got closer, I began to get serious about my choices and about who I was. I started working in the Montessori school in the basement of the house where we were living. I was staying in the living room because we couldn't share a room yet, until our consummation ceremony. I also worked out in the gym every day. I got a trainer and took some herbs the trainer was selling. She was a body builder and I was impressed with her muscles and I wanted muscles, too. I was also watching lots of TV and came across Susan Powter and her "Stop The Insanity!" program for weight loss. She empowered me with her in-your-face passion and independence. I also saw the comedy show by Mo Gaffney and Kathy Najimy on TV, *The Kathy and Mo Show: Parallel Lives*, which talked about women's rights, and I was slowly becoming aware of the oppressive forces that were controlling my life and my choices as a woman. Gradually, I lost a lot of weight, had lots of energy, and was finding a power inside myself that I hadn't ever known was in me.

Our Montessori school closed and I found a new job working at a preschool on a military base. That's where I met a Latina woman. We bonded over the following three months. During that time, I snuck out to the local bookstore and hovered around the lesbian section. Among other books I discovered there, I read a book called *Finding the Lesbians*. I also discovered an LGBT center nearby in White Plains. I went to a coming out counseling session there, and realized it wasn't for me; I already knew I was lesbian. But I was trying to figure out how to reconcile my church stuff and my religious beliefs with who I was as a person, my lesbian self. At this time, I also checked the classifieds and found my first female date. All of this was done so clandestinely. For instance, I had to use a public phone outside our house to figure out where to meet her.

I found my way to midtown Manhattan and walked to the lesbian bar where we had agreed to meet. I think it was called Pandora's Box. The bass and beat were pulsating the entire building. My date was a Black butch woman who waited outside. We introduced ourselves and went inside. Everything was so new and strange. I couldn't keep my eyes off a very tall, Black guy dressed in women's clothing doing a dance I had never seen done before. Very sharp, hit a pose on every beat, wow, he was good at it! She asked me if I wanted something to drink, and I asked for water only. I never really drank alcohol in my twelve years in the church, and before that, I was too young.

She invited me to the dance floor to RuPaul's "Work It Girl." The dance floor was crowded. In the midst of my culture shock, I thought I was blending in. Then she said, "Why don't you move your body?" I thought I was! I had been so repressed that I couldn't make my body move more than a few inches to the music. I felt shame and guilt with each inch of movement. I was doing something very radical for me, actually going on a date, and dancing at a gay bar, on lesbian night, with a woman! It was outright revolutionary!

I never heard from my date after that one night, but that experience emboldened me. I began working out more, and as part of my routine, I went to the local bookstore and read more books. I got a hold of a book called, *For Lesbians Only*, and it blew my mind. Before reading this book I had never thought critically, nor understood in such detail the systems of our female oppression; in this case sexism and patriarchy. I was hungry for knowledge, to have actual words to name my experiences, and I couldn't get enough.

I empowered myself more and more by continuing to read and understand the layers of my oppression. Then I found the book, *When God Was a Woman*, and began exploring other religions which actually accepted me, all of me. This path would eventually take me to atheism, which helped me examine and question all of my previous religious programming and indoctrination.

I was just about to move in with my latest Latina crush when I saw evidence of violence in her house: hammer holes in the wall leading to the room of her former roommate. I stayed at her house only one night and woke up to find her walking around my cot with a Glock pistol in her hand. I thought about these two experiences in one day, while sitting in my car surrounded by all of my life's belongings, considering what to do next.

In that moment, I decided to just drive down the road, get on the highway, and leave, without saying a word to her or to anyone else. I now see that decision as just another step on the road to my freedom, the freedom of becoming my full self, and finally getting all the way out of the lesbian closet on a beautiful spring day in March 1993. I was beginning my life, freely and on my own terms at thirty-three years old.

A MAD KANSAS CITY WOMAN
LOIS RITA HELMBOLD

Lois Rita Helmbold is an activist, martial artist, quilter, historian, retired women's studies professor. Upwardly mobile, working-class, Pennsylvania Dutch/Polish/Lithuanian preacher's kid. Radicalized by teaching in a Black college in Mississippi in the late 1960s. Academia was the only job that paid me to read, and I loved teaching and students. I co-facilitate a study and activist training group on white supremacy for white women in Oakland. I'm looking for a girlfriend. "A Mad Kansas City Woman" is a true story.

MARTHA ALWAYS SAID she fell in love with the books on my shelves before she fell in love with me. She met them first, at a book group scheduled at my house which my job compelled me to miss. I arrived as the gathering was breaking up and quickly noticed the warm, smiling new woman.

Months later, when we both showed up at a lesbian seven minute date night, I asked her out. *Bend it like Beckham* earned me praise for picking good movies. Her standards were low. She had reared two teenagers and she also went to all the movies her middle school students saw.

During the next week of daily phone calls, e-mails, and dates, she told me about her inflammatory breast cancer, stage 3B. Her litany of chemo, radiation, mastectomy, chemo, radiation, was hardly new to me. Dozens of women in my life had had cancer. Several had died. I could handle it. My father had been a rural fundamentalist preacher with five churches, so death and funerals were familiar rituals of my childhood.

That Friday, I e-mailed her, "If you want to come over and watch me pack, I'll make you dinner." My school year had ended, and I was traveling to a conference in the Bay Area, my previous home. Over Thai chicken salad, Martha asked, "What time is your plane in the morning?"

"I'm driving, not flying."

"Six hundred miles in one day, alone, no way! Don't do it! It's too far. It's too dangerous alone."

"I've done it before."

"I'll drive with you."

Saturday, we drove all day, and that night we made love for the first time. Nobody had ever done anything so romantic for me: driving six hundred miles to ensure my safety–and for sex, of course–at the most hectic time of her school year.

When I took a job in Las Vegas, Bay Area friends had made jokes about my finding a chorus girl for a girlfriend. "Yeah, right, one in her fifties with good politics." Martha was no chorus girl, with her meltingly soft body, outdated glasses, boring wardrobe, and styleless hair. Her type had attracted me before: dyke drab with excellent social skills, commitment to social justice, and a wicked sense of humor.

I had already planned a trip to the UK that summer, and we decided to meet in London. Martha's mother loaned her a prized, vintage beaded purse. Martha never used a purse, and I advised her to leave it home and lie to her mother. Protesting all the way, she carried it to the theater, for a hilarious play about Dubya Bush, and dropped it in the toilet by accident. The purse episode, I realized later, was one of the ways in which Martha remained in thrall to her mother.

Too soon, cancer reappeared, now in her liver. After surgery at UCLA, Martha greeted her mother, sister, and me with a long list of errands and chores for her children, Rose and Richard, and her "should-be-ex-" husband, Jim. No doubt, she was a tough cookie.

Martha, her previous girlfriend, her kids, and Jim had all lived together. After her first round of treatments, her kids persuaded her to move out, because Jim was less than helpful. A computer nerd, Jim had been diagnosed, by Martha, with Asperger's Syndrome. He was, she informed me when I had grilled her, a good friend. Her mother had financed a house for her, and she had subsequently dumped her girlfriend for lying to her about a clandestine affair. When we met, the sixteen-year-old and eighteen-year-old, as she referred to them, were living with her. They had advised her that it was time to look for a new lover.

In our first year and a half together, Martha had three liver surgeries, and I got to know the City of Angels and her family much better. Martha's recovery from the third surgery took months, but she returned to work sooner than expected, using a walker to protect her body from darting missiles (aka seventh graders) projecting themselves wildly about the halls. School reminded her that she was alive and kept her from thinking too much about her mortality.

She returned to chemo and I helped her shave her head. The kids at her school had a riddle: "Who wears baggy jeans, shaves their head, and speaks Spanish?" The description fit many of the boys, but the answer was "Mrs. D." While her own children had attended magnet high schools for the arts and technology, she reveled in teaching the "thugs and slugs." A student who had cursed her out the final day reappeared one June in her room. When Martha asked why, she said, "Because you're the only teacher who really cares." She called parents regularly, traveled to Mexico to work on her Spanish grammar, and battled with administrators to send notices to parents in Spanish.

The women I have loved have been unconventional, and Martha fit that mold. Her high school buddies were the guys in the band. During the Vietnam War, she played taps on her trumpet for the funeral of every soldier's body returned to the local military base, but refused to cash the five-dollar checks the feds sent her, thinking she could at least mess with their accounting. She entered a convent, a bane to her Presbyterian mother, and left the convent by mutual consent. Blacklisted by the archdiocese of Los Angeles for leading a teachers' strike, she switched from high school to elementary school, where she flew under the radar.

Martha's disorganization, which she attributed to "chemo brain," drove me crazy. She was always losing or forgetting something vital. As she cycled on and off oxygen, I came up with a mantra for her—"a Kansas City woman:" air, keys, cell, wallet. When I asked her about a Kansas City woman a few weeks later, her blank look told me everything. Then, one day she said to me, "a *mad* Kansas City woman," having added "m" for meds, of which she was taking dozens. Her chaos was hard for me, and we never lived together.

By our fifth summer, Martha's mother had been diagnosed with stomach cancer. She wanted to sell Martha's house in order to divide her estate evenly among her children. So Martha moved into Jim's place, planning to buy a condo.

"Sweetie, I really do not like your living with Jim!"

"Get over it. You know I haven't slept with him since Richard was born."

"But he gets to see you so much more than I do. And his house is thirteen miles away in the opposite direction of everything else."

"It's my house, too."

That was true, but I still didn't like it. I decided not to spend nights there. I could make that decision because her school was close to my house in that endless suburb called Sin City, so she frequently came over to my place.

Martha grew increasing less able to live alone, her chicks had flown the coop, and the condo never happened.

In our fifth September, Jim brought his mother, who was in failing health, to live with them. I yelled at Martha, "You don't have the energy for this!"

"Jim will take care of her."

"Sure, Jim will take care of her, but you're the one who will be telling him what to do every step of the way."

Martha, her siblings, and I celebrated Thanksgiving at her mother's house. On our way back to Vegas, Jim called Martha constantly, his mother having had a stroke. Martha talked him through every step. His mother died several days later. Martha's mother died in February. Martha was sunk in grief. She had talked to her mother daily.

Martha continued to teach. Her health problems multiplied. She had a doctor for every organ and countless side effects. Cycles of hair, bare head, and baby fuzz were reflected in annual school photos. During our fifth year, with two deaths and her deteriorating health, we saw less of each other. It took all her energy to teach. Clark County School District requires ten years in order for a surviving spouse to collect retirement benefits, and she completed ten years. Then the district decided she owed them seven weeks for time she had taken off years earlier for daily radiation at UCLA, before I knew her. So she returned to school in the fall of 2008, determined to teach the first quarter and to provide for Jim after her death.

I had won a sabbatical in 2008. If I stayed in Vegas, I knew I would see her very little. Martha urged me to move to the Bay Area, so I decided to do so. But I flew to Vegas every other month to see her. On Labor Day weekend, I helped with sorting, alphabetizing, grading, and recording sixth grade math papers. There were eight papers apiece from over 150 students. It took us three days. When I left, I said, "Jim, you've got to help Martha with grading." Unemployed and depressed, he was not much help.

After Halloween, she gave up her classes and classroom and became a wandering teacher, pushing a cart through the halls, carrying her stock in trade, helping where needed. She welcomed Obama campaigners to the spare bedrooms in their house, and when she felt energetic, she cooked huge vats of chili and delivered them to campaign headquarters.

Martha insisted on making Thanksgiving dinner for Jim and me, and I went to Vegas for the holiday. "Sweetie," she called to me, "can you go to the supermarket for butter and milk?"

When I returned, the table was still buried under the detritus of daily life.

"Jim, why didn't you clear the table?" I asked.

"No one told me to." I knew there was a reason I'd purchased a rare bottle of hard liquor while I was at the supermarket.

In January Jim got a good job, with a six-figure salary, in Boston, and left immediately. Martha and Jim began researching houses to buy and Martha flew to Massachusetts to approve or disapprove Jim's choice. It was business, she explained to me.

Martha *really* could not live alone. I visited. Richard visited. Rose visited. Richard and his wife, Samantha, came together. A student stayed with her. The Massachusetts house fell through, and they bought another, sight unseen by Martha. In March, she decided to move to Massachusetts, where Jim, Richard, and Samantha were now living. It made no sense to me; she was dying. Martha explained that she wanted to be with her family. She did not want the last face she saw to be a neighbor or acquaintance.

In April, I flew to Vegas to say good-bye. Knowing that chaos would reign, I planned to spend only two days. When I drove up to the house, Martha was standing in the front yard, surrounded by seven movers, who had appeared days early, Richard and Samantha, and other people. Martha's legs were bound with elaborate bandages to keep flesh from bursting through skin. She was the center of the whirlwind, as always. We had maybe an hour alone together, minutes snatched in doctors' waiting rooms and late at night. At the airport, her final words to me were, "Stay in touch with Rose." I felt numb.

She died five weeks later, after pneumonia put her in the hospital. Jim was on a business trip, and Rose and I lived in California. Richard and Samantha were at her side. When Jim and Rose arrived in Massachusetts, they held a small memorial, at a nearby state reserve called Purgatory Chasm. Martha would have loved the choice. I spent the day hiking along the Hayward regional shoreline in California, meditating on Martha.

As expected, my grief was more intense after I returned to Vegas, our scene. I kept imagining that I saw her on the street or disappearing into a doorway. From Martha, I learned how I do not want to die. She eagerly embraced the debility which western treatment of cancer creates because she was determined to raise her children. Inflammatory breast cancer leads to death, on average eighteen months after diagnosis. Martha's persistence and willingness to undertake the worst possible regimens gave her eight and a half years. Her children, Richard and Rose, were thirteen and fifteen when she was diagnosed. She saw her children graduate from high school (her initial goal), ensured her mother did not have to her bury her (her second goal), and left her pension to her husband (her third goal). She attended her daughter's college graduation and her son's wedding.

I could not understand Martha's allegiance to Jim. Her favorite joke was that she was keeping a plane ticket to Brazil handy, because that country does not extradite people to the U.S., and she would be forced to flee there after she had murdered him. While he and I developed a kind of familial friendly relationship, his single-minded focus on topics which attracted only him did sometimes make him hard to bear.

I loved Martha's generosity, her eccentricities, her staunch loyalties, our love-making. She brought me coffee in bed every morning when we spent the night together although she never touched the stuff herself. It was her most conventional sides that hurt. Her mother had instructed her that a husband is a business partner, and she followed that path for twenty-five years, even though her desires led her to women. She had to ensure that Jim got her pension, because she did not trust his financial skills. Rose told me that when she flew to Massachusetts after Martha died, she could not bear to stay at the new house. It was littered with post-it notes in Martha's hand, directing the unpacking in every room. If dying with dignity means staying true to yourself, Martha died with her dignity fully intact.

I spent the first couple of years after her death angry at her, angry that she had, on some level, chosen Jim over me. I also felt guilty for abandoning her, going off to Oakland on sabbatical. I could not have foreseen Jim's new job in

Massachusetts and how that set in motion the wheels that led to her demise three thousand miles away. I was angry that her death had been rendered as a family drama, not as a lesbian tragedy. It took my leaving the country for a year to allow myself to remember her love for me.

Last fall, Rose went to Massachusetts to help her father clean out the house to sell it. Unemployed again, he decided to retire to western Washington. When Rose posted a yard sale ad on Facebook, I asked if I could have Martha's fabric. One of the ways I had rubbed off on Martha was that she, a non-domestic woman, became a quilter. On one of our vacations, she made a snowflake and sunflower lap quilt for her mother from a non-beginner pattern in one of my quilt books. Later, she tackled a king-size bed quilt for Richard and Samantha as a wedding gift. When the box arrived from Massachusetts, it contained not only fabric, but a few items of my clothing, the cap Martha wore to cover her baldness at Richard and Samantha's wedding, a photo of the two of us on a camping trip, and a jar with some of Martha's ashes, the pickle label still intact. Rose e-mailed me that Jim had paid for the postage.

I remain on friendly terms with Martha's sister and with Rose, visiting with them annually. The box Rose packed in Massachusetts felt like the first time that anyone in Martha's family had acknowledged our relationship after her death. Perhaps her friends and family included me in messages of condolence they posted on a Facebook page Richard created as she was dying. But he took the page down before I figured out how to use Facebook and he told me it could not be resurrected.

Today, I celebrate Martha, our love, and the complicated relationship that we shared for six years.

FROM TOMBOY TO WOMAN TO FEMINIST TO RADICAL LESBIAN: MY LIFE'S JOURNEY
CHANTE SHIRELLE HOLSEY

Chante Shirelle Holsey was born in Dominguez Valley Hospital across the street from Compton, in California. She has a B.A. in Criminal Justice and is a self-published author of a religious spiritual inspirational book called *Longings of My Heart*, under the author name Ashirah. Her piece in this book is memoir.

GROWING UP IN a society where restrictions are put on children based on their sex at birth caused much confusion in my life. Being a girl who hated dresses and dolls, as well as other girly things, I was what some would call a "tomboy." I liked to play with "boy toys," my favorite color was and is blue, and I hated having to sit still with my legs uncomfortably crossed. From my experiences, I find the expectations of the female child, and the restrictions placed on her, to be appalling.

I remember thinking to myself, "I should be a boy," as early as the age of five. I really had no idea what I was talking about. I just knew I hated the fact that I was restricted in the things I was allowed to do. I was sick of having the weight of the world on my shoulders. For example one day, before my dad came to get me from kindergarten, I was waiting to climb up the ladder to go down the slide. A boy named Franklin looked up my skirt. My dad saw, and later I was whipped because a boy had looked up my skirt. To this day, I don't understand the logic of punishing the victim for what the perpetrator has done to her. My father was blaming me for the actions of another, when all I wanted to do was be carefree, like any child. I also remember sitting for hours on end, getting my hair pressed with a hot comb, also known as a pressing comb. My outward appearance was one way, while inside of me was a wild child desiring to burst free.

At one time, I identified with the character of Pippi Longstocking, the 1969 Pippi Longstocking who I saw on TV and read about in books. There were no stories about strong black girls back in those days, so Pippi was the image I found that I could identify with somewhat. I imagined myself as fast as the wind and as strong as Wonder Woman. I was beating up bad guys and doing amazing things with my body. In my exuberance, I even once jumped off my bed and hit my head on a table. I ended up with twenty-one stitches. Yes, I was a wild child.

During my young adult years, much like my childhood, I felt isolated from other girls. I always felt weird around them, like I was not a part of them, even though we shared similar experiences. But somehow, I knew I was different.

At one point as an adolescent I was trying to wear makeup, and from time to time my mom would guilt trip me into wearing dresses. During these times when I wore a dress, I felt uncomfortable; I felt like a drag queen. I'm bow-legged and pigeon-toed. I'm also hippy and fluffy, the type of black woman whose images are usually mocked in the media. I was not the type of woman others would call pretty. At best I was cute. I think the worse compliment I have ever gotten was when someone told me: "I wish I could put your personality into your sister's body. That would make the perfect girl." *Thanks a lot!* I thought. *You just made my day with your polite insults.*

Through a woman I met at work, I found a synagogue and joined. I soon became a gender-conforming, Holy Ghost-filled, spiritual dancer. I had to wear dresses and shirts in order not to "offend" the men in my new religion, or risk making them stumble or shake their confidence. I wasn't a tomboy anymore. Instead, I started looking like a respectable, decent Christian lady, (a synagogue is Jewish but we were the type of congregation that believed in Jesus. Many "Jewish believers" are called "Christian" as an insult.) Deep down inside, I was once again feeling miserable. To prepare for these religious services, I found myself sitting with my legs uncomfortably crossed for hours on end to get my hair "did," an expression us black girls use from time to time.

Yes, I soon discovered that even as an adult, just like when I was a girl, I was being subjected to gender roles and dress codes for females. Yet, even then I knew that my life as a female had nothing to do with any outward apparel, nor with any physical restrictions imposed on me from others. I have always felt the notion that I have to look a certain way or dress a certain way to be considered female, is not just uncomfortable and restrictive, it's wrong. I was born female, and that's what I am. No phony accessories required.

It's wrong to push young girls to fit into an outward appearance that is someone else's ideal version of "womanhood." Womanhood is a life based on biological factors at birth with certain characteristics that apply to all females, including but not limited to, mammals, insects, reptiles, amphibians, and primates. That is to say, we are born female because we have the ability to reproduce and to bear young. But this doesn't give anybody the right to tell us how to dress, behave, and fit in. Nor does every female desire to have children. In fact, some females for biological reasons cannot bear children, and that should be just fine and quite acceptable. No woman should be told we have to bear children.

Being born female, like most other females, I have reproductive organs and a system within my body which happens to be designed to bear children. I may have this biological system inside me, but it isn't my one and only purpose in life, nor is it my destiny. My shared experiences with other females give me comfort. Learning that many other females also hated dresses and liked to play hard and rough is a huge comfort for me.

From childhood to adulthood, I've faced enormous social pressures. I've been told at every age and at every stage of my life how I should look and act in order to be female. Given these conditions, I consider the fact that I survived from girlhood to adulthood to be an act of courage and strength because my girlhood was filled with true hardship. My survival to an adult woman was not a given, which is a concept that seems to float right over many people's heads. When it's all said and done, I have a deep and thorough understanding of what I lived through and what I've surmounted.

For example, as it happened, on the day of my birth, May 25th, 1974, I was the only female baby born out of nine babies birthed at Dominguez Valley Hospital, in Los Angeles County. Of course, when the doctors told my parents what I was, they simply looked at my genitals. Based on this biological fact, they announced me as a girl child. In that one moment, the weight of this sexist society and the enormity of all its social meaning was foisted upon me, and so it was to be from then on. Little did I know, but my life had been pre-planned without any input from me.

However, to my credit, from a young age I rebelled and I broke this socially constructed gender straitjacket. Now as an adult I'm still breaking their restrictive gender rules, for I am a free woman and I decide what that means and who I am. No amount of fantasy, socially prescribed face painting or female costuming can change that. I am who I am, because of my own identity, which I've created from within myself, and not from any outside pressures which too often have gone completely against my natural way of being.

As I got older, I realized that I have always been attracted to women, and in some ways I call myself a "political lesbian." By this I mean I have love toward and the desire to care for women without the need to have a sexual relationship with them. Being attracted to women has not always led me to desiring a sexual relationship with a woman, although at this point in my life, it actually does. At this time, I'm madly in love and sexual lust with an amazing woman, but I will never disclose this to her.

I attribute my slow-growing awareness of my lesbian identity partly to my having witnessed various women, including my own mother, being abused throughout my life. My mother has suffered abuse from my father because of what he considers to be her "place" as a woman. Watching this most of my young life has had a huge impact on me. It has affected me in terms of delaying my ability to form my own distinct female identity, and it has affected my choices and my life's journey in terms of my coming out as a lesbian.

My entry into the religious organization, the synagogue I mentioned above, happened two years after my mother's death. Four years after that, I became involved in another extreme religious organization called TOLI or Tree of Life International church and ministries, and I ended up devoting five years of my life there. Later, I became a member of A Messianic Synagogue. But five years into my commitment there I was forced to face their lies and racism, which I discovered were a deeply embedded part of this synagogue. In all three congregations, I confronted the "leadership" and was either, kicked out or asked to leave. Since I so desperately wanted to serve God and be a blessing, I continued to join congregation after congregation.

Upon first joining this one organization, I worked for a time with young people. However, my work, as I gradually discovered, was not valued. Instead, I was being undermined and invalidated because, as the religious authorities told me, "You are not Jewish," and "You are not an 'ordained' spiritual leader." Therefore, they explained, "Your dealings with these high school kids are nothing." When one of these young women with whom I was working came to me for support and to vent her concerns about being mistreated by her group, my efforts to help her were discredited and invalidated by this religious organization. I had to face the fact that they didn't trust me.

It first came to my attention that mistrust was afoot at the annual camping trip we held during Labor Day weekend for our youth group, called Dor Segulah. Although I was not among the official leadership, the youth, both male and female, would come to me for edification, comfort, correction, and advice. They knew I was fair and non-judgmental, and they trusted me.

On this weekend of our camping trip, I was told in no uncertain terms by the rabbi and his wife that I was too old for this group of young people. They said that they would instead make me "The Davidic Dance leader" upon my return the next weekend. This turned out to be a big lie. They simply did not want me influencing their youth, nor encouraging them to question and to think for themselves. They especially disliked my encouraging the youth to have their own relationship with "God," apart from their parents and apart from the leaders of this congregation. To have an independent relationship with "God" was a scandalous perspective, and they wouldn't permit it. As I came to understand, they were threatened by my individual approach to spirituality.

The next weekend I discovered someone else was put in charge of the young people's dance troupe, not me. I wasn't even allowed to be the assistant. In fact, I was completely removed from my previous service work. Something finally clicked for me and it culminated years of their treating me as if I was their servant, even while relying on my integrity to uphold their reputation as fair, true, and "Christ-like" in being non-judgmental and accepting of all. They wanted to project this image of their temple, even though it was untrue, and they had been using me in the process.

At this time, I had enormous zeal and really believed I'd found my calling with my membership in this congregation. However, as I gradually learned, this was not how they viewed me. So naturally, I was getting more and more alarmed and frustrated, thinking to myself, "Just because you may not see me as having credibility, and just because you don't recognize my authority, does not mean I don't have any. I know who I am!" As I was getting angrier and feeling more and more betrayed by these so-called religious authorities, I decided to pray to see what God, as I understood God, wanted for me. It took some time for me to understand what was going on and why I felt the way I did. I felt that I was being made to hide my talents and I wasn't being recognized as the leader I knew myself to be. I couldn't do my job with my kids at work, whom I cared deeply for. Basically, I could no longer be of service to them.

In the end, their betrayal of me was too much for me. I saw no way to work within the confines of this religious organization and keep my integrity and self-respect intact, so I left. It was a very painful time in my life.

After this, I vowed never to place my trust in religious people again. But this organization wasn't the first one, nor was it the last one. In all, I wasted twenty-three years of my life in and out of various congregations like this one, where the "man of God" clearly did evil, or did whatever the hell he wanted to do, and the women stuck by him, devoting themselves to his bidding. After that much time, I was devastated and disillusioned. Finally, I wanted nothing more to do with any organized religion.

Shortly after I parted ways with all things religious, I did a complete 180 and got involved in watching porn, lesbian porn in particular. I realized I had been single and celibate for a total of seventeen years in my life. I was thirty-eight at the time, a young woman. A big part of me wanted to run the opposite way as much as I possibly could, and become totally consumed by porn. However, on one occasion, and only by chance, I came across a blog on the internet written by a woman who called herself "Evil Feminist." It was on Tumblr. I started reading it more and more frequently, and eventually I was surprised to find out that I was allowing this feminist stuff to interrupt my usual "entertainment" (watching porn). At the same time I had also found other blogs, such as one called: "Feminism-and-iggys" and a third blog known as "Vivanity. These writings by women I'd never met captured my attention. They were like infomercials disturbing my porn distraction, until gradually I was convinced that I must be going in the wrong direction with the porn, and instead, I started following their blogs.

At about the same time, I was taking a class called Intro to Psychology at New England College Online School. I was completing my B.A. in Criminal Justice and this was a required class. I had an essay due, so I decided to write it on the effects of pornography on women. I saw it as a chance for me to describe my new found feminist analysis in order to explain it both to myself and on paper, while simultaneously fulfilling the purpose of finishing an assignment for this class. Once I finished the paper and turned it in, I was amazed at the harm I had caused myself by watching so much porn.

I'm an introvert and can become very obsessive with something that captures my interest. In this case, I had been single for a long time, and the hope of ever having a relationship with a real person was fading. It seemed as if I would always be single. While sucked into this world of porn, my social skills suffered. No one wants to be known as a porn watcher. As well, I was realizing the harmful effect it has on women. By finding these feminist writers online, I felt I was now on the road toward a deeper understanding of what feminism meant to me, and I felt excited and alive. What a great new direction this was for me!

Shortly after finishing my class paper, I found the feminist organization called WoLF (Women's Liberation Front), online via the Tumblr blogs I had been reading, and after watching several YouTube videos done by Lierre Keith. WoLF is a radical feminist organization which opposes pornography and prostitution, and seeks to implement the Nordic Model to address these misogynist social problems. The Nordic Model is successfully being used in Sweden. Under this model, the laws on prostitution in Sweden and Canada make it illegal to buy sexual services, but not to sell them. Pimping, procuring, and operating a brothel are also illegal. The criminalization of the purchase of sex, but not the selling of sex, was unique when this model was first enacted in 1999. Since then, Norway and Iceland have adopted similar legislation, both in 2009, followed by Canada in 2014 and Northern Ireland in 2015. As I discovered, WoLF also believes in the abolishment of the notion of gender, seeing gender roles for men and women as socially constructed and too limiting. These rigid roles don't necessarily fit us but they're imposed on us whether we like it or not, and they basically serve a sexist, racist society.

The mission of WoLF is to end male violence and to make sure that women have reproductive sovereignty over our own bodies. I went to a local meeting and soon got involved. I was excited to find that their values deeply resonated with me. Having come from a place of believing in covenants that ask you to be honorable and to have integrity, I agreed to the principles I found in WoLF and to the terms in which they described their principles, once I learned what they are. Their perspective and values suited me much better than any other outlook I had previously ascribed to in my life. I was thrilled to finally be a part of an organization that I truly resonated with, and felt good about, and whose focus was on the liberation of women.

During an annual feminist event called Michfest (The Michigan Womyn's Music Festival) which happened in the summer of 2015, I met several other members of WoLF and we participated in a radical feminist gathering during which I came to know the organization more fully and also gained the trust of the remaining members on their board. Later on, to my happiness, they asked me to join their board and I agreed. As time passed, I became more familiar with some of the founding members as women, and with what the WoLF vision and philosophy stand for. Their vision resonates so well with my own. I vow to uphold it as long as I'm on the WoLF board.

Actually, because these particular values and vision fit me and my own individual outlook as a feminist and a lesbian, I feel that as long as I live, I'll walk in the truth and integrity of this ideal. For as long as I live, I'll continue to work for the total liberation of all women.

HER HANDMADE KENTE CLOTH JACKET
TOKE HOPPENBROUWERS

 Toke Hoppenbrouwers was born in the Netherlands just before WWII and completed undergraduate studies at the University of Utrecht. In 1965, she immigrated to the United States to attend UCLA. Her strongest identity is as a Neuroscientist, but she studied Clinical Psychology as well so she could probe a deeper truth. As a Clinical professor at USC, she focused on SIDS and taught at California State University at Northridge. The search for the etiology of SIDS has brought her to cultural research in Indonesia. *Autumn Sea*, an autobiographical novel received a Small Press Award in 1997. "Her Handmade Kente Cloth Jacket" is a personal essay.

I LOVE YOUR taste in jackets, Nehanda—you look great in that colorful Kente cloth, but you live in the North West—that is too far away. Good luck in your search." Toke (Hershekisses.com, the Match site for lesbians).

In 2007, I wasn't in a hurry, so to avoid finding someone on my doorstep too soon, I decided to contact only women beyond a radius of three hundred miles from Los Angeles. I had already waited until my limp was fixed by a hip replacement and an implant remedied the hole between my front teeth. This online dating thing was new to me and since my last relationship ended, I had gotten used to a queen size bed all to myself, where the room temperature befriended my core body temperature. However, upon the urging of a happy couple that had found each other online, I went ahead.

" am yearning for somebody who can meet me with emotional intelligence and wisdom, who not only covets an elusive spiritual luminosity, but has an inkling of how to arrive there occasionally.

Not confident that the commonplace "sitting by the fireplace with a glass of chardonnay and late afternoon walks at the beach," would deliver this magical person, I began my internet profile:

A day might find me reviewing some neuroscience literature or freeing my two yellow labs, Rajata and Intan from their basement "bedroom" for their one hour hike across sage-covered hills. During a week I'll have worked on an item from my to do list, such as a Saturday planting in the garden. In a month I may have done rattlesnake aversion training for the dogs or tax preparation. Within a year I will have visited my family and friends in

Holland. During a decade I am lucky if I've discovered more of my shadow and less girth. An hour may find me reading the newspaper, listening to music or sound asleep. In a minute I'm absorbed in what I'm doing, while a second flies by without noticing.

One woman who responded to me lived in the Bay Area. She wrote: *"I live the simple life of an academic: teaching, research, conferences, travel abroad."*

I trekked up to her beautifully appointed home a few times where I discovered that she was true to her word: *"More interested in meeting potential friends in the Bay Area than in tracking down some phantom perfect match."* That association lasted just long enough for me to discover that the Bay Area was the absolute maximum distance I could negotiate on any regular basis with two large yellow labs in my car.

"You live too far away," I had written to Nehanda.

"Not so fast now," she replied. She was the attractive woman with the beautiful jacket, who responded to my email. She lived in the Pacific Northwest. *"I regularly visit my mother in Santa Barbara,"* she said.

It turned out Nehanda hadn't much cared for my profile, but my intense blue eyes in one of the profile pictures riveted her, so she took the risk of engaging in an e-mail correspondence.

FROM AUGUST SECOND to October second we checked each other out leisurely in an in depth e-mail exchange. What do I want in a woman? I wrote: "Autonomy is one of my big items; it would be nice if she liked my writing but that's not essential. However, I continue friendships with my ex-lovers, and that should not be a deal breaker for a new woman in my life. What's on your deal breaker list?"

I was glad I asked her. I received a file with more than thirty qualities such as:

- Inability, unwillingness, or disinterest in talking about feelings and ideas.
- Intolerance for silence—having to fill every moment with talk or TV.
- Indicating anger or displeasure by silence and sullenness rather than expressing it directly
- Physical and sexual repression or inhibition.
- "Rabid" extraversion
- Unmanaged or poorly managed bipolar disorder
- A deeper level of narcissism than my own (ahem)
- Uncleanness of person or place
- Taurus and Leo (half joking)

I felt fairly certain that I passed this test, except in cleanliness. One of the pictures on my profile showed me with dirty nails from working in the garden, holding a five week old puppy, offspring of Intan. On that item I gave myself at most a B+.

On my way to Holland in October 2008, I decided to make a stopover in Seattle to meet Nehanda for the first time. One of her profile pictures had shown her delivering a sermon at the Unitarian Society; she was wearing a tunic handcrafted of Kente cloth, made and bequeathed to her by a friend who had died. Now here she was, that statuesque and regal woman, walking toward me at the airport.

Later, I would discover this stunning beauty's gifts for acting, singing, and reading her poetry, all gifts of which she was well aware. At that moment I just felt her presence, with the intelligence and energy of Flo Kennedy tempered by the propriety of Shirley Chisholm. I was impressed, delighted but not intimidated.

One night in a fancy hotel gave me all the assurance I could want about our chemistry. After this brief visit, I was prepared to tell my family and friends in Holland: *"I'm bonded anew."*

I was to fly out of Seattle the next morning, which provided us with a test we hadn't anticipated: Nehanda gave me a ride to the airport but she missed the ferry that would guarantee my timely arrival for the flight. Relieved that I could reschedule the flight by phone for later that day, I managed to conceal my annoyance. Thus, she didn't get to see me "express my anger directly" or be silent or sullen (one item on her deal breaker list). I have always liked the clarity that expressing my annoyance directly provides. Luckily, my anger has a good chance of petering out promptly. However, I suspect that Nehanda has since discovered that she might prefer less directness. It's "Be careful what you ask for."

Nehanda's more lyrical report of our meeting read:

> She kissed me full on the mouth right there at Baggage Claim. But before that, when at first we pressed close to embrace, a refined aliveness lit up everywhere in me, a ribbon fuse running in all the places where regular human insides used to be. It was then that she stretched up to kiss me, softly, but with a dead center surety that made me feel claimed.

> I followed her as she headed toward an airport elevator—just any old elevator—in that brisk, "Well, let's get it done" way she has. I wouldn't have had to do that. I could have touched her arm or shoulder and said, "No, no. This way. Our car is parked near a different elevator."

> Wandering lost in an airport parking lot with no points of reference, no sense of direction, no map back to where my real life is, marked by an indigo

Honda, I call "Belle Noir." That's nightmare land for me. And that's exactly where I landed.

I think that will not be the last time that she confidently hustles me off in a direction I hadn't aimed to go.

Sure enough, I dragged her off to a poetry workshop with Jane Hirschfield in Tassajara, a remote Zen Buddhist retreat in the Santa Lucia Mountains. That was one of the first times I pushed her envelope. She covered her eyes and ears so as not to see the precipitous drop, during our one hour ride down a dirt road to Tassajara's deep canyon. Nonetheless, her poems burst forth in the workshop, and she shared them with panache.

It was a mercilessly hot summer that year, and Nehanda found it unbearable. She softly complained about the flies and that her feet got dirty in the Tassajara dust. By now, I have learned that when it comes to enjoying nature, we are different. She quotes Oscar Wilde:

"I do not play games outside. Although I once played a game of dominos outside a café in Paris."

ABOUT FIVE YEARS ago, Nehanda did move to Santa Barbara, so that she could be closer to her aging mother, closer to me here in Los Angeles, and in a more benign climate for her aging bones.

Over the years, she has supplied me with antiseptic hand soaps and wipes, bottles of bleach, special purpose cleaners, scrubbing potions, extra strength hypoallergenic deodorant, rubber gloves, loads of plastic bags and heavy duty sponges. When we travel she is armed with a suitcase dedicated to products for warding off microscopic and macroscopic bugs, topped off with a battery driven bug zapper. My hygiene has been designated "European," which is not to be construed as a compliment.

During WWII in Holland, gas and electricity were not reliably available, and we as children often shared the same lukewarm bath water, once a week at most. Even during my student days in Utrecht, a rental didn't always come with a shower or bath, so we made do at the sink. I admit, since retirement I jealously "protect the oils in my skin," as I justify to myself skipping a shower. I'm sure I have been downgraded to at best a C- for cleanliness.

On my part, I have decided that she has a smidgeon of the obsessive in her.

When we hit other manifestations of our incompatibility we remind each other of what the comedian, Elvira Kurt, said: "You can be lonely or you can be annoyed."

On my seventieth birthday celebration Nehanda, a mezzo soprano sang Schumann's *"Woman's Life & Love."* Her dark voice has a rich lower register and pure, ringing high tones. Her finale was a complete change of pace and costume; she belted out *"You're Good to Mama"* from the musical *Chicago*, an irrepressible, rousing performance in leather that she reprised in 2011 on a two-thousand-women Olivia cruise to the Mexican Riviera we enjoyed together. She basked in the ovation and the compliments she received from jury members Kate Clinton, Suede, Vicky Shaw, and Karen Williams: "This is how it is done, you younger dykes!" Or, "This is who I want to be when I grow up." At seventy, she became probably the oldest Idol winner in Olivia's forty year history. All the while I was beaming: "I get to take her home!"

Nehanda is a psychotherapist by profession, a field with which I'm quite familiar. In the seven years that we have now been together, we have made frequent inner journeys. On outer journeys, we stood in front of the only gay monument in the world in Amsterdam. In Saint Petersburg we visited the Hermitage, a museum of art and culture in Russia. In Puerto Vallarta, she lost her driver's license. The best is when we meet my old friends, who immediately embrace her as a new one.

Our future:

> Toke: *"Where are my hearing aids, Nehanda, and my glasses?"*
> Nehanda: *"Where are my pills?"*
> Toke: "What did we hear that comedienne say—what's her name?"
> Nehanda: *"Oh you mean Wanda Sykes?"*
> Toke: *"Yeah."*
> Nehanda: *"She said about needing her meds: I'm not talking about over-the-counter stuff; it takes some serious shit to keep me going!"*

How do we negotiate that deal breaker cleanliness item? For one, thus far we have kept our own domiciles; that takes a lot of wind out of the sails. When I last checked how we were doing on this issue, she answered: "It's because you are so very, very extraordinary that I can tolerate it." What more can I wish? Who says lesbian life at this age, or at any age for that matter, can't be glorious?

ON BEING LESBIAN FEMME IN A HETEROSEXUAL WORLD
HAPPY/L.A. HYDER

Happy/L.A. Hyder, *"artivist,"* is celebrating a forty-five year affair with photography. Her photo, "New Country Daughter/ Lebanese American" appears in the 4th Edition of *This Bridge Called My Back, Writings by Radical Women of Color* (Kitchen Table: Women of Color Press, 1986). Her essay, "Dyke March, San Francisco 2004: Many Are Intrigued by the Fact that I Am Also a Belly Dancer," appears in *Arab & Arab American Feminisms: Gender, Violence & Belonging* (Syracuse University Press, 2005). Hyder's current activist work focuses around issues of lesbian identity and on the Boycotts, Divestments and Sanctions movement for justice in Palestine. This piece is her personal philosophy.

THIS IS NOT my coming out story, it is more my philosophy about coming out, when and how we may each choose to take that step. These are my thoughts on our lives in the multi-faceted queer world of today. I came to this philosophical position through sexual experience; through feeling a woman's fingers reaching for my depth while she tongued my clit, enticing my hips off the bed with legs spread wide in invitation.

Beginning with the sexual revolution, mired in compulsory heterosexuality devoid of depth for me, of emotional caring, I came to this Lesbian identity and philosophical position, and carried it with me into my late sixties. Still highly sexual, if I'm so inclined, I reach easily for my vibrator, stand with my back against the wall, and buzz off, after lifting my skirts out of the way. I have truly come a long way, baby.

Raised as girl children, we are expected to love the color pink and wear dresses with puffy sleeves. (Neither made my "favorites" list.) Raised as girl children, we are given baby dolls when we are still babies ourselves. Raised as girl children, we are asked at a young age: "Do you have a boyfriend? How many children do you want?" This latter question is posed to us before we have learned where babies come from, and certainly before we even care.

Raised as girl children in the 1940s and '50s we were steered toward waiting, toward being quiet and passive, toward wanting our prince. Even most of the hardheaded "dames" of the 1930s and '40s films I saw on TV every day after school were waiting for their prince. Or they had already found their prince in their best male friend, their office colleague, or the boy next door. They were always portrayed as butting heads, but by the end of the film they're spun head over heels in love.

Thank goodness for those few dames who didn't follow the rules. I say thank goodness for the dames of every generation–the ones who manage to find a different path. Thank goodness for the lesbians hidden in those films, showing up in a tux every so often and eyeing their best friend, their bosses' wives, or a lone woman who catches their fancy. They paraded our hidden desires with style, grace, and grit.

How many of us were influenced by these role models to leave our parents' homes for reasons that had nothing to do with marriage or war? I certainly was influenced by them. Those women helped me to develop "gaydar" before I really understood what it was or what it meant. Had I known, I may have found my own path to lesbianism much earlier than thirty-three.

Coming out publicly and proudly in record numbers in the 1970s, we continue to come out as lesbian as we age, bringing a woman lover into our lives and beds. Being healthier and living longer, we will hear even more from newly out older dykes, just as we hear about the younger generations claiming queerness before they hit their teens. I note how they generally refuse the term lesbian, being influenced and encouraged by their peers to use the word "queer," though "dyke" may be embraced for its transgressiveness.

For those of us in our sixties and older, the very word "lesbian" was neither spoken nor seen in print until we reached our twenties, thirties, or even forties. For most of us, it took a long time to recognize our true sexual identities. When we rarely heard the word "homosexual," it always referred to men.

Of course, whatever portrait of lesbianism you managed to discover was certainly not nice. And if there was anything a good girl was supposed to be, it was "nice."

When I look up the word "nice," Webster's Dictionary designates to it the following:

1. Obsolete use: a. wanton, dissolute; b. coy, reticent.
2. Having finicky taste, or exacting requirements or standards.
3. Possessing, marked by, or demanding great or excessive precision and delicacy.
4. a. Pleasing or agreeable; b. appropriate or fitting.
5. Polite or kind.
6. a. Socially acceptable: well-bred; b. virtuous or respectable (for example, "Nice girls don't do that!")

In other words, if you accepted your female socialization to be a "nice" girl, you might never find your "dame," let alone your dyke self. Personally, I'll take the obsolete definition of "wanton," though "kind" need not be left behind.

I recall my fourteen-year-old self—in the midst of my heavy heterosexual and "nice girl" socialization—on a particular Friday night making sure I was home by nine o'clock from a teen meeting at the church. I wanted to catch a

TV special about homosexuals that had been advertised, most likely on the late night TV I often watched with my mother.

As I remember it, all of the still images in the program, some taken on a nude beach "where homosexuals gathered," were in negative format. Only men were mentioned. Even though the images were in this format, dark black strips were put over eyes (and of course, genitals) to disguise the men being shown. But what I remember most is being excited by the mere existence of this difference, and that it was being revealed on television, as veiled and shame-filled as it was.

Nowadays, some young women are declaring themselves to be lesbian by the age of fourteen, something that I didn't achieve until thirty. I wonder: can it be said that a young teen comes "out of a closet" when they call themselves queer? Is a child actually "in a closet"? Apart from those who are at the very ends of the homosexual spectrum, do children experience that "closet" before they begin to feel the surge of hormones and start to care about or experiment with sex?

The feeling of being different comes to many of us, no matter our sexual preference, long before we are confronted with the concept of sexual preference. This is not the same as being closeted, yet may be construed as that. I remember a sense that I was not like the other kids without understanding why, and feeling odd about that.

In some ways I envy the young their early knowledge of queer existence, and thus they have a possibility I did not know I had as a young person. (Although I do *not* envy the sexual misinformation the young are absorbing, nor the sex they are engaging in at younger and younger ages.) Those difficult younger years of my coming out were filled with internal conflict and processing—as have been all major decisions in my life—and led to my growth on many fronts. Also, I am concerned with the cultural phenomena of heterosexual parents naming their young child trans if their boy is dressing up in mommy's clothes or wants to play with dolls or their little girl wants boys' clothes and toys. I wonder how many butch dykes and fey gay boys, while wanting the freedom to play as they wished as children, are glad their parents did not decide to change their gender identity for them.

Recently I awoke and thought, "I'm actually closer to seventy than to sixty!"

Being of a certain age, and being most comfortable with identifying as a lesbian femme, my being a dyke commonly goes undetected by some in my generation who are unfamiliar with the queer community. I often find myself having to come out to them. They do not perceive me as lesbian of course; I think most simply they don't perceive *any* women of a certain age as lesbian.

Even having to educate people about what lesbians look like, I don't experience my lesbian identity as a burden in any way. I do, however, have to choose who to come out to, as anyone on the queer spectrum must do. Personal safety is the concern here.

I'm grateful to know clearly who I am. Some women may never be able to come out, even to themselves. Some will only be able to confess it on their deathbeds, out loud or to themselves. If so, I hope any tears of regret mingle with tears of joy for finally embracing themselves wholly.

Sadly, there will perhaps always be women who cannot come out as lesbian. Either it's much too dangerous, or they are too isolated and can't find their own kind, or both. I grieve for them, and I send them my strength and my joy. It's my fondest hope that someday we will all see a better world, one in which every girl and every woman can embody her fullest self, claiming any identity she chooses.

Nowadays, lesbians face a new dilemma. We are often accused of not being trans-inclusive when we choose to use lesbian as our identity, and claim lesbian space as valid. But being asked not to use "lesbian" is erasing our identity. It seems that most self-identified trans people claim trans as their identity, and will introduce themselves as such, while I believe we can all claim to be genderqueer. But if I don't claim my own chosen lesbian identity, then I become guilty of self-erasure.

I have been in venues listening to a trans poet or spoken word artist, admiring their work, when the word lesbian, or cis, is spit out like a slap in the face. For this reason, I refuse to use the term "cis" and encourage others to reject it also. I am not Mother Nature; I did not choose anyone's gender assignment. I am not responsible, as one who has learned to accept anyone's personal choice, for injuries done to any genderqueer person.

This acceptance, may I add, largely comes from times of not being accepted for my own choices by society and by personal acquaintances. Acceptance of others' choices does not come easily, raised as we are in an intolerant society. It's especially difficult when those who feel disenfranchised, in turn disenfranchise members of the very group of people they feel must accept them/allow them into the "club." It leaves no room for dialogue; luckily this is changing.

Erasure by being ignored is nothing new to someone of my age; to persons with visible disabilities; to children. Erasure is nothing new to lesbians, including purposeful erasure from our own queer community, and sometimes denigration goes along with it. Erasure from the mainstream has been happening as long as lesbians have existed, which is always.

I believe lesbians in particular, from our non-obeisance to the almighty penis, are quite powerful, and that is why erasure, from ignoring us to killing us, has been deemed necessary by the patriarchal system. It's hard enough to be lesbian (anywhere on the spectrum of what this means) in this heterosexual world without our own community telling us who we can and cannot be. Only we as lesbians can truly define ourselves.

MALENA THE MADDENED ONE
BEV JAFEK
An excerpt from a novel, The Sacred Beasts

Bev Jafek has published about forty-five of her short stories and novel excerpts in the literary quarterly and university press publications. Some have been translated into German, Italian, and Dutch and won many literary awards, including publication in the annual "prize" anthology, *The Best American Short Stories*. She also won the Carlos Fuentes Award and the Editor's Prize for fiction from *Columbia: A Magazine of Literature and Art* as well as first prize in the 2001 Arch & Bruce Brown Foundation short story competition for "redemption of gay history" through creative writing. The Overlook Press, distributed by Penguin-Putnam, published her first story collection, *The Man Who Took a Bite Out of His Wife*, and reprinted it in paperback two years later. It was cited as one of the best story collections of the year in *The Year's Best Fantasy* (7th edition, Teri Windling) as well as being selected as a finalist for the Crawford Award (best new fantasy fiction writer of the year). She was also a Wallace E. Stegner Fellow in Fiction at Stanford University. She is a third generation American. Her story included here is an excerpt from her novel, *The Sacred Beasts*, published by Bedazzled Ink Publishing, October, 2016.

MY MOTHER WAS a *tocaor*, a gypsy flamenco singer. Her stage name was Malena and they called her Malena the Maddened One and sometimes Malena the Singing Beast. When she came onstage, she yelled, "I've got ten times the balls of any man here!" and the pandemonium began. Many things then happened almost at once: her whole body tensed and sometimes her feet pawed the ground like a bull, one arm threw itself out to the audience, her mouth opened and a sound came out of it that was low, guttural, bass and churning. It was deep and thick and ragged, a voice made of blood, gravel and agony. It made you think of the force of a flooding river or rancid butter or the world's biggest bullfrog crying out as a knife was shoved into its gut. The audience went crazy with shock, ecstasy and pain. The hair rose on their arms, and my mother lived for that moment. From then on, they were all in a trance led by my mother.

She sang only *cante jondo*, deep flamenco, the oldest version of the art and most emotional, unlike the flamenco fusion music you hear today, and she was very well-trained by her own mother. She knew all the *palos*, whose different styles and rhythms numbered into the forties. Some were songs sung at fiestas—*alegrias, rumbas, tanquillos*. The most complex of these were the *soleas* and *siquiriyas*. Some of the oldest were originally written for blacksmiths as they pounded metal into shape—the *martinetas*. Other old ones were the *deblas* written to goddesses. There were many of these since gypsies are a matriarchal society. Newer songs were the *carcilenos*, prison songs, since so many gypsies use illegal drugs and end up in prison. You would probably recognize some of these songs by their rhythms—*tangos, fandangos, rumbas, guajiras, milongas*. So, despite my mother's effect on audiences, her art did not lack discipline, and she was actually a very gentle person, particularly with me. But, there was a great creative violence in her soul, and it poured from her in every performance.

It has been said that as much as two thirds of gypsies never go to public schools and are therefore illiterate. This was not true of my mother. She often rewrote the lyrics of her songs, composed music for more songs, and even sang spontaneously. The flamenco songs I heard from men were often misogynistic and sadomasochistic, but my mother's songs were most often about the strength of women. Several agents wanted to sign her up for a recording contract, but my mother could read the documents' language, which was always absurdly exploitative. She immediately demanded better terms, which shocked them. They were used to illiterate gypsies who would sign anything.

So, my mother never made a record or album. She performed all over Spain, most often in Andalusia, where we lived. I always attended school under strict supervision by my father's sister, and then I could not accompany her. But over holidays and summers, I went everywhere with her, and I loved our life on the road. My mother performed in the *tablaos,* night clubs in the big cities, in *aventas* or inns in the countryside, and also in festivals and competitions across Spain. Some of them, like the *Bienal,* could last a month. In Andalusia, she performed at *romerias*, fiestas that accompanied pilgrimages, as well as fiestas after hunting in the countryside.

Some holiday and summer flamenco concerts were elaborately and expensively staged events with seats selling for top prices. These had huge audiences from North America, Japan, and Germany. Only a fourth of the audience was Spanish, because so few Spaniards could afford the ticket price. At one of these, my mother performed with a very famous flamenco dancer—a woman like Eva Yerbabuena—and she was so moved by her beauty and dance that she kissed her on both of her thighs and ended up being punched in the nose by her—to the raucous delight of the audience. You see, my mother loved only women and in that I follow her. I was proud of her for it, though I had to ice her swollen nose. The dancer later apologized and said she was only startled and not angered, but the promoter loved the press that concert got. The scandal increased attendance at the next one.

My mother only spoke to me a few times about her women lovers. One was a gypsy flamenco dancer she met on the road and this woman, she said, was as wild and passionate about music and love as she was. If you are passionate about art, you will also be passionate about many other things, including sex, she said.

The relationship was always stormy and could not last for that reason. It is very difficult for two artists to be simply companionable together, she said, and this is what makes relationships last. She also loved a woman who lived in *Tres Mil Viviendas*, one who admired her singing and music but was not an artist. This lasted longer, but my mother's many absences because of her performance schedule eventually made them both sad and the relationship ended. I felt my mother's pain when she could not always have the love of a woman, and I came to Barcelona so that I would not suffer in this way. I know I can love a woman in a relationship that lasts, without long absences. I work here and I love my woman here; we've been together more than fifteen years now.

When school wasn't in session, it was up to me whether I went on the road with my mother or not, so you can be sure I always went. I saw everything a child is never allowed to see: completely uninhibited life at all levels of Spanish society, including sex, drugs, drunkenness and brawls. The gypsies who performed with my mother learned to slowly recede from the party, however. While it was in progress, everyone wanted to be a gypsy. They loved us for the pure wild life only we could give them; but once it was over, they couldn't stand to have us around. They never wanted to know anything about our lives, and we made no friends. My mother, of course, was one of the most fascinating singers and she was beautiful for a long time, too, but no one cared to know about the poor barrio she would return to. So, we felt the hot embrace of life and the door slammed in our face in very rapid succession. I must say, though, that I loved every minute of it and wouldn't have missed a bit of that life on the road with my mother. I had no respect for the people who were so ambivalent about us. They feared their own deepest urges, not us.

The government was uncomfortable about flamenco, too, even the socialists who were from Andalusia. All other performing arts got extensive government support, particularly the ones drawing international attention or even showing the faintest potential for that, like Spain's pathetic failure to create a national ballet. Not us, even though we were one of Spain's most successful and enduring performing arts. Spain wanted EU membership then, and the government found flamenco embarrassingly primitive, a reminder of a less than ideally civilized past that kept coming back to haunt them. The heart of this life is as wild and raw and full of tempests as the earth, and flamenco draws on this more directly than any other Spanish art. Civilization will always have its ways of stilling the heart—those endlessly flickering little screens you watch on every table and now in the palm of your hand–that's only the latest maneuver. But that wild heart will never be stifled. It will always demand expression, and my mother's life showed this to me in a unique and extraordinary way. I am grateful for this, because it has taught me to trust things that raise the hair on your arm: they are telling you something about yourself and the world that nothing else will reveal to you. This I know: my mother was a great artist, though she came from a poor barrio.

And, our barrio was Spain's most notorious—*Las Tres Mil Viviendas*—on the outskirts of Seville. All the famous flamenco singers come from here. To get to our barrio, you would have to drive away from the city's beautiful old haciendas and jacaranda trees, all the way out to Triana and then to a place where there are piles of refuse, junked cars, and nothing else but dusty earth. Then you would begin to make out a city of run-down apartment buildings, all as poor as the dust. Some have blocks of eight story buildings that have been abandoned. Farther on, the gypsies who live here are called People of the Flood since the river has overflowed and destroyed the area several times. The river is not done with us, either. Eventually, it will overflow again. Like those Indonesians who live near active volcanoes, we didn't have the money to leave, so we lived breathing in death and danger.

Our barrio is the result of a government real estate scam. The government wanted the gypsies out of their houses in Triana. It had adjoining patios that enhanced the contact between families, which our culture is based on and which gives us our strength as a people. So, the government offered to build new homes for us and buy our old properties. Naively, we agreed to it, and the 3,000 apartments—crowded and physically separate that together look like a bombed-out pit in a war zone–are the result. The notorious photo of a donkey looking out of an apartment window comes from our famous barrio. The owner kept the donkey outside in an empty field during the day–his former house had a lawn with a small stable–but he had no choice but to put the donkey in a room of his apartment at night or it would run away or be stolen. Now, when an apartment house for gypsies goes up anywhere in Spain, people claim to see a donkey looking out a window.

Las Tres Mil Viviendas is also notorious for drug abuse and crime. It well deserves its reputation for drug abuse. Spain's gypsies gave up their wandering lifestyle a century ago and mainly worked as farm hands in the countryside during the nineteenth and early twentieth centuries. As those jobs disappeared, they came to live in urban shantytowns where drug dealing was often the main way to earn a living. So, if you were walking through our barrio, you would see walled gardens, many of which are barred cages to keep out addicts, drug lords, and gangs. Moving on, you would come upon a wasteland that leads to a fence with a hole in it. Over the hole is a sign that says "Church," and through the hole is a nearly empty building with a basement for gypsies who have just shot up. I'm told there are pictures of Christ on the walls. You'll see a lot of emaciated junkies around there with bandaged limbs. They're called *los mutilados*, the mutilated ones. The worst spot for drugs, though, is the section called Las Vegas, but I've never been there. Church and the mutilated ones were quite enough for me: I didn't need any more local color.

As to our reputation for crime, I don't know what to say. Sure, you can find gangs of young gypsy boys who sometimes set bonfires on the street. Occasionally, they attack the cars of strangers driving through, break windows, demand money. But if you're just walking through, and particularly if you live here, the crime rate is no worse than any other area called a "project." There are people on the street all the time, day and night. You see lines of colorful washing everywhere, and what I do love is that you hear flamenco music everywhere. It's pouring out of kitchen windows, bars, bedroom windows, open doors of houses, street corners. A gypsy can just start singing and instantly others join in, beating out the rhythms we've all learned as children. Inspiration is catching, and a full performance, or *juerga*, can start anywhere. Gypsies start and stop whenever *la ganga*, the urge, comes upon them.

On the street, we finally have the direct contact with others that we need, though the government built us a Civic Center for that purpose. The foundation or skeleton was built first, of course, and then the rest was just forgotten for many years. That's how much the government wanted to restore our group identity. The name, *El Esquelito*, stuck. No one goes there. So much for life in a skeleton.

MY FATHER, WHO I never knew, was a strange gypsy. He spent most of his time reading and writing. My aunt, his sister who lived with us, was a big reader, too. There were books all over the walls, and a number of his stories about gypsy life had been published. He earned a small income teaching other gypsies to read and write, though he taught them for nothing if they couldn't pay. He sang flamenco, too, but he wasn't the professional my mother was. According to my mother, he was very gentle but prone to intense and uncontrollable depressions. Eventually he became a drug addict like so many other gypsy men.

When he went to prison for the first time, my mother visited him as much as she could. They would sing flamenco together through the bars in their low, throaty voices and they always set the place on fire. There were so many gypsy prisoners thumping out rhythms and crying out, that they had a full *juerga* every time. The whole prison loved my mother's visits. My father couldn't tolerate prison at all, though, and he died of a drug overdose shortly after being incarcerated. My mother had tried to keep him alive with music, but she could not erase so much despair. She always said that he was a great man in his way, and she very much respected him, but he was not strong enough to live the life of a gypsy. My mother never took drugs, she said, because she had her music and me, and no amount of sorrow could take them away.

Later, when she had more money, we moved to *Cerro Blanco*, another crumbling gypsy barrio but much more pleasant than *Les Tres Mil Viviendas*. All those books went with us, because I was an avid reader by then and wanted to be a writer like my father, though I had never known him. We were happy there, but after a while my mother developed cancer and died. I always wondered what might have been in the river when it overflowed and in the soil at *Les Tres Mil Viviendas*, but how can you ever know a thing like that? I eventually sold the house, went to the university and graduated, which would have made my mother fiercely proud. I would give anything to hear the song she would have sung about it!

When I think of my mother now, I see her face surrounded by vivid sounds, music, floating colors, strangely beautiful lights that haunt me. I don't know why I always see her that way; my mind just creates it. But in this world, there has never been a color or a light or a sound as vivid as my mother.

LIFELONG LESBIAN
BEV JO

Bev Jo is a working-class Butch, ex-catholic, mostly of European descent, with some Native American ancestry. She's from poverty class culture, a Lifelong Lesbian, born near Cincinnati, Ohio in 1950. She became lovers with her first lover in 1968, became part of a Lesbian community in 1970, and became a Dyke Separatist in 1972. She's worked on some of the earliest Lesbian Feminist projects, such as the Lesbian Feminist Conference in Berkeley in 1972, and the newspaper "Dykes and Gorgons" in 1973. (See more below). Her work is in several journals and anthologies, including *For Lesbians Only, Finding the Lesbians, Lesbian Friendships, Amazones d'Hier, Lesbiennes Aujourd'hui, Mehr als das Herz Gebrochen, The Journal for Lesbian Studies, Lesbian Ethics,* and *Sinister Wisdom.* She's named in the book, *Feminists Who Changed America, 1963 to 1975.*

With Linda Strega and Ruston, she co-wrote our book, *Dykes-Loving-Dykes: Dyke Separatist Politics for Lesbians Only,* available online at her blog. They focused on figuring out how to improve Lesbian Feminist communities and relationships in ways no one else has done.

She's currently working on a full history of her Lesbian life. She's also writing a book about how fear of nature leads to hatred of nature and is part of why men are destroying the world. She leads nature wildflower and wild animal hikes to share a love of nature. She records these with photographs, at her Facebook page. The following piece is memoir.

I'M A LIFELONG Lesbian and proud of my choice. My life's work is defending Lesbian culture and existence from those who oppress us. Our Lesbian history is being erased and re-written. Lesbians who weren't even born in the seventies tell us what my old seventies Lesbian Feminist community was like as if they were there. Even worse, men pretending to be Lesbians are writing books about our history, completely distorting communities as well as reality. We have to be the ones to tell the history about our own culture and people before it's too late.

It's natural for girls to love other girls, but we are punished if we are discovered. Some young Lesbians' lives are destroyed. Some are institution-alized and killed. Meanwhile, girls who choose boys are rewarded and gain status.

I could not, would not stop loving other girls. Nothing was going to make me be interested in the boys who harassed and attacked me and other girls, and who often tortured, sexually assaulted, and killed animals.

I was in love with other girls from my earliest memories, when I was three years old. That powerful force distracted me from the fear and boredom of my working class girlhood. Soon after starting catholic school, I fell in love with Rosemary when I was five and she was ten. One day I told my mother about her and she said, "You're in love with that girl!" And so I had a name for my intense feelings. I told Rosemary I wanted to kiss her. Years later, I realized she was another rare Butch little girl like myself, paying the price for refusing the rules of male-identified femininity. But we were just trying to be our natural wild female selves, which was forbidden in 1955 Cincinnati. We had no books, no beloved Lesbians on television, not one positive image (like now). But there were still Lesbian-hating characters and comments in the media.

As a girl, I had been confused that the definition of "Lesbian" was only about "sex." I didn't identify with feeling "sexual" because it was a cold, het, and male-identification, which had nothing to do with the love I felt for other girls. I don't feel a passionate attraction to Lesbians without a strong love or an in love connection. For example, I find "Lesbian" striptease and burlesque and sado-masochism to be repulsive and boring.

Most women who choose males first loved females but then opted for the privilege of heterosexuality. I've seen these women later dismiss and trivialize those few of us who, alone and without support, chose our own kind early on, as "lucky." But luck had nothing to do with this decision made at great risk, and which branded us as unacceptable, abnormal outcasts and permanently traumatized us.

As oppressed as we were by classism, in my neighborhood we were still in a community with others reflecting us back to ourselves. But most young Lesbians are completely isolated as Lesbians during our most vulnerable years. It's even worse for Butch girls, who are so recognizable as young Lesbians and never fit in as "normal." Yet we daily re-made the same decision, following our hearts against oppression and hatred, to love our own kind. Some of us didn't survive.

I continued falling in love, which made life worth living, like breathing the magic scent of fresh air after the rain, like plants blooming after a drought, like tasting life itself. When I started high school at thirteen, I fell in love with Ann, who became my best friend. I loved her wit and perceptive dark eyes, and how she questioned everything, including our religious training. But my parents moved me from Ohio to California, separating us.

When we were sixteen, Ann came to stay with me for two magical weeks. We spent every day together, going to the ocean, sleeping together each night, talking endlessly. I told her I loved her, and she said she loved me too, but later she pointed to the men's restroom, asking if I wanted to use it. I was both horrified and terrified that she interpreted my loving another girl with wanting to be a prurient man.

Ann decided that to have a good life she needed to find a lucrative career as well as a husband so she was trying to teach herself to learn what didn't come naturally, which was to flirt with boys. I never forgot what a calculated, cold decision that was. When I saw her twenty years later, she was miserable and divorced, but with a career, money, and security that I would never have. She told me she had been too afraid to respond to loving me, but now she was ready to try being a Lesbian. I had a lover then, and Ann's beautiful, intense glow was gone, replaced by a sad, lonely, hard, emptiness. I still have the photos of her from our early days together, so it's not just my memory. What a waste of her brilliance and passion.

I soon made friends at my new high school and some girls seemed to be in love with other girls too. But they slowly realized they would get more approval and status if they started talking about boys, though it didn't come naturally to them. I still kept falling in love with other girls, but when I was seventeen, questioned myself about why I didn't fall in love with girls who would be courageous enough to love me back, and realized that I was in love with my best friend, Marg. I'd made a conscious decision to love a girl who I trusted to be kind and caring. So I do know that we can escape the trap of being attracted to those who don't deserve or reciprocate our love.

Like with Ann, I loved Marg's wit and willingness to think and question. We also talked about our alcoholic mothers, though I was allowed much more freedom than Marg, who was barely allowed to go anywhere. In the fall, I started going to the University of San Francisco, but went back home each weekend to be with Marg. She soon fell in love with me too and wrote me beautiful love songs. We had never felt such ecstasy. Without any book or person to support us, we followed our feelings and hearts, and knew exactly how to make love. Het men and women's determination to prevent most girls from ever experiencing that ecstatic mutual first love together seems like a universal patriarchal female-hating plan, just as does the plot across the earth where men and boys work together to sexually harass all females and sexually assault most of us.

Both Marg and I were underage, and her bitter, fanatically religious mother watched how we looked into each other's eyes. (Much later, I remembered her also making bizarre, sexually inappropriate comments to me). We had so little time together—a few magical trips to the ocean, a few times with our friends, a few nights in her room, and one safe night in my room when we listened to the rain outside and talked about how someday we wanted to make love in the rain when we were finally free. Our passion and life force were opened up and we were desperate to be together.

But Marg's mother searched her room and found my letters. After that, we were forbidden to see each other ever again. My father, embarrassed, told me what happened. My mother wasn't told, but said, years later, that she would have beaten up Marg's mother if she'd known and heard her say bad things about me.

Our closest friend, Jean, helped us to keep writing and meeting secretly. But, in desperation, Marg met me only to run away to Jean's mother, who was a social worker. She was the only adult we spoke to about our relationship. I'll never forget the pain in Jean's mother's eyes as she told us how she had once loved another girl too, but now was happy she had stopped or she would never have had her husband and daughters. The irony was that she was so visibly contemptuous of them and couldn't even say she loved her daughters without qualifying it by saying in spite of how they looked. Yet, she warned us, "You must never start making love or you won't be able to stop, and then you'll have such a terrible lonely life."

Like the other het women we knew, she was desperately lonely. We had never known why she was so unhappy until that moment when she told us about her lost Lesbian love from when she was a girl.

Marg went home, my new letters were found again, and I wondered how Marg let that happen. Did she want us to be discovered? I'd transferred to go to a school she wanted to attend, which was hours away and a place I dreaded, starting out alone and lonely again while Marg was kept from leaving her parents' house. (Her parents did win in the end. Marg never married, but is now an extreme right wing fundamentalist christian).

Another thing that made it very hard for me as a young Lesbian has continued to this day in a way I never would have imagined, which is that the men who joked that they were male Lesbians and wanted to fuck Lesbians are now accepted as actual Lesbians. This is one of the most destructive forces in our Lesbian communities.

While at the University of San Francisco, in 1968, a man kept pushing me to be his girlfriend. He had no understanding of, nor respect for, my being in love with my best friend. In spite of feeling repulsed, I made the mistake of feeling sorry for him and tried to be friends, but he acted like I somehow belonged to him, and soon became obsessed with Lesbians, even though he'd never known we existed and had never questioned his own being male. As he went after other Lesbians, he decided to claim to be a Lesbian. He later stalked me into the Lesbian community and immediately got into power positions as a "Lesbian."

He was elected vice president of the Daughters of Bilitis, which was the first Lesbian civil rights organization in the U.S., formed in 1955, and he basically destroyed the San Francisco chapter in 1971. Then he was invited to "sing" at the West Coast Lesbian Conference in 1973, and he later lied to "off our backs," the feminist newspaper, to get them to print his article, "Lesbian Sex." Unlike now, where our communities have been almost destroyed, most Lesbians were outraged at the arrogance of a man saying he was a Lesbian and erasing real Lesbians. His identifying as a "Lesbian" was even more upsetting since he writes racist letters and is a porny sado-masochist.

He still makes it impossible for me to safely go to our few "women only" spaces in the Bay Area. The last time I went to women's open mic to read poetry, I was subjected to his usual off-key "singing," but this time his lyrics were about a woman crawling on the floor, desperate to reach his "kitty cat" (pussy). He's an example of how forty-five years of being on estrogen and in a Lesbian community doesn't begin to change men into women.

Women putting men before women by supporting these men is destroying our last women only spaces and is one of the most destructive things happening to our Lesbian communities worldwide.

I kept searching for others like us. I went to a Daughters of Bilitis (DOB) meeting and a Lesbian bar, but I was underage at eighteen. DOB was the first lesbian civil and political rights organization. It was formed in 1955. In 1970, when I was nineteen, I finally found the Lesbian Feminist community of the San Francisco Bay Area. It was like falling in love again—there were more of us than I could ever have dreamed possible, with a blossoming of creativity that included Lesbian music, concerts, poetry, books, and newspapers. I'll never forget the thrilling ecstasy of the women only dances. In spite of all the pain and oppression, Lesbians survive and continue. It's a celebration that never ends. Our choice to be Lesbians was, and remains, a choice of pride.

I joined the collective for A Woman's Place Bookstore, which first opened in Oakland, CA in 1972. I was also part of the collective that created one of the first Lesbian Feminist Conferences in the world in 1972 in Berkeley. I worked on the first issue of *Amazon Quarterly*, and I became a Dyke Separatist in 1972.

Separatism is about choosing Lesbians and women when we have the option, and saying no to contact with males. There are different kinds of Dyke Separatists, but we are not a privileged elite who live in the country. That is a classist stereotype. In spite of how Separatism has been slandered by many feminists and other Lesbians, it was still the basic politics that built feminist culture and our movement. Women only space was a given—and a relief from the men perving on us. In patriarchy, where men are destroying the earth, with species going daily extinct, being a Dyke Separatist makes the most sense also in terms of the safety and happiness of all females. If all women became Separatists (even celibate Separatists) when I did, most of the problems that are now catastrophic would not exist.

In 1973, I co-wrote and published one of the first Dyke Separatist newspapers, *Dykes and Gorgons*. I also worked on the Lesbian Coffeehouse collective, went to an all women's dojo, taught self-defense to women and girls for ten years, worked to organize Dyke Separatist gatherings, made connections with Lesbian Separatists in other countries, and lived for a while with my lovers in Aotearoa (New Zealand), England, and Ireland. I continued writing articles for Lesbian publications and anthologies. In 1990, I co-wrote our book, *Dykes-Loving-Dykes: Dyke Separatist Politics for Lesbians Only*, with Linda Strega and Ruston, which I updated twenty-five years later and which is now available online at my blog, along with new articles.

As I wrote in the beginning of our book:

> *The story of Lesbianism is the story of magic and survival. In almost every part of the world, we're either said not to exist, or we're hated and lied about. Yet we persist in surviving. Lesbians come from every culture and country. We appear where there are no others of us, coming from people who try their hardest to make us committed man-lovers. We create ourselves out of nothing, appearing like weeds that cannot be destroyed. We crack open the foundations of the enormous structures of male supremacy.*

It's terrible to see constant assaults on our once powerful Lesbian Feminist community. "Women Studies" at colleges have almost all been destroyed and replaced by "Gender Studies" or "Queer Studies," which are often run by men pretending to be Lesbians. The term "LGBT" includes us against our will with our oppressors, Gay and bisexual men, bisexual women, and het men (the "T"). Organizations which are supposed to be for Lesbian rights focus more on helping men who claim to be women, or even more outrageously, who claim to be Lesbians.

But it will never be as bad as it was before Lesbian Feminism even existed. We will not return to the time when Lesbians were categorized as mentally ill by psychiatrists, imprisoned, given drugs, shock treatments, and lobotomies. No longer can anyone say they don't know we exist. We have an enormous international Radical Lesbian Feminist community that includes all ages. On Facebook alone, I moderate five groups for Radical Feminists, with hundreds of members ranging in age from twenty to seventy-five.

Lesbians are involved in larger numbers than other people in various organizations fighting for people and animals and every cause imaginable, but it's time for Lesbians to also fight for Lesbians.

In the midst of mourning what we have lost historically, I'm also seeing what we still have. Though we are not allowed to have women-only space without guilt-tripping, shaming, and rape and death threats from men claiming to be women, we still meet in public spaces, at concerts, dances, films. Very few of my new friends even know basic Feminism, yet, like in the early days, most came out because of their love for other women.

I still see a love and warmth and community among Lesbians that is beautiful. Let's bask in the warmth of all of us as Lesbians and keep our culture thriving.

Additional Resources

My blog, with most of our book, *Dykes-Loving-Dykes* and newer articles can be found here. Our chapter four is about Butch oppression: https://bevjoradicallesbian.wordpress.com/

For more links about how the trans cult harms women and Lesbians: http://bevjoradicallesbian.wordpress.com/2014/07/22/please-if-you-love-lesbians-and-other-women-think-about-this/

There are a lot of troll/fake "feminist" groups on Facebook, including some run by government agents, but the groups I moderate are truly Radical Feminist. They are:
The Radical Feminist Coffee House, Womyn-Born-Womyn Radical Feminist Warriors, Lesbians for Lesbians, The Harmful Transgender Agenda, Dykes-Loving-Dykes Discussion Group (co-moderated with Megan Mackin).

This website is a list of old Lesbian and Separatist classics. Keep scrolling or click to the next page to continue: www.lesbianseparatist.tumblr.com

A FEMINIST BUTCH IS NOT AN OXYMORON
LENN KELLER

Lenn Keller is an African American, butch lesbian feminist, and earth citizen. She was born a tomboy and raised in the northern suburbs of Chicago. She has lived in New York City, Chicago, and since arriving in Northern California from Chicago in 1975 as a single mother, has been primarily based in the Bay Area. She is a multi-disciplinary artist, activist, and cosmic explorer. A few things she finds expression in and is passionate about are archiving, curating, design, photography, filmmaking, music, oral history, promoting, and writing. She is the founder of the Bay Area Lesbian History Archives Project, based in Oakland, CA. Her essay included in this anthology is part memoir. Her work and visual art can be viewed at www.lennkeller.com.

CONSCIOUSLY CLAIMING A gender identity can be a complex process that for some happens during childhood, for others during adolescence, or at later points in their lives, and for some it may never happen. Gender identity as I understand it, is how you experience, behave, represent, and think about yourself related to your biological sex. Reflecting back on my own process around claiming a gender identity, I can now clearly see why it was difficult for me to accept and claim being butch (female, lesbian, masculine) when I first came out as a lesbian feminist in the mid 1970s.

I choose female, lesbian, and masculine for my self-descriptors because I don't see "femininity" or "masculinity" attached to the body. I know most people use "masculine" to refer to male bodies and "feminine" for female ones. But I don't do that. I believe both feminine and masculine energies can be expressed through any body (female, male, intersex) and I believe everyone has a ratio of both energies (yin/yang). I also believe most people have more of one than the other and a very few folks have equal amounts.

In 1974, the year that I chose to "come out of the closet," the gay liberation and women's liberation movements were less than ten years old. I was aware of what was going on with feminism, and I was definitely down with it, but wasn't directly involved yet.

I was living in Chicago, a closeted, bohemian, black, single mom with a three-year-old daughter trying my best to be straight, and failing miserably at it. I lived in a building that was literally a few yards from Lake Michigan. The building was full of activists, hippies, Hari Krishnas, and other counter-culture types.

I was working at an educational publishing company, and hanging out with musicians, artists, and a spiritual community when I wasn't working. A few years prior, I had started a meditation practice, was studying metaphysics and comparative religion, and I'd gotten involved with the Bahai faith. I was just ending a year of celibacy and was going through the classic angst and confusion that typically precedes coming out.

Now, I have been a "tomboy" for as long as I can remember, and though my masculinity was never validated, from the time I was very small, I remember feeling like a different kind of girl, and just as masculine as my younger brothers and many of the boys I regularly played with. I found kindergarten stressful when I saw that the toys had been separated based on gender. I knew I'd have to pretend that I didn't want to play with the trucks, Legos, and Lincoln Logs. Fortunately, I could play with "boys" toys at home. Whatever! Toys are toys. I didn't have many role models, except for the few I saw on TV, like Annie Oakley, Zelda on Dobie Gillis, or the asexual Miss Hathaway on the Beverly Hillbillies.

The summer before fourth grade, my mom died, so I was raised by my father. I have two younger brothers, which made me the lone female in the family. I believe growing up in a mostly male household served to make me militantly proud of being female.

Starting in elementary school, I remember having secret crushes on some of my friends, various girls at school, movie stars like Natalie Wood and a couple of my teachers. By sixth grade, I was clear on the concept that I was supposed to be liking boys and was aware that it wouldn't be a good idea to let anyone know that I was having sexual feelings for girls. Junior high was awkward. I still had a little leeway, but that summer before my freshman year of high school, the heat was on to start "acting like a girl." The pressure to date boys had built to a nightmarish degree.

I tried to comport myself the way most of my friends did, and the way I knew I was expected to as a teenage girl. I tried to cultivate an interest in *Seventeen Magazine*, and I ditched the clothes I had grown comfortable wearing–dickies under my button-down shirts, mock turtlenecks and plaid pleated skirts with bobbie socks and boys' Keds. Despite being really good at sports, I was terrorized by the locker room and showers, fearing that I might uncontrollably stare at some girl's breasts. I lived in constant fear that someone would notice I was "kinda funny." I had read somewhere that girls can go through a homosexual phase, so I hoped and prayed that my impending lesbianism was something I'd grow out of–that I'd wake up one day magically transformed into a nice, normal big lady. Though I never had dreams of being a bride or a wife, I thought that because I enjoyed hanging out with boys, there was still a chance for me. I'd figure something out. It was too much for me to bear—the thought of possibly being that most damned of creatures, a bulldagger, as they called us in the black community. That would mean I was both a pervert and a failed (i.e. non feminine) female. Not good!

Now racism, of all things, came to the rescue—it saved me from the pressures of dating in high school. After our house was foreclosed on during my freshman year, my father moved us into an apartment nearby, in a very affluent suburb of Chicago, where there were very few black families. There were only four black kids in my class of over a thousand students—two girls and two boys. White boys didn't generally date black girls at that time (the mid sixties), which meant I was spared the horrors of compulsory heterosexuality for the rest of high school.

Life at home had become unbearable for my father and me. I knew I couldn't survive another second in that house with him. He was overbearing and abusive. My best female friend Max and I both dreamed of Harlem and Greenwich Village, so, we saved our babysitting money and made our getaway plan. A few weeks after I graduated high school, two black kids with 'fros, bell bottom jeans, and hippy sandals, boarded a Greyhound bus and ran away to New York City, not knowing a soul there. It was the same summer as Woodstock and Stonewall. I was seventeen and she was sixteen.

A couple weeks after landing in the Big Apple, I had the misfortune to cross paths with a guy who was hanging with some black activists we met in Harlem. They were squatting in protest at the site of the proposed state building. This guy was completely crazy and believed that raping me would feminize me. The rape was my first experience of sexual intercourse. I was kind of in a rage against men after that.

Soon after my eighteenth birthday, a few months after the rape, I got pregnant. After much initial denial, I came not only to accept it, but to embrace my pregnancy as an opportunity to raise a revolutionary. The thought has occurred to me that the trauma of my rape, my inability to accept my sexuality, and my insecurities about not being feminine enough, all possibly contributed to my getting pregnant at age eighteen.

A couple of months shy of my nineteenth birthday, I joyfully gave birth to my daughter. When she was less than a year old, I made the decision to leave New York and return to Chicago to raise her.

I remained a tomboy and from the ages of eighteen through twenty-two, I was intermittently involved with a few guys, more than a couple of whom were bisexual. I put myself through excruciating gyrations trying to look like a bonafide heterosexual, more than once pretending to like a guy who hung out with a guy who was hanging out with a girl that I wanted to be near.

By the time I was twenty-three, I was completely exhausted by the effort to be straight, and bursting at the seams to come out of the closet. I had been having recurring erotic dreams about women almost every night. Though the sexuality in my dreams was tame, it was profoundly powerful. Beautiful women kissing my forehead caused me to wake up on the verge of orgasm. When I awoke, I'd say to myself, "Okay, girlfriend, I believe you've got something to deal with here."

Inching up on accepting my lesbian sexuality, I took refuge for as long as I could in celibacy, while engaging in covert conversations with my "straight" girlfriends. I tried to be intellectual and very nonchalant about it all. While having tea, I'd casually bring up Anais Nin, and ask their views on bisexuality. I hoped they'd say they thought it was cool, so we could get into a discussion about it. A couple did admit experimentations, but much to my disappointment, they were dismissive of their experiences. They said things like, "Oh yeah, I tried that in college. It was okay."

Meanwhile, I remained conflicted about my sexuality. One day, hanging in downtown Chicago on State Street, I saw two gorgeous young black women holding hands and gazing into each other's eyes. Something inside me clicked, and a voice screamed inside my head, "Yes! This is it! This is beautiful! This is right! This is who I am!" In that moment, I made the decision to come out of the closet, and it was one of the most liberating moments of my life. After that, I became desperate to meet other lesbians. Despite the fact that I lived in the city, I was completely isolated and in the dark about where to find them.

Not long after that, I was browsing in Kroch's & Brentano's bookstore, when I came across a copy of *Sappho Was A Right On Woman*, the lesbian classic from 1972. After paging through it for a few minutes, I knew I had to have it. I took the book up to the counter and, still coming into my new identity, endured the embarrassment of having the young white male clerk assume I was a lesbian. I couldn't drive home fast enough to dig into it and I stayed up most of the night reading.

That book became my Bible. It validated and affirmed me in ways that I had been wanting all of my life, and confirmed so much that I had thought about yet wrestled with in isolation. Soon afterward, I somehow found out about a lesbian support group, which I promptly went to. I checked out the lesbian "uniform" that everyone there seemed to be wearing. After that, I quickly dispensed with my bohemian/hippy unisex look, and donned my dyke uniform—flannel shirt, t-shirt, Levis and Frye boots, so the dykes about town, wherever they were, could easily spot me. Despite my already well established status as the office weirdo, everyone at work was shocked at my changed presentation.

Things started happening really fast after that. I was tight with this cool black straight woman who also worked at the publishing company. She was always telling me about a female cousin of hers who she said I should meet because she thought we had a lot in common. I didn't understand what she meant by that, but finally the cousin who had been living in Denver returned home. One day after work, my friend dropped by my apartment with her cousin and I could not believe my eyes. She was a foxy, chocolate brown sister with a wild Afro, and huge magnetic eyes. She was fine. She was very feminine and had a bohemian style—she wore red lipstick, a hippie dress, and cowboy boots. She was irreverent, brainy, witty, eccentric, sexy and flamboyant, and I was a goner.

My co-worker friend couldn't stay long, so during my brief conversation with her cousin, I did my best to impress her with my knowledge about jazz and a musician that was coming to town. I could tell she liked me. She invited me over for lunch, and I accepted without hesitation. She lived about ten minutes from where I worked, so it was convenient for me to visit her during my lunch hour.

The first time we had lunch together, she made us delicious grilled cheese sandwiches. We took them up to her bedroom to eat, and I was so turned on by her I could barely contain myself. We sat on her bed and talked about everything, books, music, and as it turned out we had a lot of common interests. I also discovered that she was a feminist. I'd always had a strong intuition about things, but I was inexperienced, and my gaydar was still developing, so although I was ready to roll, I wasn't one hundred percent sure she was into women. When she went downstairs to get us something to drink, I noticed a book face down on her bed. It was *Our Bodies, Ourselves, 1st Edition,* and it was open to the chapter on lesbians. Taking this for a sign, or a surreptitious communication, I decided to make my move.

For reasons I didn't understand at the time, I felt completely confident in pursuing her. A day or two later, after some nervous procrastination, I mailed her a sexy cryptic note asking for a real date. She quickly wrote me back a witty reply accepting.

Sparks soon began to fly between us, as we went out to the movies, concerts, picnics at the Skokie Lagoons, and walks on the beaches of Lake Michigan. One weekend, she took me out bar hopping, and gave me a tour of all the lesbian bars in the city. What a mind blower it was to find out that right under my nose there was this whole lesbian culture with numerous bars, bookstores, cafes, and tons of cute dykes. She was a book junkie like myself and she turned me on to lots of books including, Rosa Guy's *Ruby*, Jill Johnston's *Lesbian Nation*, and Emma Goldman's *Living My Life.* She was sensuous, seductive, and impossibly flirtatious. Being with her was exhilarating. She inspired in me the full expression of sexual feelings I had been working hard to suppress since the sixth grade, when I used to run up to girls I had crushes on, and punch them in the arm, or smack them on the butt because that was the only kind of physical contact I knew how to safely have with them. At last, I didn't have to suppress what I wanted to do. Instead, I could feel with every fiber of my being that all she wanted was for me to ravish her.

Even though neither of us would have said it, we both knew that I was decidedly more masculine and she more feminine. We were attracted to each other in part because of our gender difference, even if we didn't realize it, know how to think about it, name it, or even be with it.

We dated for a few months, then she left for college in California and I joined her about six months later, landing first in Santa Cruz just after New Year's, 1975. Six months later, I re-located to the Bay Area because my daughter was about to start school and there were no kids of color where we had been living.

I'm sure there must have been some, but I don't remember knowing any feminist dykes during that period who were thinking and talking about gender differences among lesbians. I think most of us were so preoccupied with coming out, dealing with our sexuality as lesbians or bisexuals, and being P.C. that we didn't get around to looking at lesbian gender differences.

Given feminist concerns at the time, it's understandable that the butch-femme dynamic was mis-read, demonized, and largely excluded from the lesbian feminist community. During the mid-to-late seventies, most feminist theory was coming from white middle-class women and their take on sexuality was a lot different than most working class lesbians and lesbians of color, whose communities continued in the bars. Even now, many lesbians (feminist or not) have ambivalent or negative feelings about both butch-femme, and using the terms "masculinity" and "femininity." For many lesbian feminists during the seventies, concepts of "femininity" and "masculinity" were associated with the heterosexist gender roles that were being rejected.

"Feminine" attire and expression was equated with patriarchal oppression, so long hair, lipstick, dresses, and heels were rejected as being the expression of women who wanted to please and appeal to men. Perhaps because more masculine-appearing women had historically made lesbians visible, we accepted the myth that all lesbians are to some degree "masculine." So it was okay to be "dykey" looking. At the same time, the contradiction was that lesbian feminists were only allowed to be "dykey" or "masculine" within certain sanctioned limits—so that you didn't appear to be "male identified," which was definitely not P.C. Concepts of masculinity and femininity were not acknowledged or deconstructed, nor re-defined from their patriarchal definitions. So the possibility that some women regardless of their sexual orientation, could simply prefer a "feminine" expression for their own empowerment and self pleasure did not occur to us. The ideal dyke gender performance and presentation at that time was to be "androgynous," that is, to express an equal blending of feminine and masculine energies.

Those of us who were naturally inclined to express and present ourselves in decidedly more feminine or masculine ways did our best to meet the prescribed standards of "politically correct" feminist dyke comportment in appearance and yes, sexuality.

One of my girlfriends and I were the same size and we could wear each other's clothing. With our gender difference unconsciously understood but unspoken, she would freely wear my shirts, but I never borrowed from her wardrobe, which included many feminine-looking items.

We joked about it, but we never talked about why I would never have, for example, chosen one of her colorful flowered strappy t-shirts, or long flowing skirts. We had no language to think or talk about our gender differences, despite the yin/yang energy between us being palpable and unmistakable. We simply did not have permission to frame ourselves within a butch-femme dynamic. Likewise, there was almost no space for us within the context of the mid-to-late seventies Bay Area lesbian feminist community to acknowledge or claim butch-femme identities or dynamics. As a result, my girlfriend and I, and others of us who might have claimed these identities, were at that time unable to be our full authentic selves or to express our deepest erotic yearnings.

I had already learned from books like *Sappho Was A Right On Woman* that butches and femmes were not P.C. and were *personae non grata* in the lesbian feminist community. Some of the typical things I heard from my friends about butch-femme was that butches and femmes were "old timey" lesbians who were ignorant. The younger ones who were into "roles" or "acted" that way just didn't know any better. I was also told that butch-femme was nothing more than a poor imitation of heterosexist gender roles, so my thought was, "What feminist dyke in her right mind would want to perpetuate that?" I'd had very little contact with butch lesbians, and what I'd heard about them was all negative. I'd heard that they were "male identified," looked too much like men (i.e. wore clothes not on the approved "dyke gear" list, such as men's hats, suits, ties, etc.), and that they were macho, controlling, domineering, sexist, gruff, uncommunicative, emotionally inaccessible, into car mechanics, motorcycles, and football. I'd heard that they didn't have children, and didn't cook, etc. Even though with my shoulder-length dreadlocks, I myself was often mistaken for a boy, I had a child, and was unable to relate to the other stereotypes I'd heard. So I concluded I couldn't possibly be a butch.

Yes, I was attracted to feminine women, but what I was told a femme was supposed to be was also quite negative. Femmes, I was told, were supposed to be passive, sexually submissive, manipulative sell outs. I had also been told that they were not to be trusted because they wore lipstick, long hair, heels, nails, and dresses only to gain special favor with sexist men and the butches who acted like those men. Consequently, for many years I was very conflicted about being attracted to feminine women. I compromised by allowing myself to "track for" and be with women who had feminine energy, but who did their best to dress and comport themselves in accordance with the lesbian feminist dress code.

Neither myself nor my peers could conceive that a feminist dyke could be naturally predisposed to appropriating and performing codes of femininity or masculinity for her personal expression, empowerment, and enjoyment, as well as a way to signal a specific kind of sexual desire for another woman. We didn't realize that the concepts we were holding about "femininity" and "masculinity" had been defined for us by a patriarchal system. Why couldn't we just appropriate them and define them for ourselves? So, in a zealous haste to dispense with anything that even remotely resembled a heterosexist model, we were unable to see anything redeemable or authentic about the butch-femme dynamic.

I think there are also other factors that have caused many lesbians, then and now, to misread femmes, butches, and the butch-femme dynamic. Some haven't learned to recognize energetic differences in people of the same sex. They are not aware that the attraction of complementary energies can exist in any sexual orientation, not just within heterosexuality. That's another myth we've all been taught to believe is the norm.

I think some of the lesbians who came of age in lesbian culture during the 1950s and 1960s had justifiably negative feelings toward butch-femme because they were pressured into choosing one identity or the other whether they resonated with them or not, which is also oppressive. Audre Lorde expressed this in 1982, in her biomythography, *Zami: A New Spelling of My Name.* It is true, that some who do identify as femme or butch can behave in ways that are imitative of heterosexist roles, because they have internalized sexism and misogyny, and/or they have no feminist butch-femme role models. Like, the fact that there are butches and studs who relate to femmes like a sexist man relates to a woman. Or, the femmes who expect and demand unhealthy masculinities from butches. Yes, all of that can exist with butch-femme, but those are stereotypes.

Additionally, a lot of early lesbian feminist theory came primarily from middle and upper middle class white women and it was often embedded with the assumptions and repressive sexual attitudes characteristic of their culture and class.

Class was another factor that caused the butch-femme dynamic to be rejected primarily by white lesbian feminists. It's notable that butch-femme culture has remained visible in many working class and lesbian of color communities throughout the country during the 1970s, and it continues to the present day. It can often present itself with heterosexist elements, which butch-femme has been stereotyped to be entirely based in. Classism and racism meant that many working class lesbians and lesbians of color were not included in lesbian feminist communities. They were either rejected or they were not exposed to feminist theory generated by white women. At the same time, many lesbian feminists were only able to perceive the surface expression of butch-femme couples. They were unable to see what was really going on, or to consider the possibility that despite the existence of sexism in some cases, that the butch-femme dynamic could also be regarded as an authentic erotic dynamic of its own; that is, an erotic dance expressed between two women, based on complementary gender energies, expression, and sexual desires.

While many lesbians were trying to heal and liberate themselves sexually, certain standards had become a part of seventies lesbian feminist culture. Many believed that politically correct sex could be prescribed, and it actually was. Certain sexual practices (penetration, frottage, or tribadism for example) and certain ways of thinking about sex were considered politically incorrect because of their conflation with sexist heterosexuality.

Throughout those years, I had moments of awareness when I knew that how we were looking at sexuality and gender wasn't quite right, but I couldn't articulate it. For example, there was the occasion when one of my girlfriends and I were at a lesbian and gay speaker's bureau gig at a local high school. An astute teenage boy in the class asked me if I was the guy, and she the girl. Of course, being there to educate people in the most P.C. fashion possible, I quickly replied no. I said that we were women in an equal relationship, and that we weren't into playing roles, which was true. Still, after saying it, I felt conflicted, feeling deep down that my statement was not completely true. I knew there was more to our dynamic, but I didn't know how to think about, or articulate our gender differences. This not knowing troubled me for years.

And then there was the time that another girlfriend went with me to a card party in San Francisco. Everyone was gathered in the kitchen, and much to our surprise, the room was filled with butch and femme couples, also in their twenties and early thirties. Most of the butches were seated at the two tables, slamming down cards, cursing, and laughing. It was the femmes who were bringing them food and drinks, or sitting on the side lines laughing and talking to each other.

We took in the scene, and gave each other one of those knowing looks that said, "What the hell is this?" I knew some of the women there from around town, and one of the black butches who was playing cards, greeted me. She looked me and my girlfriend up and down, and said something about butch-femme. Then she asked me, "So, you a butch? What's your story?" Surveying the room again, I looked at her, smiled and said in a somewhat superior tone, "No, I'm not into that. We're not into roles." She chuckled, rolled her eyes, and looked at me like, "Yeah, whatever. You'll figure it out." Little did I know how prophetic that moment would prove to be. It took me over a decade to figure out and accept that I was butch and that I was and had always been attracted to femmes. I think now that some of what I saw in the kitchen that day were expressions of butch-femme dynamics of play that I didn't understand, and also, some that were sexist and just didn't work for me.

So, during the 1980s and most of the '90s, though I was having intense sexual and deeply intimate relationships with women, I spent many confused and agonizing years continuing to suppress my butch lesbian identity and sexuality and not fully understanding what I was really wanting in a lover. Only in retrospect have I been able to understand why this happened, and how much my life has been impacted by fear of discrimination and violence, homophobia, butchphobia, sexism, misogyny, and repressed sexuality. I have come to realize how much my relationships suffered because of my and my partners' inability to fully acknowledge, accept, claim, and present our gender identities, and just be the way we really desired to be with ourselves and each other.

The 1980s became famous for the "sex wars"—a time of fierce debates in the feminist community among lesbian and bisexual women over a number of issues related to sex, including lesbian sexual practices, porn, and BDSM (bondage & domination, and sadomasochism).

As these debates were in full swing, BDSM practices were becoming more visible in the lesbian community and our community became divided over this issue. Samois, a lesbian feminist BDSM organization based in San Francisco, started in 1978. There were books published pro, such as *Macho Sluts* by Pat Califia and con, such as the anthology, *Against Sadomasochism*, a radical feminist anthology that came out in '82. The authors in this anthology saw sado-masochism as being rooted in "patriarchal sexual ideology." These fierce debates resulted in a polarization that was never resolved.

While these debates raged on, the prescriptive and repressive 1970s' standards around lesbian sexual practices were rapidly loosening their hold on us and there was a sexually liberating feeling in the air. Those who had been suppress-ing identities and desires not previously sanctioned began to tentatively express them.

Butch and femme identities and dynamics were being now defended by butch and femme identified lesbian feminist writers, cultural workers and activists, like Joan Nestle, Margaret Sloan, Cherie Moraga, and Jewelle Gomez. They were becoming vocal in challenging the negative assumptions that many lesbian feminists had accepted about butch-femme during the '70s.

The "lipstick lesbian" phenomenon that showed up during the mid '80s seemed to me, not so much a claiming of femme identities, as it was a practical response to the growing right-wing conservative economic and politi-cal climate in the U.S. With the presidential election of Ronald Reagan, and the passing of Prop. 13 (it reduced the property tax rate in California in 1980), for many lesbians, the country's economic base was shifting from a counter-culture orientation with non-profit sector jobs to a clearly more corporate one. Many lesbians decided they needed to go back to school and get more serious about their careers and their futures. It was clear, that in order to succeed in the business world, it would be necessary to conform as much as possible to gender presentation rules for women, which often meant wearing makeup or even dresses. Presenting in makeup and dresses is easy, even preferable for some lesbians. For others, it's doable, and for some of us, it's torturous and downright impossible short of the threat of death. During that time, many lesbians went back into the closet in order to survive in "professional" environments. I saw myself and other masculine lesbians struggling with negotiating our gender presentations in society and the professional world. I had a teenage daughter to support, and I was very worried about job discrimination, which also became social discrimination in the lesbian community. Some lesbians did not want to be socially or romantically associated with anyone who looked "too obvious." It was common to see personal ads that said, "No butches or alcoholics need apply." So my strategy, like a lot of butches at that time, was to present as feminine—or at least as much as we could stomach (Many blackmail worthy photos resulted from these attempts.) But that strategy for most of us proved to be unsustainable.

I believe as result of the "sex war" debates of the '80s, the 1990s became the decade of being "sex positive." In the San Francisco bar and club scene, those lesbians who were tentatively embracing their butch identities, began to gravitate more openly toward women who had been emboldened by the "lipstick lesbian" phenomenon. This was seen particularly in a lesbian-owned place called Clementina's Baybrick Inn in San Francisco, a popular spot on the weekdays for the "professional" crowd. It was a place where you could find lesbian feminists who were starting to express their "femininity" in ways they had always wanted to, but would never have dared to in the '70s. Now, they were also more openly signaling their attraction to masculine presenting women. There was a "high femme" woman I met at The Baybrick Inn, who I dated. I was attracted to her feminine energy and she was attracted to my butch energy, yet she would always insist I "soften" my look by dressing in tailored women's clothing instead of the men's clothing I had preferred. She'd sometimes put eye liner and lip gloss on me when we went out in public together. I allowed it to please her and because I was still fearful and conflicted about looking "too butch." But I wasn't at all comfortable doing it.

By the 1990s, the "sex positive" movement and butch-femme culture had fully emerged in lesbian clubs in the Bay Area. There were the Drag King contests put on by Aché, an African American lesbian organization, and a few clubs had opened that encouraged drag kings, butches, and femmes to come out in full regalia. One of them was called Club Confidential, where there were drag kings and butches who sported short-cropped hair cuts, suits, and ties, and femmes wore dresses, makeup, and heels. In these spaces lesbians were finally allowed to camp it up and boldly signal our butch-femme desire. It was also around this time that lesbians in significant numbers first began to transition "female to male" and to claim transgender identities.

I knew I was butch, but I continued to struggle with it. I was deeply conflicted and fearful of the consequences and repercussions of being a gender non-conforming lesbian. My experience was that because of the political atmosphere during the '70s, it was no big deal to present a gender non-conforming look as a dyke, but during the '80s as things got increasingly conservative, lesbians began moving more toward assimilation and going back into the closet. There was a lot more fear and expression of our internalized homophobia, which meant policing of our own presentations.

I was also aware that in the lesbian community, black lesbians in particular were often sexually objectified and assumed to be butch. In the early '90s, I moved from Oakland to escape the homophobia into San Francisco, where I experienced an alarming amount of blatant racism and sexual objectification in clubs and other lesbian social spaces. I was also still afraid of experiencing discrimination, hostility, and violence for being gender non-conforming. Those fears coupled with my resistance to being sexually objectified by other lesbians, were sources of confusion and internal conflict that further delayed my ability to claim a butch identity. It took a mind-blowing sexual experience with a self-identified femme to give me both the clarity and the courage to claim my butchness and my affinity with the butch-femme dynamic.

I attended the Femme Conference, held in San Francisco in 1998, and that increased my understanding of what I and many others had been struggling with. I realized that to me, a femme lesbian is more than just "feminine." She is a woman who has thought about her femininity and has made a conscious decision to claim and express her femininity the way she wants to because it's empowering for her to do so. I also realized that there are many erotic dynamics that are available to us and that the butch-femme dynamic is one of many.

So, in the late '90s, out I came again—this time as a proud feminist butch. For me that meant an embracing of the masculine energy that is natural to me and expressing that energy in ways that are comfortable and empowering for me, while also having a feminist, non-sexist, female loving consciousness.

The butch-femme erotic dynamic for me has been a continuing process of joy and self-discovery. It has been as liberating as when I first came out as a lesbian. Claiming butch as a feminist has made me a much freer and happier person, because I have given myself full permission to relate to the kind of women I have always been attracted to, and in the ways that I have always wanted to. Since claiming butch, I have felt more empowered and attractive than ever before in my life. I feel I'm my most authentic self now, by accepting and owning masculine energy expressed through my female body—that is my butchness. I see this acceptance as a radical act of self love, of liberation by resisting society's dictates of how I as a female should show up in the world. I'm busting through those limitations and claiming my female masculinity—embodying it, honoring it, and acknowledging it.

I can also now without hesitation affirm that I love and appreciate femme lesbians–feminine lesbians who are conscious and revel in their feminine power. I love being butch for a femme who loves and appreciates butches. I now know, and I want others to know, that it is possible to be in a butch-femme lesbian relationship that is not only not sexist, misogynist or homophobic, but one that has no power over dynamic and that is radically feminist. I know now that to be butch and feminist is not an oxymoron.

FIRST KISS
HEIDI LAMOREAUX

Heidi LaMoreaux has published in a wide variety of genres including a short play, creative non-fiction, and poetry. She has a Ph.D. in Physical Geography and is interested in overlaps of academic disciplines, particular science, writing, and art. Heidi has taught courses at The University of Georgia, in The Hutchins School of Liberal Studies at Sonoma State University and at Santa Rosa Junior College. Her contribution in this anthology is creative non-fiction.

LISA TURNS RIGHT unexpectedly to pull the Cougar into a parking lot entrance less than a mile from my house. I was expecting us to drive farther tonight. Usually we go downtown to The Grill, a '50s restaurant that never closes. I read the sign near the entrance as we drive into the lot, "Charter Winds."

"Charter Winds? As in the 'If you don't get help here, please get help somewhere' Charter Winds?"

"Yeah."

"Why here?"

"I figure there won't be much traffic at a place like this late at night."

"Makes sense." I grin. "But it is a mental hospital. You just never know."

"Yeah, especially this close to the holiday season."

The parking lot is empty except for a few cars parked near the hospital entrance. Lisa chooses a remarkably unilluminated space at the back end of the lot. You'd think Charter Winds would worry about poor lighting giving escapees a convenient cover of darkness. We can see the entire lot from where we're parked. No one can sneak up on us.

I glance at the trees to the right and the words *Liriodendron tulipifera* pop into my head. I wince. Even at night I can identify the trees. Another tree, its roots trying to escape an encircling confinement of bricks, recedes to a shadow as she turns off the headlights. I recognize the tree as a *Albizia julibrissin*, or mimosa. I can't turn off the science. Ever. I'm such a geek.

Lisa turns off the ignition and turns toward me.

"Come here you," she says. She puts her arm over the back of the seat to make room for me. I lay my head on her chest. She starts running a hand through my hair, slowly. I breathe in her Amarige, hoping the smell will remain on my clothes after she drops me back to my stagnant duplex. Back to the responsibilities. Back to the boredom. Back to him.

She turns on the radio. One hand continues to comb through my hair. R & B as always. Not my favorite. She looks down at me. "I haven't talked much to you today. How did it go at the lab?" Her fingers keep stroking my hair.

"Okay I guess. I've almost finished processing the pollen from the first site."

"Good. Any more problems with the acids?"

"No more than usual."

"Good."

She takes my hand with her free hand and we interlace fingers. She actually talked me into getting my nails done. Definitely a first. Out of character for me, but I like it. This week my fingernails are grey, hers blue. "How did *your* day go?" I ask.

"Not bad. After work I went out to my mom's to give Dixie a bath and trim her nails. Then we played fetch for a while. I was glad mom wasn't there today. I wasn't in the mood."

A thump on the hood of the car startles us both. A tabby cat sits down, leg up, and starts licking. I'm not surprised. Every time we park the car somewhere the neighborhood cats come out and head toward us as if drawn by some secret frequency. Lisa is a cat magnet.

The cat finishes licking itself and starts walking toward the windshield, still unaware of us. Lisa lets go of my hand and reaches to the left of the steering wheel. "Watch this." The cat looks up and finally sees us. Just as it realizes the car is occupied, Lisa flicks on the windshield wipers. The cat jumps a few feet into the air and lands running off in another direction. We both laugh.

"Cats are wound so tight." She takes my hand again and motions for me to put my head back on her chest. Soon the energy from my cheek and her chest blend. I cannot feel where she ends and I begin.

"Lisa, I feel so open with you."

She smiles, stroking my hair again. "You can call it that if you want to."

"What do you mean 'I can call it that if I want to'? What would you call it?"

"I don't know. Something like 'attracted to,' or 'aroused by.'"

A long silence follows. I find myself suddenly struggling to breathe, but not enough that she'd notice. "No. I don't think so. Not arousal anyway. This can't be arousal because that would mean this is sexual. It isn't. What we are doing is perfectly fine. I even prayed about it. It's sisterhood. Intimacy. Arousal would be against God's will."

"Yeah, I know. Remember I'm a Mormon too. It would be against the commandments. Hey, I just know what I feel. I've felt this before with men and I call it arousal. But, I don't think it really matters what you call it. It just is."

She strokes my face, which feels even better than her hands did in my hair. I put my cheek on her cheek, my lips near her lips. I want to kiss her. I want to kiss her more than I wanted to marry Roy, more than I want those amazing chocolates my grandma sends me for my birthday, even more than I want to get this damned dissertation finished.

We break apart so she can see into my eyes. "What are you afraid of, Heidi?"

"Oh, not much. Just not making it into the Celestial Kingdom when I die, having to confess to the Bishop, getting excommunicated, losing my family, you know, minor stuff like that."

Her focus onto me intensifies–like light from a magnifying glass burning a hole. "Does this," she lifts our interlocking hands upward, "feel right to you?"

I look down. Nothing has ever felt more right. Not going on a mission, not marrying Roy in the temple, not having my child. Nothing. "Lisa, this just isn't something I'm supposed to do. I'm not supposed to kiss a woman except on the cheek or something. All the scriptures and the prophets say it's wrong."

She shakes her head. "Heidi, what do *you* think? Do you really think this is in any way wrong?

I look down at our hands and the pattern alternating blue and grey fingernails. I put my lips near hers again. Such a beautiful mouth; I want that mouth, want to taste her. I wonder what is inside her, what it would feel like to merge with her, to connect, like ancient humans did through food sharing and sex before words existed like "Mormon" and "can't" and "homosexual" and "abomination" and "darkness" and "sin." Back when instinct was what kept us alive, when women in clans may have shared space for survival, and what they did at night was their business. Could my polygamist ancestors have shared a bond like I do with Lisa? Did they exchange kisses on nights when their husbands slept with another wife?

"It does feel right. So right. So righteous even. But I can't. It wouldn't be fair to Roy. This is just something I shouldn't do. Something I can't do."

But it is something I want to do. She strokes my face again. I put my lips on the corner of hers and whisper, "I can't can I?"

"I'm tired of this, Heidi . . . I'm not playing games anymore." She grabs my hair, pulls me to her, and kisses me hard. I don't pull away. I kiss her back. Her intensity is so unlike the teasing lips of Gary, the first person I kissed, who gave me a peck on the lips at my doorstep in Utah, so I wouldn't have to say I was still sweet sixteen. Unlike the reluctant lips of Jim who wouldn't kiss me until the night before he left for two years to serve a mission in Uruguay. Unlike the spit-covered lips of LaVar on New Years Eve. Certainly unlike the serpentine lips of my husband, mustached and scratchy. Her lips are anti-male–delicious, gentle, passionate, unbelievably soft.

She runs her tongue slowly over my lips. I keep my mouth closed–too many lessons at church when I was young about the sins of French kissing. She pulls away slightly. "Heidi, give me that tongue." I open my mouth and am suddenly inside her–the suction grabs my tongue hard, pulling at the connecting skin. It hurts. I like it. She is forceful in a way my effeminate husband could never be. Urgent. Confident. She releases my tongue and I take in hers—thick and strong. It completely fills my mouth. She kisses me quickly three times and we break again.

"Loosen up, Heidi. You're so stiff." She pulls back slightly so she can look at me and smiles. "I'm what's called a lazy kisser. Not stiff. Try to keep your mouth open just a bit and relax. Like this." Her lips slide over mine. She bites my bottom lip and takes my tongue into her mouth again. I try to be more relaxed, but it's hard to. This whole scene is not even supposed to be happening.

She speaks between short kisses. "Good. Better. Oh, Heidi, you taste so good." She kisses my eyelids, my nose, my neck. With each kiss, past taboos surface: the sleepover with Samantha when our clothed bodies, groin to groin, ground hard into each other until I panicked and pushed her off of me; the nap when I tried to get Sage to kiss me as "a token of our friendship" and she said she wouldn't kiss anyone but her future husband (but kissed Samantha a few weeks later); the night in Kansas when I held a woman I had just met at a mutual friend's wedding until just before my red-eye flight; and all the times I rushed to the mailbox hoping to find another long letter from my beloved Rayna. Stifled synapses finally fire.

Later, we will leave our husbands, Mormonism, and Georgia to create a new life with our daughters in California. I will grow a backbone and find my voice. She will cultivate compassion and gentleness. Together we will survive excommunication, alienation from our birth families, and chronic illness. We will laugh about these first kisses—especially about the corniness and drama of my now infamous, "I can't can I?" line. She will tell me that the first kisses weren't great for her. That I kissed just like she imagined Roy would kiss, tight lipped, uptight, like a snake, tongue darting in quickly. And she will tell me one day, much later that I've become a good kisser. Slow and relaxed. More like her than him.

This future, though set in motion as the friction of belief gives way to the gravity of passion, doesn't matter now. In this moment there is only R&B on the radio, tongues, and teeth on my lip. Only breathing, shadows of leaves on the windshield, fog, darkness, green light from the dashboard, stars through the sunroof, long lashes edging her closed eyes, fake blue fingernails, and her curly brown hair on my cheek.

ORGANIZING LESBIANS IN AOTEAROA/NEW ZEALAND, INCLUDING AMERICAN INFLUENCES
ALISON J. LAURIE

Alison J. Laurie is a New Zealander of mixed European and Māori heritage. She has been active in lesbian, gay, and feminist politics since the 1960s, and has published on lesbian history and politics, including as co-author, with Julie Glamuzina, *Parker and Hulme, a lesbian view*, on the 1954 teenage murder case, which was later the subject of the film *Heavenly Creatures*. She was editor of *Lesbian Studies in Aotearoa/New Zealand*, and with Linda Evans, co-editor of *Outlines, lesbian and gay histories of Aotearoa* and of *Twenty Years On*. She was guest editor for the special issues on lesbian history of the *International Lesbian Studies Journal*. She was a founder of New Zealand's first lesbian organisation Sisters for Homophile Equality (SHE), and of the first lesbian magazine *Circle*, (1973-1984); she was also a founder of New Zealand's first lesbian radio programme, which she co-hosted for over sixteen years. Now retired, she was Programme Director of Women's Studies at Victoria University of Wellington, where among other courses she offered lesbian studies, auto/biography and oral history. Her article here is memoir.

WHY DO SOME of us become activists? I came out at the age of sixteen, in 1957, in Aotearoa/New Zealand, far from any centres of lesbian and gay urban culture and organising. My first lovers knew no more than I did about the possibilities of organising or of building our own communities. I began by trying to find whatever I could about traces of same-sex love between women in our past, and in our present. Some of what I found I'm relating here. I'll also tell you about my own need to find and build lesbian communities, and of what inspired me and informed my activism, including the generation of lesbian activists who came of age in the post WWII United States, who were part of a wave of progressive change.

To begin with, same-sex love relationships have a long history in Aotearoa/New Zealand. However, we do not always know how women of the past arranged their lives and relationships. In A/NZ we know that before colonisation by the British, same-sex relationships seem to have been commonly accepted in Māori societies. Māori were the original inhabitants of this land, and they referred to people in such relationships as takatāpui—intimate friends of the same sex. Europeans introduced Christianity, and British colonizers brought laws and legal controls of women's role in society, and of male homosexual behaviors. Many controls were used to restrain women, who under nineteenth-century British laws, had no legal identity, no property rights, no access to higher education, and few employment opportunities enabling them as women to become economically independent of men.

Reforms in the later nineteenth century and early twentieth century rectified some of these aspects of women's situation. A/NZ enacted universal education and there were acts enabling women to keep our own wages and property, and women's suffrage was achieved in 1893. We were the first country in the world to achieve this. But women's situation was still so inferior that no laws were considered necessary to control lesbianism. However, because male homosexual practices remained a criminal offence up until 1985, this also affected lesbians. When any form of homosexuality is criminal, all forms will be seen as undesirable and verging on the illegal.

Despite restraints, some women in the past lived as lesbians, especially as educational and employment opportunities for women increased. There was farm work, including working in sheep shearing gangs, cooking and laundry work on farms, coastal freighters, and in hotels around gold mining towns, etc. More opportunities came with nursing and teacher training. A/NZ's participation in two world wars created more work opportunities as women replaced men serving overseas, in government departments and emerging industries. Increased urbanisation meant that by at least the 1950s, small "kamp" communities had developed in the main cities. We used the term "kamp" in A/NZ and also in Australia, before the American term "gay" was introduced in the late 1960s.

We had no equivalent to U.S. or European lesbian bars. Until 1967, A/NZ licensing laws prohibited the sale of alcohol after six p.m. and on Sundays, and allowed alcohol to be sold only at hotels. Also, women were not permitted in most hotel bars. The few city hotels serving women meant that we socialized in a mixed "crowd" including Kamp women and men, drag queens, and straight women. These early publicly visible communities were predominately Māori and Pākehā (European descent) working class.

Much of our socialising was in private homes, around guitars and singing, a keg of beer and food to share. Or we met in coffee bars. Older and more middle class lesbians met privately often in occupationally based networks, including nurses, teachers, post office employees, and those in the military. Lesbian members of women's organisations and clubs, including peace organizations, socialist organizations, etc. networked discreetly. The first actual club was the Kamp men's Dorian Society, set up in Wellington, the capital city, in 1962. Eventually, in 1972, Auckland lesbians set up their first lesbian club, the KG Club, named for "Kamp Girls" and for the Karangahape Rd premises.

The main influences on early Aotearoa/New Zealand culture came from the United Kingdom. American influences were slight, apart from the introduction of cinema and American films, and popular American music, including jazz. However during WWII, U.S. forces were stationed in A/NZ for "rest and recreation" during the Pacific war, increasing our awareness of American films, popular music, food, comic books, and culture. Following the war, improved communications increased our exposure to American influences. There were A/NZ subscribers to One magazine, the monthly publication from the gay rights organization One, Inc., established in the U.S. in 1952. There were also A/NZ subscribers to the Mattachine Society magazine. The Mattachine Society was founded in 1950 and was one of the earliest gay rights organizations in the U.S.

Myself and a few others obtained copies of *The Ladder*, the first nationally distributed lesbian publication in the U.S., published from 1956 to 1972. From *The Ladder*, we also heard about the Daughters of Bilitis (DOB), the first lesbian civil and political rights organization in the U.S. Then I heard about the London based Minorities Research Group (MRG) and their magazine *Arena Three*. MRG was Great Britain's first national lesbian organisation, holding monthly meetings in London. They had contact with women in many other centres. Others and I joined MRG and received their magazine. In 1964, I went to the United Kingdom, and began to attend MRG meetings. Once I had a job and a flat, I volunteered to hold the book discussion group there, and also the Christmas party. At MRG, we called ourselves "homosexual women." Then, in 1965 I joined a group going to Amsterdam to attend the women's conference of the COC–the Dutch homophile organisation that started in 1946. COC originally stood for Center for Culture and Leisure, which was meant to be a cover name for its real purpose. Founded in 1946, it's the oldest existing LGBT organization in the world. The Europeans called themselves "homophiles," or lovers of the same sex. This was my first introduction to a large, well-organised group, campaigning for political and social rights for homophile women and men. Travelling further around Europe, I made friends in Copenhagen, Denmark. I moved there and joined the Forbund af 1948, (F48) their large homophile organisation, and learned still more about the importance of organising for political change.

From the 1960s, the introduction of television and improved communications brought news to both Europe, and to Aotearoa/New Zealand, of the U.S. civil rights movement, hippies, the New Left, drugs, flower power, protest music, Black Power, the women's liberation movement, anti-Vietnam war protests, and then gay liberation and lesbian feminism. I visited the U.S., and on a visit in 1972, got inspired by groups like the Redstockings, a radical feminist group founded in 1969, the Furies, an American collective giving voice to lesbian separatism, and several other groups. I gathered their newsletters and magazines, and in 1973 I travelled back to Aotearoa/New Zealand, taking these along in the VW van that I and my Norwegian lover, and an American friend, drove overland from Europe, shipping the vehicle overseas.

Lesbian-feminism

WOMEN'S LIBERATION STARTED in 1970, in Wellington, the capital of A/NZ. The first newsletter mentioning international influences was *Women's' Liberation Front,* published June 26, 1970. During the following years, women's liberation groups were set up throughout the country, and a group started a new publication called *Broadsheet,* our first feminist magazine. Gay liberation began in 1972, following protests after Ngahuia Te Awekotuku, Māori lesbian and feminist, was refused a visa by the U.S. embassy, as she was a "known homosexual." At that time, and perhaps even still, known communists and homosexuals could not enter the U.S.

Gay Liberation Front groups were set up in the main cities to promote the radical new ideas of outreach and pride which they had read about in U.S. magazines. These U.S. ideas included wanting to "bring out the lesbian and gay man in everybody's head," as stated by U.S. author and activist Martha Shelley. However, lesbians in the Gay Liberation Front became disenchanted by the sexism and misogyny of some gay men, while lesbians in women's liberation groups were often experiencing lesbophobia and heterosexism, as was happening elsewhere. So we began our own lesbian organizations. Sisters for Homophile Equality (SHE) began in the city of Christchurch in 1973. I was visiting Christchurch, and suggested the term "homophile," which I'd learnt in Europe, as newspapers at the time refused advertisements containing the word "lesbian." One of their activities was to start the first Women's Refuge, which provided safety for women leaving violent or difficult marriages to men. They were inspired by American ideas, including slogans like "All women are lesbians except those that don't know it yet," as expressed by U.S. author and lesbian separatist Jill Johnston, and "In societies where men oppress women, to be a lesbian is a sign of mental health," (Martha Shelley). SHE members welcomed women to their Refuge, explaining that they should now leave their marriages and become lesbians. Interestingly, many did. And to give the New Zealand Women's Refuge credit, they have never denied that the first Women's Refuge here was started not only by lesbians, but by a lesbian organization.

A few months later, while living back in Wellington, I was part of the founding group that began SHE Wellington, and we affiliated to SHE Christchurch, establishing New Zealand's first national lesbian organisation. We soon had branches and individual contacts in many smaller centres. Then we began New Zealand's first lesbian magazine, called *Circle,* producing the first issue in December 1973. It was pasted together in my flat. We wrote some original articles, but clipped others straight from the U.S. lesbian feminist magazines that I had brought home. This meant that from its first issue, NZ lesbians were reading articles coming from *The Furies* magazine in Washington, D.C., among other publications. Soon we had magazine exchanges with many U.S. publications, providing our readers with regular access to emerging ideas from the U.S.

Guided by U.S. ideas of creating Lesbian Nation, and through outreach to all women, we encouraged them to become lesbians. We sold *Circle* in the streets, to women, and even to men, suggesting that they pass it on to their women friends. The title Circle was suggested by artist Viv Jones. She explained that it was from "the women's symbol, minus the cross at the bottom, as a circle can grow bigger and bigger and include everyone." I wrote the first editorial, proclaiming, "It is our purpose to unite the lesbians of New Zealand as part of the ever-growing international movement of gay women . . . our prime responsibility, time and energy must be directed towards improving the conditions of lesbians, and for all women." (*Circle*, December 1973)

My friend Diana Sands and I approached Carmen, a Māori entrepreneur, who had some premises available for sale. Four SHE members put up the money, and we began Club 41, the first lesbian club in Wellington, open to all women, and advertised in *Circle*. Lesbians from the older Kamp cultures and the newer lesbian feminists socialized together, building an ever stronger community. A telephone contact service called Lesbian Aid was set up, operating from lesbian households, and our contacts were advertised through *Circle*, enabling isolated lesbians throughout the country to build social and political lesbian communities. Though Club 41 eventually closed, it was the forerunner of several collectively run lesbian clubs in Wellington, continuing up until the early twenty-first century. SHE eventually ceased to exist, but was followed by numerous lesbian groups and organizations, including sports teams, cultural groups, Lesbian Centers, and events such as Lesbian Liberation Week. We were politically active on human rights, homosexual law reform, abortion rights, anti-racism, and peace, among other campaigns. We worked in coalitions with many other groups, including the National Gay Rights Coalition (NGRC), an umbrella organization for lesbian and gay groups working on political and social issues, including human rights and homosexual law reform. We were also part of the broad peace and anti-nuclear movements, the women's liberation movement, and much else.

The last issue of *Circle* magazine was published in 1986, though interest had begun to wane earlier. Two others and I began the Wellington Lesbian Radio Programme in 1984, realizing that radio gave many closeted and isolated lesbians a way to hear our news safely, while listening privately. We knew that some were afraid to receive lesbian magazines in case family or friends found them. Again, A/NZ lesbians were exposed to many U.S. influences, through the lesbian and women's music produced by Olivia Records, a U.S. music collective founded in 1973, and other companies. Our theme tune was, and remains, since the programme still broadcasts, the famous song by U.S. musician Alix Dobkin: "Women Loving Women." We regularly played lots of other music by U.S. lesbian artists including Alix Dobkin, Meg Christian, Maxine Feldman, and many others. I co-presented the programme for sixteen years, until I retired.

It still broadcasts, and is now presented by a broad collective of lesbians. The same policy continues: they play only music written or sung by lesbians, and interviews with lesbians.

The development of women's publishing, especially in the U.S., and the establishment of women's bookshops in A/NZ, gave us regular access to lesbian novels, magazines, music, and culture. And our own lesbian writers produced lesbian newsletters locally, as well as books. Herstory Press published local lesbian writing, and The Women's Press published some local lesbian novelists.

The Homosexual Law Reform Campaign from 1985 to 1986 unleashed another kind of U.S. influence. This Bill decriminalized male homosexual acts, and sought to include sexual orientation in the Human Rights Act. A campaign against this Bill was launched nationally, with a Petition taken door to door and into workplaces by anti-gay groups. It became obvious that this anti-gay campaign had strong conservative U.S. influences. This was a cultural imperialism that was hard to oppose. But we were assisted by our own U.S. contacts, including my friend Eleanor Cooper of Lesbian Feminist Liberation in New York, who visited A/NZ, as well as made herself available by telephone to provide information about the U.S. right-wingers who came to NZ to advise our local opponents of law reform. To fight this, we worked in coalitions with gay men, and in a broad based Coalition on the Bill (COB), that included trade unions, progressive church groups, and activists from peace and anti-racism groups. In the end, law reform was achieved. Lesbian and gay human rights were achieved in 1993—I was also involved in this campaign. Then came civil unions in 2004. More recently, our same-sex marriage and adoption rights were achieved.

However, now in the twenty-first century much lesbian culture, developed through those exciting years of the 1970s, '80s, and '90s, has declined. There are only a few lesbian organizations still in existence. Most events are now mixed, and we have followed the U.S. into an alphabet soup of LGBTIQ, etc., where lesbians are becoming invisible, as men dominate such mixed organizations. Our broad based coalitions of the past worked well, as lesbian organizations could participate more effectively as groups, not as just a few individuals.

I am personally grateful to the generations of radical lesbian feminists in the U.S., who inspired and influenced the development of our lesbian culture and community here in Aotearoa/New Zealand. We took up those influences and ran with them, developing our own strong lesbian communities here. Though some organizing has been lost, future generations of lesbians may create new and even stronger cultures than ever before.

THE DAY MAYA WENT MISSING
MO MARKHAM

Mo Markham is a lesbian feminist pagan French-Canadian middle-aged emerging writer who has lived in British Columbia, Quebec, and New Brunswick, and now makes her home in Ontario. She has had some non-fiction published, and is beginning to get recognition for her fiction. She believes in magic and intention and story. "The Day Maya Went Missing" is a piece of fiction.

IT WAS LETITIA'S idea the day my new baby sister Maya was kidnapped. Not that *we* kidnapped her, of course. We just brought her across the street so Alicia—that's my best friend, besides Letitia—could finally get to see her, and Mama was out like a light and Delia was at work taking care of somebody else's mémé, so I don't really see how it was wrong. I'm allowed to cross our street, and I'm allowed to pick Maya up carefully. But now Mama has said that I'm allowed to cross our street *alone*, but not with Maya, and I'm *not* allowed to pick Maya up when I'm alone. New rules all the time! It's exhausting.

Me and Letitia kind of get in trouble a lot for being smart. Smart-mouthed and smart-alecky, Mama says. To the rest of the world, Letitia is an elegant purple stuffed pig with a white bow tie, but she's really trouble through and through, Delia says.

Delia's my new mama who I call Delia.

Like it was Letitia's idea for us to hide in the back of the car when Delia brought Mama to the hospital to have Maya. Why should we stay at the neighbour's? We've been around much longer than Delia, after all, and she got to go. And that worked out, eh, because we got to see Maya being born, against Mama's better judgment. "It was really gross and bloody, and Mama just screamed like her head was going to pop off," I told Alicia the day of the kidnapping, "but it was way cool too. This whole other person came right out of my mama's vagina thing!"

And it was Letitia's idea to plant grandma Mémé's fancy teacups with all the different roses on them all around the tree where we had spread Mémé's ashes, because she loved those cups, and there were no other flowers in the garden then.

Mémé—my mémé and my mama's mama—died when Mama was going out with Dennis. Mémé didn't like Dennis much, but she loved Delia, and loved Delia taking care of her. Delia was Mémé's nurse, and she came to stay over a lot at the end, so Mama could get some sleep and go to work and have some help. Mama was stressed and exhausted and she got in the family way by accident and then figured out she was in the family way after Mémé was pushing up roses–well, rose-covered teacups. And by then Dennis was gone, and good riddance, she said, and everybody else pretty much agreed. And then Delia was staying over a lot, and then she just stayed for good.

I don't blame Letitia for getting me in trouble, mind you. I'm always a "willing accomplice," Mama says, and it's true. Letitia's just the idea girl is all.

What I said when Letitia and I saw Maya being born was, "But she's . . . she's black!" Which was kinda dumb and obvious, and Mama and Delia laughed and laughed at the look I gave Delia, but who knew? Mama hasn't really decided on a name for my new baby sister, but her name's Maya, I'm here to tell you. It just *is*. Maya smells like powder and sweat and roses, and has dark brown skin like Delia's, though she came from my Mama's belly. And she wrapped her tiny little fist with its itty bitty sharp little nails around my finger and held on really tight as soon as I touched her. She knew right away I was her big sister Lily. And she moved her lips around and sucked at the air, and Letitia told me later that it looked like Maya was trying to say my name.

When our neighbour Wendy saw Maya, or baby no-name, she said to Delia, "Girl, how did you *do* that?" Delia, who was Wendy's friend/girlfriend before she started being Mama's partner girlfriend, just laughed. Delia didn't actually do it, though, Mama did–I saw, and it looked like a *lot* of work. But I knew what Wendy meant, because I kinda wondered that myself.

So anyway, the day of the kidnapping, Alicia was jumping up and down when I brought Maya over, because she finally got to see our new baby. And Maya grabbed Alicia's finger too, which was nice of her. But then she fell asleep again–she does that a lot–and she was just being boring, so we moved on. We weren't dumb enough to bring Maya into the treehouse–you have to climb up this groovy rope ladder, then pull it in after you so no one else can come up–so Alicia went up to the attic and got her old doll carriage. We're way too old to play with dolls now, of course, and now we have Maya anyway. We just put her under the tree in this pretty white carriage where we could hear her if she started to cry or anything, which I'll tell you now, she did not.

To celebrate Maya being born, Alicia was fixing us tea and crumpets in the treehouse–well, Coke and Twinkies, anyway, because we don't really know what crumpets are, and probably don't have any. The Coke looks just like my mémé's strong tea used to, and we can refill the tiny little china cups with the bears on them over and over as many times as we want, and no one is there to stop us.

"You remember Dennis, Mama's last boyfriend?" I asked Alicia, and she did, of course.

"Well, Mama says Maya's black because of *him*, not Delia! Weird, eh?" And of course she thought it was.

"Dennis wasn't really dark at all, not like Maya and Delia, so I don't believe it. I didn't even think he was black. That's probably another one of those stories adults tell kids, that Dennis brought Maya," I told Alicia, "like the Easter Bunny and Santa and that? Except Dennis didn't bring good stuff like they do, so what's the point?" Alicia couldn't think what the point might be at all.

"You know how the book says the sperm thingies come from boys and go into girls' tunnels? And kind of attack their eggs until the eggs open up and let one in? Well, I saw Delia doing things with Mama–one time when I had a nightmare and I went to find Mama–and it looked like Mama was letting her in too."

"What do you mean letting her in?" asked Alicia, who won't be ten for another three months, and doesn't know much about these things.

"Well, Delia had her face between Mama's legs and Mama was saying 'Oh god oh god oh god' with her eyes closed. I just didn't mention that part to Delia or Mama because I'd probably get in trouble and I'm not stupid or anything."

"'Course you're not," said Alicia, who is a very loyal friend, I must say. Mama doesn't talk about God very often, so I was a bit surprised that night with what she was saying to Delia. "For god's sake, Lily, don't be smart," is one of her favourite expressions though, so maybe I shouldn't have been. Her god talk doesn't always make sense. Don't be smart? Well, I know she doesn't want me to be dumb either.

"I don't know about the eggs, because I didn't see them or smell them, but I kinda noticed it smelled fishy before I sneaked back out into the hallway. And now we have a dark brown baby girl, so you do the math!"

"It was Delia, for sure," Alicia agreed, nodding and biting into her third Twinkie. Her mama always has stacks of yummy things around, so we have some really good picnics in the treehouse.

And right then, along comes Delia, looking like an angel all dressed in her white uniform with her shirt flying behind her into Alicia's yard, and Mama with her big red maternity blouse all crumpled and her black hair all big and wild and sleep-messed, making her look a bit crazy. And the two of them yelling and cursing something inappropriate, but mostly yelling "Lily Marie Desrochers, where the hell is that baby?!!!" And lo and behold, no doll carriage and no Maya, and me and Alicia and Letitia just looked at each other with our jaws dropping and our eyes all popping out.

Alicia and Letitia and I knew right away it was Lovey and Tootsie, Wendy's kids. Who else could it be? Lovey hates it when we roll the ladder up into the treehouse and she can't come up–not since the time she kidnapped Letitia–and Tootsie's a boy so he can't come up for sure. They just like to get our goat, as Wendy says, though we've never even had a goat, and really prefer stuffed pigs.

We searched and searched, and I hung on tight to Letitia to keep her safe from Lovey. But Lovey's kinda sneaky, so we couldn't find Maya or Tootsie or the carriage, and Mama was starting to talk about calling the police. Their mom was helping us look, because she figured it was probably them too, and so she just started walking up and down the street and the alley yelling at the top of her voice, "Lovey Eldridge! Tootsie Eldridge! There's a real baby in that carriage, and you'd better appear this second or your life is over! *DO YOU HEAR ME??*" And at the best of times it's a voice that can make your hair stand up, even when she's just yelling, "Lovey! Tootsie! Supper! Get home!"

Then a little voice in the Cunningham's tree called down right over Letitia and me—"It is *not* real," and I hissed back up, "It is *too* real, Lovey—it's my new baby sister, now *give her back*!" I guess they hadn't looked so close when they stole the carriage, but just to be sure, I hissed up there again, "My mama's talking about calling the police, you stooge, so hurry!"

And then I didn't see anyone at all, but I heard rustling over my head and a thump on the roof of the Cunningham's garage, then nothing. I was about to tell the adults where Lovey was when the door in the side of the garage opened with a squeak, and the white carriage with the lace skirt wheeled out really slowly, smelling like grease and cars and dust, and I could just see one of Tootsie's grubby little hands pulling the door closed again. "She's here! She's here! She's here!" I yelled, and me and Maya and Letitia were mobbed by adults cooing at Maya and shaking their heads at Letitia and me and swearing about Lovey.

Mama says I'm grounded for the rest of my life. As if this was *my* fault.

I'll have to ground Letitia too, of course, and I hate that!

WHERE ARE MY PEOPLE?
ARIELLE NYX MCKEE

Arielle Nyx McKee is a Feral Femme and Counter of Unhatched Chickens. Arielle is a professional by day and nerd by night. A multi-faceted artist, she has published poems in the *International Library of Poetry*, knitted her way across Etsy, performed in several West Edge Opera productions, and created original art for the SF Olympians. She currently resides in Oakland and is pursuing her Masters of Divinity at the Berkeley Chaplaincy Institute. This piece is her *personal philosophy*.

JUST BELOW THE surface of this feral lesbian femme exterior is a girl looking for a place to belong. I'm on the periphery of the periphery, looking in from the outskirts. I am like the child with my face pressed against the glass tank in the restaurant, watching lobsters whose claws are clamped shut. I'm the schnauzer with her head to the ground, sniffing for connection.

I am a femme—a female-identified female, a lesbian who presents typically in makeup and skirts; invisible to would-be lovers; faceless in "The Community." I'm invisible to the straight world as a lesbian because my look is not specifically edgy enough to push me out from the crowd. Even though I volunteer for Pride every year and my Facebook pages are littered with me in rainbows, "You're gay?" is a common comment in my daily life. I am also a gamer; nerdy, feminine, and introverted. I'd sooner pick up a book than a date in a bar.

So where are my people? *Who* are my people? I can't find them. I am not sure there is a lesbian community anymore. With the social media phenomenon—Facebook, Twitter, OKcupid, Suicide Girls, and Tumblr—there's a cluttered clusterfuck of social networks, but what of them? Are these really our lesbian communities? What happened to our coffee shops, our bookstores and bars, the physical spaces where we found each other, wrapped our ideas around each other, and cruised?

> . . . community is running away to the suburbs. The media has become our pseudocommunity. People don't belong, but if they're part of a sound bite, they feel part of a larger world. It's the false idea of the media as a public forum. People take their intimate stories on talk shows, replacing political engagement and community, which would actually bind people. [1]

Growing up in post punk Philadelphia in the 1980s, I knew what I wasn't. I was not a preppie, blonde, skinny, country club girl, and definitely not straight. I did not fit in. Attending an all girls' school from kindergarten to twelfth grade, you'd think I'd have found some like-minded girls; nope. In the all girls' summer camps I was sent to, surely there would be another lesbian hiker or ballet dancer to share my camp experiences with. Nope.

In the mid 1990s I became an early adopter and joined the untethered world of ICQ (one of the first person-to-person instant messaging systems, purchased by AOL. It literally means "I seek you"), where there were one-to-one chats and message boards (both precursors to our current social media). I was looking for other women to relate to, even in the cyber world. This approach worked well at first until I arranged to meet a virtual pen pal and the person turned out to be a guy masquerading as a woman online. Perfect. I was further adrift than ever, seeking connection and visibility even in the unseen, unreal world of the early internet. So I went "afk" (away from the keyboard) and set out to meet people in the "real world."

College in Washington, D.C. was not much better. The one dyke bar (Hung Jury) was not the hotbed of community I was seeking. Mostly I met butches and sports dykes who were into other butches and athletes. I was neither. I'd grown up thinking that being a lesbian could only mean appearing in the world as butch. At that time it was easy to identify a butch lesbian by her combat boots, torn baggy jeans, oversized plaid shirts, and military style buzz cut. Clearly I wasn't butch.

I was raised with an older brother and got his hand me downs. My parents cut my hair short (think Mary Lou Retton on her Wheaties box). I hated it. In my brother's jeans and bowl haircut, people complimented my parents on their "cute little boy." I'd cross my arms defiantly and proclaim, "I'm a girl, not a boy."

I am a girl. I want to be noticed for being female. Not in a lecherous or aggressive way, but to be a female in the world, wearing my femininity proudly and enjoying my female body. Carving out my identity and securing myself in my female body took a lot of work. It was arduous moving past the labels and body hatred that made me afraid and kept me from truly being myself in the world.

I'm attracted to butches, but don't want to be one. The James Bond movies shaped my image of what being a strong, fierce lesbian femme could be. Those females were my role models. I idolized them, not for their giving into Bond's advances, but because they were women in total control of themselves and their situations. They were self-contained, possessing prowess, fierce femininity, and they rocked some seriously powerful outfits.

Off television, in real life, butches seemed to have all of the power, striking badass poses James Dean style, in a masculine-identified way. The idea that a femme lesbian could be as strong, as powerful as a butch, was not available as an archetype. Strong, smart femme dyke role models were nowhere to be found. I had to find my own way. I still do. I meet baby dykes who say to me, "Wow, I didn't know a lesbian could look like you."

> Community requires tools that cannot be built. Community exists in one place—in your heart. Without passion, without a feeling of belonging—what is there? You cannot build heart. It's either there, or it's not. A community grows its own leaders. Community is inside of you—but it's not about you. It's about other's experiences with you. Community is everywhere, and it starts inside of you. [2]

This describes lesbian community in a larger sense, but what about in the smaller, more intimate and emotional world? Being a non-monogamous, bottom-leaning femme means I'm cast out even further from my own community. I am not part of this heteronormative couple-up-and-settle-down paradigm which somehow makes me further distanced from other lesbians. Is assimilation becoming the measure of community and acceptance? How can simply fitting in and matching up with the people I work with even come close to my relating to another woman? It doesn't, it can't—I am in relationship with women. I don't want it to be the same or even close to what straight couples share. We are different, and that difference isn't bad or a reason to be ashamed. Women together have different ways of communicating; different ideas of conflict resolution; we simply don't have the luxury or the laziness that straight people have in their traditional relationships.

Also, success to me is independence. But my need for independence seems to be the tipping point, keeping me out of many dyke social circles. I don't want to steal your girlfriend, I want to be friends with her.

The trouble with online connecting is that many sites are focused on dating—read: finding your mate and settling down. But I'm using the sites as a way to connect, to join virtual hands and make those connections that might otherwise be lost. Several times though, when I've met someone online, we'll meet in real life and hit it off, but then it turns out that person is looking for a girlfriend, not a friend.

I have had butch friends end their friendships with me because they have a girlfriend who feels threatened by my presence. Then there are my partnered lesbian friends, who are so insular that they've become judgmental and frown on my independence. It's always one thing or another, and I end up alone.

> Rebel girl rebel girl, you are the queen of my world. Rebel girl, Rebel girl I want to be, your best friend. [3]

In the San Francisco Bay Area (I affectionately call it the Area of the Gay) there are more women supposedly like me. There are even meetups geared toward femme lesbians meeting other femmes. So why does my foraging for connection (both platonic and romantic) prove harder than calculus?

Sometimes I wonder if my own success is part of the problem. Maybe my own striving toward financial independence, emotional emancipation, and the freedom to be a nerdy femme instead of a doormat, means I've lost my ability to trust that if I'm sick, a neighbor will bring me soup; or that I will be able to reach out beyond my own social anxiety and make that connection myself.

With all of my tweeting, Facebooking, instant messaging and texting, I am not any closer to the elusive community I seek. Repeating profound observations you've read somewhere else (aka re-tweeting) doesn't make you smart. It just makes you a culture vulture. It doesn't tell me where you're at or how you're growing. It tells me you have opposable thumbs and can use them to copy and paste.

The women who are online and creating virtual communities are still mostly marginalized. Those who do get through the mainstream display have to be so socially or sexually outspoken that they can become commodities of the system. It seems impossible to be a stand-alone lesbian persona without your sexual and bedroom activities having to be factored into the equation of your worth. I want a community where we are with and for each other not because of what we do with each other's bodies, but because of how we inspire each other's minds. I want to grow an actual community of real people who do prosaic and poetic things together. I fear that true friendship is a lost art. But we need the connection of friendship to build our community, to instill and bolster that sense of belonging. Are we losing this connection?

> People are looking for community in all the wrong places. It's not goodwill and like-mindedness, it's daily experiences in workplaces and neighborhoods and civic groups."[4]

Searching for my lesbian people is about clearing the space and acknowledging how much is on the line if we don't get this right. I'm a Gen X'er, that post-boomer generation full of pity, loathing, and accusations about how the world has been irreparably damaged. This is not because we are generally depressed or pessimistic. It's because there is a simple truth in our perspective. Positioned between two mega generations, full of noise and vigor, my group is smaller, resilient, and forced to see the world from a new vantage point. We have lost the community and the family and the comfort of earlier generations. As a femme lesbian, I have lost my spaces.

The choice is clear—community is about actual connection, not a social media quip. I challenge you: Put down your iThing and step away from your devices. Look up and connect with someone, yes, an actual someone around you.

Sources

1 Susan Faludi - http://www.motherjones.com/politics/1994/05/what-community
2 Chris Pirillo - http://chris.pirillo.com/what-is-community/
3 Bikini Kill - http://bikinikill.com/about/
4 Francis Moore Lappe - "The Quickening of America," 1994

OTHER: DRIVING THE LAND IN BETWEEN
HEAL MCKNIGHT

Heal McKnight lives in Arcata, California, with her wife Maggie and two kids. Her work has appeared in *Brevity*, *Poem–MemoirStory*, and *Brain, Child*. She holds an MFA in Nonfiction Writing from the University of Iowa, and teaches composition and creative writing at Humboldt State University. Her essay in this book is an excerpt from a book length memoir, about an older child from a previous relationship, back in the darker days of lesbian family history.

WE'RE IN THE car. I'm taking her back, and the sun has slid west but the day's heat hasn't broken. We're rolling past vegetable stands, hosed off tractors, farms with tidy blue silos and trim lawns, our car rattling loosely over bumps. Rennie's riding next to me, wiggling and shifting and adjusting the back of her seat every few minutes. She's been holding her hair out the window and it's become a big light brown tangle, a shiny tumbleweed she will complain about later. Her bare feet are splayed on the dashboard. She peeled her socks off a few miles ago and now the whole car smells dark and sweaty.

"Mama, you need some fresh prints?" she asks, inching the bottom of her foot toward the windshield. I told her an hour ago about the footprints I found there—the ones she left last month. How they showed up when I thought I was driving alone, along humid back roads with the radio blasting.

"I turned on the defroster," I had told her. "The whole windshield cleared off, except for the prints of two little fan-shaped feet."

That made her laugh. "Yep, when you were taking me back I pressed them in and held them there. And you were like, 'bub, are your feet actually *touching* the windshield?' I told you they weren't, but they were. Sure you don't want me to freshen them up?"

I'm pretty sure they're actually touching now.

"No thanks. I'm sure," I tell her.

But really, I'm not at all sure. Because sometimes after she's gone, I just want some proof of her around. She leaves notes on the chalkboard *please get me hair stuff*, or *think about a kitten*, and I don't erase them until it's time to go pick her up again. I keep the elaborate scorecard she makes for marble games; most of what we draw in Pictionary; the signs that she and the neighbor kid make for her bedroom door: "Acorn Club, Meeting to Save Nachur." I hold on to these things quietly, because it's all gotten so complicated. So I tell her not to stamp her sticky feet on my windshield, and later, looking through clean glass at the stars above the highway, I'll know that was wrong.

Instead, I reach over and pat her leg, the knee that's sticking up like a strong brown mountain in front of her. She's ten. Her face is becoming lovely, her mouth wide and elegant, her adult teeth starting to look like they belong to her. She's tanned to a glowing brown—her great-grandmother's even, olive skin—ripening in long summer sun. She prides herself on being able to pick me up. She's been in gymnastics for years now and her body is fiercely strong; her legs and butt the same determined curve of muscle my sister had when she was ten. So she hugs me just below my waist and lifts me for a few seconds, awkward and proud. She likes it when other people watch her do this.

"I saw this great thing on TV," she's saying now. "Do you ever watch—no, wait, you don't got cable. Anyway, there's this one show, *Emergency Response Team*, and there was this guy. Who'd been in a car crash, I think it was, and his leg was *cut almost off*."

Her hand is chopping away at her own thigh, sawing along the bottom of her shorts. She's talking fast.

"I don't know how it happened, but the bone was broken off, and his leg was just dangling by two blood things—Mama, two of those things that hold your blood in? They're like straws?"

"Arteries?"

"Yeah, arteries, just two arteries were holding his whole leg on. Nothing else. *But he could still move it!* They were like, 'bend your knee!' and he could bend his knee. And they were like, 'move your toes!' and he could wiggle his toes. He could swirl his leg around when they told him to. You wouldn't think that was possible, but he could *do* it."

She's rocking in her seat now, swirling her own leg and wiggling her toes, her whole body helping tell this story, convincing me, though at this point I don't need convincing. Since she got cable at her other house, she's become an eyewitness to stuff like this.

I step on the brake a little, trying to quiet a rattley noise in the front wheels. "That's wild," I say.

I'm thinking about a message traveling from his brain, jumping through thin air and cut-off nerves, still somehow getting through to the leg. I'm trying to think how to say this without sounding educational or metaphorical—two things she currently hates coming from me.

"I'm just thinking about how that could work. How all the cut off nerves could still hear what the brain was telling them."

"He was probably in shock," Ren declares. "Weird things happen when you're in shock. Can we stop for shakes?"

Shakes sound good. We pull into the place that's half gas station, half fast food place, and she runs in to order while I fill the tank. By the time I come inside, she's made it to the front of the line.

"That'll be $3.93," she says over her shoulder, not even looking up to see if it's me.

We don't have far to go before we cross the river and do together what I used to do as a kid: pull in a big lungful of one state's air, hold it across the bridge, then breathe it out in the new state, mixing where we used to be with where we are now. Once we do that, we'll be halfway to her other home, where we all lived together once.

I'll come back by myself when it is pitch black, the dashed center line pulling me home. What did we do with our time? In my head I'll make a list, fold it over and over and over on itself: we played cards, made pizza crust, listened constantly to that Cher CD Ren really likes. The neighbor kid was there for most of it; I showed them both how to tie a bunch of new knots, simple and orderly and strong, and two mornings in a row we made pancakes. They cleaned out my desk drawer and found stuff we'd all forgotten about: bug tattoos, enough for all of us. I popped the hood on the Honda and showed them what was inside. We called my mother. We sewed an oven mitt for a stuffed penguin who, apparently, needed one.

On the way back, I'll wonder if that was enough. I'll wonder if that was the right stuff. I had her for a week; what all should have fit in? Was that real parenting? Is this it?

Because this wasn't part of the plan. Two moms, one kid—an invented family—chosen in that way we thought lesbians could just choose. We thought we could make our own vows, lock our ethical hearts together as surely as any wedding ceremony; lock together as a family, in spite of what the state recognized legally.

Ten years into the relationship we failed; a slow, painful leak of failure. And now, two moms: one child, plus a river and 178 miles in between.

"You were never a real parent anyway," my partner said to me in the last, deflating days. "Legally, you're nobody's mom. It makes the most sense to align our emotional reality with the legal one."

Two moms, two savings accounts wrung out, turned into too many hours with lawyers and the most painful document I have ever seen, studded with words like "former partner," and "visitation order," and "parent-like relationship." Two moms who are, finally, something legal to each other: "Petitioner" and "Respondent."

Right now we're at a stoplight waiting to get on the bridge. Rennie's trying to suck her shake through the straw, though it's still so frozen that none of it is coming up, and the insides of her cheeks are nearly touching each other.

"Mama," she asks suddenly. She's looking right at me. "Why do you think the foot could still hear what that guy's brain was telling it? How'd it know what it was supposed to do?"

I've been wondering that too. I'll bet there are real answers, and I could guess at them: neural synapses, measurable chemical reactions, something that makes it sound like I know. Or not.

"Maybe some things don't only work like science says," I tell her. "Maybe there's something like . . . not magic, exactly, but surprises." I glance over to see whether she's still listening. "Maybe legs and brains work in ways we don't understand yet."

I look at my kid. She doesn't call me much, doesn't like getting mail from me; wants to keep her two lives with her two moms separate because she tells me that's much easier. But she's always waiting at the curb when I come to pick her up.

"Heck, I don't know," I tell her. "Maybe the leg really loved the man."

She's looking at the shake lids, with their little bumps on top, the ones the employees push down so they don't get your drinks mixed up: Diet, Regular, Iced Tea, Other.

"'Other,'" she says, pushing down the little dome, then leaning over to push mine. "We both got an 'other.'"

Together we take a deep breath and hold it while we cross the Mississippi River, on the way to where we're going tonight.

SEALED WITH A KISS
HELENA LOUISE MONTGOMERY

 **Helena Louise Montgomery,** a Black Native American lesbian writer, was born with something more precious than a silver spoon: a lifetime supply of the #2 pencil. She holds a BA in Writing and Literature from Burlington College. Her book reviews appeared in the *International Lesbian Review of Books*.

She was one of the contributing writers for the *Contemporary Lesbian Writers of the United States: A Bio-Bibliographical Critical Sourcebook*, by Denise Knight and Sandra Pollack. As one of the staff sistahs for *Imani*, a monthly publication by lesbians of color in Atlanta, Georgia, she was also one of its contributing writers. Her essays and poetry have appeared in *Crossroads, The News of The African American Lesbian/ Gay Alliance* (ALLGA) in Atlanta; *Mama Raga* in Gainesville, Florida, and *ONYX A Black Lesbian Newsletter* in San Francisco. She has read her works in progress at Olde Wives Tale in San Francisco and Charis Books & More in Atlanta. She's conducted creative writing workshops for children in Georgia and for adults in Virginia, and American University in D.C. Most recently, she have reinvented her writing wheel to include songwriting. Although new to playing the guitar, singing, and songwriting, she has ventured out to perform at open mic nights at the Greenwich Hotel and Lounge in East Greenwich, Rhode Island. Career-wise, she's spent almost twenty years working as a counselor for our youth at risk in California, Georgia, Virginia and Rhode Island; and as an outreach worker for adults with mental health and substance abuse issues in Dorchester, Massachusetts. She's just returned to the Massachusetts/Rhode Island area after spending a year in Vermont. The new hat she will soon wear is that of a Certified Professional Dog Trainer. "Sealed With A Kiss" is memoir.

WHO WOULD HAVE thought in 2013, almost sixty-four years to the day since I took my first breath, that I'd be here to say, "I'm a Proud Black Native American Lesbian Bury Girl?"

"Bury Girl." Roxbury, Massachusetts, that is. Home of the once-upon-a-time-screeching elevator rails at Dudley Station, memorialized in the opening scene of Spike Lee's 1992 film *Malcolm X*. Truth be told, by the time they filmed that movie the elevator rails at Dudley Station had long since been dismantled. Wikipedia tells us, "The actual scene was of New York City Transit Authority 'D' type museum cars that were built in 1927 and ran on the New York City BMT Subway Lines."

To this day, Roxbury remains as real as it gets. Like any part of Boston, or any major city, life in Roxbury encompasses the full spectrum of humanity's beauty as well as its ugliness. Bury parents, whether single or together, continue to raise incredible children who are not predestined to grow into gangsters, felons, or any other kind of perceived failures. But to be successful in Roxbury is to be born as healthy as possible, to be blessed with a steel will strong enough to hold on to your passions, and to have at least one parent or other adult who will have your back while you ride the waves of the economic system, the school system, the lost mind system, and the jail system, all of which Roxbury living will make you ride. Then you have a chance to not only live to grow up, but to actually be proud of who you become in life.

My first ten years in Roxbury were a blast. We owned our yellow two family house at 10 Wyoming Street. Roxbury was going through its racial transition in the late forties and early fifties, turning over from Jewish to "Colored." By the time I came along there was only one Jewish family left in our neighborhood, the Weinbergs. Two Weinberg sisters, Susan and Alice, matched me and my oldest sister Terry in age. They lived across the street from us, in a big red two family house.

Also across the street were Reggie and Jerry Denny and their little sister Beverly. Their grandmother lived in their upstairs unit; and my Granny, my father's mother, a Black Nipmuc Indian, also lived with us.

The Perini family also lived across the street, a couple of houses up to the left. They were the only Italian family left in our part of Roxbury. Their son David was old enough to have given up playing with the little kids on the block, so we didn't see much of him. The Perini adults stood barely five feet tall and were thereby the smallest adults I knew. They also spoke faster than any other people on earth, and always in Italian. We called them Mr. and Mrs. Gabba-Gabba behind their backs, because we never understood a word they said—which is not to say that we didn't know what Mrs. Perini *meant* when she yelled down to us from her second floor bedroom window. Just like we understood the identical twin sister/nurses on the other side of the street who would call out every Saturday morning: "Shhhhh!!! Don't make so much noise. Move on! Our patients are still sleeping." Mrs. Perini's admonitions, spoken in Italian, were quite clear.

The sisters, a pair of freckled, "redbone" women (which is to say, fair-skinned Blacks) operated the "old folks home," as we used to refer to it in that day. "The home" was a big white house surrounded by a six-foot wrought iron fence, and was guarded by two identical red-haired Doberman Pinschers. These were large, lean, intimidating dogs with sharp pointed ears and cropped tails. Mr. and Mrs. Gabba-Gabba didn't have patients, but they shared the twin nurses' craving for a bit of peace and quiet early on Saturday mornings. Who could blame them?

If you include a kid named Richard who lived at the corner of Wyoming and Warren Streets, who we called "Football Head" for obvious physical reasons, and whose last name I never did know, and my cousin Michelle, who lived at the top of Wyoming Street, there were nine of us old enough to play outside without parental supervision. All outside toys were shared between families.

Like clockwork, every Saturday morning, we'd meet in the middle of the block. We'd line up in start positions at the top of the hill, with groups of four on opposite sides of our semi tree-lined street, ready to race full speed to the bottom. The odd one out always stood at the bottom and threw down an imaginary flag to start the race. One blue tricycle with an orange seat, one red wagon propelled by a pushing leg (the other leg resting inside the wagon bed), one red bike with training wheels, and five pairs of roller skates-all careening down the uneven red brick sidewalk, past the nursing home and the Perini's, heading to the large open field which separated the Weinberg's house from the last big house on the corner, which was the Winter's family home. What a racket we made! But never a broken bone.

The Winters had the biggest house of them all. Their family was the community's saving grace in the summers. They owned and operated the summer day camp that we, and almost all the neighborhood kids, attended every single summer until we were old enough to attend overnight camp. And when that time arrived and we were all older, the Winter family was prepared: they started an overnight camp in Amherst, MA.

And that, my dear people, was the beginning of my introduction to the world beyond the Boston Children's Museum, The Boston Science Museum, the Franklin Park Zoo, the MDC (Metropolitan District Commission) ice skating rink, and the local Roxbury movie theaters.

It was also the end of my ability to fit in.

That first summer at overnight camp, Char, the Winter's oldest daughter, was our lead camp counselor, and my first girl crush.

Talk about the unexpected. A flash of raised goose bumps went up and down my arms. Heat rose in my ears, making them warm to the touch. A wide grin that wouldn't quit took hold of my face as a group of us stood in front of Char, while she explained to us the camp rules. I heard very little. Instead I was totally transfixed by her tall, toned, athletic physical presence. Her bright yellow sleeveless V neck shirt, with black block letters spelling "Camp What's Up?" on the front and her dark green shorts, made my breathe skip. Till that moment in my life, not one thing, not one boy had ever caused the excitement that came over me as I stood planted in place, staring at her. The only thing that broke the spell, that made us all double over in laughter, was reading the back of her shirt as she walked away. "Doesn't Always Come Down!" Come to find out, she had a different shirt, in different colors, with different sayings on the back, for every day of the week, and more.

When camp ended that summer, I found every possible reason to visit the Winter's house, just to see Char. Luckily, Mrs. Winter was the neighborhood adult that everyone, old and young, gravitated toward. Kids would knock on her back door just to say hello or visit with her on her screened back porch while she sat shucking beans, husking corn, or getting her hands dirty in the garden.

My time with Mrs. Winter was like a cool sea breeze that shook the wrinkles from all my kid concerns. But suddenly, I was experiencing this new feeling. I knew enough to keep this new experience to myself. I didn't know what it was but I sure didn't want anything I did to make it go away. Little did Mrs. Winter know, visiting her became my excuse to be around Char and to experience my newfound joy.

During one of our many conversations, I discovered that Mrs. Winter knew how to cook a fresh fish whole. After that, fishing became my new hobby. I didn't have a fishing pole, but my mother had a pile of S&H green stamps that the A&P grocery store gave her every Saturday with her receipt. These stamps were redeemable for merchandise at any S&H store. Now, I never was a goody two shoes, so using her stamps without asking came naturally. Asking would only produce a guaranteed "No." A fishing pole required very few stamps, so I helped myself.

After that, every chance I got, I would go to Houghton's Pond, because Mrs. Winter let me bring my fresh caught catfish to her house. She taught me how to clean, season, and fry them. And this is how I got to see Char without having to say a word to her.

In reality I couldn't have spoken a word to Char even if I'd wanted to. When she'd enter the kitchen where I was visiting with her mother, I became a sweaty, uncontrollable, shaky, clumsy kid. Smiling felt like the safest thing to do and I hoped my wide grin didn't give me away.

The end of that summer at overnight camp introduced me to another new feeling. Missing someone. Char went off to college and wasn't around through the following fall, winter or spring, except for holidays. As it happened, those were the same holidays my family spent at my grandmother's house, so I didn't see Char again for more than a year. But I knew she was around. And those memories became my best way to get through the following school year and all the adolescent drama that came with it: boys, girl friendships, peer pressure, school, grades, and teachers comparing me to my sister's high intelligence.

Then suddenly, everything changed. Somewhere between my eleventh and thirteenth birthdays, life indoors at number 10 Wyoming came to resemble a gyroscope spinning out of control. My parents divorced shortly after my father was accepted to the MDC Police Force (now merged with the State Police). This began the end of order in my life.

Between summer breaks I found myself looking at people differently. I was searching, trying to discover what else might bring that same fun joy good sensation my way again. My friends at school started talking about boys. My sister, eighteen months older than me, was simply boy crazy. No one even hinted at having a crush on a girl. So I kept my difference to myself.

One day, near the start of my interest in people watching, I caught a glimpse of something I later would realize had been there all along. There were people in our church, members—both women and men—who were identifiably different from most of the rest of the congregation. The men were said to be "effeminate"—a word I learned later. The women, in their finest Sunday threads, wore what our men wore—tailored two or three-piece pants suits, crisp pastel or white shirts with thin silk neck ties. They were more easy on the eye–my eyes at least—than some of the handsome, young fathers of our church.

In my growing awareness, I also began to detect a very subtle uneasiness in the adults I knew. By this I mean my family members and family friends. At twelve years old, reading adult body language was a skill I was rapidly acquiring.

While these different-looking men and women didn't hide, I noticed that they were invisible in a manner that, initially, I couldn't figure out. Conversations among my own family members, when people did speak about "them," were not of the straightforward kind. My mother's sisters–there were seven sisters and two brothers–spoke about "those" people in whispers or hushed tones.

What came across clearly was that in and around all the whispering involving "those people," who were "that way," there was little pleasantry expressed. At least not when they discussed the women. The whispering sessions resembled a football huddle, but instead of calling out plays, there was a lot of eye-rolling, lip-smacking, and elbow nudging, not to mention the giggling, head nodding, and camouflaged finger-pointing, directed at the "different" women. Clearly, they weren't altogether accepted. Needless to say, all this signaled to me that my own good joy feelings would not be accepted either. (Years later I would learn to my amazement that one of that same gossiping gaggle of women, my Aunt Ruby, had been in the closet.)

Most of my mother's conversation with her sisters took place during their frequent knitting gatherings. Those knitting circles, to this day, conjure up a cigarette smoke-filled atmosphere. Pall Mall, Chesterfield, and Lucky Strike ashes filled the large square glass ash trays set between each chair or at their left elbows, depending on if they'd settled into one of their kitchens or in their living rooms. Lit cigarettes were always lying in wait for a long, lung-filled drag between the countless clicks of their needles.

Their sharp rhythmic clicks held double duty. First of all, they created some of the greatest character sweaters—like my bright red, short-sleeved Sleeping Beauty cardigan, featuring all seven Dwarfs on the back panel. The second duty of their clicking needles was to provide cover for their conversations, shielding them from the prying ears of children. These conversations encompassed everything from what would be on a dinner menu, to a coveted recipe, to their offspring's accomplishments, to the inevitable town scandals.

Yet the one conversation that I never heard discussed, muffled or otherwise—the "missing" conversation—would have involved yet another aunt of mine, my Aunt Ruby, the sister that moved to Alaska. She was the lesbian aunt. Though I was very skillful at eavesdropping on my mother and my aunts, I didn't learn about Aunt Ruby until long after I had come out of the closet myself. I wasn't surprised, because nothing about my family could surprise me by then. But it saddened me to think that she felt she had to move so far away in order to live. As it was, she remained closeted, married a Native Alaskan man and had multiple children. I don't know if she ever found happiness.

Curiously, I noticed, the "effeminate" men were not always shunned, even when they were outwardly flamboyant. Somehow they were allowed to fit in, while the male-dressed women were treated as social outcasts by our church community.

The unspoken acceptance of the gay men and the pointed ostracizing of the lesbians played out also within my own immediate and extended family. Neither my younger brother, a gay man, nor I, a lesbian, ever attempted to hide our sexual orientation from the family once we were adults. Yet while he was never forbidden to spend time with our nieces and nephews, I was told in no uncertain terms not to go near any of them, with or without other adults around. This would take an incredible toll on me over the years.

Yet during this period there was a silver lining. I met Susi Learmonth (Dr. Susi Lamdin at the time), a single mother of three boys, and a friend and music student of my father's second wife. As we got to know one another, she became the single most important presence in my life. From Susi I learned what a loving family actually looks like and feels like. She would provide the maternal love I needed to grow into myself. Our friendship would span more than fifty years.

I WANT TO rewind a bit here, and re-focus on my new found passion for people watching and the growing keenness of my young eyes. One day near the Dudley Street Station, I noticed an establishment that I gathered had been there all along, but was just out of sight of the place I typically stood waiting for my bus. It was the Red Line, and I was waiting for the Warren Street bus, heading home. One day, this place caught my attention because I saw a pair of sharp, male-dressed women on the street, heading toward and disappearing into an inconspicuous, dark-windowed tavern. I wondered what it was. Later I would hear the tavern referred to as the "bulldagger's bar."

At the time I simply enjoyed watching these women come and go on days when I waited for my bus. I'd hear snippets of conversations from other observers of this foot traffic, who were often loud in expressing their offense, and I quickly realized that I did not share their sentiment. I liked how the women walked, how they dressed, and the supreme confidence with which they seemed unbothered by those who objected to their lifestyle. In their own way they did fit in, because they didn't give others the satisfaction of stopping them from expressing who they were. As I got older, I came to understand myself better because of observing those women. Today, I identify neither as a butch, nor a femme lesbian. I tend to dress in a variety of ways that feel comfortable and suitable to me at any given moment, depending on where I'm going. But I will be forever grateful to those women near the Dudley Street Station for opening up another world for me, one in which I could imagine my own more authentic self-expression.

There is no direct line between my first real crush on Char, and those moments when I watched the Dudley Street Station butches, but I know for sure that all of it made me begin to feel more comfortable about my newfound fun joy good feeling for Char. What is unquestionable is that these experiences led me into a world I felt at ease with, and remain so, although this was a world I never saw on TV, heard about on the radio, nor heard spoken of kindly in my family and their supposedly "polite" society.

It was many years before I got any indication of acceptance for who I am from my parents. In my late twenties, my mother called to tell me that she loved me, "even though you're that way."

In the same way I can tell you exactly where I was standing in school when I learned that President Kennedy had been assassinated, I can remember every detail of the little magnets on the refrigerator in my Mission District, San Francisco flat that day. That's what I focused on during that phone call. What I cannot tell you is how long I stood staring at that refrigerator after her call ended. I can tell of the numbness I felt as her words penetrated to my heart. I can also tell you it has taken me many, many years after her sudden death to understand what it must have meant to her to speak her heart to me that day. Sadly, the mother-daughter bond that had detached between us shortly after my first girl-crush never came close to fully mending in this lifetime.

In May of 2013, my father made a similar call to me, in which he said: "I hope the Supreme Court rules in your favor in June." He meant the marriage equality decision. That was the first time he ever openly acknowledged my lesbian lifestyle, although he has known for decades. I told him long ago. His recollection of that long ago conversation is that "I said nothing when you told me." I reminded him of what really took place: he had turned away from me and said, "That's not my fault." More recently he said, "Oh, I don't remember saying that." Even today, he prefers that we never speak of it—nor of all the years I was excluded from family gatherings. Basically, he let me know that he prefers that I just dismiss those feelings that arose and settled in my heart each and every one of those painful years of my exclusion.

Even now there is no room for conversation that includes my sharing with him how I have felt as a result of the exclusion, nor does he offer any explanation of what was happening on his end during those years. I don't know how to dismiss those years. I don't know how to pretend it didn't happen. I especially don't know how to do so when I'm still excluded; still not allowed to share my love with my nieces and nephews and the newborns in their families. To this day, when announcements are sent out heralding the coming of a new grandchild, I am not included in the telephone tree.

I must end this tale by telling of my saving grace. That has been the degree to which the emotional impact of being ostracized by my own family was softened early on, by my being embraced and loved by Susi Learmonth, the music student. By the time I met Susi, I was desperate for an adult in my life to let me know I was not broken. To that end, I give thanks that I met her when I was thirteen years old and the oldest of her three boys was eleven. I give thanks to her with all my heart for listening to me when I told her that I liked girls. She didn't walk away, she didn't stop listening; she didn't tell me that I could not come to her house anymore.

Moments before I came out to Susi my heart pounded, fiercely, as though it might beat straight through my chest. I felt much as I had on a day, years earlier, when I stood directly over an open gutter at the curb in front of St. Francis de Sales Church holding in the palm of my hand the host I had received during communion. Since the nuns and priests never answered my doubting questions, I decided then to speak directly to God myself. "Forgive me, for I do know what I'm about to do." I turned over my hand, releasing the host, and watched it fall through one of the open slats of the gutter; my eyes squeezed tight, my head bowed as I waited for His instant wrath. Telling Susi I was a lesbian was the second time in my life that I held my breath in that particular way, waiting for my life to crumble at my feet in an instant.

But God didn't strike me dead with a lightning bolt. And Susi sealed normalcy back into my life by giving me a light kiss on my forehead.

Years later, I often wondered why Susi's heart did not close off to me because of my sexual orientation, as was the case with my own family. I do know that she knew firsthand what it was like to be an outcast. She was born in Vienna, Austria in 1926, after the Anschluss—the occupation and annexation of Austria into Nazi Germany. In March, 1938, Susi's family escaped to the United States through Italy. Her father, Dr. Otto Ehrentheil, was one of thousands of citizen-soldiers who did whatever they could do during that period. He was instrumental in sponsoring Jewish families and in finding many other American sponsors for Jewish families fleeing Europe.

Susi is the one adult who nourished and encouraged my authentic girl spirit and who brought me to where I am now. Just after she was diagnosed with brain cancer, at the old age of eighty-four, Susi shared that it was her experience with me and my coming out, and the way she had to work through it within herself way back then, that eventually helped her many years later to assist Jack, her once very conservative second husband, to accept his own son's coming out as gay. Jack has since then turned around 180 degrees in his heart. When the state of Vermont recognized same sex marriage, Susi's husband Jack was the Justice of The Peace in Corinth, VT. He has now wedded many same-sex couples at the Town Hall and in their home.

It was Susi's acceptance of me, during my young coming out years, that finally allowed me to openly own and embrace my fun joy good feelings for other women.

To this day, I look back and remember fondly my first girl crush on Char. I remember her, and I grin like a Cheshire cat when I recall how my heart would leap each time Char entered the kitchen, as I stood beside her mother, learning to fry catfish.

In loving memory of my dear friend, Susi J. Learmonth

MOTHERTONGUE
DR. BONNIE J. MORRIS

Dr. Bonnie J. Morris is an out lesbian professor and author, and for the past twenty-one years have taught women's studies and lesbian history at both George Washington University and Georgetown in Washington, D.C. She is the author of thirteen books, three of which were Lambda Literary Award finalists: *Eden Built By Eves, Girl Reel, Revenge of the Women's Studies Professor.* "Revenge" is also a one-woman play which she's staged all over the world from Iceland to New Zealand. When not teaching or writing, she lectures on Olivia Cruises, works as a consultant for Disney and the State Department, and gives workshops at women's music festivals. She's about to publish a new book on the vanishing of lesbian spaces, titled *The Disappearing L.* Her story "Mothertongue" is memoir.

TO BE A writer and gay, lesbian, or queer at the turn of this last century is to live in the overlap between corporate publishing and numbers of unknown zines. It's to labor moodily over your doctored resumes, wondering "Do my lesbian books COUNT? Do I mention them? Does publish or perish apply in my situation?" To be a lesbian writer today is to harbor aspirations of perhaps becoming a FAMOUS homo, or to possibly write about the body in ways that most straight folks would find unpoetic, no matter how you express it.

Let's face it, today the bloom is off the rose of radical lesbian literature. The heyday and explosion of our acclaimed women writers from the 1970s and '80s has passed. However, many of us are still writing, and yes we're still being published. But the struggle is harder for us now. Women's bookstores, like D.C.'s now-closed Lammas Bookstore, once showcased the mass wave of 1970s/'80s women authors long before Borders, Crown, and Barnes & Noble discovered us. Considering us the "cliterati," those bookstores have now remarketed women writers under "gender studies." Now a few top famous gals get big reviews while all over the nation women's bookstores are disappearing, vanishing, nearly extinct, like magnificent saber-toothed tigers. One store is shutting down after the other, like clams stranded at low tide, and newcomer women writers and readers have no space to find and read the dykey words that Hyperion simply won't publish.

Thankfully, in the 1990s poetry slams and open mics emerged in a renaissance of lesbian coffeehouse culture. In this arena, our writing took off once again, this time on caffeinated wings, serving up heaven and hell in bar-stooled dives named Heaven and Hell, and in poetry and theater salons named Works in Progress, Mothertongue, and Women's One World, scattered throughout the U.S.

I first discovered poetry slams at the OutWrite gay and lesbian writers' conferences and through the Lambda Literary Foundation's journal, *Lambda Book Report,* during the mid-1990s. I tried one slam and won fourth prize. After that, I woke up in January 2000 and told myself I was going to use that first year of the century to be a writer in the city where I live: Washington, D.C.

After producing volumes of stories, essays, poems, manuscripts from age five on, finally I was now a writer, especially once the haunting question of "Will I ever have a BOOK of my own?" had been settled. I got my first book published in 1997: a series of interviews about my parents' Los Angeles high schools, reviewed favorably in a great spread in the *L.A. Times.* I was being interviewed and reviewed and profiled regularly, soon learning that "fame" is a mixed bag. For instance, one month my picture actually appeared on the cover of one of D.C.'s free gay weeklies, and while this was terribly thrilling, I had to adjust to seeing the homeless men and women of Dupont Circle sleeping on spread-out copies of my face.

Between 1997 and late 1999 I published my first three books to good acclaim, but I belonged to no writers' group, and had no peer membership. What confidence I gained (Look, Ma, a book a year!) had been sapped by late 1999, when I was living through a very horrible year of being trashed in several reviews for my big book on lesbian music festivals. I was consequently freaked out, defensive, and lonely. Somewhat perversely, I was dating only those women who knew nothing about me or my work.

Despite my attempts to be somewhat low-key as a lesbian writer, I kept dragging the women I was dating to open mics in basements, or to trashy films about authors. Then, suddenly, a Jewish woman I'd met at the last event of Lammas Women's Bookstore, and an African-American woman I'd met at a debate about the Human Rights Campaign's "Millennium March" both e-mailed me, asking if I'd serve as an impartial judge for some poetry slam at "Mothertongue." And that is how I first found my beloved literary community, and managed to come back from the dead.

Mothertongue was a monthly women's open mic. It began in the fall of 1998 and lasted until 2013. When I first walked into the Black Cat nightclub where it took place, I'd only missed out on the first year-and-a-quarter. The nightclub was on 14th Street NW, in Washington, D.C. On that frozen night of February, 2000, hundreds of unbelievably attractive young poets in hip-hugger pants and pierced navels were lining up to read at the Valentine's Day "anti-love" slam. Despite my twenty-five years in queer D.C. I knew almost no one in the room, perhaps because they all seemed to be college age, and I was pushing forty. But here I was, the "real" lesbian author, brought in as a judge. I bought myself a glass of wine, and as soon as I sat down to drink, poet Noabeth

Bruckenthal stood up. That instant is frozen in my memory. It's what I'll always picture as the start of my Mothertongue journey.

Until Noa flexed her arms and opened her mouth, I had forgotten that such a woman was possible: young, out, loud, proud, Jewish, and built like an athlete. She took up space twice as well as I did, at twenty-two. Everyone in the room was screaming her name, "NOA, NOA," as though this really were the Ark and we were the last of the lesbian species to be saved for the Goddess's greener pastures. But Noa was a nice dyke rugby player, not an old man with a ship. She stood and posed and laughed and yelled, and I slid off my chair and stopped being bored with anything ever again. After her followed two dozen women, each as compelling as Noa, and their prose and poems shouted YES: I am the woman, Jewish and Black and Latina and mixed; I am the Native, invisible/seen. I am the foot on racism's neck. I am the one they raped who lived to tell about it. I am the young lesbian/queer scene writ large. It was an open mic Garden of Eden, and Adam discreetly tended the bar. Eve was in every line of spoken word, and all the fruit was luscious, ripe, split open by our common language.

And everyone knew everyone. I wondered, how long had this been going on? Where did they all come from? All these hip and curvy, scruffy, buffy dykey girls with notebooks, printouts, tender pages clutched in sweating palms, silver rings on fingers, nose rings, bulging competent Rosie the Riveter arms; red henna hair tossed back from tight young faces, throats cleared. Ready/set/GO. This was passion, written out by hand, memorized, delivered. Slam it, then sit down. That's what they did.

"Wow, you're really good," I said to Noa's back, but she left too quickly and I had to wait a full month to see her again. This open mic came each month like every woman's blood flow—Mothertongue, third Wednesday night, at the Black Cat nightclub, doors opening at eight or so, $5 sliding scale. There was always a line of creased black jackets stretching down the block. Inside was low lighting, dark walls, drumming and announcements, round tables, and scream-ing crowds. "THIS IS THE ONLY SCENE IN TOWN," I e-mailed all my loved ones. "THIS IS THE REBIRTH OF IDEAS, COMMUNITY, FRESH WORDPLAY."

Month after month, I never heard anyone bomb onstage, although half the readers hung their heads in shyness, as women writers can do. But I was in perfect awe of everyone. However, spreading the word as I did brought mixed results from certain middle-aging pals of mine. I brought one friend whose nervous comment was "Young crowd," meaning, NOT FOR US. But maybe you had to be a writer, because it was very much for me. I had an ageless hunger that got fed each month, and so of course I kept going back.

The nerve-wrack of Mothertongue was this: once I started getting up onstage and being the "old dyke" at the party, I started seeing a line of my own students march in and sit down just before I launched into an erotic piece. All right! Fine. Let them know their professor gets laid. But still, seeing the same faces in class the next day could bring a blush to my blazered throat. "Turn in your midterms, please, and oh, how did you like that seduction scene I read last night?"

But living in the groove of good lit, ah, how sweet. When I was in my twenties I also had a "scene" like this, but not so literary. From 1983-1991, I belonged to Herizon, a lesbian social club in Binghamton, New York. We had a bar and talent shows, and that was home for eight years of my life. When it closed I thought, never again will I have such a place. Mothertongue *was* different from Herizon, but it became a second current home.

It was my home because it served me in times of grief and ritual. I experienced this more than once. Mothertongue fell on Yom Kippur one year—a tragic snafu of schedule. It was Wednesday night, and this was the first Mothertongue after September 11th, 2001, you see, and our lives had been rocked and split. We all needed our friends, to hug, to hear our poems, to be together. All over my D.C. I could feel Jewish dykes debating whether to attend Kol Nidre services or to slam some anti-war verse at Mothertongue. Pray or play? Fast or party? The end of the world might be near. We needed to cry out for the dead in our memories. Which site served these goals?

This was just after "Reverend" Jerry Falwell had made his infamous remarks blaming feminists and homosexuals for the attack on the World Trade Center. Yes, reclaiming our own holiness on this night—instead of ritually blaming ourselves—became a dyke imperative. And I became a bad girl, storming to the club. But I thought, *I will not fast tonight. I can't.* So while American flags fluttered from every cafe on 18th Street, and gay men in yarmulkes walked toward Congregation Beth Mishpachah, I was thinking, "Blessed is my writing community," and I went there.

As it turned out, I wasn't the only one. Inside Mothertongue the Jews present found each other like magnets, saying "Good. You came anyway." Emcee Lauren Schumer, endlessly stylish in a smart black suit, was scribbling away on a tablet—our slim Moses, our Moishe Rabeynu. Lauren introduced the somber post-bomb evening by waving her long statement on the meaning of Yom Kippur. But, she quickly added, she'd decided not to read it. What she wanted to say was that she was very sorry about the timing of the show falling on the holiest night of the Jewish calendar, but that she was really glad we all came to Mothertongue to find some solace in our beloved lesbian community, and that she, Lauren, was leaving soon to go to shul and pray. There was a collective hum and sigh among us women. Right on. Someone of our number goes to God tonight, to be in Jerusalem. The rest of us will break every commandment: eat, drink, smoke, fuck, dance and wear perfume and leather shoes. We're tired, so tired of organized religion, its mullahs, reverends,

Taliban; time to break some rules and be among each other, as women, and not self-deny.

So the parade of sacrilege began. Onstage, in wild defiance, I shouted that I found the pious Orthodox of organized religion to be behind all of the world's most major problems.

"Tonight *you* are my temple," I proclaimed. "The writing life is my spirituality, and I'm having a drink on Yom Kippur in the name of *all* our dyke ancestors." Actually, no bolt of lightning hit me, only sweet applause. I hugged Natalie so hard I accidentally dropped her, and both of us got bruised falling down.

Later on, I rode over to Club Chaos in my student JJ's little red car, and ended up getting drunk on vodka shots, and dancing, in true erotic disaster. I got crushed between two much younger women, a gay guy and a drag king, and thrown back and forth by Noa and her joyous gorgeous muscles. Everyone pressed up against me, bumping and grinding, in this orgiastic sandwich, all of us on the dance floor behaving disgracefully, until at last I peeled off and said, "That's it: I'm leaving now," and wobbled home.

Since it was really Yom Kippur, I would not eat or drink for another eighteen hours. In Hebrew, eighteen is the number value of the word *chai*, which means life. I was hungover, bruised from falling down, from dancing pelvis to pelvis, and from being a bad girl in wartime with all my lesbian poet buds. Now eighteen hours of fasting, and my last shot at heaven, before the Book of Life slammed shut on me. Mothertongue—blessed art thou, my beloved women's community. May you be inscribed in the Book of Life, as Jews wish each other at High Holiday time.

After that night, I experienced month after month of being a writer onstage, introduced by our robust and energetic emcee, Heather Davis, saying, "Next up, Dr. Bon," and me saying, "What's up, women?" and launching into my spoken word. Heather and her friend Lauren did an almost comedy act of hosting, witty and sharp, loving and flirtatious, holding the all-important List with names of readers waiting to go up. And go up we did, like climbing mini-steps to heaven, because once you left your tabletop and found the side of the stage and walking and blinking your way to the mic with hopefully good applause to welcome you, it was *let's try out this piece of writing that I've never shared before. Let's read what's scariest, most personal. Let's regard the audience as family, gene pool, datelife, critic, agent. Now or never. Is my hair okay?*

Offstage, we held meetings, had a BOI (a Board of Instigators) determining which women's charity we'd donate to each month, no matter how modest the intake at the door. Heather's briefcase bulged with organization applications, those hoping to be our beneficiary-of-the-month. Our stories and open mics funded women leaving prostitution, writing programs for women and girls of color, girls in the sciences, battered women's shelters, rape survivors, peace groups, arts foundations that struggled even more than we did to stay solvent in those last years of George W. Bush.

Then one day came a shocker. On my father's sixty-seventh birthday, 20 December, 2001, I was out West, celebrating with my family in Santa Cruz, California, blissfully unaware of events unfolding back East. On the morning of December 21st my parents were still asleep when I rose up bright-faced in California, to saturate my eyes and my heart with the swollen creek of our family's backyard, dripping with Santa Cruz oak and redwood trees. The misty morning dew hung on every spider's web. Just as I sighed with pleasure into my steamy coffee, the phone rang, and Karen Taggart and Lauren Schumer from Mothertongue in D.C. broke the news to me. The night before, Heather, our emcee, had died in a car crash on the Beltway. Heather Davis, the friend whose house I partied at, who introduced me on countless nights, calling me onto the stage with excitement and panache. Heather was gone in an instant. She had died soon after the one monthly Mothertongue show that I missed, the Wednesday when I'd flown West to visit my parents.

Heather, the onstage mistress of our matrix, one of our own, GONE. "Sorry to ruin your vacation," Karen and Lauren said. At first, I could barely feel anything, except the instant whisper in my head: *"Be careful now, and mind your own mortality."* This winter solstice: the longest night of the year, this long night's journey into sleep, and that poet's voice was now silenced. It was the year's end, and it was one month shy of Heather's thirtieth birthday. I struggled to take this in.

I pictured Heather, big and smiling, holding the Mothertongue clipboard, motioning me onstage, reading announcements laced with her deadpan humor, folding brochures for our next event; a living, walking body. How could she ever know as she drove away from the pre-Christmas Mothertongue show, that her work with us was done? There was no way. No one could know.

The sudden loss of Heather made me think. What about us? All of us. Who will remember us? What do we need to do to live forever? This is what I thought in frantic stupidity as Karen cried into the phone long distance, "What is the lesson, Bon? That it's easy come, easy go? What is God telling me?" Our Heather was gone, after that great last show, with the pressure of our whole community's hugs still upon her back. *"Take it with you, girl. Take us with you."*

I marveled at how quickly it can end. You can go from poet organizer to heavenly angel in an instant. How could Heather be dead? I recalled twenty-two months of Heather saying into the microphone, "And next up, we have Dr. Bon," and me jumping on stage to recite my work. This was impossible to digest; the end of an era.

That day, I drove away from my parents' house to look at the ocean, and ironically I was behind a hearse the whole way. This had never happened to me on any road in my life. Coincidence? Not. Heather was always my emcee; now was I her escort to another world?

When I returned to D.C. in January, we held her memorial tribute. It was the party to end all parties, with the rumble of *"Value each other, value each other,"* looping like a Chinese dragon through our women's community. On Wednesday night, January 16th, everyone lined up against the brick wall outside the Black Cat nightclub in gorgeous lesbo finery, including cleavage in winter, and elegant clothes of black and red. Inside, candles flickering. There were dykes with journals, and weeping Jewish girls. There was flirtation in grief and loss, in love's response to death. Beautiful young butches, and bois, whispering softly to one another the single exhaled word, *"Dude."* Everyone flipping through whatever ripped-out pages they had brought to read in praise of Heather's life. Our purpose lay as sharp as splinters in our palms. Lauren Muser, Heather's roommate and friend, reminded us, from under her sombrero, that humor and sexiness were our obligations tonight, or Heather would start sneering. So everyone was touching, drinking, exchanging phone numbers, and exposing lacy bras. This was our sendoff—the sounds of drumming and didjeridoo, old video clips and anger, dancing, photos, and words. Of course, there were words.

There's a sort of inward gasp when you see your community at its best. I felt proud of us. I felt comforted. Should anything happen to ME, I thought, I too would be remembered by my community. It was a night to feel *at home*, rather than sad; we'd all been sad for weeks. How do you thank the woman who did so much to make this our home but now is only present as a ghost? With noise and tears and sensuality right up to closing time. Drum the girl up on her golden way. And we did.

Days later, there was a Mothertongue board meeting and we even had a grief counselor present, should anyone be wrecked. But mostly the vibe afterward was: *"That was great!"* No doubt, now, that we women had the greatest scene in town. "I was never prouder in my life," said Taggart, meaning how our community came together and dressed up to recognize Heather. Our women's community, our dyke literati. And even a few more days after that, when she and I were walking together after a cycling workout, Taggart suddenly turned to me and said: "I get chills just thinking about it."

I smiled. I knew what she meant. Those of us who even then were scorned and rejected, few laws yet in place to protect us and no same-sex marriage, were finding our family in poetry and word, transcending our loss and binding our love around a microphone.

Later on, Noa e-mailed me: "Tell me about life on Earth vs. preparing for the afterlife," she said. Then she added: "How about that full moon last night? A solitary goose sat on the water, puffs of condensation emanating as she honked."

LET IT BE KNOWN: MY COMING OUT STORY
ASHLEY OBINWANNE

**Ashley Obinwanne** is a Nigerian-American writer and film-maker. She was born in Yonkers, New York but spent most of her childhood in Port Harcourt City, Nigeria. She studied biology at The State University of New York at Albany, but ultimately decided to pursue a career in writing. She moved to Los Angeles in 2014, created a web series called *Lavender Collective*, and co-founded LesbiansOverEverything.Com. She is currently writing a screenplay for a short film called *Adapting*. "Let it Be Known: My Coming Out Story" is memoir.

Part 1

THE FIRST REAL crush I had was on a girl named Joy. Before that, I'd had "strong feelings of attachment" toward my nanny without knowing what those feelings were. All I remember is that I liked spending time with her and I thought it was a shame that she was getting married. I must have been six at the time.

Joy and I attended the same secondary school in Port Harcourt, Nigeria for a year. We were both in the seventh grade, but we were in different classrooms, so we never really spoke. I noticed her because she was taller than most of the other seventh graders. The fact that she was really pretty might have also been a factor.

I changed schools at the end of that year for no particular reason. I stayed at my next school until I was done with the nineth grade, and then I changed schools again at the start of grade ten, because everyone else was doing it. This time, I went to a boarding school that my two older sisters had previously attended.

A twelfth grader who was friends with my sisters helped me carry my bags up three flights of stairs. She walked me into the room that was meant for the girls in grade ten. Before she left, she handed me off to another girl that she had selected at random.

"Hey you! Help her get settled in!"

That girl looked awfully familiar. I hadn't seen or thought about her in over two years, but it didn't take me long to realize who she was. Joy pointed me in the direction of an empty bunk bed, and then we caught up on each other's lives as she helped me unpack.

A week later, all the girls in my grade were being punished because some of us hadn't done our chores. A senior student called us down to the dining room to "serve our punishment." When it was your turn, you would put both hands on the wall and let the senior use the flat side of a broken clothes hanger to flog your ass.

Most of the girls took their punishment in stride. Some of them cried, but they were at least able to get the whole thing over with relatively quickly. Not me. I couldn't stand still. I'd try, but then she'd raise the hanger to hit me and I'd panic and move away. I was a sweaty, a terrified mess. Then out of nowhere, Joy said, "I'll take it for her." She said it in the coolest way too. If I wasn't crushing on her before, I definitely was then.

I could go on to write about the things that Joy and I experienced together in the three years that followed, about the time when we locked the guidance counselor in her room because she was annoying, or the time when we hid underneath a bed because the vice principal was looking for us, or how we argued over the silliest things, but this story isn't really about Joy. The last time I saw her, it was someone's birthday, and we were outside a movie theater saying goodbye. We had just finished secondary school, and I was leaving Nigeria for good a few days later. We hugged for a long time. I left for the United States. I haven't seen her in six years.

When I was sixteen, I got on a bus from New York City to Toronto so I could visit my best friend Daniel. He was openly gay. I went to Pride for the first time. I hung out with a lot of gay and bisexual people, but if anyone asked, "I was there to support my friend." The following summer, when I was again in Canada, and we were playing truth or dare on the beach, Daniel's friend grilled me about my sexual orientation. She wanted to know if I was gay, straight, or bisexual. At the time, I was only comfortable admitting that I liked girls. I wasn't quite ready to take on any labels yet. That wasn't a good enough answer for her, so she badgered me with questions for about an hour. My answer remained the same. The night ended rather dramatically. Everyone involved—the woman who kept asking me questions, her girlfriend, Daniel, and myself—ended up getting upset in some way.

A few months later, when I was back at school, I wrote a "Coming Out" poem. I remember it having the lines: "This is me finally saying it out loud. This is me finally coming out." I shared it with Daniel and his friend even though I was sure they already knew. I came out to my roommates and my college friends casually. It was never a big deal for them.

The hardest part was coming out to my mother. I didn't have the heart to do so in person. I didn't want to get into a huge fight. I lived with her for three months after I graduated college. I cut my hair off in that time. She didn't like it. On one occasion, she hinted that people might think that I'm gay because of it. I quickly changed the subject.

I wrote her a letter in February, 2015, when I was thousands of miles away in California. It's funny, she called me on the day that I put the letter in the mailbox, a week before she was set to receive it. My aunt had seen me post something lesbian-related on my Facebook page, and she had called my mother to warn her. Apparently two other unnamed people had also told her about their "suspicions." My mother wanted confirmation that I wasn't . . . she couldn't even bring herself to say the words. I knew what she wanted to hear. I knew that everything would be a lot easier for her and a lot less awkward for me if I could just say, "No, Mum, I'm not a lesbian." But I couldn't do that. I couldn't keep pretending, so I said, "Yes, I am."

She yelled at me.

"Don't you know where you're from? You're being influenced. It's this country. It's America. What will people say? This is a disgrace."

I hung up. We didn't speak for weeks. In that time, I came out to everyone who mattered. I told my dad via text. He thought I was joking at first, and then he thought I was just saying that to piss him off. I didn't really care what he thought. I told one of my sisters, but she already knew. She sent me a supportive text. It was short and straightforward, but it made me cry like a baby. I was grateful for it.

I am twenty years old. I've been completely out as a lesbian for a year now, and I don't regret it in the slightest. I feel as if a weight has been lifted off my shoulders. My parents and I get along now. We talk about everything except the fact that I'm a lesbian, but they call to say that they love me, and that is enough.

Part 2
Just Let Me Be: A Personal Look at Being Gender Nonconforming

AS A KID, getting dressed for church, or for weddings, or for pretty much any formal event was always a battle. When left to my own devices, I would throw on a pair of jeans, a T-shirt, and a comfortable pair of shoes, and be done with it. But that was never good enough. My mother would want me in a skirt or in a dress. I at least had to wear earrings. I had to change out of "those shoes." And I did. I'd pout and I'd complain, but I ultimately had to wear whatever outfit my mother had deemed appropriate.

As a teenager, this trend carried on. My two older sisters had begun wearing makeup, and I was "childish" for not wanting to. I "lacked a fashion sense." My mother chided me for being so strange. I started wearing my older sister's clothes to compensate. I wore high heels even though I hated them. I occasionally wore makeup. When I did, the compliments came flooding in. My mother was pleased, and I was happy to be doing something right.

During my last three years in college, when I lived away from home, I found myself wearing clothes that I actually wanted to wear. Without my mother or my sisters standing over my shoulder and scrutinizing my choice in clothes, my T-shirt collection grew tremendously.

In the weeks leading up to my graduation, my mother grew concerned about what I would wear on the big day. She called me to ask about it.

"Uh. I think I'll wear a blazer, and maybe a pair of black pants."

That didn't cut it. She was sure to pack a dress and a pair of heels in her suitcase for me.

I was eighteen. Two years have passed since then. In that time, I have cut my hair, moved across the country, and officially come out to my family. I haven't worn anything that I haven't wanted to wear since May, 2014.

I thought we had all come to terms with the fact that I just didn't like to wear certain clothes, so imagine my surprise when I got a call from my mother last week informing me that she had bought me a dress to wear to my older sister's graduation. (She's getting a Master's degree. Go sis!)

It's completely ridiculous to me that my mother and I spent over five minutes going back and forth about it.

"Why won't you wear the dress?"

"I don't want to."

"What if you just wore it for a few hours and we got some pictures of you in it."

"No."

"I spent a lot of money on that dress."

"I didn't ask you to."

"Just wear the—"

"No. No. No. No."

I could probably just wear the dress (and the heels that I'm certain will accompany it). I could make myself uncomfortable for a few hours so I can keep the peace. Pose for a few pictures so that my mother can upload them to Facebook and pretend for a while that her daughter isn't a butch lesbian. But I've done that for too long. I'm sick of pretending to be someone that I'm not. I won't do it anymore. I can't.

PRISON DYKIN': SHE WORE A DIFFERENT UNIFORM
TONYA PRIMM

Tonya Primm is an underground lesbian voice, currently writing from prison in Tennessee. We are grateful to have her story in our collection.

FINDING A LOVER while I was in prison was not at the top of my priorities. A woman wearing a guard's uniform completely failed to make the list, considering the time I spent avoiding even casual conversation with our jailers.

She worked the maximum security unit as a prisoner escort; I worked there as maintenance. In the max unit, I had to be escorted and supervised at all times—by her. This was an unwelcome pairing at first. I was an inconvenience to her rigid schedule—something she did not fail to remind me of frequently. She was a hard, by-the-book challenge to my willful nature. Our personalities clashed as we both pushed to be in charge.

Over time however, I was surprised to see her stiff façade fading, and a gentleness begin showing through. After some months, instead of a strip search, we started greeting each other with a smile and parted with a "good evening." As time passed, the orders she barked at me as an inmate were transformed into conversations between more or less equals.

I became attracted to the flirtiness of her laughter when I said something silly, her thoughtfulness in the little things she did, like folding the shirts I shed as I worked. I was even attracted to her callousness—as long as it wasn't directed at me. There were even times when her interactions with me seemed to possess the suggestion of something more. I was unsure as to what this meant, plus I questioned her sincerity.

One day during what should have been a routine strip search, I took a chance. Leaning back on the sink, I reached out, pulled her to me, and kissed her. It was gentle enough to not freak her out, yet deep enough to gauge her response to this action. My instincts were confirmed when she did not resist, and instead pressed into me and returned my kisses.

After this icebreaking moment, my working in maintenance became a job of pure convenience for us. I was allowed the clearance I needed to move from one building to another without any questions being asked. There happened to be a lot of "work" that needed to be done in max; more so when she was there. She would have me called in for non-existent emergencies at night during her overtime shifts. These included a washer in the laundry room that would not turn on and needed to be repaired before morning; a water leak in a storage room that could not wait; a light out in management's office that would cause far too much inconvenience to fix the next day. Our favorite "emergency" occurred on rainy nights, when the air units would shut off and not reset properly. At these times we were granted a trip to the roof in complete privacy with no chance of being interrupted or seen. Part of our daily routine became finding clever ways to snatch a moment for the simple physical contact we both craved.

There were many frustrating moments as well, when I wanted to share myself with her either verbally or physically, but could not because we might be seen. Instead, I was forced to restrain myself. One of the harshest reminders of the barriers we faced was when we got too comfortable and called one another by our first names, which drew far too much attention and suspicion from those around us. Thankfully, those lapses were few. We learned to put on a good show by maintaining stringent boundaries. It also helped that she was one of the strictest officers here, so no one expected otherwise from her.

Obviously my circumstances limited and strained the relationship we had. Sadly, there were no conversations or dreams of what the future held for us. To be honest, I saw no purpose in dreaming, considering the length of time I faced here and the dim chance of that changing. Sure, we had mail, phone calls, and our brief hideaway moments whenever we could steal them. However, that all seemed superficial to me compared to what could actually be. The reality was that this could not be a lasting connection. There was no future for us.

We eventually both realized we had had all we would ever have, and that was not enough for either of us. She deserved more than I could possibly give her; I wanted more than she was able to offer me, given the huge risks she was already taking with her job. After several months, we ended our relationship the only way we knew how: she transferred to another institution.

BEYOND THE WOODEN SPOON
Excerpt from an Italian-American Memoir
FRANCESCA ROCCAFORTE

Francesca Roccaforte came out as a lesbian during the 1970s in New York City. She relocated to the San Francisco Bay Area in 1979, joining other activists in the growing LGBTQ rights movement. Besides writing essays and poetry, she is a longtime photographer, exhibiting and publishing her work for the past five decades. Her website is: www.rocknfranny.weebly.com This story about her late mother "Vee" is a true recollection of her mother and their family in New York.

MY MOTHER VIRGINIA, Big Vee, (Virginia, Vincenza) and her delicious eggplant *parmigiana* and Neapolitan cooking were the center of our family home when I was growing up. Big Vee was the Italian Matriarch. She ruled with a wooden spoon in her working class kitchen, one of the many realms of her matriarchal power. Our kitchen decor included silver and beige triangles of sanitex linoleum and stained wooden cupboards, hand built by my uncle Joey Florio, the carpenter.

That 1950s gray linoleum floor knew how to handle the quick clicks of my mother's imitation leather slippers moving from sink to stove in one swift motion. Vee's peasant feet sounded heavy, as if her slippers had heels on them. She sat down only occasionally, stealing a moment to take a drag on her Winston cigarettes. Maybe it was the power of her motherhood in my small child's vivid imagination that made the sound of my mother's footsteps feel so powerful. As the youngest child, I was attuned to the footsteps of everyone in the family, especially my mommy's and daddy's.

My mother was a great cook and a fantastic baker of assorted goodies when we kids were young. She enjoyed it immensely, spending hours in the kitchen creating cheesecakes, cream puffs, honey-drenched *struffoli*, and all the other Italian holiday pastries and sweets. Vee took motherhood and cooking very seriously.

Big Vee wasn't actually big in height; she was only five feet tall, but she was strongly built, sturdy, and robust. We all looked up to her. She was the matriarch of the gang of girls and boys who surrounded her in our family kitchen. She was the domineering force in our household, controlling the men in the family with her food and nourishment.

Smart mouthed, sharp-tongued, fiery, generous, kind hearted, and warm, my mother also fed the many neighborhood children and various stray animals that my brothers often befriended. She had them all licking their fingers when she cooked and baked in our family home in Brooklyn's East New York.

In the 1960s, East New York was then a small urban village full of Southern Italian immigrants who brought their old world family traditions to those over-crowded city streets. The orange brick and shingled family row houses stood nestled together on our block with a few stoops for sitting and small front yards. Our family home was built by the weathered hands of my mother's grandfather, Vincenzo, a bricklayer from a small town outside of Naples. My grandmother, Antoinette, tended her Italian garden full of herbs, vegetables, and large, fluffy roses. She often sat under the shaded grapevine with the other old ladies. She and her *paesane* spoke only in Italian.

Regarding my mother, one of Big Vee's best recipes was definitely her egg-plant *parmigiana* hero on sweet Italian bread with sesame seeds. She bought the Italian bread freshly baked from the Colonial Bakery across the street from our house. I remember her methodically cutting the deep purple eggplant slice by slice, then stacking the slices between two plates and resting the clothes iron on top to give it weight. She said this released the bitterness from the eggplant. So I copied her method years later when I made eggplant in my own kitchen, calling her up and getting her family cooking secrets. She told me that the cheese was her main secret, and of course the spices.

"Use *mozzarella* with oil in it, not the non-fat kind that the skinny Americans eat," she said.

She told me to buy the *Locatelli* cheese, an aged *Romano* cheese that is very sharp and pungent. Even my father and brothers could tell you her most important details, since she had trained their stomachs with her wooden spoon, the one that she used to stir the gravy for macaroni every Sunday morning, bright and early.

The gravy, or sauce, she'd make ahead of time on Sunday for her eggplant on Wednesday. This allowed the flavors to mingle and simmer longer and it was richer tasting for our second round of *Ronzoni* macaroni during the week. She tried to train her family to be respectful of her hard work and our good fortune. She taught us to be grateful that we didn't eat "the same old shit" like the other peasant families who couldn't afford the luxury of freshly butchered steaks, Italian sausages stuffed with herbs and cheeses, veal cutlets, and seafood dinners which my father's salary afforded us.

My father, Frank Roccaforte, commuted daily to his supervisor job in an electronics factory in lower Manhattan. Along with Uncle Joey, they also earned extra money from selling seasonal holiday trees, wreaths, and Easter baskets made from palm leaves. They fashioned these seasonal items themselves, and sold them from our garage, located conveniently on a busy street *en route* to the Evergreen Cemetery on Bushwick Avenue in Brooklyn.

The fact that we had some lower middle class privileges around food, clothes, and education was a form of ethnic pride, and my family displayed it and tried to share it with others at their many open houses in our neighborhood. They liked to party and share our good fortune with everyone. At these parties, my mother received many compliments for her great cooking and her fun-loving spirit.

Vee was often the life of the many parties we held in our front yard and garage. We had weekend clambakes, barbecues, and wine tasting contests. Gallons of both red and white homemade wine lined our garage walls to be consumed at these block gatherings. We took great pride in the quality and strength of our family wine, sometimes having wine taste-offs with the other neighborhood winemakers. It was a family tradition to make wine each year, with even the kids participating in this process, including tasting the wine. Plenty of heated arguments arose over which family's wine would get you the drunkest!

As a kid, Mom sent me off to Catholic grammar school and later to high school with her amazing eggplant and meatball hero sandwiches on fresh Italian bread. It was one way she showed that she loved me. I felt special, since many of the other kids ate the crappy American cafeteria food. When I opened my brown paper lunch bag and saw an eggplant or meatball hero, I was particularly happy. It felt so good eating our Italian food. My mother would also tuck a Milky Way bar in with it. Sometimes I went home for lunch and she would make me a chocolate malted with ice cream. Oddly, I was still petite and muscular as a young tomboy, probably due to my vigorous athletics, rather than the rich Italian foods we ate on a regular basis.

Remembering myself at this age, as a young girl living within a family of three males and my Alpha mother, Vee, I knew that I didn't quite fit the stereotype of the girly-girl. I realized early that the men had more privilege, power, and freedom—things which I certainly couldn't have as a girl. As a female, I already felt the inequities within our family, so it was to my advantage to behave like a boy and dress like a boy as much as I could get away with, much to Vee's chagrin. I was often teased by others with the repeated taunt: "Are you a girl or a boy?" It annoyed me to have to answer such a ridiculous question.

I had very close bonds with other girls throughout my girls-only grammar school and high school years. My girl-on-girl crushes were exciting, even though sexual relations at that young age were forbidden and taboo. But when I observed various girls in the neighborhood, a frequent fantasy running through my mind back then was, "If I were a guy, I'd definitely go for her!"

Even though I had boyfriends as a teen, this desire and longing to experience lesbian love lingered in me until I was eighteen years old. It was only then that I could begin to explore and express my sexual feelings with

Carol, another young Italian American woman. Fortunately, she readily accepted her own lesbian identity even though she had never had a female lover. We kept our relationship a secret from our families, in the beginning, but I knew that Big Vee with her sharp eyes never missed a thing. Actually both of our mothers had their suspicions, because of the obvious closeness of our so-called friendship. Despite their suspicions and concerns, my first lesbian relationship, as young and fledgling as it was, had definitely gotten off the ground and for this I was thrilled.

We used to meet each other at a youth center in Greenwich Village and ride the subway home at night to Brooklyn. Our train rides home were filled with flirtations, small seductions, and tantalizing teases, with Carol brushing up against me and kissing me good night on the lips, which aroused my curiosity. It wasn't long after this that we rode out to Rockaway beach in the dead of winter, parked the car, and kissed each other long and passionately. No other rush of sexual excitement compared to this since there was so much seduction leading up to that first passionate kiss. The touch and feel of a woman made my head spin. I never felt this way with any guy, that was for sure.

We had to remain in the closet in Brooklyn. We only felt free to be ourselves in the Village and in the lesbian bars (The Dutchess & Bonnie and Clyde's). Coming out was physically dangerous in the 1970s. Homophobia was in full swing and we valued our safety. For this and other reasons, not many people knew about our relationship, except for our closest friends.

Besides parking in desolate spaces, we spent countless days and nights in Carol's basement room amidst her hippie black lights and pot smoke. We slept entwined in each other's arms, experimenting sexually with every fantasy we could think of. It became our private den of lust and love, the secrecy making it all the more exciting.

Because of the enormous time we spent in Carol's basement, coming upstairs only for food and drink, Carol's mother Lena grew suspicious of us. She tried to figure out what exactly we were doing down there. One night, she crept around in the darkened room while we slept, trying to catch us doing something. Fortunately we had heard her steps and quickly separated our bodies.

We kept this a secret from our families in the beginning, but I knew that Big Vee and her ever watchful eyes never missed a thing. However, somehow I don't think she put all the pieces together about Carol and me. Nevertheless, both of our mothers maintained strong suspicions about us, because this "friendship" of ours was so close. Either way, it didn't matter to me, because my first lesbian relationship was so exciting and engrossing.

A few years later, I actually did tell my mother the truth about Carol. Even though she liked Carol, she felt the whole lesbian thing was disgusting. In spite of her feelings, she did meet all of my girlfriends over the years, and she treated them well. My father was more open minded and accepting of my identity, but he feared for my safety from the haters.

Getting back to Big Vee and her influence, to this day I'll always remember my mother, her sharp, watchful eyes and her matriarchal power within our family, and of course her eggplant *parmigiana* hero. She passed away far too young, at the age of only sixty-two and our entire family was bereft.

Today, I think of my mother every day with gratitude. I'm dedicating this story to her: Virginia Diorato-Roccaforte, or Big Vee, born April 11, 1926, and died Oct 21, 1988. *Mille tante grazie Mama! Con amore, tua figlia, Francesca.*

LOST ON THE LAVA
LILITH ROGERS

Lilith Rogers writes in multiple genres. Regarding her own background, her father was Jewish but this didn't play a part in her youth as he converted to Christianity when he moved to Texas in the '40s. So she is a Caucasian raised in Texas who happily moved to California in her early twenties. "Lost on the Lava" is a chapter from her memoir in progress. It reflects upon the several months she and her partner Luna had spent on the Big Island studying Hawaiian culture and spirituality. This study reinforced for them both their long-held embrace of the power of the goddess in her many forms, and led them to call upon Pele in their time of need. And that call was answered. To find out more about Lilith's other works (including children's books and lesbian erotica) you can reach her at: Earthymamapress@gmail.com

WANDERING AT NIGHT with our tiny flashlights, we walked across the old lava flow on the big island, in Hawaii. We went over rough ground and smooth, uphill and down, holding hands, alternating leader and follower, thinking the car must be here? No, then over there? Hour after hour, toes getting sore from bumping the ends of our shoes, which filled with tiny glass shards that had to be dumped out over and over. Our ankles and knees started to ache from the constant up, down, up, down. Watch out for that crevice! My right wrist was hurting from you holding it so tightly, but I didn't want to tell you that.

"Oh, watch out for that hole, Lilith!" you called out as I almost stepped into it.

"Whew, thanks, Luna," I said to you. "How the heck did you see that? I sure didn't!"

"I didn't see it, honey. Just felt it was there. Pele is playing with us for sure. She wants to take us to the edge and see if we can figure out all her tricks."

On we wandered, calling out to the friends we were supposed to meet, hoping, despairing, getting colder and colder as the wind rose and the full moon slipped in and out behind clouds.

Oh, please Goddess Pele, don't let it rain, I silently prayed, protecting Luna from my fear by not speaking it out loud. We took tiny sips of the precious water we'd brought in little bottles, adequate for the short hike we had planned with our friends, but not for this endless wandering; just the two of us, hour after hour, up and down *over there, no, over there.* We never expected to get so lost.

Finally I said, "We're not finding the car tonight. We're exhausted. This is dangerous. Let's lie down and wait until morning."

You reluctantly, miserably agreed. "I guess you're right. Pele is playing with us tonight, and she's winning." In all the years I lived on the Big Island, the times I was allowed along with other haoles to attend Native Hawaiians' rituals, I could feel Pele's presence.

"Maybe it's me she's annoyed with, Luna," I said. "Maybe She feels I doubted her power. I mean, I've understood intellectually that when Kilauea goes off, what used to be solid ground, green fields, and sandy beaches can become molten rock, fiery flows like what we can see over there in the distance; the smoke. But wow, I didn't accept how awesome Her power is until tonight, when with one false step, we could go down."

"I can tell you're finally getting it, deep down inside . . . and I hope and pray Pele can tell."

"I sure am, honey," I answered. "In fact, why don't we say a prayer to Her now? I'll beg forgiveness for my arrogance. You offer one of those chants you learned from that Hawaiian kahuna, that shaman you used to study and pray with when you lived here."

"Good idea," you said. Lifting your arms and looking toward the distant flow, you called out, "Pele, Pele, Goddess of Fire, Creator of this island on which we stand. Lover of lovers, Giver and Destroyer. Have mercy on us. We know You can give as well as take. Please give us the gift of continuing our journey together and we promise to hold your fire in our bellies. To praise You and offer You our eternal gratitude. Aloha, dear Pele."

"Aloha, dear Pele," I shouted out, too.

Amazingly, a flood of sheer pleasure washed over me that had to come from Pele. The Goddess was listening, to the devotion in Luna's prayer, to my own best efforts. Luna carried deep faith in the wisdom of the teachings she'd absorbed from all the wise ones she'd studied with: in India where she had traveled long before we'd met; in Hawaii during her years here on the Big Island; in California where we live together now; even from the Catholic nuns and priests who taught her as a girl. I knew suddenly, her faith would see us through this trial as well.

With deep sighs and great weariness, trying to escape the cold wind that seemed to spring out of nowhere, we hunkered down in a tiny ball together on the glassy ground, under a small overhang of one of the taller hills.

You were shivering. I almost cried for you. I covered you with my long-sleeved silk shirt. It gave you just a shred more warmth, but it seemed to help.

I'll never complain ever again about any lumpy pillow, or any hard bed, I promised myself as I lay there waiting for this endless night to end. I watched the moon dance in and out of the clouds, still silently begging the elements to have enough mercy on us not to send rain.

Amazingly, we both fell asleep.

A few hours later, the sun woke us as it rose slow and red over the gray landscape. We got up too, so stiff we had to help each other to our feet. I was half afraid we'd find ourselves within easy reach of the parking lot, that if we'd only kept going last night, we'd have been spared that terrible evening.

But no. We both shed a few tears of dismay as the sun rose in a clear sky above a vision of nothing but more rolling gray lava mounds in every direction.

Every direction except one.

"Look, the sea is over there," you said suddenly, pointing. "We know we can follow the coast back to somewhere. Let's go." It was the first surge of hopeful energy either of us had felt in hours.

We walked and walked, uphill and down, hopping over and around deep crevices, amazed and grateful that we hadn't fallen into any holes the night before. The gray lava took on patterns, colors, and shapes we hadn't seen in the dark. Underfoot they were strange beasts and goddesses complete with Pele's long flowing tresses.

Now that we knew we were bound to arrive somewhere sooner or later, we finished off the last drops of our precious water. We sang songs of thanksgiving. We even laughed at our foolishness for going off alone so near sunset when we'd missed the group of women we had planned to hike with.

Finally, I pointed in the direction of the still distant sea. "Look, can you see that shiny thing over there? I think that's our truck!"

It was. Still far away, another hour of up and down, up and down and around.

Just as we got very near, we came upon a stone altar someone had set up in a large basin in the lava, perhaps put there by another lost soul. We stopped to pay our respects.

"Pele, Pele! Mahalo nui loa," we sang over and over as we added our own stones to the piles. Then simultaneously we shouted,

"Hurray! We did it! We did it! We got back safe and whole and alive and together." We hugged each other tight, laughing and crying with relief.

The remaining few yards to the truck took only a few more moments and we climbed in, started her up, and rushed through the few short miles home to our cabin.

We made it home, drank lots of water, feasted on papayas and bananas, and slept and slept. The next day we saw Helen, one of the group we'd missed for the hike to the flow. She told us the group had waited for us for a while and then gone off, wondering where we were.

"We must have missed you by only a few moments," she said. "I'm so sorry we didn't wait longer."

"It's not your fault," you told her. "We were late. And we had a strong encounter with Pele that night. She showed us who's boss around here, didn't she, Lilith?"

"She sure did, honey. I witnessed firsthand the power of faith."

"Well, I'm glad it all worked out well for you two in the end," Helen said. "I'll see you next week at the chanting circle."

"Yes, see you next week," you said, giving her a hug goodbye.

"Oh," I said to you as Helen drove away. "If only we'd have gotten there a bit sooner and found the group, we wouldn't have had that horrible night."

"Horrible?" you said. "I don't think it was horrible at all. For me it was magical. Wonderful and amazing. I could really feel the reach of Pele's power, how she challenged us and protected us at the same time. She showed me how vital it is to ask for help in times of great need.

"And most of all, sweetie, it brought us together in a way we've never been in our ten years as lovers. I'll never forget what generosity of spirit you showed by wrapping me in your shirt, when you were so cold yourself. I say, *Mahalo* to you for that, and *Mahalo*, Pele."

I realized then, as usual, Luna was right. That journey of many hours tested our relationship and our ability to stand by one another in a challenge and face it squarely. We succeeded and it strengthened our bond of love as a couple. *Mahalo*, Pele. Thank you for all the lessons and blessings you gave us the night we got lost on the lava.

Some Hawaiian Words

Aloha. Hello, goodbye, blessings
Haoles. Hawaiian for non-Hawaiians, especially Caucasians
Kilauea. Volcano on the Big Island of Hawaii that has been active since 1992
Mahalo nui loa. Many, many thanks
Mahalo. Thank you
Pele. The Hawaiian goddess of volcanoes, fire, passion, and creativity

MESS WITH TEXAS
RUTH A. ROUFF

Ruth Rouff is an English instructor and freelance writer living in Collingswood, New Jersey. After earning a BA in English from Vassar College and a MS in Education from Saint Joseph's University, she taught for a number of years in Philadelphia and Camden, NJ. Her work has appeared in various literary journals, including *Exquisite Corpse, Philadelphia Poets*, and *Wilde*. In addition, she has written two young adult nonfiction books for Townsend Press: *Ida B. Wells: A Woman of Courage* and *Great Moments in Sports*. Her story "Mess With Texas" is non-fiction.

I'VE TAKEN THREE vacations in the past six years, and two of them have been just awful. They weren't awful for the usual touristy reasons—missed connections, bad hotels, passport theft, bad weather and the like. No, the reason my vacations were terrible is that I went with the wrong person. That is, I didn't go with someone I was attracted to. I went with someone with whom I *tried* to be attracted to. If you've ever done that, you probably know that it just doesn't work out.

Let me tell you about my Alaskan cruise. I went with Connie, a perfectly nice middle-aged lesbian. I'm a middle-aged lesbian, too. I don't know how nice I am, but I try to be. Connie and I had been going together a little less than a year when we went to Alaska. The thing was, I should never have dated Connie in the first place.

The first time I set eyes on her, she was standing in the parking lot of the Holiday Inn on Route 70 in Cherry Hill, New Jersey. She had cropped brown hair, and she was wearing an Oxford type shirt and men's trousers.

Oh, no, men's trousers. I know this isn't politically correct, but I tend to prefer women who are more traditionally feminine—I guess one would call them "lipstick lesbians." Or maybe soft butch. But I was hungry for companionship, so I thought, *what the heck.*

Connie had seen my profile on an online dating site and emailed me to ask for a date. She was working in Moorestown as an information systems consultant for a huge defense contractor. She worked in South Jersey during the week, then flew down to her home in San Antonio, Texas on Thursday afternoons. I was amazed at her grueling schedule, but she said it wasn't uncommon these days.

"There's plenty of us," she told me. Connie had good incentive to commute halfway across the country; she made $130 an hour. This was about what I made in an entire day, working as a freelance educational writer.

"Isn't it kind of weird being a liberal lesbian, working for the defense industry?" I asked over dinner at an Indian restaurant.

"Oh, I don't work for the weapons side of the business," she assured me. "I work for the procurement side."

But it's still the same company, I thought. But then, who was I to judge? My father had worked as a metallurgist for the U.S. Navy for 35 years. You might say that my upbringing was paid for by the military-industrial complex.

As we continued to talk, I decided Connie had a nice personality. I was also intrigued by the fact that she was from Texas. I had never met anyone, gay or straight from the Lone Star State. She had that Texas twang, though since she had lived in California for a while, it wasn't too pronounced.

I learned that Connie liked baseball and reading about dead presidents. That was funny, so did I. Since she had lived in San Francisco for a number of years, her favorite team was the Giants.

"I can't stand Barry Bonds," I opined.

Connie shrugged. "In San Francisco we say, 'That's just Barry being Barry.'"

As the evening wore on, the thought occurred to me that I should try not to be turned off by superficial things such as personal style. My pattern was to be attracted to women who weren't emotionally available. My therapist had suggested this was because I'd had to tend so much to my mother, who had been chronically depressed for years. Apparently, children who have to nurture their parents often view intimate relationships as oppressive. That's why we develop unrequited longings for people who won't give us the time of day. Hence, my goal was to have a relationship with someone who was actually available. Perhaps I would grow to become attracted to Connie.

A few days later, the phone rang. It was Connie, asking if I wanted to go out to dinner again. Why not? No one else was beating down my door, as they say.

"Sure," I said.

So we dated for a month or so. We were sitting in a coffee shop near Rittenhouse Square in Philly when Connie invited me down to San Antonio for a long weekend.

"I'll pay your fare with my frequent flyer miles," she said. She seemed quite proud of her ability to do this. After I got over my surprise, I agreed. The fact that I hadn't known her for long didn't deter me. She seemed nice; she *was* nice. In some ways, nicer than I was. She was much more outgoing, anyway, always talking about her co-workers and her friends at home with genuine warmth. I found this refreshing. Besides, I had never been to Texas, and I'd heard San Antonio was by far the prettiest city in the state.

When I landed in San Antonio, Connie was standing near the exit, a big smile on her face. After driving me to her home, a two story, vaguely Spanish style tract house, we had dinner at a nearby restaurant. The next day, she showed me the sights. We strolled around San Antonio's famed River Walk, which was colorful and busy. We toured the site of the 1968 World's Fair and saw the Tower of the Americas. And of course we saw the Alamo. It was smaller than I had imagined it, but impressive nonetheless with its rough mission architecture. Since tall office buildings now surrounded it, it was hard to associate with a bloody battle.

That evening, Connie introduced me to her friends. We sat around a fire pit at her neighbor Danny's house and drank wine. Danny was a government worker who was married to Laurie, a nurse. Their friend Mark worked in communications for the University of Texas, San Antonio. He also played bass for a jazz combo that performed at the River Walk. Mark was divorced. Danny and Mark were good guys. They were both that endangered species: Texas liberals. Neither had a problem with gay people, however Connie said Laurie was a devout Catholic and she didn't really like her. She just put up with her because of Danny. Connie had known them all since high school. It said something about them that they had remained friends. Connie said she didn't have any gay friends in San Antonio. She missed not having them. Evidently the gay scene in San Antonio wasn't all that hot.

That Saturday, we drove to Lyndon Johnson's ranch in the Hill Country. On the way, I asked Connie about the phrase, "Don't Mess With Texas," I had noticed on bumper stickers. I said it sounded belligerent.

"Oh," she laughed. "That was just a slogan from an anti-littering campaign."

I was a relieved. You never knew about Texas, what with that disaster, George W. Bush.

When we got to the LBJ Ranch, we saw the tiny house where LBJ was born and the Pedernales River, which twisted like a corkscrew among the live oaks.

"You call that a river?" I kidded Connie. I'm chauvinistic about the Delaware.

"Sometimes it floods," she replied.

As our guided tour bus pulled closer to the Texas White House, we saw a group of people sitting out front on the porch. The bus driver mentioned that Lady Bird Johnson—who was now in her nineties—still came out here from time to time. Just then, from out of the crowd, a woman waved to us. Although we weren't close enough to get a really good look, I suppose it could have been Lady Bird. For a lifelong liberal, this was about as good as it gets.

"I read that LBJ's mother was extremely religious and his dad drank too much," I told Connie.

"That describes half the couples in Texas," she replied.

I laughed.

That evening, Connie and I sat drinking beer on her couch and watched comedy videos on her new, huge, hi-def TV. Connie was a big fan of certain stand-up comedians.

"Is Wanda Sykes gay?" I asked Connie.

"I don't know," Connie said. This was before Wanda had come out.

The beer we were drinking put both of us in a mellow mood. Although the plan that night was for Connie to sleep on the couch and me to sleep in her bed, we began getting intimate on the couch after I kissed her. It was probably the alcohol—a brand of Texas beer. Also, I hadn't had sex with anyone for ten years. *Ten years!* It felt good to wrap my arms around someone substantial— even if she was wearing an Oxford shirt. I was shocked at myself, since I had made the first move. Connie seemed a little taken aback, too, but pleased. Afterward, I felt like throwing up.

"I feel queasy," I told Connie.

Needless to say, she was disconcerted. She had probably never made anyone sick before simply by having sex. It wasn't her, per se. It was nerves and alcohol. The whole thing had been too abrupt. Here I was two thousand miles from home, having sex with a woman I hardly knew. I hastened to assure Connie that I wanted to keep seeing her.

So I did. Connie would come up to South Jersey on Sunday afternoons and leave for Texas on Thursday afternoons. Sometimes I'd spend the night with her at her room in the Holiday Inn.

"You live an anomic life," I told her.

"What?" She hadn't heard the term.

I told her that *anomie* meant disoriented and disconnected. But she didn't mind her life. It didn't seem to bother her to spend so much time in hotel rooms and airports and rental cars. In fact, she seemed rather proud of commuting such a long distance. She spent a lot of time listening to podcasts on her iPod. She was a big fan of NPR. Also, she said if she continued earning good money as a defense consultant, she could retire in a few years.

As our relationship continued, I became much more comfortable around Connie. But it was clear that I was never going to be passionately attracted to her. I liked her, but she wanted more. She had every right to expect passion. So did I, but at this point in my life, I thought I should settle for less—like simple companionship. If Connie and I broke up, who knew how long it would be before I met another woman I could even talk to? It wasn't as if I was living in a hotbed of lesbianism like Northampton or San Francisco.

It was awkward. Still, we continued to see each other. That summer we decided to take an Olivia Cruise to Alaska. Except for the crew, the whole ship would be lesbians. Connie graciously offered to pay for half of my fare. Since she was making much bigger bucks than I was, how could I refuse?

There's nothing like breaking up on a cruise ship. It's not as if one can go anywhere, and those tiny cabins with double beds! The ship sailed from Vancouver, Canada. The crunch came our first night out of harbor. We both got drunk, Connie more so than I.

That night, when we were in bed, Connie said, "This is awful." I had tried to reciprocate her passion, but it was clear to Connie that my heart just wasn't in it. By the way, anyone who thinks lesbian sex is by nature hot, is living in a dream world. Ever heard of lesbian bed death? That's how my relationship with Connie started out.

Connie was by now very angry with me. Her romantic vacation was not meeting her expectations. I should have told her sooner I wasn't into her physically. But I liked her company. I liked her warmth. I was afraid of being alone again.

Seeing all this spectacular scenery in the company of a person who doesn't want to be around you is a bittersweet experience—more bitter than sweet, actually. I knew Connie resented me. She began giving me the cold shoulder. Still, she tried to make the most of the trip. We saw the totem pole village outside of Juneau. Connie developed a cold, so I did the tour of Skagway, the gold rush town, alone. There were lots of little shacks there, lining a lane. The woman who conducted the walking tour said they had been used by prostitutes for quickies. Prostitution was a big thing in gold rush camps. We learned the miners paid the women in golden nuggets.

A day later, Connie and I went on a whale watching excursion together. We saw plenty of whales blowing out water and breeching in spectacular fashion. We also saw bald eagles, swooping above the deep blue water and alighting on the pine trees that lined the shore. I was torn between feeling awe for the breathtaking scenery and wildlife, and embarrassment at being with someone who thought I was a jerk.

The next day, we took a birdwatching hike in Sitka. Since it was raining, we didn't see many birds—just a few kingfishers. But we did see a lot of salmon that had been half-eaten by brown bears. Then we took the train ride to Anchorage and endured the long flight back to Houston, and then Philly. Connie had her iPod in her ear so she didn't have to talk to me. I tried to keep busy reading Zora Neale Hurston's *Their Eyes Were Watching God*. After a lousy marriage, Janie finally met her true love, Tea Cake. I still hoped something good like that would happen to me.

After getting the rental car at the Philly airport, Connie dumped me at my house like a sack of potatoes. Then she headed to the Holiday Inn in Jersey. She had to work the next day. I knew she was deeply disappointed. She certainly deserved more than my lukewarm ass.

It's hard to disappoint a nice person. I knew my therapist meant well in advising me to become involved with someone who was emotionally available, but one can't fake desire. On the basis of my awful Alaskan vacation, I resolved never to become involved with someone to whom I wasn't passionately attracted. But I broke that resolution fairly quickly when I met another Texan named Dawn.

As for Connie, we stayed in touch long enough for her to tell me she went on another Olivia cruise and thoroughly enjoyed herself. This time she went alone.

FIGHTING BACK:
THE STRUGGLE TO RECLAIM MY WOMANHOOD
HEATH ATOM RUSSELL

Heath Atom Russell is a radical lesbian feminist activist living in Northern California. She graduated in 2011 from Humboldt State University with a B.A. in Sociology. She works as a developmental disability rights advocate. In 2014, she gave a speech about gender abolition at the conference Radfems Respond, in Portland, Oregon. Her story has been featured in a
recent *New Yorker* article, entitled "What Is a Woman?" by Michelle Goldberg, and also in the book *Gender Hurts: A Feminist Analysis of the Politics of Transgenderism*, written by Sheila Jeffreys. Her piece is memoir.

I WAS BORN a girl, then became a boy, then grew into an adult female lesbian. If you feel confused or alarmed by this, then you're on the right track.

My mother once told me a story of when I was an infant sitting at the dinner table. A friend who was sitting with my mom said that I "looked like a lesbian" because of how I was exuding an air of assertiveness in my posture while sitting in my chair. Mom shushed her, but dejectedly agreed with her friend's statement. This lesbophobic atmosphere was rife, and it continued into my childhood and adulthood. In spite of it, by my teen years I had still managed to come out to my family as "having attractions for women." At the time, I didn't even use the word "lesbian" in fear for my safety.

I had every reason to be terrified about my safety regarding coming out as a lesbian. Throughout my childhood and even now, into young adulthood, memories of my childhood abuse still feel like singed ashes blanketing my existence. My mom, being a product of a horribly abusive environment as a child, merely passed on the patriarchal legacy she herself had internalized. I have been slapped, punched, burned, bruised, cut, sexually violated, beaten over the head with a hair dryer, screamed at, had objects thrown at me, and had my hair pulled out in clumps. In addition, I was subjected to numerous beauty practices so that my mom could make me conform to society's expectations of how a woman should look (dolled up) and how we should act (submissive to authority).

The abuse in my household occurred on an almost daily basis. My dad was not much better as a parent because of his failure to protect me from harm. If anything, he enabled the abuse to continue. I sometimes wonder if Mom had not been there abusing me, if he would have been the culprit instead.

His attitudes toward women were equally abhorrent. If you're ever in need of a "dumb blonde" joke, or information on how "women can't drive," he's your man.

When I wasn't getting abused at home by my parents, I was getting indoctrinated by the church we attended for five years, starting when I was only seven. The first time I cried and expressed sadness and anxiety over the prospect of dying some day, my parents took that as a cue to introduce me to this Baptist church so that I could be "saved." At the church we attended, even reading books containing fantasy characters made me worthy of eternal hellfire. You can imagine the congregation's stance on lesbians and gays. If anyone at my church was lesbian or gay, nobody knew about it. They were forced to stay in the closet or risk ostracism, reparative prayer, or exile from the church. The chance of my "coming out" in that kind of environment was unlikely.

I briefly attended public school from kindergarten until first grade. One day I gave myself a haircut. It ended up being very unevenly cut. It was innocent child's play. However, my mom was horrified by how people would treat me, and more importantly what people might think about her. So she took me to get my hair "fixed" that same afternoon. The hairdresser ended up cropping my hair to an inch in length on top, with the back buzzed a bit shorter. As the stylist and my mom stood there lamenting over my handiwork, they decided to add a half-heart design at the nape of my neck, to make me feel better about my short hair. I wasn't sad about my hair at all, and had no idea why I should have been.

My peers at school began taunting me and seized every opportunity they could to call me a boy, shove me onto the pavement, pick fights, and attack me at recess. Clearly, it was dangerous to be gender non-conforming, as I was learning. Everyone in my life reinforced that message to me. Since I was being badly mistreated simply because of my appearance and behavior, it was impossible for me to consider "coming out" any younger than I did.

But eventually I did fully "come out," at sixteen, in the middle of a one-sided argument with Mom. She kept screaming at me and berating me; she just wouldn't let up. Finally, I drew in a sharp breath and bellowed out, "I like girls by the way!" As she sat on her bed, her facial expression morphed from raw fury into confusion. Her jaw dropped and she looked at me with wide, sullen eyes. Finally, she spoke.

"So, what are you saying? What do you mean? You mean you're a lesbo?"

I froze with fright. After all, if she was already using the word "lesbo" around me, I knew I couldn't be open with her. Instead, I choked up inside, but managed to sputter out, "No, I mean, I think I just might be into girls too,"—I paused, carefully considering my next words, and murmured—"along with guys."

Mom stared at me, her face unreadable. "Get out of my sight, you dumb fuck!" she snarled through gritted teeth, and waved her hand, dismissing me.

I walked into my bedroom and sat at my desk. I could hear mom still rambling away, tossing various slurs left and right under her breath. She screamed about what a worthless whore I was, and how she couldn't believe any daughter of hers would "turn out this way." I knew at that moment that our relationship would become even more estranged than it already was. I didn't ever approach the subject of my sexuality with Mom again after this. I was worried about being thrown out of the house. Even though my home life was filled with violence, at that young age my fear of the great unknown beyond the walls of my childhood home felt more ominous to me than anything that happened within it.

A year later I was in a bookstore with Mom. We went up to the cashier, who was a tall woman with her hair in a ponytail. She was wearing a gray dress shirt and a purple paisley vest over it. On her hand, written in pen ink, was the transgender symbol, which was a combination of a male, female, and combined female-male symbol inside a triangle. By this point, I was already researching transgender people online because I thought that maybe the reason I was a lesbian, and the reason I wasn't a particularly "attractive" woman was because I was *really a man on the inside*. I realized that the cashier's preferred pronouns for herself were "he" and "him/his."

I very discreetly pointed to the symbol on "his" hand and whispered, "Mom, that's the transgender symbol."

My mom spoke up, but enthusiastically so that everyone could hear, "Oh, is that what you want to be?"

I replied in earnest, "Mom, transgender isn't something I *want* to be. I *am* transgender. I'm a guy on the inside." Surprisingly, she seemed open to the idea, but she didn't have much more to say about the topic. *Well,* I thought to myself, *at least it's better than being called a "lesbo."*

At eighteen, when I got accepted to Humboldt State University, I was happy to be moving hundreds of miles away from the homophobia I had grown up with, although, at that point in time, I thought I was dealing with transphobia as well.

Mom was dropping frightening remarks like, "You better watch what you do in your life. If you end up in prison, you'll go to a man's prison, and you'll end up dead." When I finally got to be around others my own age who were part of the LGBT community, I was both relieved and ecstatic to be meeting people who may have had negative experiences in their adolescence like those I'd had.

During my first couple of years at school, most Humboldt State students were following an ideological standpoint known as "queer theory." I didn't realize this at first, but was soon to find out. This postmodernist outlook is rooted in the assumption that gender is an individual choice and a malleable identity. The belief is basically that anybody can adopt the gender identity they choose just by claiming a label for themselves. For example, someone can claim he or she is "genderfluid" if he or she does not identify with the terms "man" or "woman." Someone born a male can assert that he is actually a woman if he "feels like a woman on the inside" or genuinely believes he was born a woman in a male's body. Conversely, a born-female can state that she is actually a man.

However, many feminists are asking a pressing question of this theory: "What does it mean to *feel* like a man or a woman *on the inside?* Isn't this just reinforcing sexist cultural stereotypes about women and men?" At the point when I was "identifying" as a man, I had had no exposure to radical feminist theory. I was being informed by my peers and instructors that in order to be politically progressive, respecting and accepting queer identity politics was a necessity.

My gradual indoctrination into queer theory in my university studies and in my personal life was very subliminal, but every bit as pervasive psychologically as is misogyny, rape culture, or porn culture. Nevertheless, at the time it felt wonderful to be accepted and validated by these new peers. It felt good to be told I could be gender non-conforming, so long as I was identifying as the opposite sex while doing so. When you are surrounded by other confused misfits, you start to feel fairly normal yourself.

I began meeting people who identified as being under the trans* umbrella. The asterisk after the word "trans" was meant to include anybody who was transgender, such as transsexuals, cross-dressers, and drag performers. I started hanging out with other trans* people more often, and asking them questions about transitioning. One of my friends at the time told me where "he" had gotten clearance for starting hormone replacement therapy (HRT). Apparently, there was a doctor in town who dealt with numerous trans* patients and could help me out. Somehow, I felt hesitant. Even when I had the name of the doctor right at my fingertips, I was still waiting for the "right time" to transition. I figured it would be best to wait until I was done with college. But as I learned more about transitioning, I realized I would want my chosen name printed on my sociology degree. I also wanted to "pass" better as a man, because I was tired of getting harassed and targeted for being a visibly gender non-conforming woman. I figured at least if I was a guy, I would look like a *normal* guy, instead of this *abnormal thing* that I currently was.

I regularly saw counselors at my university, and I was seeing a psychiatrist as well. When I made an appointment with the doctor who would later go on to provide my HRT, he said I needed clearance from my psychiatrist before he could prescribe any hormones for me. My psychiatrist wasn't familiar with the condition known as "Gender Identity Disorder" listed in the DSM-IV, so she asked me to explain my symptoms. When I saw her again the following week, she informed me that she had done some research online and she agreed with my self-diagnosis. She gave me her permission to begin testosterone therapy, and my primary doctor then gave me a little booklet of information about the positive and negative effects of cross-sex hormone therapy. I read the entire packet when I went home and signed my name at the bottom to indicate that I had read and understood the risks of this treatment. Despite understanding these risks, I was sure nothing negative would ever happen to me as a result of my taking these hormones. However, I was wrong.

I took my first injection in January, 2011, just a few weeks before my twenty-second birthday. I remember leaving the doctor's office feeling a surge of euphoria because I was now on the track to fully "passing" as a man.

Within six months, I had changed my name legally and on most of my records in order to reflect my new identity. I had read all the literature that I could find regarding transsexuals and there was not a shadow of a doubt in my mind, nor in my doctors', that Gender Identity Disorder was what had plagued me all these years.

Six months after my first injection, I was passing 95% of the time, and I had found a support group in my community for others like me. However, to my consternation, that group quickly dissolved, since it consisted of individuals laden with narcissism and identity problems, which often led to conflicts in the group. In this trans support group, I also got my first taste of being on the wrong side of a trans "woman's" anger. (That is, he was a man in the process of transitioning.)

He and an elderly female heterosexual ally got into an argument online. During their argument, I interjected my opinions. I couldn't help but notice the outright aggression coming at me from this trans "woman." Not surprisingly, the way I was treated was indistinguishable from behavior I had experienced coming from angry men at the bars. Still, immersed in queer theory, I saw this as a chance for me to "be a man" and stop these "ladies" from fighting. He saw it as a chance to kick my ass. The very next time we saw each other, he smacked my lit cigarette from my hand and removed his jacket, egging me on to fight him. I walked away, because that is what women are trained to do when faced with the possibility of male violence.

Also during this time, within the first few months of starting hormones, I had met another trans "woman." He was a very socially awkward young man. In fact, he often relished a fantasy of becoming a self-made "lesbian." On a social media account, he openly admitted that he was "jealous of all the girls who would go skinny dipping together." On one occasion, when he was visiting me at my apartment, he pointed to some refrigerator magnets I had. One of the magnets said, "You too can be a lesbian" and "Why are all the cool girls lesbians?" As he pointed to my magnets, he asked me directly, "Are you a lesbian?"

I replied, "I don't know. I guess I was."

He pointed to another magnet, which declared me a feminist (even if only a liberal feminist type), and asked me, "How can you be a feminist if you're a trans man?"

"What?" I replied, feeling confused.

"Well, you're transitioning to a man. How can you be a feminist if you're transitioning to a man?"

I had never considered this before, and suddenly I felt wrong for ascribing to *any* feminist ideas. Then again, I also felt defiant that my moderately feminist convictions were now being challenged by someone born a male. So, I told him, "Well, I figured I can be one of the few good men out there who is a feminist." I didn't really know what else to say. I was completely taken aback. But it made me think. In that moment it became clear to me that society would view my identification as both a man and a feminist to be disingenuous. It was an oxymoron. It hadn't occurred to me till then that I would be expected to give up my feminism, and many other ties to females in the process of my "becoming a man." I still hadn't fully realized at that point just how alienated I was going to become from all things female as a result of my transitioning.

While on hormone replacement therapy, I experienced both desirable and undesirable effects from the testosterone. Even though I anticipated that my facial and body hair would grow in, and my voice would deepen, other effects were very troubling, and frankly quite foreign to me. I was unprepared for not only what it did to my libido, but how it changed my sexual fantasies entirely. I began fantasizing about death and about having my corpse defiled after I died. I reasoned that if a mortician was desperate for sex, he could just defile my body. Maybe then another corpse would be spared, and that other deceased person and their family wouldn't be disrespected.

I later learned through my reading that radical feminists have long understood that men have a patriarchal culture built on necrophilia, whether necrophilia is expressed as a sexual urge or not. As author Valerie Solanas once wrote: "The male likes death—it excites him sexually, and already dead inside, he wants to die." Additionally, author Mary Daly also addressed the subject of mens' preoccupation with necrophilia in her book *Gyn/Ecology: The Metaethics of Radical Feminism*. Daly notes that men sap women of life energy and resources. In this way, they are slowly killing the female as their host. Mary Daly wrote that men idolize "those victimized into a state of living death."

In retrospect, for a young woman like me to say, "I hope a man rapes my corpse when I die" is similar to prostituted women saying, "I'd rather he just pay for my services than go out and rape other women."

In the years leading up to my transition, and the time during my transition, I was highly suicidal. By the time I had begun hormone replacement therapy, I had already gone through three suicide attempts and two hospitalizations in mental facilities. Perhaps fantasizing myself as a necrophiliac's victim simply reflected my own suicidal impulses due to my profound depression at this time, rather than a result of the HRT. I still don't know for sure.

While on testosterone, I also started heavily consuming porn videos, eventually getting to the point where I could no longer masturbate without them. (Since taking the testosterone, I now masturbated more than a few times a day). There were random times when, even unstimulated, my clitoris would spasm. I was told this was proof that I was trans because it was the same as men getting erections. I still don't know whether it was the porn, the hormone replacement therapy, my own depression—or possibly all three—that had caused my necrophiliac fantasies.

My porn movie of choice was one short independent film which featured a prolonged scene of corpse defilement. I justified viewing this at the time because it "wasn't real" and was only a fantasy. What I know today is, theses fantasies stopped once I discontinued the HRT and the heavy porn consumption.

In addition to these bizarre sexual fantasies and my annoyingly high libido, I was also experiencing heart palpitations and an elevated blood pressure. Before the hormones, I had never felt my heart palpitate, and in fact after I quit, I never experienced the palpitations again. Unfortunately, my ill health effects weren't just byproducts of my hormone use. I had also been binding my breasts with a chest compression vest for six years. Despite using a properly fitting chest compression binder and only wearing it for eight hours or less per day, I had still done obvious damage to my rib cage. My girlfriend Carolynn noticed this once when she ran her hand over my ribs. I flinched in pain. One time I even screamed in agony.

In fact, the physical and mental changes that transitioning induced in me not only had an adverse effect on me, but on Carolynn as well. She had been telling people she was straight, and this suited me well enough because at the time I identified as a heterosexual man. However, our friends still considered us a "queer couple," which meant that they actually did not really acknowledge me as a legitimate man.

Shortly after Carolynn and I began dating, I moved back to my childhood home in southern California. My relocation didn't last very long. After a year of long distance dating, I moved back to northern California to live with Carolynn. It wasn't long after moving in with her that I started noticing how Carolynn would get triggered whenever we'd have sex. It would leave her in tears, cradling herself on the bed. She finally told me that she just couldn't be with someone who *pretended* to be a man, and that she was wrong for previously calling herself straight. She was also annoyed with me wanting to "prove my masculinity" by pursuing more stereotypically masculine activities like hunting, fishing, barbequing, and watching sports. Later, I realized that women could do all those things too, along with wearing plaid shirts, having short hair, and forgoing make up. I realized that doing all of the above activities doesn't magically make us men. At the time, neither Carolynn nor I knew what to do about our feelings surrounding our issues. It would take both of us some time to figure these things out.

Two years into my hormone therapy, I began to purposely "forget" my next dose. I didn't like sticking myself with a needle in my thigh twice a month. Nor did I want to switch to testosterone topical gels. On a very fundamental level, I really didn't want to be on hormones for the rest of my life. In terms of eventual "top and bottom surgery," I blanched at the idea of having my breasts cut off, even given the numerous times that I no longer wanted them. I didn't want someone digging out my reproductive organs either, and the photos of surgically-created penises horrified me. Not only did the penises themselves look awful and frightening, I couldn't imagine offering up a skin graft from somewhere else on my body to create such a disgusting looking *thing*. I began to wonder openly, "Will I myself become this . . . *thing*? Am I destined to not be a person at all?"

During this time, I was working on my senior project, entitled, "Cisgender Feminist Perspectives of Transsexuals within the Feminist Movement" (Yes, I was definitely drinking the queer theory Kool-Aid). This is when I first learned about author Sheila Jeffreys. In my report, I ended up citing passages from her book, *Unpacking Queer Politics,* basically to prove that she was horribly misinformed. Meanwhile, I had also begun browsing the online blogs of notable "transphobes," otherwise known as radical feminists. What they said angered me, but I kept coming back to read them. These were feminist writers who had the courage to question the "queer theory" of the day.

In hindsight, I realized there was truth to their words and I heard it, even with my vehement insistence that these women, these *feminists,* were wrong about me. Regarding those writers, I used to like to say to myself, "Me thinks the lady doth protest too much." But looking back, I understand now that I was drawn to a more comprehensive explanation for the problems I was experiencing. Radical feminism offered me that explanation, as well as solutions and alternatives to this patriarchal society. I was finding that perhaps the answer I sought for my gender dysphoria was closer than I had thought.

One day, I saw a notification from a "genderqueer" friend of mine that celebrity Roseanne Barr had made some "transphobic" remarks on her Twitter page. I jumped onto Twitter and expressed my disappointment to Roseanne. I snapped a picture of myself with a month's worth of beard growth and asked her whether she would be comfortable with me in a women's restroom, since I "look nothing like a woman." A radical feminist activist replied to my photo and said, "Congratulations, you're a woman who presents as a stereotypical male. Good for you. Women don't rape with their beards." At first, I was pissed off by this. But I had a back-and-forth correspondence with this woman over the course of the following days. We gradually became more friendly. While I was absorbing these pro-female messages from my new online friend, I also reflected on Sheila Jeffreys' gender-critical position. It was starting to make sense. Things were becoming more clear for me.

Eventually, with my growing feminist knowledge, along with the horror of my deteriorating physical health, I made the formal decision to quit hormone therapy altogether. Not only that, but I told Carolynn that I wanted to detransition back to a female, including socially. This was perfect timing to disclose such news to her because she was planning on coming out to me as a lesbian. Prior to this, I had thought she was straight. We were both worried that the other one would want to end the relationship after we each shared our news. Thankfully, a breakup didn't happen. In fact, our relationship has only gotten stronger from that point on. Carolynn and I have now been together for four years, I'm proud to say.

After going public with my detransition on a friend's local access television show, I began getting flooded with hateful messages. Some people told me that I was "never really trans" and "never a true transsexual" because I detransitioned. Angry men told me I was a "failed male" and sent me rape and death threats. A local MTT (male-to-trans) stalked me for weeks due to my outspokenness about detransitioning. I had to seek a restraining order against him. Someone who I suspect was from our local queer community slashed the tires on Carolynn's car, and followed up this property damage by keying "dyke" into her bumper. Carolynn and I were also instructed to relinquish our positions on the local Pride March board because members of our community now felt "personally attacked" by my new gender abolitionist stance.

A gender abolitionist believes in the destruction of gender as a societal institution. She believes in stripping away socially defined categories based on gender. Where the queer theorist tends to adopt multiple, seemingly endless gender identities, a gender abolitionist feels there really is no set way for a man or a woman to act. Gender, they say, is just a presentation based on sexist social constructs that prescribe our behavior. It's limiting, and it should just be abolished.

At this time, Carolynn and I had decided to keep our politics separate from the Humboldt Pride March, attempting to remain neutral. Ironically, we had already decided to put in our resignations from the board, but before we did so, we were asked by the Pride March Board to step down.

In the midst of this opposition I was getting from those I used to consider my friends, I was also starting to get messages of support from radical feminists and lesbian feminists. They were thanking me for my courage, and expressing their joy that I had stopped transitioning. Their messages about body love, self-acceptance, and self-esteem came pouring in. I also started getting notes of solidarity from other women who had given thought to transitioning or had stopped transitioning too, once they discovered my story. I was surprised that my particular experience had had such an impact on them.

Today, five years later, I'm vocal and strong about my decision to detransition. It was the right decision for me and I'm glad I figured this out. Yet, trans activists still get very angry with me for continuing to go public about the harms of transition that I experienced. They want me to shut up. These trans activists either deny the existence of detransitioners like myself, or they repeatedly demand to know if I claim to speak for all detransitioned people, which I do not.

Sometimes trans activists claim that detransitioners have transitioned in haste, without giving the decision much forethought. If trans activists want to believe that, fine, but it doesn't invalidate the fact that sometimes people realize they made the wrong decision to transition. They deserve support and resources too. It is a great disservice and it's dishonest to just sweep all of us detransitioners, "transition regretters," or "retransitioners" under the rug simply because it's more politically convenient to try to shut us up.

When people have detransitioned in the past, they did so in silence, thinking that their discomfort and confusion was just their own problem. They believed that they were alone. When pro-trans advocacy groups are faced with the existence of detransitioners like myself, they admit they aren't knowledgeable about the subject, or that the statistics on people who detransition are too insignificant to mention. They're actually correct. Until very recently, nobody has taken the time to study or examine the life stories of detransitioners, or transition regretters, so the numbers and information about us simply don't exist yet. This is why I'm putting my story out there, so that others will know that if they're going through a similar situation and they want a way out, they can stop if they want. They do not have to feel coerced to continue that process.

It was a painful journey for me to try hormones and try transitioning so I could feel secure about myself in the world. This is a part of my life that I have to accept, because my physical and mental health mean a lot to me, especially in terms of healing from my past traumas.

Today, I tell women my story so that they will hear another perspective; one that isn't in the mainstream (in terms of the all too common "happy transitioner" narrative). Actually, it's much more of a struggle for me socially to live as a butch-appearing lesbian named Heath than it was for me to drug myself, bind my breasts, and try to mold myself into the "man" that everybody, including myself, told me that I should be. But I'm not a freak and I'm not a man. I believe we should be exactly who we are. Change the world, not your body. Today I remain a proud female-born woman, a proud lesbian, and a strong feminist.

CONSTANTINE, MICHIGAN 1959
BARBARA RUTH

In the small, Midwestern towns where **Barbara Ruth** grew up, she always felt queer, even before she fell in love with a girl at age seven. Since early childhood she has written to uncover secrets, resist assimilation, and explain what she could not understand, to the world and to herself. She is disabled by diseases and disabilities too numerous and aggravating to name. She still believes in propaganda by the deed and revolution within the revolution, preferably one she can dance to. Access in all its permutations, challenges and inspires her. She primarily write biomythography; such as the piece herein, "Constantine, Michigan, 1959."

MR. GLASS KNEW. Maybe no one else in Constantine suspected we were anything other than white Protestants, but Mr. Glass knew. Just like he knew that the man who applied for the high school English teaching position was a Negro, even though the prospective teacher included no photograph and didn't fill in the line on the form marked "race." No one on the school board had ever heard of the Alabama college on the resume. Since Mr. Glass was from the South, the school board called him in to look at the incomplete application. He knew right away it was a Negro college. "Send the application back to him," Mr. Glass told them. "Include a note: "'Please designate race.'" Sure enough, it turned out Mr. Glass had been right. The school board didn't give the man an interview, not because he was a Negro, but because he'd lied to them, tried to trick them into believing he was white.

I learned all this because my parents were teachers at the one Junior-Senior High School in Constantine. Mr. Glass told my dad, and he talked about it at home. I couldn't figure out which side Dad was on, exactly. He was mad at Mr. Glass for knowing about the college, mad at the school board for asking the guy his race, mad at the teacher for applying in the first place. Anger was my father's default position in those days. My mother didn't say much. Staying quiet meant staying under the radar. That was her way.

My reaction was certainty of impending doom. If Mr. Glass could tell someone's race just from the name of a college no one else had ever heard of, he'd know all my secrets.

That fall in eighth grade History class I had Mr. Glass as a teacher for the first time. I hated him. He teased us about our defects: stutters, thick glasses, pimples, too fat, too skinny, too tall or too short—he was merciless. "Timothy, I'd like you to read to the class, beginning on page 143."

Tim reddened, opened his book, hands shaking. "Sick . . . sex . . ."

Titters from the class.

"No sick sex, Timothy," Mr. Glass oozed. "That's for queers. The word is 'secession.' Now stand up and continue reading."

I looked up. Mr. Glass angled his poisonous smile directly at me, from behind the fortress of his oak desk. Did he think I was queer? Did he somehow know about me and Laura, me and Chrissy, me and Maryanne—how we'd played doctor and patient, husband and wife, space alien and woman? That was kid stuff, back in elementary school, and they all had boyfriends now. So that just left me.

I turned my attention to Tim. He looked like he might throw up, still standing there, as the class agonized with him through the paragraph containing the word "secession" over and over.

I could tell my father thought Mr. Glass was a jerk. While he did not encourage me to battle with Mr. Glass, he accepted it as inevitable that I would. After all, I was his daughter, and he feuded with him all the time. "You can't fight City Hall," Dad said, year after year. But you could challenge authority in the workplace, which for him meant the faculty, the principal, the school board. Since at that point in my life I had never lived in a town with a population larger than 1000, I had only a vague idea of who or where "City Hall" might be. But I sure knew where my Dad worked: I went to school and challenged authority there every day.

My mother avoided Mr. Glass. She recognized him as a threat and tried to do what she could to protect herself and her family. She would never be able to stop Dad from saying or doing anything, but me she could try to control. After all, I was her daughter.

"Don't argue with him," she'd tell me, her fingers pushing my hair off my forehead. "You only have him for an hour a day. Just sit and be quiet. Don't make trouble." I sighed and picked at my food, as we both pretended my suppertime silence signaled consent. I bowed my head and my bangs fell back over my eyebrows.

Don't make trouble: my mother's formula for every situation. If you didn't say anything, if you didn't call attention to yourself, then no one would know. And as long as they didn't know, terrible things wouldn't happen. But if they found out you were a Jew, your father would lose his job, and then he'd get cancer and be sick all the time and you'd always have to tiptoe and whisper so you didn't disturb him and he would die young. These things had happened to my mother in her Chicago childhood. I didn't understand the details but I internalized the message that Chicago was a dangerous place for Jews. My mother never wanted to live in a city. "It just makes me think of Chicago."

I don't know why my father felt no fear of Mr. Glass. Perhaps it's because he absorbed a different emotional overlay along with his "dark past." Straight black hair, burnt umber eyes, alcohol as drug of choice: these and being "dark" are what he brought with him from the Potawatomi Reservation.

Dad told me when he went to school off the reservation he got beat up for being Indian. "So I decided not to be," he concluded, in that unnervingly calm way he had of explaining logical impossibilities. In Constantine, it simply didn't come up. There were no Indians. No Jews, either. We were just—dark.

In the 1980s my father explained to me his theory that all skin colors and all shapes and sizes of noses, lips, and eyes are found in every ethnic group. Therefore you can't possibly determine a person's race just by looking at them. I made no comment.

Which is what he'd given me when I came out to him: No comment. I learned the value of words from my school teacher parents. I also learned the strategy of silence.

When I came out to my mother, her first response was disbelief. "You marched in those demonstrations for Negroes," she reasoned, "but that didn't make you Black. You just like causes." But because she had closeted lesbian friends—a couple she'd met in college and remained close to until their deaths—I convinced her that even though I had married (and divorced) a man, I was, in fact, like her friends. "Maybe it's better," she said at one point. "You're so sensitive. You're more likely to find a woman who won't hurt your feelings." Loving women made sense to her; but those "causes"—and radical dyke activism was full of them—did not. "Why can't you be like Dagny and Nita? Just be the kind of gay person who pays their taxes and doesn't *bother* people."

Questions of race, ethnicity, sexuality, and taxes have always bothered me. Back in Constantine these coalesced into: What *am* I? I was eight when we moved there. I figured out I wasn't a Negro—all the African-Americans in Constantine lived on farms and were first or second cousins to each other. So even though I was as dark as one or two of them, I knew I couldn't be Black because I lived in town and wasn't related to them. That made me white. White with grandparents who Mom and Dad called "old-fashioned."

"You can smell Grandma's food in the elevator," Dad would say on our way up to her Chicago apartment.

"They all cook that way," Mom said. "This whole building stinks of cabbage and beets and brisket."

"I'm sure glad you don't cook like your mother," Dad chuckled.

"I never will," she vowed.

My father corrected his own parents' accents when we visited them. "We don't talk that way now," he'd tell them.

"Dick doesn't care for our ways," I heard my grandmother say to my grandfather.

"I know," he replied, putting his hand on her arm as she cried. "I know."

In the car on the way home Dad said, "They're so old fashioned. And they tell the same stories, over and over. Ridiculous stories about coyotes and the moon and who knows what. It's the 1950s for crying out loud. They're afraid to join the real world."

My mother was afraid for me. I was darker than her or my brother. More like my father.

And Mom was afraid of Mr. Glass. She feared the cruel power of the man my father argued with, the same man I argued with, of necessity, within a month of being in his class.

Mr. Glass knew, I'm sure of it. Why else would he stare at me when he made his remarks about Jews? When he talked about "the colored" he looked at the Black kids. When he talked about "the Jews" he looked at me.

I would always mouth off at him. I had to. Mr. Glass told lies, taught prejudice; I was required to protest. Not because I was an Indian or a Jew ("Don't *say* that!" my mother's fear rang in my mind) but because Mr. Glass was evil. My father always became enraged, spoke out, when he encountered what he thought was wrong, and so did I.

I didn't know the word "solidarity" back then, but I had the concept. I just wasn't sure how to apply it. Lois and Junior, two of the African-American kids, were in my history class. Mr. Glass brought literature to the curriculum through weekly readings from *Uncle Tom's Cabin*, clearly for the opportunity to perform lines like Topsy's "I just growed." Junior and Lois put their heads down on their desks when Mr. Glass took out Harriet Beecher Stowe's book. I wanted to do the same but—should I?

After another "learn about the South" day, I caught up with the two of them after class. Lois was a good friend, Junior not so much. "I hate it when he reads that book too," I said. "Should I put my head down when you do?"

They looked at each other but didn't say anything.

"We could all go together to the principal and report him," I tried.

Junior shook his head. "Our parents talked about it. They said we should just put our heads down on our desks. We told them you walk out of his class sometimes and they said, 'No. Don't do that.'"

Lois put her hand on my arm. "It's sweet that you want to put your head on your desk too. And if our heads are down, well, I guess we won't see what you do."

In Mr. Glass' class my mother's terror and my father's rage warred in me. I spoke out, while fear gripped my belly and sucked out my spit. Mr. Glass played with me, enjoying my agony.

Fridays were the worst. Thursday night was faculty bowling and my father and Mr. Glass would spend the evening drinking and trading insults. Friday mornings at the breakfast table Dad would tell us about "the good one I got over on Glass last night." I wanted to stay home sick—most Fridays I *did* feel sick, but I knew my parents would call the house every hour to tell me I really should be at school with them. "I come here plenty of times when I don't feel good," either of them would say. "It's what people do. You go to school, then you grow up and go to work. If you become a teacher, it's the same thing."

In class on Fridays Mr. Glass' beady eyes bore into all of us. He'd start with speculations about dates students in the class might have planned for the weekend. Whatever he said, you were screwed. "Poor Anna. I guess she'll be staying home all weekend, as usual. But Chrissy and Paul, they'll be K-I-S-S-I-N-G." If either of them made the slightest gesture of denial, he would follow up with: "Oh, I guess it must be Paul and Tim. Chrissy and Barb."

Then would come the "cross" jokes. "What do you get when you cross a rooster with a snake?" "What do you get when you cross a monkey with a Chinaman?" "What do you get when you cross an Indian with a Jew?" "What do you get when you cross a queer with a queer? That one's easy—a big fat zero." Did he really say that? Do those words come from my memory or imagination? Is there a difference?

Most Fridays Mr. Glass and I would race to see if he could come up with grounds to kick me out of class before I felt justified in walking out on my own. I never knew what my weekend homework was in History.

I don't know what became of Mr. Glass. The next year we moved to a slightly larger town in Michigan, where my parents lived until my father's death. There are Jews in this slightly larger town. Still no Indians. My family's white. Just— dark. It could happen to anyone.

TELLING
MARY SARACINO

Mary Saracino is a novelist, memoir writer, and poet. "Telling" is an excerpt from a longer, unpublished memoir. Mary's most recent novels are *Heretics: A Love Story* (Pearlsong Press 2014) and *The Singing of Swans* (Pearlsong Press 2006). She co-edited (with Mary Beth Moser) *She Is Everywhere! Volume 3: An anthology of writings in womanist/feminist spirituality* (iUniverse 2012). She is the editor-in-chief of the e-zine, *Return to Mago*. www. marysaracino.com and http://www.pearlsong.com/mary_saracino.htm

I WAS THIRTY-FIVE years old before I told my father that I was a lesbian. Eighteen years before, when I was a senior in high school, I had kissed my best friend Cheryl, after we professed our love for one another. While I had considered coming out to my father many times over the course of the intervening decades, the right moment always eluded me. At least that's what I always told myself. In truth, my silence had always been fueled by my fear that this essential, yet secret, detail of my life would stymie whatever wee progress I had been able to eke out in my ongoing quest to establish some semblance of a relationship with my father. Having grown up in an Italian American, Catholic, working class family, I feared my sexuality would cause him to ostracize me.

My father and I had no precedence for shared confidences; our tenuous bond failed to foster the type of intimacy that would have enabled me to tell him. Other familial wounds also impeded our progress. When I was thirteen, my mother left my father, after nearly twenty-three years of marriage.

My parents' relationship had been rocky for a long time—it was eroded by constant fighting, financial strain, and the fact that my mother didn't love him. She had carried on an affair with our town's parish priest for almost seven years. My father and we children knew about her affair, as did all our small town gossips. In 1962, two years into the affair, my mother had a child, a daughter, with this priest, even though she and my father acted as if the baby was my father's. Five years later, on a balmy September afternoon in 1967, my mother and her priest boyfriend decided it was time for her to run off with him. They wanted to raise their daughter, my youngest sister, together. My mother left a note on the kitchen table for my father and my four older brothers—two in high school, two in college. On that fateful day, my mother piled me and my eight-year-old and five-year-old younger sisters into her priest-lover's car and we sped away. He took us 1500 miles from our home in western New York to

Minnesota. I didn't see my father or my brothers for two years; I never lived with them again.

The physical distance made it difficult to maintain any sort of meaningful relationship, and, as a teenager, I lacked the skills and the courage to build a bridge back to my father's heart. By the time I came out, at seventeen, four years after I had been abruptly taken from him, I still didn't know how to tell him who I truly was. I didn't know where to begin. And so I simply didn't.

When I was a teenager, living in Minnesota, my father and I rarely wrote to one another. Our infrequent correspondence meagerly consisted of short notes I'd scribble on a sheet of lined notebook paper informing him about the superficial particulars of my life. I stuck to neutral subjects—my grades or the weather. After I graduated from college, I'd throw in a tidbit or two about my job or my soccer games, omitting the fact that I played on an all-lesbian team called the Amazons. To fill up space, I'd supply a sentence or two about my sisters' lives, who they were dating, how they were doing in school. Sometimes my father would write back, on the same letter I had sent to him, scribbling a one-or-two sentence reply in the corner. Once in a while he'd tuck a five dollar bill inside the envelope and sign off with his shorthand kind of tenderness. *Buy yourself a coke. God bless you. Love, Dad.*

My father wasn't longwinded when it came to telephone conversations, either. Except for major holidays and birthdays, we rarely talked on the phone. This man who could wax tirelessly about saving unborn babies from the brutality of abortion fell nearly mute when it came to chatting with his living, breathing daughter. Our conversations lasted about thirty seconds.

He'd say, "Hello, how are you, I'm fine, well, good talking to you."

Bye. Click. That was it.

Such anemic efforts weakened my resolve to tell my father about my sexual preference. Still, I ached to have him know. I struggled to construct the right moment, find the perfect pause in even the briefest of conversations that would allow me to slip past the gates of resistance and speak. Should I wait for a face-to-face meeting, so I could more accurately calibrate the timing of my message? Should I tell him over the phone—if I were able to extend the length of our brief conversations? Or would a long letter suffice? Numerous books on how to tell one's family advised the latter route. It was easier on one's loved ones, the authors had claimed. It offered them a reprieve from the exposure of immediate reaction. In the hiatus, they could better digest the newfound information and respond; it also allowed the letter writer the luxury of finding the right phrase, composing the right sentence that would ease the news, make it more palatable.

Of the three coming out options suggested by the experts, in person held the most appeal. I feebly clung to my resolve to tell my father and I bided my time until the next trip to my hometown, Seneca Falls, in western New York. Even in his house, where I assumed he'd feel safer about hearing such potentially unsettling information, the right moment continued to elude me. Someone—one of my brothers or sisters, my father's new wife (for he'd remarried by then), his wife's daughter—was always present—in his kitchen, his living room, his car, in his back yard. The few conversations I was able to initiate never lasted longer than our unremarkable phone calls, and they covered the same tired, old ground. Even though I had traveled a considerable distance to visit him, he never rearranged his schedule to accommodate me. Each day he would fill his time with other people and other activities. The patterns set so long ago in my childhood prevailed. He disappeared into the mystery of his separate life to attend a political meeting, say a rosary at church, grab a cup of coffee with some crony—sabotaging any chance for a deeper connection between us.

The wide spaces between his life and mine were crowded with something that language, like love, failed to name. We used the constant presence of others to keep the odious monster at arm's length. Each of us nursed our own hidden wounds—my sisters, who'd traveled with me, my brothers who stopped by to visit us, our father who looked at us through eyes that promised more but could never deliver. We tended our broken places, separately, unconsciously buffing the raw edges to a makeshift smoothness we could endure. What verbs, what nouns, could we pull from the air that would build a path into the deeper places we needed to travel?

The diversions of people and activities were only part of the reason I hesitated to tell my father about my sexuality. Each missed chance guaranteed its own sweet relief. If he didn't know about *IT,* he couldn't reject me. I could still pretend to be the young daughter who possessed the aspiration, if not the power, to reclaim the father she had lost, the young girl who could restore his love and finally receive his approval. I did not know how to hurdle the fear that my disclosure meant losing him forever.

It didn't help that I was also haunted by memories of how hard it had been to come out to my mother when I was seventeen.

One afternoon, the summer after I'd graduated from high school, my mother had pilfered the top drawer of my dresser and pulled out a steamy hot, love letter, written to me by my lover Cheryl, who was also my best friend. I couldn't deny it. I was guilty as charged. My mother and my stepfather, who was by then a defrocked priest, were both convinced that I was damned to hell. They forbade me to see Cheryl. They threatened to withhold my college tuition if I persisted in *that lifestyle.* I had thought they might be more understanding of my love for someone outside the bounds of what was "acceptable," since they themselves had broken so many "rules" with their own illicit love. But I was wrong. With the brazen boldness of teenage defiance I refused to cooperate with them. I don't fully understand how, but I found a way to unearth the mother lode of courage I needed to defy them.

All summer long, I sneaked time with Cheryl. We met clandestinely over my lunch hour at work. With all the fervent love our teenaged hearts could muster, we talked and cried and pledged to find a way to keep seeing each other. I prayed in churches, begging God to give me some sign if he disapproved of my love for another woman. I never got one. Instead, my fierce passion for Cheryl ignited a self-respect that I had kept at bay; I began to uncover a self-defining determination that I had denied.

I left for college that September. Although Cheryl and I went to separate local schools, she visited me in my dorm room every chance she got. Hoping to save my sinful soul, my ever-vigilant mother spied on me. Mom called a high school friend of mine, who happened to go to the same college that I attended, and probed her with questions about whether Cheryl was visiting me at school. My friend innocently confirmed my mother's worst fears. Feeling angry and betrayed, my mother called Cheryl's mother and disclosed the nature of our relationship. Afterwards, Mom called me in tears, not to repent, but to chastise. *We might not be able to control who you see when you're away at college but when you come home this summer, you'll live by our rules.* No contact with Cheryl would be allowed.

The doting daughter I had always been felt shocked, shamed, furious. But, I felt something else, too. Defiant. Declaring my right to my sexuality was my first act of treason. I had disobeyed my Catholic, Italian American family's proscription: marry, have children. But my offense was more audacious, more dangerous than that. My true crime was to assert my separateness, to trust my needs and make them more important to my sanity than the needs of my family. For the first time in my life, I put my own needs before my mother's. I was not prepared for the onslaught that ensued. My mother spent the next fifteen years trying to suppress this information from her brain and from the rest of my family, while simultaneously punishing me for being queer. As threatened, my mother and stepfather disowned me financially.

At eighteen, I landed a job as a fry cook at a local breakfast and burger restaurant to pay for my living expenses and the college costs not covered by my scholarships and student loans. Cheryl and I rented an efficiency apartment in a seedy part of Minneapolis, near downtown, decades before that sector became trendy and gentrified. We juggled work and school, love and guilt, for while I would not be deterred in my right to love whomever I pleased, I could also not be dissuaded from shouldering the burden of consequence.

By some act of grace and luck, I managed to make the Dean's List and maintain an A average, tapping out English Lit papers with the same drive and determination I used to flip burgers, fry French fries, and shout, "You're order's up!" We lived from paycheck to paltry paycheck, staving off hunger with four-for-a-buck boxes of Kraft macaroni & cheese and free meals after every shift at the restaurant at which we both worked. Looking back, I marvel at our tenacity; we survived because we had to. We lived on the borderline, in a cockroach-infested efficiency, struggling every day not to give in to fear—or its stepbrother, failure. The choices we made, and the ensuing fallout, were not easy; in fact, those years were among the hardest, most challenging of my life. Thankfully, Cheryl's parents were more tolerant than my mother and stepfather. Her mother would buy us groceries from time to time, and when our second-hand yellow Dodge Polaris would break down, which happened often, Cheryl's father would come to our rescue.

The fierceness Cheryl and I displayed, the necessity of getting up each day and carrying on, sowed in me the seeds of something astonishingly life-altering. The world might be cruel to us, misunderstand our love, deny us rights and respect; my own flesh and blood might disown us, brand us outlaws, urge us to change our ways, but nothing could take away our will to live from the center of our truth.

Every Sunday, after our breakfast and lunch shift at the restaurant was over, Cheryl and I hauled our weary bodies into our car and drove across town to muddle through separate visits to our families. As we sped over the highway we listened to the radio and held hands until Cheryl dropped me off at my mother and stepfather's townhouse. Cheryl was never invited in. She would deposit me out front, and then drive away. I'd wave good-bye, turn the knob, and enter a world where my lesbian skin was unwelcomed and invisible.

All through dinner the conversation held fast to safe topics—work, school, the latest news about my brothers and other family members back East. After supper we would lounge in the living room, watching TV—my mother on the couch, my stepfather in his recliner, my sisters and me on the floor. I can't recall what was on, only that I felt relieved for the diversion of sitcoms and commercials. Around nine p.m., Cheryl would return for me. She'd honk the car horn and my mother would announce, "Your ride's here," barely glancing up from the TV screen. I would gather my things, kiss my family, and be off.

Sometimes during these Sunday evening visits, during dinner or in between TV shows, my sisters would casually ask about Cheryl. Although they knew she was my best friend, they didn't, at that time, know that we were also lovers. I tried to feign composure, even though their questions rattled me, for I knew that her name provoked ire in my mother and stepfather. Still, I did my best to periodically slip my sisters a little news, thankful for the opportunity to utter Cheryl's name out loud in that house.

Each Sunday, I took the leftover love that my mother and my stepfather threw me and sucked it clean to the bone. Lying, to myself and to them, was easier at their dining room table than in the car on the way back to the apartment across town that Cheryl and I shared. At supper, I became a complacent and compliant partner. See no evil, speak no evil, hear no evil. I knew the *evil* pertained to me, or at least to my *lifestyle*—as if my budding queer sensibility were as fleeting and as frivolous as last year's fashion trends. Surely my need for my mother's acceptance and approval would become passé, like the cut of last year's jeans. In the mid-1970s, the banner of cultural diversity had yet to be waved. I stood, a lone dissenter, waiting for my mother's heart to soften. My watch was cold and lonely. I felt ashamed to have acquiesced to her rules—*when you are in my house you will pretend to be something that you are not*—even as I ran through the moves in her playbook. In the half-hour drive back to our apartment, I did my best to re-attach my tongue, re-assert my identity, re-orient my perceptions.

It took decades to unlearn the lies, undo the subterfuge.

Even though my father still lived far away in Seneca Falls, NY, I feared that he would discover my sexuality and shun the truth of me, as my mother had. She had discarded those parts of me that did not fit her version of what or who her daughter should be. I had grown up believing that my mother was the one true source of unconditional love and understanding in our family. If ignorance could have suffocated her ability to cherish my lesbian self, how could I expect any better from my pious Catholic father? I conjured images of churches filled with vigil candles, my father leading doily-headed old Italian women in a rosary for the redemption of my sinful soul. Catholic vengeance, would no doubt, overrule any acceptance his heart might be able to hold.

In my twenties, I honed my coming out skills. I told friends; I told colleagues. I built a life amid the lesbian community in Minneapolis. I learned that we were not sinners, damned to hell, as my Catholic faith had taught me, but humans made to live in a world that fears us and hates us; a world that would rather stifle our essence, erase our culture.

Eventually, I grew strong enough to defy even my mother's edict of silence. In time, I came out to each of my siblings. One day I told my sisters about me and Cheryl. They were cautious, but accepting. They confessed that they had long sensed that *something like that* was going on. Telling my four brothers was harder. For too many reasons and in too many ways, the realities of my life were out of context to them. They lived halfway across the country and did not know Cheryl. One by one, each of them learned the truth—and, to their credit, none of them rejected me.

Years later, nearly two decades after I had come out to myself, I returned to Seneca Falls to celebrate my father's seventieth birthday. By then, Dad was the only remaining family member who hadn't a conscious clue that I was a lesbian. While the time had come to tell him, I had no idea as to how or when I would be able to broach that subject.

My secret found its own escape route.

The night before my father's birthday party, I sat around the kitchen table with my sister Teresa, my dad, and his wife, Rose, sipping coffee, eating cookies, and talking about the day my mom took us girls from our father. This conversation was a continuation of another that Teresa and I had initiated with Dad earlier that year in Minnesota, after our youngest sister's wedding. At that time, we'd asked Dad and Rose to join us for lunch; we confessed how deeply our separation from him had impacted our lives. Something began to shift that afternoon. Somehow we'd found a way to begin the arduous task of speaking the unspeakable. At that quiet lunch, my sister and I bravely attempted a truer intimacy with our father. After a fitful start, in which he retreated then finally acquiesced, he eventually broke his own imposed silence.

Months later, in the quiet of his kitchen, Dad took the next step. He told us of the ways in which he had tried to be a father to us in the aftermath of our mother's desertion. He had sent Mom money to help pay for our braces. He had sent money for Easter dresses and plane tickets for trips back home to see him and our brothers, too. His forlorn eyes glanced at us, willing us to accept his fatherly actions, demanding that we decipher the code of love they concealed. We nodded, recalling the incidences, knowing he was being truthful, assessing whether or not it was enough, for we had needed so much more than straightened teeth, frilly dresses, and summer vacations. When he was done making his case, my father took another swig of coffee and sat back. Then, he let go a small sigh, leaned forward, and looked directly into my eyes.

"Why'd they kick you out of the house?" he asked.

He was referring to my mother and stepfather. He was talking about the summer after my freshman year in college when I was eighteen. The official story, the one my mother had relayed to family members back East, was that I had moved out because I wanted to be more independent. I had no idea that my father was aware that a murkier reason might have existed. My mother and her husband had made it clear: if I came home from college that summer, they forbade me to see Cheryl. I couldn't abide by their ground rules. On the evening before the day they were scheduled to pick me up at my dorm, I called and told them not to bother. Weeks before, Cheryl and I had rented an efficiency apartment, found jobs, prematurely sprouted adult wings and flew in the face of parental authority.

"Why'd they kick you out of the house?"

I looked away from my father's asking eyes. I grabbed another cookie, took a bite, and changed the subject. I wasn't ready to tell him that my mother and stepfather disowned me for being *queer*. Old fears arose. Would my father shun me? Would my confession awaken the Catholic finger of damnation that I worried lay dormant in the center of his dark brown irises?

Not now, I told myself. *Not now. It's too soon.*

We had come so far, I tried to convince myself. We had just finally arrived at being able to acknowledge the hard places; so close to catching an honest glimpse of one another's lives. We were poised for real change, perched on the cusp of expanding beyond the *Hi how are you?* stage of familiarity. I didn't want to blow it. He was within my reach, and I couldn't bear the thought of his hand pulling back, recoiling at the truth of me.

I clung to my lesbian secret, making the silencing of it more important than my need to be whole—as if there was only room for one truth at a time in our family.

I looked away, tried to smile. I pretended I didn't hear his question. My father was insistent. He asked, again. "Why did they kick you out of the house?"

I stared at the thin line of his lips, the slight gap from which his question had escaped. I couldn't speak. My mind raced. *Maybe, he's looking for some dirt, something nasty to pin on my mother and stepfather, something to add to their long list of transgressions.* I knew such mean-spiritedness was not typical of my father, but still, I was wary. I took a deep breath and looked at Teresa. I wanted a way out, a back door, an escape hatch. My sister shrugged and offered, "It's your call."

My heart sank. I wanted her to open her mouth and tell him for me. I wanted her to fashion the words into something sweet and easy to swallow. I wanted her to make my lesbian secret respectable, dress it properly with her heterosexual acceptance. To my pleading eyes, my sister offered nothing but a reassuring *you-can-do-it.* I stared at my clenched hands, stealing seconds from what I knew was inevitable. My eyes scanned the long length of table toward my father's insistent face. I sucked confidence from the air, and said, as calmly and as quietly as I could, "They kicked me out of the house for being gay."

Something in me chose the safer word *gay* rather than the charged word *lesbian*, thinking it might ease the gale-force response that I expected to be hurled back at me. I waited for the reproach, for the Catholic hell-fire-and-brimstone outrage at my deviance. I looked at Dad, then at my stepmother Rose, then at the table top, then at my own shaking hands, then back at Dad.

"So what," Dad and Rose said, in unison.

"What difference does that make?" Rose added. "It doesn't matter to me."

I believed her, not simply because I so needed the tender touch of her acceptance, but because her eyes exuded kindness.

My father echoed his wife's support. "It's just how God made you. He makes us all different."

I don't know if my father had plucked that line from a list of politically correct responses floating in the collective unconscious sea of TV talk show airwaves, but I was suddenly grateful for Oprah Winfrey and all the others who had reached into the living rooms of small town America and helped break the taboo about the existence of people like me. Relief washed over me. Maybe the walls weren't going to come crashing down after all; maybe I'd misread the signs; maybe I was dead wrong about the outcome I'd so long conjectured. As

my mind eased to accept my father's words, the aftershocks of my announcement hit him and bounced back into my hopeful face.

"Just don't act on it," he said.

He had done it; just as I had feared. My father had delved into the recesses
of his Catholic faith and dredged up the Pope's encyclical on homosexuality.
From the dark brown pools of my father's eyes sprang righteous testimonies
from countless sermons about how homosexuals are children of God and aren't
innately sinful. The sanctimonious platitudes howled at me, line for line. The
sin is in the act. God hates the deed, not the doer.

I stammered, "I have a good life. I'm very happy. I have very wonderful
friends. Jane is very good to me."

I had invoked my partner Jane's name, calling on the powers of sanity and
grace to pacify my raging spirit, let me know I was still the good, loving
person I knew myself to be. I rambled on, trying to hold a magnifying glass to
my heart to let my father witness the hidden kindness inside, the sure, steady,
normal beat that made me who and what I am.

Lesbian blood is just like everybody else's.

"Jane's wonderful," my sister Teresa said, trying to help. "We all think the
world of her."

I doubt that my father cared about how wonderful Jane was. He had met
her. He knew of her generous spirit, knew that she was intelligent, responsible,
kind, and loving. But once the lesbian veil was lifted and Jane and I stood
before him in a revealed light, the simple truth of our impeccable characters
didn't matter. My father's struggle was evident. I watched as his mind whirled
and twirled. *She's my daughter and I love her. But she's queer and a sinner.* His
irises deepened then lightened and deepened again. Every once in a while he
seemed to resolve the paradox and say, "It's just the way God made you. He
makes us all different."

I can't remember much about the remainder of that evening. I was lost in a
post-coming-out coma. Eventually our conversation changed to other things,
but my skin felt tight and hot. As I sat in the kitchen chair, I reverted to old,
unproductive ways. I became ten-years-old again, afraid of losing my father's
affection. I managed to chat about work and other benign topics even as my
mind flew around the house, bumping into the lamps, the walls, and the door-
jambs. *How can I stay here all weekend? Oh-my-god I want to call Jane. Oh-my-
god what did I do? I came out to my father. Finally.*

I felt relief, yes. I was lighter from having the secret lifted. But I also felt
trapped. If he truly believed that *God makes us all different,* I would be able to
stay at his house and not feel alien or alienated. If the Pope's encyclical took up
permanent residence in his skull, my sense of belonging would grow even more
tenuous. What would happen in the morning when he'd had more time to
digest the information, after he'd had the chance to go to mass and pray about

it? What if he came home from church with a gallon of holy water ready to drown me in Catholic dogma? What if he opened my mouth and poured the blessed water down my throat, choking the lesbian life right out of me? Blessed be God. Blessed be His most holy angels.

Later that night before I went upstairs to bed my father pulled me aside in the kitchen. "Didn't you ever like boys, Mary?"

Although it had been hours since we had talked, his mind, like mine, was still ruminating on the lesbian revelation.

"No, Dad. Never. I was never interested in boys."

"That's just the way God made you," he said to the air. Perhaps some saint or angel stood beside him, intervening on my behalf, helping him see that his daughter was not a monster.

"Are you careful?" He paused and added, "About AIDS?"

His question astounded and embarrassed me. That he saw me as a sexual human being, an adult capable of contracting AIDS, that he would even think about AIDS made me feel anxious, exposed.

"Yes, I'm careful, Dad."

I wanted to flip into intellectual mode, bide my time, give myself space to cover my heart, keep it from spilling out onto the floor at his feet—as if statistics and data could shield me from his piercing eyes. I could talk to him about groceries, the weather, and other social topics of discourse, but how could I talk about sex? He could see me, now, kissing Jane, holding her close in my arms, touching her in lesbian ways. My brain reeled with defenses.

While lesbians are not immune from the disease, I wanted to lecture, *we are in a lower risk group, and the fact that Jane and I have been in a committed, monogamous relationship for many years further lessens our risk of contracting AIDS.*

I said none of those things. Being in the kitchen with him, the walls quiet and listening. It was too much for me to bear.

For so many years I had visited my hometown and fumed, thinking that all my Italian American relatives assumed I was a lonely spinster. *When ya gonna get married, Mary? Who ya dating?* I had no boyfriend's name to wag in their faces, no fiancé to placate their hopes for grandchildren, progeny, normalcy. So many times I'd daydream about blurting out the names of all my female lovers. I had so badly wanted them to know that I had a circle of lesbian friends, a family of women who loved me and cared for me and knew me more deeply and fully than any of them would or could. Face-to-face with my father in his kitchen hours after the truth was revealed, my righteous fury evaporated. I pinned all hope on his mercy, his tender acceptance of my different-ness. I knew if things got really ugly, I could leave. I was an adult with a Visa card. I could book a room in a motel, rent a car, eat at restaurants, far away from him. The one thing I wouldn't escape was the fear that he would throw me away.

The next morning, after Mass, as I sat around the kitchen table with my sister Teresa, two of our brothers, and one of our sisters-in-law, my father announced that he had been saying novenas for everyone in our family. It is one of his ways of showing that he cared about us, or at least our Eternal Souls. My father believes that if he attends Mass and receives Holy Communion every day for thirty consecutive days, he will save the soul of the individual to whom he dedicates the novena. He prays for us all, his children, their spouses, his grandchildren, his mother, my aunts, and uncles. That morning, after Mass, my father rattled our names off on his fingers—David, Steve, Mike, Pete, Mary, Teresa, Peg. When he reached the end of his long roster of those in need of saving, he emphatically announced, "When I'm all done with everyone on the list, I'm gonna say an extra novena for Mary."

A door slammed inside me; not the closet door I had so recently opened, but a different one, inside the deep interior passageways, the thick bronze portal that hid itself behind bone and muscle, DNA, and breath. That door fiercely safeguarded me from pollutants and toxins. At its entry, a sentinel stood guard, requesting the sacred password from those who approached, refusing anyone or anything that would deny me my basic humanness. I would not be my father's lesbian pariah. I would not be seen as his tainted one.

"Thanks a lot, Dad," I seethed.

The coffee turned in my stomach. I wanted to poke out his beatific eyes, one at a time, and lay them on a tray, beside the bananas and grapes in the center of the kitchen table, to stare back at the world, like St. Lucy's. An offering for the promise of hindsight and foresight; a reminder of his vision eschewed.

"Gees, Frank," my siblings griped.

Their protestations fell on closed ears. I had become my father's personal holy mission, his soul to save, his damned lesbian daughter to convert back to the fold. I stared at the floor, stood up, and walked out of the kitchen. The rest of the day I found it difficult to look at my father. I avoided him, often leaving a room when he entered. When I could not elude Dad's physical presence, I hovered near my sister and brothers, seeking their invisible protection. Nothing more was said of novenas or AIDs or wayward daughters, yet I floundered in the silence. A numbness set in that protected me from collapsing entirely, but it was too soon to gauge whether or not my father and I would be able to repair this newest tear in our relationship.

The following day, my sister and I said good-bye and flew back to Minnesota, as scheduled. Jane met me with a hug and a kiss at the airport and she drove me home. I opened the back door and stepped into our house, a home not unlike those of my siblings'. Our lesbian lives are not dissimilar to theirs. We have bills to pay, lawns to mow, rooms to repaint. We love and fight. Kiss and make up. We honor the truth of one another's lives and find the courage to claim the path that has chosen us. What passes for hate in those who would brand us as evil is, in reality, ignorance and fear. What marks our difference is that we are two women with a passionate love for one another who believe in opened doors and uncluttered shelves; who believe we have a right to be in the world. To some, that kind of comportment is outrageous, dangerous. Perilous.

Since that fateful coming out day, my father's acceptance of my lesbian identity has slowly progressed. I've visited him many times. Rose has remained true to her original, authentic response. This woman, who is not my mother, has always loved me as if she were. She showers me with hugs and opens her heart without judgment. She has always been warm and welcoming to Jane as well. While my father has never been rude or cruel, his support has been slower in surfacing. Back in 1990, he completed his double novena for me, just as he had promised he would.

Saving my queer soul was hard work, but some headway has been made. When I called him for his seventy-fifth birthday in 1995, he closed our brief conversation with "Say hello to Jane." It was the first time that he acknowledged her importance to me. Perhaps it was his soul that needed saving, not mine. By some ironic twist of fate, his novena prayers worked a miracle of a different sort. Now, in 2016, he always asks about Jane when I talk with him on the phone, or when I visit him in Seneca Falls.

I like to think that my father has fully reconciled his love for God with his love for me. Although, it is unlikely that I will ever know that for certain. Still, when the time comes from him to pass on, it will be enough for me to know that no secrets remain between us. I know that I am not the daughter that my father needed or wanted. I know that he has failed me as well. What-ifs may haunt the remainder of my days, even as I recognize and accept that things do not always turn out as planned—for fathers or for daughters. Had the early years been different, he might not have abandoned me to the wounded places in his own heart. Had the circumstances of our lives been anything other than what they were, I might not have received the fierceness required to dive into the hell of grief and emerge, reborn and mended.

I have known, it seems every minute of my life, that sometimes love can fail us, sometimes it can teach us to fly. The creaking closet doors are fully open, now, unencumbered. Telling is as powerful as a month of novenas, and as grace-filled as anything divine or secular could possibly be.

HIGH TIDE
CHEELA "ROME" SMITH

 **Cheela "Rome" Smith** was born in Selma, Alabama. Since moving to the San Francisco Bay Area in 1981, Rome has served an apprenticeship at a dyke-owned tattoo shop in SF; sampled every variety of drama in our Oakland lesbian demi-monde; and made her living variously: as record store clerk and calligrapher; rubber stamp designer; indie comix artist and writer; serving on the board of directors at the late, great, employee-owned distributorship BookPeople, where she operated a forklift and sadly watched as Amazon.com slouched toward small, independent book shops. After BookPeople, she worked warehousing produce at the lesbian-owned organic wholesaler who kindly financed her rehab and web-design training. An avid journal keeper for the past forty-five years, she's now up to volume 176. Rome lives in Oakland with her long-term partner and their two very bad cats (and possibly her mother's ghost, who signals by flickering the dining room chandelier.) "High Tide" is memoir.

MOM WAS ALWAYS late for everything: doctors' appointments, PTA meetings, parties. You name it, she was going to be late for it. The only event I ever noticed Mom make a genuine effort to show up for in a timely manner—in fact, not merely right on time, but even ten years early—was dying. It was one of her pet topics, this getting-ready-on-time-for-death business. What were my plans, she wanted to know, when her time came? Did I intend to stay in California as she lay dying—*alone!*—in Selma, Alabama?

"I took care of my mother when *she* died. It's what daughters *do*," she said, as if she had just read it in the latest edition of "Emily Post's Handbook on Deathbed Etiquette."

"A mother changes her infant's diaper in the middle of the night whether she feels like it or not; a grown daughter cares for her mother when she can no longer take care of her own self. Whether she *feels* like it or not."

"That's what *you* did, Mom, because you were already living in Selma. In your mother's house! But tell me the truth: if you'd been living out here in California at the time, would *you* have gone all the way back to Selma to take care of her?"

"Well, now. Would I have?" She gave it a little thought. "Okay. You win. Probably not. I mean, it's true that when my best friend Betty Taylor was dying in Andalusia—which isn't even all that far from Selma, I'll admit it—I couldn't bring myself to . . . to go see her. Oh, I just felt awful about it."

That was one of the best things about Mom: her self-awareness, owning when it was time to just 'fess up. And she always tried to put herself in my shoes, even when it didn't serve her purpose.

We'd had this same conversation many times. She was welcome to move here, I always countered, adding that I could go on for days reeling off all the reasons why I would rather live in the Bay Area than in Selma, Alabama: I'm a dyke who takes for granted the freedom to be "out" anytime, anywhere; I have a long-term *female* partner; my job is here, my friends are here, this is my *home*. I have no desire to start all over somewhere else. Even if only temporarily, while she runs late for her impending death. Sometimes I would even do my Fred Sanford imitation of "impending death":

"Oh—now you went and did it! You said 'No!' This is the Big One! I've never felt so much pain! I might die tonight!" And then we'd both laugh—usually, anyway. That was something else really cool about Mom: she knew when she was licked, and she'd back off fast. She had learned to be a good sport. At least, until she got the itch to try a new strategem.

All of which is not to say I don't feel a deep and abiding affection for Selma and all the people I know and love back there, all the rich complexity and horror and beauty and just plain Southern Gothic *je ne sais quoi*-ness of the place. But the East Bay has been my home for thirty-five years and this is where my roots are now—my job, my girlfriend, all my friends, my older brother and his family, my cat, my twelve step meetings. Anyway, what butch dyke in her right mind would willingly leave the San Francisco Bay Area to become caregiver for her dictatorial and agoraphobic mother in Selma, Alabama? A mother who doesn't like to be left alone, who throws a hissy fit any time I try to stay out after sunset? Or when there's a storm watch? Especially when that mother is so challenging that most of the family is no longer on speaking terms with her? This would be a sacrifice greater than I am capable of making. I've attended way too many Co-Dependents Anonymous meetings to sign up for that. Recovery has wrecked the early promise I showed for altruistic self-neglect.

That Mom and I understood each other's side almost made it worse. Each time this topic came up, the undercurrent of sorrow which flowed back and forth between us felt just a little bit deeper, swifter, and darker.

I wonder sometimes that if there had been a lot less mutual understanding, and a whole lot more hollering and insult-hurling, would things have ended more bearably for me? Because, despite how well she understood my reluctance to give up my life here to become her live-in caregiver for an undetermined length of time, in the end, she went out kicking my ass anyway, making me feel like the most selfish daughter *ever*.

This is how it went, her last ten years: her repeated attempts to guilt trip me into moving back to Selma, my usual patient and reasonable explanations for why it was not a good idea, followed by my customary counter-offer that she

Dispatches From Lesbian America

move out to California, all of it finally concluding—whenever possible—with the same concession. The one that always appeased her.

"I'll be there as soon as I can, Mom."

"Oh, that's wonderful! How long can you stay, honey?"

"Maybe ten days this time."

"Ten days! Oh, Cheela—I mean, 'Rome'!—that's just *wonderful!*"

It kept my life in a constant whirl of unpredictability, this never knowing when I would have to rush to Selma to help her with an urgent health crisis. Still: it sure beat moving there.

Even after being diagnosed with cancer by her physician—Dr. Overstreet, a dapper ninety-year-old who was her last heartthrob—death seemed inconceivable. He'd predicted that she had another good ten years on her. None of us were buying into her certainty that the end was near; not even her own doctor.

But then—what about her *previous* MD, that pit viper, Dr. Delgado? He had shared none of Dr. Overstreet's optimism regarding Mom's health. Right before she fired him, he had spit out a very different prognosis. My brother Hain had offered to come get Mom and move her up to Charlottesville, Virginia, the town where he'd been born, and to which Mom had always hoped to return someday.

"No. Absolutely not! That's a very bad idea—" Dr. Delgado had said, looking Mom up and down with incredulous disdain, as if he'd never before encountered so imbecilic a patient in all his years of practice.

"Why," he'd continued, "that would be tantamount to hauling a broke down old jalopy all the way up to a car shop in Virginia to get an oil change. You probably couldn't even make it halfway there!"

Later, when she and I discussed Dr. Delgado's bedside manner during one of my many emergency visits to Selma, she asked if I remembered Dr. Brown, the psychiatrist she sent me to when I was a fourteen-year-old pot-smoking, shoplifting heap of teen misery.

"Who could forget the shrink who says to your mom, 'You know what's wrong with *you*, Mrs. Laramore? *You don't have a* penis!'?"

"That's the one!" she said. "'Someone ought to sew one on you,' he told me!"

"Dr. Brown! What a nut job, huh, Mom? Did I ever tell you he offered me a joint in one of our sessions?"

We could hardly speak, the memory had us laughing so hard. The kind of laughter that makes you cry, which then makes you laugh even harder, maybe even wet your pants, especially if you're past a certain age and knocking on toward incontinence. But for a few giddy minutes we forgot about Dr. Delgado and his shockingly unprofessional diagnosis. We even made a joke about his skill at taking the Hippocratic Oath and twisting it so deftly into a nasty little "hypocritic curse."

I knew how riled up Mom could drive anybody, having once been the primary target of her barbs. But now that the hormonal peace of post menopause had descended upon me in a mellower biochemistry with late-blooming individuation, I was no longer so quick to take offense. And yet even I—long after having trained myself to ignore the occasional cruel quip by pretending I was Thich Nhat Hahn—*even I* still found myself sometimes itching to shut her up by any means necessary.

Mom and I recovered from our laughing fit, dabbing our eyes and passing a box of tissues back and forth.

"We've had some fun times, huh, Mom?"

I try to forgive myself for not being there with her when she died. For missing her last weeks. Days. Hours—that one final minute. To have been there, just in case she'd been aware of the fact that she was dying—alone at 5:15 a.m. Just in case she had been afraid. To have wrapped my arms around her, offering the comfort of company, a witness, the assurance that she had been loved; holding her close enough to help her let go.

How different I would feel, now—or so I imagine—if I'd been there for the Great Role Reversal, that flip of the magnetic field which binds mothers and daughters and rocks us in its centrifugal cradle; just to have been allowed to hold her mother, soothe the one who'd given her life, offering a safe refuge from the raw infantile horror one imagines must arise as neurons cease firing, and darkness swallows the dimming lights of the Self.

"It's natural to be in denial about a parent's impending death," I was being told by a grief counselor from the hospice facility that had served Mom. Reverend Sam, a young Baptist preacher who visited Mom at the nursing home where she died—someone she mentioned often, and who she clearly adored despite her resistance to accepting Christ as her Savior.

"Denial is common," he was saying. "Denial, and especially, regrets. No matter how much people do, when a parent dies I always hear the same thing: 'I had no idea she was about to die,' and: 'If only I had realized she'd be gone so soon, I would have done things differently. Been kinder. More available.' And sometimes—from people who are unusually self-aware—I'll hear something like, 'But—how could I *not* have known? What's wrong with me? Why am I so . . . *selfish?*'"

I'm in my car, parked near the bird sanctuary in Alameda. Today the San Francisco skyline is a featureless and soft-edged strip, unmistakable in its subtle beauty, ruling unassailably from its panoramic throne across the Bay. Right now, its metropolitan profile wears my favorite look: moody, insubstantial as a band of fog looming low over the financial district. Its smoky blue-gray silhouette reminds me of the Blue Ridge Mountains that had often seemed, to my fanciful child's eyes, to encircle Charlottesville, Virginia, cradling my hometown like a giant mother of everybody. Except, instead of the gently rolling maternal slope of those ancient mountains, San Francisco is laid out in geometrical shapes: masculine, an urban fortress; its watchtowers standing guard against threats to its citizens. Dominated by the towering TransAmerica Building, the City skyline's one concession to dreamy beauty is the softly twinkling Golden Gate Bridge.

I came here with the hope that I might actually open my guilty heart enough to receive comfort and maybe learn to forgive myself for my failure to be with Mom at the end of her life. Can this really be me, talking to a Baptist preacher, hoping to be absolved for letting my mother-the-agnostic down?

I furtively hit the mute mic icon on my cell phone just in time to sustain a violent barrage of tears. A surprise offensive launched from a dark place, point blank. All the full metal jackets of numbness behind which I've sought protection since losing Mom are no defense against this grief.

The preacher responds to my silence with a quietness so spacious and deep, that I feel safe riding this tide. Feel safe . . . *feeling*. How can I thank him any better than by unmuting my phone and sharing with him the relief I've received from his skillful lancing of my emotional infection? A temporary balm, we both know, but over time these short reprieves can lengthen and even heal.

Beyond the tangle of dune grasses and wildflowers that serve as a buffer against the constant breeze, the bay sends a steady volley of waves toward the shore. Creeping incrementally farther ashore with each tidal pulse of the San Francisco Bay, the surf submerges a little more beach with each incoming wave. It's high tide.

I hear Reverend Sam exhale on the other end of the line, and then draw in a deep breath.

"It's *never* enough—no matter how much anyone does—because it's just human nature to have regrets when you lose someone you love. And who knows?" he says. "Hiding behind all our regrets and self-blame for our failure to save our parents, may lie the stark awareness of our powerlessness over our *own* death."

You did what you could, is what this man is telling me. *And that's good enough.*

Reverend Sam falls silent again. His breathe is soft and steady, soothing as the tide.

I take a deep breath, and let it out long and slow. I take another, and another. How good it feels, this intentional breathing. It's as if I have been holding my breath for a very long time, and am now finally getting some air.

PROVINCETOWN
TESS TABAK

Tess Tabak lives in Brooklyn. She currently works as a ghost writer (boo!) and co-edits *The Furious Gazelle*, an online literary magazine devoted to art and fury. Her publishing credits include *Athena's Daughter's II* and *Narrative Northeast Magazine*. You can learn more about her at tesstabak.weebly.com "Provincetown" is a work of fiction.

1.

WHEN MOM WAS five, Grandpa told her the world was going to end that night. It was a joke, but she's never forgiven him.

They were in the car driving to Provincetown, their annual vacation spot. The kids loved the beach there; the little cottage where they stayed felt outside of time and space.

Grandpa said, "Hey, Sally."

Mom looked up.

He pointed out a large three-legged metal structure as it whizzed by the side of the road. "Those are aliens," he said. "The tripods are waiting for all of us to fall asleep, and when we do they're going to kill everyone."

Mom can remember the tripods better than anything else: the rusted legs, the grotesque way they rose into the sky, towering over everything. She was horrified. Her brother and sister recognized the story from Orson Welles's *War of the Worlds*, and they laughed at the joke.

Even Grandma played along. "Surely there's some way to stop them?" she asked, joking.

Grandpa shook his head. He said, "I'm sorry, there's nothing I can do."

That night at the cottage after everyone went to bed, Mom stayed up late that night, waiting for the tripods to come crashing down on her through the adobe-tiled roof.

The next morning she arose, shaking, and inquired to her father why she was still alive, and why the world was not a jumble of flaming wreckage. He replied, "Oh, Sally, didn't you know it was only a joke?"

Whenever Mom tells this story to us, my brother and I, this is her moral: that all parents disappoint their children, in big ways or small. She always said, "So if I do something like that, and I know I will, I apologize."

2.

SHUVO BROKE UP with me the Friday before spring break.

"It's not working out," he said in the hallway between third period and gym. There were people passing all around us, everyone going to their own corner of the high school. I wish he had chosen a moment when we didn't have class together, so I didn't have to stand like this, with him lingering and waiting for some response.

"Okay." I breathed out.

"Okay?"

"Yeah, okay."

"I'm gay," he said. "Sorry."

"No hurt feelings."

Truthfully, I was baffled more than hurt. It had only been a day and a half since he asked me out in chem class. He was my very first boyfriend. I might have said no had he not asked so publicly—how can a girl turn someone down when everyone is listening and grinning at you like you're the most adorable thing ever? He can't have known anything at all about me; we'd never talked at all before that, never exchanged any words that were not directly related to a class assignment or something taking place in front of us. If asked for a word to describe me, I'm sure he'd be utterly speechless to come up with any adjective except for *quiet*. The very first thing he said after our first dry-mouthed, chapped-lipped kiss, was, "My parents would kill me if they knew I was kissing a Jewish girl."

Maybe that's all I was to him, an experiment and a chance to piss off his parents. But now he's topped that. What better way to aggrieve Shiite Muslim parents than by coming out to them?

I WALKED AWAY into the girl's locker room. Laurell met me in the back row, already out of her t-shirt. She had on a white cotton bra, a B cup, she told me. If she knew the effect that bra had on me at that moment, our friendship would probably be over forever. Pale and wispy me never stood a chance with Laurell. She liked girls who were tall and lean, muscular, large breasted, confident.

"What's up?" Laurell asked.

"Shuvo and I broke up."

I pulled off my shirt, self-conscious in my navy blue bra. A bunch of other girls filled the row of lockers, laughing to each other; girls in panties and bras, bits of bare butt jiggling under panty lines. I turned to my own locker. Laurell grinned, noticing me noticing the other girls.

"Are you upset?" Her voice lacked inflection, as if she already knew that I wasn't. I shook my head "no" and pulled my grey baggy gym shirt on. It swallowed me whole, covering my slim frame.

"Good," she said. She leaned over me on the wall. While I wasn't looking, she had changed into our school's gym uniform. It looked good on her, the cotton stretched over her breasts, the shorts showing off long voluminous legs. She waxed so often that the hair never grew back on her calves anymore. She said I should try it, but I was scared of the pain: a hot, searing burn, and then something ripping you apart at the seams. Laurell wasn't scared of anything, except maybe her mom.

I took off my pants, leaving myself vulnerable. Did all girls feel like this in front of other girls? No one else seemed bashful. They could all talk to each other, underwear-clad, their eyes instinctively facing the right places.

"Do you want to come ice skating with me and my friends later?" she asked.

Yes, I screamed in my head. As I pulled on my gym shorts, I mulled it over. Skating with her *and her friends*. Not a date. Still, the possibilities: Laurell and me skating together, my hands warm in hers. She and I talked all the time, in school and online, but we rarely went places together, except maybe Roma's down the block from school where we ate greasy pizza and talked about our lives at home: my gnawing feelings of inadequacy and her experiments with tomboy-ism. Her mother made her keep her hair several inches below her shoulders, and she hated it. I loved it, the black and silky sheen of it, but of course I never said so. She only appreciated the trappings of femininity when they were on other people, not on herself.

"I dunno," I said. "My mom mentioned something about her parents' anniversary. Let me ask her."

"Okay." Laurell had the decency to look disappointed. "Maybe you can get out of it."

I whipped out my phone. "Can I go sk8ting 2nite? Be home by 8." Were my fingers trembling? Maybe. I imagined us twirling around the rink. I was terrible at skating, a wall hugger. Maybe she would ask me to hold onto her, to balance myself against her weight.

Laurell glanced at her watch. "I gotta go," she said. "Weight room calls." She rolled her eyes. "See you later."

Although we had gym the same period, we were in different classes. She'd opted for weights, trying to buff up her arms.

"Bye," I said. Then I ran out of the room, prepared for forty minutes of torture that goes by the name of volleyball.

MR. G. DRIBBLED the basketball in my direction. "Look sharp, hun," he yelled, and threw it to me. All girls were "hun" to him; he remembered the boys' names. I raised my arm over my face instinctively, batting the ball away. It fell to the ground, and Mr. G. sighed.

"What's wrong today?" he asked.

"Cramps." I clutched my stomach protectively. He waved me to the bleachers. "Cramps" was the ultimate excuse. A girl could have cramps four days a week, every week, and Mr. G. would ask no questions. He wouldn't touch the inner workings of the menstrual cycle with a ten-foot stick. Every class the bleachers are half-filled with girls supposedly being visited by dear Auntie Flo.

I chose a nice deserted place on the blue plastic benches and sat down. I flipped open a book and let myself imagine Laurell with her hair flying in the wind as she whizzed by in the ice skating rink at Chelsea Piers. My heart skittered.

A volleyball landed next to me on the bleacher, a stray. Mr. G. put out a hand for it, and I tossed it gently down to the main gym floor.

He blew his whistle. "Come on, girls, let's get those bikini bodies in shape! You all want to get boyfriends for the summer, don't you?"

I tried to space out, doing my best to ignore Mr. G's unhealthy obsession with his fifteen-year-old pupils. As a gym teacher, every day he is confronted with two dozen girls, bodies bouncing beneath the grey-and-blue uniforms. The popular ones, like Darla DeVito, rolled up their shorts to accentuate their figures. All I wanted was to muster the courage to yell at him, "No, I do not want to get a boyfriend for the summer, or any other time, and no, I do not want to wear a bikini." But for now I was content to sit and watch the flashes of white and tan and black legs go by.

My phone buzzed, and I picked it up eagerly. It was Mom.

"Have you forgotten about P-Town?" the text said. "I hope this is a joke."

My heart fell. Mom had mentioned Provincetown three weeks ago. She said her family used to vacation there every year, and it would be the perfect anniversary present for her parents. But she hadn't reminded me about the trip in weeks. What kind of person thinks someone can remember a date three weeks in advance, but has to be reminded to charge her phone every day? It was unfair.

LATER THAT DAY, when the school bell rang its final toll, I ran upstairs to my locker. Laurell and I had lockers next to each other, in first period English. That was where we met earlier this year. This was my favorite part of the day, when I got to see her again. Even if our paths never crossed after gym, she would be here.

She was already there when I walked into the classroom, rifling through her locker. Her silky black hair was pulled back in a ponytail, caressing the square of her shoulder blades that wasn't covered by the pink tank top. What I wouldn't give to be those fibers of hair touching that skin.

"Hey," I said when I got close.

She smiled when she saw me. "Hey. Are you coming with us?"

I shrugged. "My mom's being weird. I'm going to ask her when I get home."

"Okay." She hefted a stack of textbooks into her shoulder bag. "We're meeting in Manhattan at five. Let me know."

"Alright." I shifted my weight. "If I don't see you, have a great break."

She held her arms up for a hug. I leaned into it. Her hair smelled like jasmine. "We'll see each other. I'll call you tonight."

"Okay."

I got on the train to go home. The tunnel stretched, infinite. Spring break was nine days long, nine long days without her.

I trudged into the house. Jake, my brother, was sitting on the window seat, his long lanky legs spread over a suitcase. I walk past him up the steps, in a bad mood.

"Aren't you going to welcome me home, little sister?" he called up the stairs.

"No," I yelled back. This wasn't his first visit home since he moved to Annapolis, but this was the longest he'd ever been away. The brother-shaped hole in my heart, already small to begin with, was filling up with other things. It was growing easier to look at him and feel nothing. I had his Pokemon poster now, and all the other good stuff from his room. Usually I felt like an only child, like he was never here at all.

In my room, I grabbed a few things for the weekend and stuffed them into a bag, then trudged back down the stairs. My brother was gone, probably packing the car with my father. Mom was out, stuffing a few last minute things into suitcases.

"So, Mom," I said, "a bunch of people are going to Chelsea Piers tonight."

"That's nice," she said. "Have you told them no yet?"

"Couldn't I just stay here for the weekend? I'm fifteen."

She turned to me. "Provincetown is beautiful. You'll love it there."

"Mom, this is important. Laurell might never ask me to go skating with her again."

"You can go next week. When are you going to get the chance to stay with your entire family for a weekend?"

Incredible. "Why didn't you give me some kind of advance notice? How am I just finding out about this now?"

"We told you last week, and the week before." She told me, I know she told me. But dates have a way of slipping up so that you're not expecting them, even when there's no surprise. She strolled out of the house with a rolling suitcase in each arm. I followed her, carrying my hastily packed bag. But I didn't say anything. She might have been right, but it's pointless to spoil a good sulk once it gets going.

Mom and I walked into the car, me next to Jake in the back seat.

"Who's excited for P-town?" Dad asked as he pulled out of the driveway and drove down the block.

"I hate you."

"Thank you, ungrateful child," he said.

I texted Laurell. "Can't make it 2nite. :(Stupid vacation. Next week?"

A minute later she responded. " :(ok. do you want to sleep over at my house next week?"

The black cloud lifted. A sleepover at Laurell's would be good. Better than skating, even.

"Mom, can I sleep over at Laurell's next weekend?"

"Yes, of course," she said.

Just like that, there's a smile on my face again.

Someone said in a song once that people love you and tell you lies. I've tried never to disappoint Laurell. Lord knows she's used to disappointment. She is constantly disappointed in her mother, who believes unfailingly in whatever Jesus said two thousand years ago; in her body, which she swears is lumpy and uneven, although to me it looks perfect; and in the world, which has so far failed to recognize her brilliance. She's only fifteen, so there's time. In the meantime I'm her self-appointed support system. We talk to each other during school and after school over texts and instant messages. Sometimes, when she has one of those moments of weakness she will call me. Her voice is crystalline over the phone, like a gust of wind on a day right before it rains. She's beautiful even in her disappointment. She weeps silently to me over the phone. "If I told my mom, she'd never talk to me again. She'd throw me out of the house."

"She'd still love you," I always say, although sometimes I'm not sure.

Laurell sniffles. "Sometimes I think she'd be happier if I just killed myself. She hates me."

I grip the phone. "Don't say that."

"I know," she says, "I know."

Her mom doesn't know anything about her daughter's identity, didn't even know the word "lesbian" in English, only Chinese. That made it easier, in some ways—Laurell didn't have to hide the button on her bag reading "three out of five cats are lesbians" when she came home from school. She just had to hide a box of sex toys in a shoe box under her bed, a small price to pay to escape high school without being disowned.

She never asked me if I was in love with her, and I never told her, because I didn't know. Don't know. I loved the way she looked, the way she carried herself, but sometimes it was hard to tell if I loved Laurell or if I just wanted to be her.

SOME PLACE ALONG the highway, the scenery has melted from city buildings to sea shore and breezy palms. There are the famous water towers, too, large and foreboding. I can see why Mom would have been frightened of them.

Hours later, we pull up at the house. It's a colonial style cottage, elegant 1700s aesthetic. It looks as though George Washington or someone equally important might have lived there.

We unpack our bags, say hi to everyone. My aunt and uncle are there with their spouses and two kids apiece, and my grandparents are reclining on the couch. By the time we get there I am tired, exhausted, and I retire to bed. No tripods come during the night to disturb our sleep.

THE NEXT DAY we go into town. There is a row of tiny shops, so picturesque, all sticking to the colonial theme. There are rainbow flags everywhere. Mom notices them uncomfortably.

"I forgot to mention this is a gay town," she says.

People walk down the street; amidst the crowd, two men are holding hands with each other. Across the street are two husky masculine women, standing kissing distance apart. More homosexual couples appear out of the woodwork. There aren't many, but there are enough.

Mom grabs me by the shoulder. "Did you see that?" she squeals. "Those two women just kissed *on the mouth.*"

I follow her gaze and see two women canoodling in front of a bus stop. Their arms are wrapped around each other, lovingly. And Mom is staring at them with a level of disgusted fascination usually reserved for squishing an insect.

"Grow up," I want to say, but the words freeze on my tongue.

"Let's go into that shop," I say instead, pointing to a dress shop with a colorful array in front of their window. She nods. I come out an hour later with three stretchy, soft pastel-colored beach gowns, and a growing sense of shame: both for my mother, and for me.

LATER, WE GO out to eat. Chinese. Every year, we do something for my grandparents' anniversary. Last year it was a giant party at our house, where Mom dredged up all of their old fossil friends. One woman named Dorothy Currant, who everybody said was a little bit insane, took a banana from our counter and stuffed it into her pocketbook. "For later," she whispered to me conspiratorially.

There are gay couples at the tables around us, chatting in casual conversation. Grandpa looks at all of them, a sneer on his face.

"You know my friend Ernie? His son came out to him, told him he was that way," Grandpa said. "And Ernie said he accepted it! Unbelievable. Of course, I would never do anything to harm my fellow human being, but there is something sick about homosexuality. I convinced Ernie that his son was sick in the head, that he needed to get professional help. And now Ernie is so upset."

I almost laugh at the absurdity. Instead of helping, Grandpa took someone who didn't have a problem and convinced him that there was one.

"It's legal in California now," Dad says. "Pretty soon, it's going to be legal everywhere, it looks like."

"Unbelievable," Grandpa repeats.

"Didn't you used to be friends with Allen Ginsberg?" I say. "Wasn't he gay?"

"Allen Ginsberg was a wonderful man," Grandpa says, "but I don't agree with his way of life. He did drugs too. He was a great poet, but I don't support the use of drugs. Sick in the head."

"But-"

Mom shushes me.

THAT NIGHT I sit on my laptop, talking to Laurell over instant message.

"SAPPHIC LIBIDO: my eyes are uneven. i want to get plastic surgery."

"QWERTYPIE: "What are you talking about?" I write. Her eyes are beautiful, small, and delicate. I love the way they scrunch up in English when we've been up till four a.m. the night before, talking.

"SAPPHIC LIBIDO: they're uneven. one has a lid crease, and one doesn't."

"Your eyes are beautiful," I write back.

"SAPPHIC LIBIDO: thank you but you don't have to lie."

I google it. Lid crease surgery is something Asian women get to fall more in line with a Western appearance. Most Asians are born with a single eye lid, one without a crease above the eye.

"Why do you need to have a lid crease on both eyes?" I ask.

"SAPPHIC LIBIDO: I can't put on makeup evenly."

It's Americanization, is what it is. Trying to fit in, to be like everyone else.

"QWERTYPIE: Getting plastic surgery would be trying to be like everyone else. Being different is what makes you special."

"Maybe," she writes. "I just hate it."

THE NEXT DAY, we go for a hike as a family. A few more snarky comments are made about the gays, but mostly they just fade into the woodwork along with the rest of the New England scenery.

That evening in our cabin, my aunt has prepared a slideshow of old family photographs. Everyone sits around the screen, watching and joking. In one, Uncle Bob gives the camera the finger, and we all laugh. But Mom shifts on her chair anxiously, looking like she wants to say something. Finally, she does.

"So, Dad," Mom says, "you know, you never apologized for the Martian thing."

Uncle Bob laughs, remembering it.

"Mom, drop it," Jake says.

"No, what?" Grandpa asks. "What Martian?"

"Don't you remember?" she says. "You told me the world was going to end. Why would you do that? I was only five!"

"I thought you knew that I was joking," he says.

"I was five. How was I supposed to know what's made up or not?"

He shrugs. "Nobody's perfect. So I made a mistake."

"I stayed up all night waiting to die," she says bitterly.

Grandpa looks thoughtfully at his water. "Well, you were always an anxious child."

She turns away, hurt. If Mom is seeking an apology for her forty-year-old grief, she's not going to get it.

LATE DURING THE night, after everyone has gone to bed, my cell phone buzzes. I pick it up, and Laurell is on the other end, crying softly.

"Sorry," she says, her voice breathy. "I just wanted to talk."

"What's wrong?"

"My mom found my box. It was in my room, under the bed." She laughs harshly. "She didn't know what most of the stuff was, but she said I was a demon. She said she's going to take me to the church tomorrow to pray for my soul. And she took my stuff away. That was *expensive*."

"I'm sorry."

She stops, shaken by a sob. "I just want to die. I can't live with her anymore. It's tearing me apart."

"She's lying to you," I say. "She doesn't believe any of that stuff about demons. She just isn't used to you, yet. She will be."

"I can't wait," she cries.

"Laurell." I grip the phone harder. "Don't make me get on the bus to Greenwich. I will, if you keep talking like that."

"I don't—"

"Promise me," I say. "Promise that you won't do anything."

"I promise," she whispers.

"Good. We're going to have a sleepover next weekend, and you need to be alive for that. I love you, you know that?"

She laughs. "I love you too."

Those words send tiny chills down my spine.

"So good night. And just keep tight till the morning."

"Night."

THE NEXT MORNING, I am on my computer again at the kitchen table. Dad comes up behind me and takes my laptop. "I just need to check my e-mail. One sec." He takes it to the couch, where his eyebrows furrow as he looks at the screen.

"What did I tell you about talking to strangers online?" he asks.

"Um . . . don't do it?"

"Who is 'Sapphic Libido'?"

"None of your business."

Mom walks over. Dad says, "Do you know what 'libido' means?"

I shrug.

He gets quiet. "I want you to block this person."

"What? It's one of my friends from school. I promise."

"Who?" Mom asks. I don't say anything.

"*Who?*" Dad says.

"Laurell."

They exchange a look. "Is Laurell a lesbian?"

"That doesn't matter," I say aloud, although I know as the words escape my lips that it's a lie. It does. Of course it does.

ON THE CAR ride home, Mom faces forward the entire time. At a rest area, she and I get out to use the bathroom.

At the sinks of the grimy public bathroom, she says, "You know, sometimes I wonder if I had the capacity to be interested in women." She pauses. "I had a girl crush on one of my friends once. Carol Zlotnik. I thought that she was the coolest person ever. I wanted to be with her all the time."

I don't say anything. I am trying not to curl up in a ball and die right here on the soggy tiled floor.

"But I think if I ever felt anything for another woman, I would have suppressed it. Does that make sense? It's easier with a man. It just is."

She catches my eye in the mirror, and I nod.

"Okay," she says. Then, "Maybe Laurell shouldn't sleep over."

I am silent, but she keeps talking. "It's just not meant to be like that, you know? I think if it was meant to be then the parts would fit. People are saying nowadays that it's not a choice, that you're born like that, but I think there's an element of choice in everything."

We walk to the car; I remain mute. She blathers, "I don't really care if you marry a Jewish man, you know that? You're Jewish, your kids are going to be Jewish, no matter what. But you need to marry a man. Please. It would kill me."

When we get in, she shuts up, finally. The rest of the trip is a grey blur.

THE NEXT DAY at school, I met Laurell at our lockers before class.

"Hey." She smiled.

"Hey." I twisted my hair nervously. "How did the rest of your weekend go?"

"It was okay," she said. "Was the anniversary thing really boring?"

"Yeah," I said. "Super. Anyway . . . I don't think my mom is gonna let me sleep at your house anymore."

"Why?" she asked. Then she got it. "Did you tell her I was gay?"

I flinched. "I didn't think it would matter."

"You can't just out someone like that!"

"I thought you were already out." I stared at the floor. "Anyway, I had to explain your stupid screen name to them. They thought I was chatting up some creepy older woman."

"Fine," she said. "Whatever."

We sit, and for the rest of the class neither of us says anything. She'll never forgive this cowardice.

Tomorrow, I will ask out Michael, whom I suspect is gay. He'll come home with me, and maybe we'll kiss on the couch, give Mom something else to worry about. She'll ask if he is using protection, and I'll roll my eyes. After a while, she'll let it go. We both know I'm not going to get pregnant that way.

It should only be a few years time before it is legal, everywhere, all across America. Probably a few years after that until Laurell tells her mom. I'll tell mine eventually, when the time is right.

Whatever happens, I will always know this: it's not the end of the world.

MY URBAN FOREST
POLLY TAYLOR

 **Polly Taylor** was an eighty-six-year-old lesbian (born in 1929, came out at forty), disabled by Chronic Obstructive Pulmonary Disease and heart issues. She lived in senior housing on what even the government calls "very low income," but was also happier than she ever dreamt of being in her straight middle class salad days. "My Urban Forest," a memoir, was how she lived her life, as well as a snapshot of her wandering elderly mind. Polly's papers will be archived at the San Francisco Public Library James C. Hormel LGBTQIA Center atchives.

FRIDAY

YESTERDAY THEY STARTED trimming the trees in the courtyard. First on their plan was the huge bottlebrush reaching from outside my living room halfway up the windows of the floor above.

For a year and a half I've eaten three meals a day, and done some desk chores, in a forest. The trees they cut today entirely covered the side of the window where I sat. It always seemed that I was among them. The birds that came close were the smaller ones, finches and sparrows, hummingbirds, and some little ones I decided were warblers that came in flocks of a dozen or more and moved from branch to branch so quickly that it was as if they simply vanished from one spot and reappeared in another. I don't care much for the mourning doves. Their constant "coo" depresses me. I prefer the cheerful birds. But who do I think I am? Queen in my tower, deciding what the sound of birds should be? Wild creatures after all.

When I first moved in I would have wished the trees away, wanting the view they obscured and finding the room rather dark and dingy. But sitting there enjoying my escape from the crowded space I'd moved from, appreciating the far more visitor-friendly seating in this new apartment, I came to feeling my forest setting as my home. Anyway, the only thing that would be visible without the trees was the other wing of the building—other people's apartments. It was only a few days living here before I realized that I didn't need to go through contortions to reach around furniture and draw the vertical blinds I despise. In my old apartment downstairs I'd been in a fishbowl, opening to the courtyard and passersby. Now I could be invisible among the trees at any time of day or night.

Mitigating my enjoyment of forest living was the likelihood that the bottlebrush was a significant contributor to my persistent, increasing shortness of breath. I'd tried to call the problem a progression or exacerbation of my COPD, but it got pretty obvious that a good bit of it was allergy. I set up high-powered HEPA filters in both my rooms, began taking antihistamines on a regular basis, and figured on living with whatever comfort I could achieve.

SUNDAY

SO LAST NIGHT the bottlebrush tree at the living room window was gone. I glanced out and was startled to see another brightly lit kitchen across the courtyard. It's the apartment Sandy and Joyce will be living in soon. We'll be close visual neighbors—at least until the trees grow back or we take to closing the blinds. Another surprise is my view of the hillside and the field of lights, in hundreds of houses in early evening; just a few lights left late at night. From dusk to dawn I see the garlands of street lights up and down and across, tracing the shape of hills otherwise invisible. A few headlights flash briefly from cars traveling on whatever their business might be.

I'll grow to love the new view as much as I loved the shelter of the forest. I can't wait to see what they do with the tree near the bedroom window and whether I can see the Sutro Tower from there and the full sweep of the surrounding hills.

TUESDAY

THE COURTYARD IS finished and the debris cleared away. There are, as always, conflicting opinions among the residents, some expressed loudly and insistently. The one resident who may have knowledge to back his assertion tells us they did it all wrong. I really don't care about that: I'll worry about the health of the plantings when and if they turn ugly. For now, it looks really nice, far sunnier for me and the courtyard than it was last week.

Birds are checking things out. I hope they will feel at home in spite of being less sheltered. I assume they couldn't care less about us, the creatures on the other side of these panes of glass. The birds here were always being tossed about by the breezes, so that won't change much for them. They'll probably get wetter, come the rainy season, than they did in the denser foliage. Whether they thrive or not, their presence or their absence will give me something to watch for, something to ponder.

The tree that covered half my living room windows and most of one bedroom window has been thinned out rather than cut shorter. As the branches move in the near constant wind I can indeed see the Sutro Tower–more or less. It is really just a practical structure for communications equipment but I love it because it is an iconic image of San Francisco, visible on the horizon of many views, on many postcards, and many panoramas of the city presented to the larger world. It is also eye-catching because of its many faces. Today its feet are firmly planted out of sight behind the "marine layer" of summer fog while the fully rigged sailing ship that forms its top floats freely in a clear blue sky.

NIGHT

I OFTEN WAKE during the night. My joints get sore and I haven't much choice about sleeping position and my mind gets busy or something has troubled me and it's hard to set it aside. I get up and walk around the apartment. I check out the apartments across the courtyard. There are five women who are often up when I go to bed: Piedad and Dusa and Nina and Shannon and Joyce. When I get up later their lights are out.

If there's a moon, I bask in its light. More often I simply gaze at the hills and the flatland rising to meet them. On one of the first of these restless nights, I discover to my surprise that the Sister Act Church is floodlit at night. I've renamed it for the Whoopi Goldberg movie that was filmed there. I'd rather not call it by whatever saint or saints it celebrates.

I'm picky about religious institutions and practices. They seem a very mixed bag of good and bad. I've heard men who went to Catholic schools make bitter, scornful remarks about nuns, blaming them for all the trauma of their childhood. I suspect the women who were their schoolmates have far more ambiguous memories, including passionate crushes.

There was a group of nuns who used to haunt our building. I don't know who originally allowed them access. Nor do I have any idea what nest they came from. Somehow they would get into the house; maybe it was just that the door had been left open. They'd evade the manager and start knocking on doors to uncover victims for their salvation. A few of us had taken to watching movies in the community room on Sunday afternoons. Juanita, a warm and humorous African American woman struggling with chemotherapy, had a boyfriend who worked in a video store and she would bring us cassettes.

One day the religious flock sailed in and began regaling us with their message. None of us wanted their services and we certainly didn't want them interrupting our movie. The rest of us sat there with our jaws open. It was Juanita who rose from her chair in spite of her serious illness and blasted them for their arrogance: what made them dare to break in so rudely and interrupt our gathering? Didn't their religion care about respect and privacy? Why did they think they could tell women far older and wiser than they how to live our lives? They scattered in a flurry of skirts and veils while we applauded Juanita.

Then there are the Women Religious whose teaching and nursing, activism for social justice, and modeling of kindness I've found exemplary. Strong, pious women. "Pious" has gone out of favor in my community of defiant impious defenders of social justice who focus on women's secular passions and pains.

Someday I'd like to take a stab at reclaiming piety as we work to achieve public respect for the varieties of spiritual belief.

But, of course, I digress. I've backed into a discussion of religion. I turned a corner up there somewhere and unexpectedly found the lighted church in my view, and the whole topic in front of me.

But then, that is what my nighttime wandering is about: a digression for my mind and body from whatever thoughts or whatever pains are keeping me awake.

LITTLE BIRDS

THIS MORNING I sat watching, more or less, the exercise program I have been following. I've made a good start at being faithful to it, but today I slept late; a good thing, given my trouble sleeping. I woke up feeling fine but I had only just finished my breakfast—necessary first thing to keep the headache that looms over my shoulder from attacking, when my alarm told me to turn the program on. I was too short of breath to try to follow the movements. I considered getting my nebulizer treatment done to be able to do the second half hour, but I can't inhale the medication properly with a stomach as full as mine without serious reflux. So I sat and considered my guilt and whether Wednesday, the "hump day" for those who work a five day week, should be one I would skip as a part of my exercise program.

Then the little birds came. Did I mention that I had feared they would not come back after the pruning? Now it is December and here they are. Apparently they don't mind that the vegetation is so sparse. They always descend in a group. Maybe a dozen or more darting from branch to branch pecking at something here and there. They're very little, longer than the bigger of the hummingbirds, but their bodies are almost perfectly round. I haven't spotted any distinguishing markings so that I can find them in my bird book. I try to get a good look this morning when they are less camouflaged by the leaves, but they still move too fast. I'll just have to be content with calling them "the little birds." But unnamed they are such a cheerful sight that they send me off to my writing work in a better spirit, with my guilt about the exercises assuaged.

MORNING

THIS MORNING WHEN I sit down for my breakfast the sky is quickly turning light. The gently moving fish and bird shapes of the tree leaves frame Diamond Heights where Gold Mine Boulevard's buildings are light-colored shapes against dark wooded slopes. Houses closer by are more distinct. The sky is becoming a deep blue, streaked with clouds touched by the rising sun.

I've never learned the names for the types of clouds. There's always something to learn and I'll put that on my list. They nonetheless charm me. Of course, blush pink and powder blue would never be my choice of color palette anywhere but in this morning's sky.

The section of sky to my right is centered by the moon. A couple of nights past full, it is just enough off round to be more interesting than a perfect orb. And a seagull makes passes across it to give the scene life. The gulls only seem to come this far inland in the morning. Perhaps it's their breakfast spot before they're off to the day's hunt.

Some people favor mountains, some prefer seascapes or lakes or fields of grain. I've heard many debates, even serious arguments about the virtues of the city or the country, a holiday in a foreign metropolis or at sea. I believe it is the ultimate in the pointless, mindlessly destructive competitive spirit to compare and judge one beautiful scene against another. Can't we all just get along? I believe the beauty of the world we live in is a major source and support of the spiritual impulse alive in us all. And that in turn has generated the virtue and beauty manifested in many religions. Drawing from all the traditions seems the best, most glorious way.

YELLOW BIRD

RETURNING FROM A long walk yesterday I was met at Marge's garden and escorted through the courtyard by a slender little bird with yellow markings. When I got to my own apartment he returned to my tree for a bit. My bird book suggested Townsend's or Yellow Throat Warbler and I had made notations on the page that I'd seen them in the city before. The bird has a black mask over the eyes with yellow stripes above and below it.

The bird's mask reminded me that a raccoon has appeared right below Colette's window in the area between her bedroom and the courtyard entrance to the building. Colette and the manager agreed to put up signs asking us to keep that door closed. A raccoon in our lobby would be too much competition for the cats that streak through there when they slip out of their apartments.

If I still lived downstairs where I was for nine or ten years I would have seen the raccoon. But the woman who lives there now seems not to sit at the window as I did, watching people and cats and birds and even the occasional rat passing by. It was a bit of a fishbowl life but nonetheless entertaining. I've retired from "people watching," although I still indulge as I occasionally walk the neighborhood.

LATER

THIRTY SOME YEARS since I moved out here from the East Coast and I'm still astonished at how things grow in this climate. In a Pennsylvania December, everything was dormant. It was a matter of faith to believe that trees would grow green again and flowers would bloom once more. Here, growing and blossoming are constants.

The trees that were trimmed are already filling more of my windows. I suppose we're talking about cycles of life here, as I think I will be getting my forest back very soon. It only takes time and rain. It's a matter of perspective. Each inch of new leaf obscures a yard of the hillside. I hope I will still have an occasional moonlit breakfast and that my view of life will only grow wider.

Although they are only breath
words which I command
are immortal

—Sappho
(Greek poet from the island of Lesbos, (c.630-c. 570 BC)